LIBRARY
OF
SOULS

LIBRARY OF SOULS

THE THIRD NOVEL OF

MISS PEREGRINE'S

PECULIAR CHILDREN

BY RANSOM RIGGS

QUIRK BOOKS
PHILADELPHIA

Library of Congress Cataloging in Publication Number: 2015939051

ISBN: 978-1-59474-758-8

Printed in the United States of America
Typeset in Sabon, Belwe, and Dear Sarah

Cover design by Doogie Horner
Cover photograph courtesy of John Van Noate
Full image credits on page 463
Production management by John J. McGurk

Quirk Books
215 Church St.
Philadelphia, PA 19106
quirkbooks.com

10 9 8 7

FOR MY MOTHER

The ends of the earth, the depths of
the sea, the darkness of time,
you have chosen all three.

—E. M. Forster

GLOSSARY OF
PECULIAR TERMS

PECULIARS   The hidden branch of any species, human or animal, that is blessed—and cursed—with supernormal traits. Respected in ancient times, feared and persecuted more recently, peculiars are outcasts who live in the shadows.

LOOP A limited area in which a single day is repeated endlessly. Created and maintained by ymbrynes to shelter their peculiar wards from danger, loops delay indefinitely the aging of their inhabitants. But loop dwellers are by no means immortal: each day they "skip" is a debt that's banked away, to be repaid in gruesome rapid aging should they linger too long outside their loop.

YMBRYNES The shape-shifting matriarchs of peculiardom. They can change into birds at will, manipulate time, and are charged with the protection of peculiar children. In the Old Peculiar language, the word *ymbryne* (pronounced *imm-brinn*) means "revolution" or "circuit."

HOLLOWGAST Monstrous ex-peculiars who hunger for the souls of their former brethren. Corpselike and withered except for their muscular jaws, within which they harbor powerful, tentacle-like tongues. Especially dangerous because they're invisible to all but a few peculiars, of whom Jacob Portman is the only one known alive. (His late grandfather was another.) Until a recent innovation enhanced their abilities, hollows could not enter loops, which is why loops have been the preferred home of peculiars.

WIGHTS A hollowgast that consumes enough peculiar souls becomes a wight, which are visible to all and resemble normals in every way but one: their pupil-less, perfectly white eyes. Brilliant, manipulative, and skilled at blending in, wights have spent years infiltrating both normal and peculiar society. They could be anyone: your grocer, your bus driver, your psychiatrist. They've waged a long campaign of murder, fear, and kidnapping against peculiars, using hollowgast as their monstrous assassins. Their ultimate goal is to exact revenge upon, and take control of, peculiardom.

CHAPTER ONE

The monster stood not a tongue's length away, eyes fixed on our throats, shriveled brain crowded with fantasies of murder. Its hunger for us charged the air. Hollows are born lusting after the souls of peculiars, and here we were arrayed before it like a buffet: bite-sized Addison bravely standing his ground at my feet, tail at attention; Emma moored against me for support, still too dazed from the impact to make more than a match flame; our backs laddered against the wrecked phone booth. Beyond our grim circle, the underground station looked like the aftermath of a nightclub bombing. Steam from burst pipes shrieked forth in ghostly curtains. Splintered monitors swung broken-necked from the ceiling. A sea of shattered glass spread all the way to the tracks, flashing in the hysterical strobe of red emergency lights like an acre-wide disco ball. We were boxed in, a wall hard to one side and glass shin-deep on the other, two strides from a creature whose only natural instinct was to disassemble us—and yet it made no move to close the gap. It seemed rooted to the floor, swaying on its heels like a drunk or a sleepwalker, death's head drooping, its tongues a nest of snakes I'd charmed to sleep.

Me. I'd done that. Jacob Portman, boy nothing from Nowhere, Florida. It was not currently murdering us—this horror made of gathered dark and nightmares harvested from sleeping children—because I had asked it not to. Told it in no uncertain terms to unwrap its tongue from around my neck. *Back off*, I'd said. *Stand*, I'd said—in a language made of sounds I hadn't known a human mouth could make—and miraculously it had, eyes challenging me while its body obeyed. Somehow I had tamed the nightmare, cast a spell over it. But sleeping things wake and spells wear off, especially those cast by accident, and beneath its placid surface I could feel the hollow boiling.

Addison nudged my calf with his nose. "More wights will be coming. Will the beast let us pass?"

"Talk to it again," Emma said, her voice woozy and vague. "Tell it to sod off."

I searched for the words, but they'd gotten shy. "I don't know how."

"You did a minute ago," Addison said. "It sounded like there was a demon inside you."

A minute ago, before I'd known I could do it, the words had been right there on my tongue, just waiting to be spoken. Now that I wanted them back, it was like trying to catch fish with bare hands. Every time I touched one, it slipped out of my grasp.

Go away! I shouted.

The words came in English. The hollow didn't move. I stiffened my back, glared into its inkpot eyes, and tried again.

Get out of here! Leave us alone!

English again. The hollow tilted its head like a curious dog but was otherwise a statue.

"Is he gone?" Addison asked.

The others couldn't tell for sure; only I could see it. "Still there," I said. "I don't know what's wrong."

I felt silly and deflated. Had my gift vanished so quickly?

"Never mind," Emma said. "Hollows aren't meant to be reasoned with, anyway." She stuck out a hand and tried to light a flame, but it fizzled. The effort seemed to sap her. I tightened my grip around her waist lest she topple over.

"Save your strength, matchstick," said Addison. "I'm sure we'll need it."

"I'll fight it with cold hands if I have to," said Emma. "All that matters is we find the others before it's too late."

The others. I could see them still, their afterimage fading by the tracks: Horace's fine clothes a mess; Bronwyn's strength no match for the wights' guns; Enoch dizzy from the blast; Hugh using the chaos to pull off Olive's heavy shoes and float her away; Olive caught by the heel and yanked down before she could rise out of reach. All of them weeping in terror, kicked onto the train at gunpoint, gone. Gone with the ymbryne we'd nearly killed ourselves to find, hurtling now through London's guts toward a fate worse than death. *It's already too late*, I thought. It was too late the moment Caul's soldiers stormed Miss Wren's frozen hideout. It was too late the night we mistook Miss Peregrine's wicked brother for our beloved ymbryne. But I swore to myself that we'd find our friends and our ymbryne, no matter the cost, even if there were only bodies to recover—even if it meant adding our own to the pile.

So, then: somewhere in the flashing dark was an escape to the street. A door, a staircase, an escalator, way off against the far wall. But how to reach them?

Get the hell out of our way! I shouted at the hollow, giving it one last try.

English, naturally. The hollow grunted like a cow but didn't move. It was no use. The words were gone.

"Plan B," I said. "It won't listen to me, so we go around it, hope it stays put."

"Go around it where?" said Emma.

To give it a wide berth, we'd have to wade through heaps of glass—but the shards would slice Emma's bare calves and Addison's paws to ribbons. I considered alternatives: I could carry the dog, but that still left Emma. I could find a swordlike piece of glass and stab the thing in the eyes—a technique that had served me well in the past—but if I didn't manage to kill it with the first strike, it would surely snap awake and kill us instead. The only other way around it was through a small, glass-free gap between the hollow and the wall.

It was narrow, though—a foot, maybe a foot and a half wide. A tight squeeze even if we flattened our backs to the wall. I worried that getting so close to the hollow, or worse, touching it by accident, would break the fragile trance holding it in check. Short of growing wings and flying over its head, though, it seemed like our only option.

"Can you walk a little?" I asked Emma. "Or at least hobble?"

She locked her knees and loosened her grip on my waist, testing her weight. "I can limp."

"Then here's what we're going to do: slide past it, backs to the wall, through that gap there. It's not a lot of space, but if we're careful . . . "

Addison saw what I meant and shrank back into the phone booth. "Do you think we should get so close to it?"

"Probably not."

"What if it wakes up while we're . . . ?"

"It won't," I said, faking confidence. "Just don't make any sudden moves—and whatever you do, don't touch it."

"You're our eyes now," Addison said. "Bird preserve us."

I chose a nice long shard from the floor and slid it into my pocket. Shuffling two steps to the wall, we pressed our backs to the cold tiles and began inching toward the hollow. Its eyes moved as we did, locked on me. A few creeping sidesteps later and we were enveloped by a pocket of hollow-stink so foul, it made my eyes water. Addison coughed and Emma cupped a hand over her nose.

"Just a little farther," I said, my voice reedy with forced calm. I took the glass from my pocket, gripping it with the pointed end out, then took another step, and another. We were close enough now that I could've touched the hollow with an outstretched arm. I heard its heart knocking inside its ribs, the beat quickening with each step we took. It was straining against me, fighting with every neuron to wrest my clumsy hands from its controls. *Don't move*, I said, mouthing the words in English. *You're mine. I control you. Don't move.*

I sucked in my chest, lined up and laddered each vertebra

against the wall, then crab-walked into the tight gap between the wall and the hollow.

Don't move, don't move.

Slide, shuffle, slide. I held my breath while the hollow's quickened, wet and wheezing, a vile black mist blooming from its nostrils. The urge to devour us must've been excruciating. So was my urge to run, but I ignored it; that would've been acting like prey, not master.

Don't move. Do not move.

Another few steps, a few more feet, and we'd be past it. Its shoulder a hairsbreadth from my chest.

Don't—

—and then it did. In one swift motion the hollow swiveled its head and pivoted its body to face me.

I went rigid. "Don't move," I said, this time aloud, to the others. Addison buried his face between his paws and Emma froze, her arm squeezing mine like a vise. I steeled myself for what was to come—its tongues, its teeth, the end.

Get back, get back, get back.

English, English, English.

Seconds passed during which, astonishingly, we weren't killed. But for the rising and falling of its chest, the creature seemingly had turned once again to stone.

Experimentally, moving by millimeters, I slid along the wall. The hollow followed me with slight turns of its head—locked onto me like a compass needle, its body in perfect sympathy with mine— but it didn't follow, didn't open its jaws. If whatever spell I'd cast had been broken, we'd already be dead.

The hollow was only watching me. Awaiting instructions I didn't know how to give. "False alarm," I said, and Emma breathed an audible sigh of relief.

We slid out of the gap, peeled ourselves from the wall, and hurried away as fast as Emma could limp. When we'd put a little distance between us and the hollow, I looked back. It had turned all the way around to face me.

Stay, I muttered in English. *Good.*

*   *   *

We passed through a veil of steam and the escalator came into view, frozen into stairs, its power cut. Around it glowed a halo of weak daylight, a tantalizing envoy from the world above. World of the living, world of now. A world where I had parents. They were here, both of them, in London, breathing this air. A stroll away.

Oh, hi there!

Unthinkable. Still more unthinkable: not five minutes ago, I'd told my father everything. The Cliff's Notes version, anyway: *I'm like Grandpa Portman was. I'm peculiar.* They wouldn't understand, but at least now they knew. It would make my absence feel less like a betrayal. I could still hear my father's voice, begging me to come home, and as we limped toward the light I had to fight a sudden, shameful urge to shake off Emma's arm and run for it—to escape this suffocating dark, to find my parents and beg forgiveness, and then to crawl into their posh hotel bed and sleep.

That was most unthinkable of all. I could never: I loved Emma, and I'd told her so, and I wouldn't leave her behind for anything. And not because I was noble or brave or chivalrous. I'm not any of those things. I was afraid that leaving her behind would rip me in half.

And the others, the others. Our poor, doomed friends. We had to go after them—but how? A train hadn't entered the station since the one that spirited them away, and after the blast and gunshots that had rocked the place, I was sure there'd be no more coming. That left us two options, each one terrible: go after them on foot through the tunnels and hope we didn't meet any more hollows, or climb the escalator and face whatever was waiting for us up there—most likely a wight mop-up crew—then regroup, reassess.

19

I knew which option I preferred. I'd had enough of the dark, and more than enough of hollows.

"Let's go up," I said, urging Emma toward the stalled escalator. "We'll find somewhere safe to plan our next move while you get your strength back."

"Absolutely not!" she said. "We can't just abandon the others. Never mind how I feel."

"We aren't. But we need to be realistic. We're hurt and defenseless, and the others are probably miles away by now, out of the underground and halfway to somewhere else. How will we even find them?"

"The same way I found you," said Addison. "With my nose. Peculiar folk have an aroma all their own, you see—one which only dogs of my persuasion can sniff out. And you happen to be one powerfully odoriferous group of peculiars. Fear enhances it, I think, and skipping baths . . . "

"Then we go after them!" Emma said.

She pulled me toward the tracks with a surprising burst of strength. I resisted, tug-of-warring our linked arms. "No, no—there's no way the trains are still running, and if we go in there on foot . . . "

"I don't care if it's dangerous. I won't leave them."

"It isn't just dangerous, it's pointless. They're already gone, Emma."

She took back her arm and started hobbling toward the tracks. Stumbled, caught herself. *Say something*, I mouthed to Addison, and he circled around to block her.

"I'm afraid he's right. If we follow on foot, our friends' scent trail will have dissipated long before we're able to find them. Even my profound abilities have limits."

Emma gazed into the tunnel, then back at me, her expression tortured. I held out my hand. "Please, let's go. It doesn't mean we're giving up."

"All right," she said heavily. "All right."

But just as we were starting toward the escalator, someone called out from the dark, back along the tracks.

"Over here!"

The voice was weak but familiar, the accent Russian. It was the folding man. Peering into the dark, I could just make out his crumpled form by the tracks, one arm raised. He'd been shot during the melee, and I assumed the wights had shoved him onto the train with the others. But there he lay, waving to us.

"Sergei!" cried Emma.

"You know him?" Addison said suspiciously.

"He was one of Miss Wren's peculiar refugees," I said, my ears pricking at the wail of distant sirens echoing down from the surface. Trouble was coming—maybe trouble disguised as help—and I worried that our best chance at a clean exit was slipping away. Then again, we couldn't just leave him.

Addison scuttled toward the man, dodging the deepest reefs of glass. Emma let me take her arm again and we shuffled after. Sergei was lying on his side, covered in glass and streaked with blood. The bullet had hit him somewhere vital. His wire-framed spectacles were cracked and he was adjusting them, trying to get a good look at me. "Is miracle, is miracle," he rasped, his voice thin as twice-strained tea. "I heard you speak with monster's tongue. Is miracle."

"It's not," I said, kneeling beside him. "It's gone, I've already lost it."

"If gift inside you, is forever."

Footsteps and voices echoed from the escalator passage. I cleared away glass so I could get my hands under the folding man. "We're taking you with us," I said.

"Leave me," he croaked. "I'll be gone soon enough . . . "

Ignoring him, I slipped my hands beneath his body and lifted. He was ladder-long but light as a feather, and I held him in my arms like a big baby, his skinny legs dangling over my elbow while his head lolled against my shoulder.

Two figures banged down the last few escalator steps and then stood at the bottom, rimmed by pale daylight and peering into the new dark. Emma pointed at the floor and we sank quietly to our knees, hoping they'd miss us—hoping they were just civilians come to catch a train—but then I heard the squelch of a walkie-talkie and they each fired up a flashlight, the beams shining against their bright reflective jackets.

They might've been emergency responders, or wights disguised as such. I wasn't sure until, in synchrony, they peeled off wraparound sunglasses.

Of course.

Our options had just narrowed by half. Now there were only the tracks, the tunnels. We could never outrun them, damaged as we were, but escape was still possible if they didn't see us—and they hadn't yet, amidst the chaos of the ruined station. Their searchlights dueled across the floor. Emma and I backed toward the tracks. If we could just slip into the tunnels unnoticed . . . but Addison, damn him, wasn't moving.

"Come on," I hissed.

"They are ambulance drivers and this man needs help," he said too loudly, and right away the beams of light bounced up from the floor and whipped toward us.

"Stay where you are!" one of the men boomed, unholstering a gun while the other fumbled for his walkie-talkie.

Then two unexpected things happened in quick succession. The first was that, just as I was about to drop the folding man onto the tracks and dive after him with Emma, a thunderous horn blew from inside the tunnel and a single brilliant headlight flashed into view. The rush of stale wind belonged, of course, to a train—running again, somehow, despite the blast. The second thing, announced by a painful twinge in my gut, was that the hollow had come unstuck and was loping in our direction. The instant after I felt it, I saw it, too, plowing at us through a billow of steam, black lips peeled wide, tongues thrashing the air.

We were trapped. If we ran for the stairs we'd be shot and mauled. If we jumped onto the tracks we'd be crushed by the train. And we couldn't escape onto the train because it would be ten seconds at least before it stopped and twelve before the doors opened and ten more before they shut again, and by then we'd be dead three ways. And so I did as I often do when I'm out of ideas—I looked to Emma. I could read in the desperation on her face that she understood the hopelessness of our situation and in the stony set of her jaw that she meant to act anyway. I remembered only as she began to stagger forward, palms out, that she couldn't see the hollow, and I tried to tell her, reach for her, stop her, but I couldn't get the words out and couldn't grab her without dropping the folding man, and then Addison was alongside her, barking at the wight while Emma tried uselessly to make a flame—spark, spark, nothing, like a lighter low on juice.

The wight broke out laughing, pulled back the hammer of his gun, and aimed it at her. The hollowgast ran at me, howling in counterpoint to the squeal of train brakes behind me. That's when I knew the end had come and there was nothing I could do to stop it. At that moment something inside me relaxed, and as it did, the pain I felt whenever a hollow was near faded, too. That pain was like a high-pitched whine, and as it hushed, I discovered hidden beneath it another sound, a murmur at the edge of consciousness.

A word.

I dove for it. Wrapped both arms around it. Wound up and shouted it with all the force of a major league pitcher. *Him*, I said, in a language not my own. It was only one syllable but held volumes of meaning, and the moment it rattled from my throat, the result was instant. The hollow stopped running at me—stopped dead, skidding on its feet—then turned sharply to one side and lashed out a tongue that whipped across the platform and wrapped three times around the wight's leg. Knocked off balance, he fired a shot that caromed off the ceiling, and then he was flipped upside down and hauled thrashing and screaming into the air.

It took my friends a moment to realize what had happened. While they stood gaping and the other wight shouted into his walkie-talkie, I heard train doors whoosh open behind me.

Here was our moment.

"COME ON!" I shouted, and they did, Emma stumble-running and Addison tangling her feet and me trying to wedge the gangly and blood-slick folding man through the narrow doors until we all crashed together across the threshold into the train car.

More gunshots rang out, the wight firing blindly at the hollow.

The doors closed halfway, then popped back open. "Clear the doors, please," came a cheerful prerecorded announcement.

"His feet!" Emma said, pointing at the shoes at the end of the folding man's long legs, the toes of which were poking through the doors. I scrambled to kick his feet clear, and in the interminable seconds before the doors closed again, the dangling wight fired more wild shots until the hollow grew tired of him and flung him against the wall, where he slid to the floor in an unmoving heap.

The other wight scurried for the exit. *Him, too*, I tried to say, but it was too little too late. The doors were closing, and with an awkward jolt the train began to move.

I looked around, grateful that the car we'd tumbled into was empty. What would regular people make of us?

"Are you okay?" I asked Emma. She was sitting up, breathing hard, studying me intensely.

"Thanks to you," she said. "Did you really make the hollow do all that?"

"I think so," I said, not quite believing it myself.

"That's amazing," she said quietly. I couldn't tell if she was frightened or impressed, or both.

"We owe you our lives," said Addison, nuzzling his head sweetly against my arm. "You're a very special boy."

The folding man laughed, and I looked down to see him grinning at me through a mask of pain. "You see?" he said. "I told you. Is miracle." Then his face turned serious. He grabbed my hand and pressed a small square of paper into it. A photograph. "My wife, my child," he said. "Taken by our enemy long ago. If you find others, perhaps . . . "

I glanced at the photo and got a shock. It was a wallet-sized portrait of a woman holding a baby. Sergei had clearly been carrying it with him a long time. Though the people in the photo were pleasant enough, the photo itself—or the negative—had been seriously damaged, perhaps narrowly survived a fire, exposed to such heat that the faces were warped and fragmented. Sergei had never mentioned his family before now; all he'd talked about since we met him was raising an army of peculiars—going loop to loop to recruit able-bodied survivors of the raids and purges. He never told us what he wanted an army *for*: to get them back.

"We'll find them, too," I said.

We both knew this was far-fetched, but it was what he needed to hear.

"Thank you," he said, and relaxed into a spreading pool of blood.

"He doesn't have long," Addison said, moving to lick Sergei's face.

"I might have enough heat to cauterize the wound," said Emma. Scooting toward him, she began rubbing her hands together.

Addison nosed the folding man's shirt near his abdomen. "Here. He's hurt here." Emma put her hands on either side of the spot, and at the sizzle of flesh I stood up, feeling faint.

I looked out the window. We were still pulling out of the station, slowed perhaps by debris on the tracks. The emergency lights' SOS flicker picked details from the dark at random. The body of a dead wight half buried in glass. The crumpled phone booth, scene of my breakthrough. The hollow—I registered its form with a shock—trotting on the platform alongside us, a few cars back, casual as a jogger.

Stop. Stay away, I spat at the window, in English. My head wasn't clear, the hurt and the whine getting in the way again.

We picked up speed and passed into the tunnel. I pressed my face to the glass, angling backward for another glimpse. It was dark, dark—and then, in a burst of light like a camera flash, I saw the hollow as a momentary still image—flying, its feet lifting from the platform, tongues lassoing the rail of the last car.

Miracle. Curse. I hadn't quite worked out the difference.

* * *

I took his legs and Emma his arms and gently we lifted Sergei onto a long bench seat, where beneath an advertisement for bake-at-home pizza he lay blacked out and rocking with the motion of the train. If he was going to die, it seemed wrong that he should have to do so on the floor.

Emma pulled up his thin shirt. "The bleeding's stopped," she reported, "but he'll die if he doesn't see the inside of a hospital soon."

"He may die anyway," said Addison. "Especially in a hospital here in the present. Imagine: he wakes up in three days' time, side healed but everything else failing, aged two hundred and bird-knows-what."

"That may be," Emma replied. "Then again, I'll be surprised if in three days' time any of us are alive, in any condition whatsoever. I'm not sure what more we can do for him."

I'd heard them mention this deadline before: two or three days was the longest any peculiar who'd lived in a loop could stay in the present without aging forward. It was long enough for them to visit the present but never to stay; long enough to travel between loops but short enough that they were never tempted to linger. Only dare-devils and ymbrynes made excursions into the present longer than a few hours; the consequences of a delay were too grave.

Emma rose, looking sickly in the pale yellow light, then tot-tered on her feet and grabbed for one of the train's stanchions. I took her hand and made her sit next to me, and she slumped against my side, exhausted beyond measure. We both were. I hadn't slept properly in days. Hadn't eaten properly, either, aside from the few opportunities we'd had to gorge ourselves like pigs. I'd been running and terrified and wearing these damned blister-making shoes since I couldn't remember when, but more than that, every time I spoke Hollow it seemed to carve something out of me that I didn't know how to put back. It made me feel tired to a degree that was wholly new, absolutely subterranean. I'd discovered a fresh vein inside me, a new source of power to mine, but it was depletable and finite, and I wondered if by using it up I was using myself up, too.

I'd worry about that another time. For now I tried to savor a rare moment of peace, my arm around Emma and her head on my shoulder, just breathing. Selfishly, perhaps, I didn't mention the hol-low that had chased our train. What could any of us do about it? It would either catch us or not. Kill us or not. The next time it found us—and I was sure there would be a next time—I would either find the words to stay its tongues or I wouldn't.

I watched Addison hop onto the seat across from us, unlock a window with his paw, and crack it open. The angry sound of the train and a warm funk of tunnel air came rushing in, and he sat reading it with his nose, eyes bright and snout twitching. The air smelled like stale sweat and dry rot to me, but he seemed to catch something subtler, something that required careful interpretation.

"Can you smell them?" I asked.

The dog heard me but took a long moment to reply, his eyes aimed at the ceiling as if finishing a thought. "I can," he said. "Their trail is nice and crisp, too."

Even at this high speed, he could pick up the minutes-old traces of peculiars who'd been enclosed in an earlier train car. I was impressed, and told him so.

"Thank you, but I can't take all the credit," he said. "Someone must've pushed open a window in their car, too, otherwise the trail would be much fainter. Perhaps Miss Wren did it, knowing I would try to follow."

"She knew you were here?" I asked.

"How did you find us?" Emma said.

"Just a moment," Addison said sharply. The train was slowing into a station, the windows flashing from tunnel black to tile white. He stuck his nose out the window and closed his eyes, lost in concentration. "I don't think they got off here, but be ready in any case."

Emma and I stood, doing our best to shield the folding man from view. I saw with some relief that there weren't many people waiting on the platform. Funny there were any at all, or that trains were still running. It was as if nothing had happened. The wights had made sure of it, I suspected, in hopes we'd take the bait, jump onto a train, and make it simple for them to round us up. We certainly wouldn't be hard to spot amongst modern London's workday commuters.

"Look casual," I said. "Like you belong here."

This seemed to strike Emma as funny, and she stifled a laugh. It was funny, I guess, inasmuch as we belonged nowhere in particular, least of all here.

The train stopped and the doors slid open. Addison sniffed the air deeply as a bookish woman in a pea coat stepped into our car. Seeing us, her mouth fell open, and then she turned smartly and walked out again. *Nope. No thanks.* I couldn't blame her. We were filthy, freakish-looking in bizarre old clothes, and splashed with blood. We probably looked like we'd just killed the poor man beside us.

"Look casual," Emma said, and snorted.

Addison withdrew his nose from the window. "We're on the right track," he said. "Miss Wren and the others definitely passed this way."

"They didn't get off here?" I asked.

"I don't think so. But if I don't smell them in the next station, we'll know we've gone too far."

The doors smacked closed and with an electric whine we were off again. I was about to suggest we find a change of clothes when Emma jolted beside me, as if she'd just remembered something.

"Addison?" she said. "What happened to Fiona and Claire?"

At the mention of their names, a nauseating new wave of worry shot through me. We'd last seen them at Miss Wren's menagerie, where the elder girl had stayed behind with Claire, who was too ill to travel. Caul told us he'd raided the menagerie and captured the girls, but he also told us Addison was dead, so clearly his information couldn't be trusted.

"Ah," said Addison, nodding gravely. "It's bad news, I'm afraid. Part of me, I admit, was hoping you wouldn't ask."

Emma's face drained of color. "Tell us."

"Of course," he said. "Shortly after your party left, we were raided by a gang of wights. We threw armageddon eggs at them, then scattered and hid. The larger girl, with the unkempt hair—"

"Fiona," I said, heart thudding.

"She used her facility with plants to hide us—in trees and under new-grown brush. We were so well camouflaged that it would've taken days for the wights to root us all out, but they gassed us and drove us into the open."

"Gas!" Emma cried. "The bastards swore they'd never use it again!"

"It appears they lied," said Addison.

I had seen a photo once, in one of Miss Peregrine's albums, of such an attack: wights in ghostly masks with breathing canisters, standing around casually as they launched clouds of poison gas into the air. Although the stuff wasn't fatal, it made your lungs and throat burn, caused terrible pain, and was rumored to trap ymbrynes in their bird form.

"When they'd rounded us up," Addison went on, "we were interrogated as to the whereabouts of Miss Wren. They turned her tower inside out—searching for maps, diaries, I don't know what—and when poor Deirdre tried to stop them, they shot her."

The emu-raffe's long face flashed before me, gawky, gap-toothed, and sweet, and my stomach lurched. What kind of person could kill such a creature? "God, that's awful," I said.

"Awful," Emma agreed perfunctorily. "And the girls?"

"The small one was captured by the wights," Addison said. "And the other . . . well, there was a scuffle with some of the soldiers, and they were near the cliff's edge, and she fell."

I blinked at him. "What?" For a moment the world blurred, then snapped back into focus.

Emma stiffened but her face betrayed nothing. "What do you mean, fell? Fell how far?"

"It was a sheer drop. A thousand feet at least." His fleshy jowls drooped. "I'm so sorry."

I sat down heavily. Emma kept standing, her hands white-knuckling the rail. "No," she said firmly. "No, that can't be. Perhaps she grabbed onto something on the way down. A branch or a ledge . . ."

Addison studied the gum-spackled floor. "It's possible."

"Or the trees below cushioned her fall and caught her like a net! She can speak to them, you know."

"Yes," he said. "One can always hope."

I tried to imagine being cushioned by a spiky pine tree after such a fall. It didn't seem possible. I saw the small hope Emma had kindled wink out, and then her legs began to tremble and she let go of the rail and thumped down onto the seat beside me.

She looked at Addison with wet eyes. "I'm sorry about your friend."

He nodded. "Same to you."

"None of this ever would've happened if Miss Peregrine were

here," she whispered. And then, quietly, she bowed her head and began to cry.

I wanted to put my arms around her, but somehow it felt like I'd be intruding on a private moment, claiming it for myself when really it was hers alone, so instead I sat and looked at my hands and let her mourn her lost friend. Addison turned away, out of respect, I think, and because the train was slowing into another station.

The doors opened. Addison stuck his head out the window, sniffed the air on the platform, growled at someone who tried to enter our car, then came back inside. By the time the doors closed again, Emma had lifted her head and wiped away her tears.

I squeezed her hand. "Are you all right?" I said, wishing I could think of something more or better to say than that.

"I have to be, don't I?" she said. "For the ones who are still alive."

To some it might've seemed callous, the way she boxed up her pain and set it aside, but I knew her well enough now to understand. She had a heart the size of France, and the lucky few whom she loved with it were loved with every square inch—but its size made it dangerous, too. If she let it feel everything, she'd be wrecked. So she had to tame it, shush it, shut it up. Float the worst pains off to an island that was quickly filling with them, where she would go to live one day.

"Go on," she said to Addison. "What happened to Claire?"

"The wights marched off with her. Gagged her two mouths and tossed her into a sack."

"But she was alive?" I said.

"And biting, as of noon yesterday. Then we buried Deirdre in our little cemetery and I hightailed it for London to find Miss Wren and warn all of you. One of Miss Wren's pigeons led me to her hideaway, and while I was pleased to see that you had arrived before me, unfortunately so had the wights. Their siege had already begun, and I was forced to watch helplessly as they stormed the building, and—well, you know the rest. I followed as you were led away to the underground. When that blast went off, I saw an opportunity to aid you and took it."

"Thank you for that," I said, realizing we hadn't yet acknowledged the debt we owed him. "If you hadn't dragged us away when you did . . . "

"Yes, well . . . no need to dwell on hypothetical unpleasantries," he said. "But in return for my gallantry, I was rather hoping you would assist me in rescuing Miss Wren from the wights. As unlikely as that sounds. She means everything to me, you see."

It was Miss Wren he'd wanted to snatch away from the wights, not us—but we were the realistic save, farther from the train, and he'd made a snap decision and taken what he could get.

"Of course we'll help," I said. "Isn't that what we're doing now?"

"Yes, yes," he said. "But you must realize, as an ymbryne, Miss Wren is more valuable to the wights than peculiar children, and thus she may prove more difficult to free. I worry that, if by some miracle we are lucky enough to rescue your friends . . . "

"Now *wait* a second," I snapped. "Who says she's more—"

"No, it's true," Emma said. "She'll be under heavier lock and key, no question. But we won't leave her behind. We're not leaving anyone else behind, ever again. You have our word as peculiars."

The dog seemed satisfied with that. "Thank you," he said, and then his ears flattened. He hopped up onto a seat to look out the window as we pulled into the next station. "Hide yourselves," he said, ducking down. "There are enemies near."

*   *   *

The wights were expecting us. I glimpsed two of them waiting on the platform, dressed as police officers among a scattering of commuters. They were scanning the cars as our train pulled into the station.

We dropped down below the windows, hoping they'd miss us—but I knew they wouldn't. The one with the walkie-talkie had radioed ahead; they must've known we were on this train. Now all they had to do was search it.

It came to a stop and people began filing on board, though not into our car. I risked a peek through the open doors and saw one of the wights down the platform, speed walking in our direction as he eyeballed each car.

"One's coming this way," I muttered. "How's your fire, Em?"

"Running on empty," she replied.

He was getting close. Four cars away. Three.

"Then get ready to run."

Two cars away. Then a soft, recorded voice: "Mind the closing doors, please."

"Hold the train!" the wight shouted. But the doors were already closing.

He stuck an arm through. The doors bounced open again. He got on board—into the car next to ours.

My eyes went to the door that connected our cars. It was locked with a chain—thank God for small mercies. The doors snicked shut and the train began to move. We shifted the folding man onto the floor and huddled with him in a spot where we couldn't be seen from the wight's car.

"What can we do?" said Emma. "The moment this train stops again, he'll come straight in here and find us."

"Are we absolutely certain he's a wight?" asked Addison.

"Do cats grow on trees?" Emma replied.

"Not in this part of the world."

"Then of course we aren't. But when it comes to wights, there's an old saying: if you're not sure, assume."

"Okay, then," I said. "The second those doors open, we run for the exit."

Addison sighed. "All this *fleeing*," he said disdainfully, as if he were a gourmand and someone had offered him a limp square of American cheese. "There's no imagination in it. Mightn't we try *sneaking?* Blending in? There's artistry in that. Then we could simply walk away, gracefully, unnoticed."

"I hate fleeing as much as anyone," I said, "but Emma and I look like nineteenth-century axe murderers, and you're a dog who wears glasses. We're bound to be noticed."

"Until they start manufacturing canine contact lenses, I'm stuck with these," Addison grumbled.

"Where's that hollowgast when you need him?" said Emma offhandedly.

"Run over by a train, if we're lucky," I said. "And what do you mean by that?"

"Only that he came in quite handy earlier."

"And before that he nearly killed us—twice! No, three times! Whatever it is I've been doing to control it has been half by accident, and the moment I'm *not* able to? We're dead."

Emma didn't respond right away, but studied me for a moment and then took my hand, all caked in grime, and kissed it gently, once, twice.

"What was that for?" I said, surprised.

"You have no idea, do you?"

"Of what?"

"How completely miraculous you are."

Addison groaned.

"You have an amazing talent," Emma whispered. "I'm certain all you need is a little practice."

"Maybe. But practicing something usually means failing at it for a while, and failing at this means people get killed."

Emma squeezed my hand. "Well, there's nothing like a little pressure to help you hone a new skill."

I tried to smile but couldn't muster one. My heart hurt too much at the thought of all the damage I could cause. This thing I could do felt like a loaded weapon I didn't know how to use. Hell, I didn't even know which end to point away from me. Better to set it down than have it blow up in my hands.

We heard a noise at the other end of the car and looked up to see the door opening. That one wasn't chained, and now a pair of leather-clad teenagers stumbled into our car, a boy and a girl, laughing and passing a lit cigarette between them.

"We'll get in trouble!" the girl said, kissing his neck.

The boy brushed a foppish wave of hair from his eyes—"I do this all the time, sweetheart"—then saw us and froze, his eyebrows parabolic. The door they'd come through banged closed behind them.

"Hey," I said casually, as if we weren't crouched on the floor with a dying man, covered in blood. "What's up?"

Don't freak out. Don't give us away.

The boy wrinkled his brow. "Are you . . . ?"

"In costume," I replied. "Got carried away with the fake blood."

"Oh," said the boy, clearly not believing me.

The girl stared at the folding man. "Is he . . . ?"

"Drunk," said Emma. "Soused out of his brain. Which is how he came to spill all our fake blood on the floor. And himself."

"And us," said Addison. The teens' heads snapped toward him, their eyes going wider still.

"You goon," Emma muttered. "Keep quiet."

The boy raised a trembling hand and pointed at the dog. "Did he just . . . ?"

Addison had said only two words. We might've played it off as a trick of echoes, something other than what it seemed, but he was too proud to play dumb.

"Of course I didn't," he said, raising his nose in the air. "Dogs can't speak English. Nor any human language—save, in one notable exception, Luxembourgish, which is only comprehensible to bankers and Luxembourgers, and therefore hardly of any use at all. No, you've eaten something disagreeable and are having a nightmare, that's all. Now, if you wouldn't mind terribly, my friends need to borrow your clothes. Please disrobe at once."

Pallid and shaking, the boy started to remove his leather jacket, but he'd only wriggled one arm free when his knees gave out and he fainted to the floor. And then the girl began to scream, and she didn't stop.

In an instant the wight was banging at the chained door, his blank eyes flashing murder.

"So much for sneaking away," I said.

Addison turned to look at him. "Definitely a wight," he said, nodding sagely.

"I'm so glad we put that mystery to rest," said Emma.

There was a jolt and a squeal of brakes. We were coming into a station. I pulled Emma to her feet and prepared to run.

"What about Sergei?" Emma said, whipping around to look back at him.

It would be hard enough to outrun a pair of wights with Emma still recovering her strength; with the folding man in my arms, it would be impossible.

"We'll have to leave him," I said. "He'll be found and brought to a doctor. It's his best chance—and ours."

Surprisingly, she agreed. "I think it's what he'd want." She went quickly to his side. "Sorry we can't take you with us. But I'm certain we'll meet again."

"In the next world," he croaked, his eyes slitting open. "In Abaton."

With those mysterious words and the girl's screams ringing in our ears, the train came to a stop and the doors opened.

* * *

We weren't clever. We weren't graceful. The moment the train doors slid open, we just ran as fast as we could.

The wight leapt out of his car and into ours, by which time we had dashed past the screaming girl, over the fainted boy, and onto the platform, where we struggled against a crowd that was streaming onto the train like a school of spawning fish. This station, unlike all the others, was heaving at the seams.

"There!" I shouted, pulling Emma toward a WAY OUT sign that glowed in the distance. I hoped Addison was somewhere at our feet, but so many people were flooding around us that I could hardly see the floor. Luckily, Emma's strength was returning—or a rush of adrenaline was kicking in—because I don't think I could've supported her weight and threaded the human stampede, too.

We'd put about twenty feet and fifty people between us and the train when the wight burst out of it, shoving commuters and yelling *I am an officer of the law!* and *Get out of my way!* and *Stop those children!* Either no one could hear him over the echoing din of the station or no one was paying attention. I looked back to see him gaining, and that's when Emma started tripping people, sweeping her legs left and right as we ran. People shouted and fell into tangles behind us, and when I looked back again the wight was struggling, stepping on legs and backs and getting swats with umbrellas and briefcases in return. Then he stopped, red-faced and frustrated, to unsnap his gun holster. But the gulf of people between us had yawned too wide now, and though I was sure he'd be heartless enough to fire into a crowd, he wasn't stupid enough to. The ensuing panic would've made us even more difficult to catch.

The third time I looked back he was so far behind and swallowed by the crowd that I could hardly see him. Maybe he didn't really care whether he caught us. After all, we were neither a great threat nor much of a prize. Maybe the dog had been right: compared to an ymbryne, we were hardly worth the trouble.

Halfway to the exits the crowd thinned enough for us to break into an open run—but we'd taken only a few strides when Emma caught me by the sleeve and stopped me. "Addison!" she cried, spinning to look around. "Where's Addison?"

A moment later he came scampering out of the thickest part of the crowd, a long piece of white fabric trailing from a spike on his collar. "You waited for me!" he said. "I became entangled in a lady's stocking . . ."

Heads turned at the sound of his voice.

"Come on, we can't stop now!" I said.

Emma plucked the stocking from Addison's collar, and we were off and running again. Before us were an escalator and an elevator. The escalator was working but very crowded, so I steered us toward the elevator instead. We ran past a lady painted blue from head to toe, and I had to turn and stare even as my legs carried me onward. Her hair was dyed blue, her face caked with blue makeup, and she wore a skin-tight jumpsuit, also blue.

She'd only just passed out of sight when I saw someone even more freakish: a man whose head was divided vertically into halves, one bald and burned to a crisp, the other untouched, hair moussed into a dapper wave. If Emma noticed him, she didn't turn to look. Maybe she was so used to meeting genuine peculiars that peculiar-looking normals hardly registered. *But what if they aren't normal?* I thought. *What if they're peculiars, and instead of the present we've ended up in some new loop? What if—*

Then I saw two boys with glowing swords battling by a wall of vending machines, each sabre clash sounding with a thin plasticky *thwack*, and reality came into sharp focus. These strange-looking people weren't peculiars. They were nerds. We were very much in the present.

Twenty feet away, the elevator doors opened. We poured on the speed and hurled ourselves inside, bouncing off the back wall with our hands while Addison tumbled in on tripping legs. I turned just in time to glimpse two things through the closing doors: the wight breaking out of the crowd and coming at us in a full run, and back by the tracks where the train was pulling away, the hollowgast leaping from the roof of the last car to the station ceiling, swinging like a spider from a light fixture by its tongues, its black eyes burning at me.

And then the doors closed and we were gliding gently upward, and someone was saying, "Where's the fire, mate?"

A middle-aged man stood in the rear corner of the elevator, costumed and sneering. His shirt was torn, his face was crosshatched with fake cuts, and strapped to the end of one arm, Captain Hook–style, was a bloodstained chainsaw.

Emma saw him and took a quick step back. "Who are you?"

He looked mildly offended. "Oh, come on."

"If you really want to know where the fire is, don't answer." She began to raise her hands, but I reached over and stopped her.

"He's no one," I said.

"I thought I was making such an obvious choice this year," the man muttered. He arched an eyebrow and raised his chainsaw a little. "Name's Ash. You know . . . *Army of Darkness?*"

"Never heard of either," said Emma. "Who's your ymbryne?"

"My what?"

"He's just doing a character," I tried to explain, but she wasn't hearing me.

"Never mind who you are," she said. "We could use an army, and beggars can't be choosers. Where are the rest of your men?"

The man rolled his eyes. "L-O-L. You guys are funny. Every-one's in the convention center, obviously."

"He's wearing a *costume*," I whispered to Emma. Then, to the guy: "She doesn't see a lot of movies."

"A costume?" Emma scrunched her brow. "But he's a grown man."

"So what?" the man said, looking us up and down. "And who are *you* supposed to be? Walking Dorks? League of Extraordinary

Dingleberries?"

"Peculiar children," said Addison, whose ego wouldn't allow him to be silent any longer. "And I am the seventh pup of the seventh pup in a long and illustrious line of—"

The man fainted before Addison could finish, his head knocking against the floor with a *clonk* that made me wince.

"You've *got* to stop doing that," Emma said, then grinned despite herself.

"Serves him right," said Addison. "What a rude person. Now quick, nick his wallet."

"No way!" I said. "We're not thieves."

Addison snorted. "I daresay we need it more than he does."

"Why on earth is he dressed like that?" said Emma.

The elevator dinged and the doors began to slide open.

"I think you're about to find out," I said.

*   *   *

The elevator doors split open and like magic the day-lit world spread before us, so bright we had to shield our eyes. I drew a welcome lungful of fresh air as we stepped out onto a swarming sidewalk. There were costumed people everywhere: superheroes in spandex, zombies shambling in heavy makeup, raccoon-eyed anime girls wielding battleaxes. They congregated in unlikely bunches and spilled into a street blocked off to traffic, drawn like moths to a large gray building where a banner proclaimed: COMIC CONVENTION TODAY!

Emma recoiled toward the elevator. "What *is* all this?"

Addison peered over his glasses at a green-haired Joker touching up his face paint. "Judging by their attire, it appears to be some sort of religious holiday."

"Something like that," I said, coaxing Emma back onto the sidewalk, "but don't be scared—they're only dressed-up normals, and that's what we look like to them, too. We only need to worry

about that wight." I failed to mention the hollow, hoping we'd baffled it by vanishing into the elevator. "We should find a place to hide
until he's gone, then sneak back into the Underground . . . "

"No need for that," Addison said, and he trotted into the
crowded street, nose twitching.

"Hey!" Emma called after him. "Where are you going?"

But he was already circling back.

"Huzzah for fortune!" he said, wagging his stubby tail. "My
nose tells me our friends were brought out of the underground here,
via that escalator. We've gone the right way after all!"

"Thank the birds!" Emma said.

"Do you think you can follow their trail?" I asked.

"Do I *think* I can? They don't call me Addison the Astounding
for nothing! Why, there isn't an aroma, a redolence, a peculiar eau
de toilette I couldn't nose from a hundred meters—"

Addison was easily distracted by the topic of his own greatness,
even when pressing matters were at hand, and his proud, booming
voice had a tendency to carry.

"Okay, we get it," I said, but he steamrolled on, walking now,
following his nose.

" . . . I could find a peculiar in a hollow-stack, an ymbryne in
an aviary . . . "

We chased him into the costumed crowd, between the legs of
a dwarf on stilts, around a pack of undead princesses, and on a
near-collision course with a Pikachu and an Edward Scissorhands,
who were waltzing in the street. *Of course our friends were brought
this way,* I thought. It was perfect camouflage—not only for us, who
amidst all this looked downright normal, but also for wights ab-
ducting a herd of peculiar children. Even if some of them had dared
cry out for help, who would've taken them seriously enough to in-
tervene? People were play-acting all around us, improvising staged
fights, growling in monstrous costumes, moaning like zombies. Some
strange kids yelling about being kidnapped by people who wanted to

steal their souls? Wouldn't raise an eyebrow.

Addison walked a circle sniffing the ground, then sat down, perplexed. Subtly, because even in this crowd a talking dog would be shocking, I bent down and asked him what was the matter.

"It's just . . . err," he stammered, "that I seem to have—"

"Lost the trail?" Emma said. "I thought your nose was infallible."

"I've merely *mislaid* the trail. But I don't understand how . . . it leads quite clearly to this spot, then vanishes."

"Tie your shoes," Emma said suddenly. "Now."

I looked down at them. "But they're not—"

She grabbed my forearm and yanked me down. "Tie. Your. Shoes," she repeated, then mouthed, *wight!*

We knelt there, hidden below the heads of the loose-knit crowd. Then came a burst of loud static and a strained voice through a walkie-talkie. "Code 141! All crews report to the acre immediately!"

The wight was close. We heard him reply in a gruff, oddly accented voice: "This is M. I'm tracking the escapees. Request permission to continue searching. Over."

I exchanged a tense look with Emma.

"Denied, M. Cleaners will sweep the area later. Over."

"The boy seems to have some influence over the cleaners. Sweep may not be effective."

Cleaners. He must've been talking about the wights. And he was *definitely* talking about me.

"Denied!" said the crackling voice. "Report back immediately or you'll spend tonight in the pit, over!"

The wight muttered "Acknowledged" into his walkie-talkie and stalked away.

"We've got to follow him," Emma said. "He could lead us to the others!"

"And straight into the lion's den," Addison said. "Though I suppose that can't be helped."

I was still reeling. "They know who I am," I said faintly. "They must've seen what I did."

"That's right," Emma said. "And it scared the stuffing out of them!"

I unbent myself to watch the wight go. He marched through the crowd, hopped a traffic barricade, and jogged away toward a parked police car.

We followed him as far as the traffic barrier. I looked around, trying to imagine the kidnappers' next move. Behind us was the crowd, and in front, beyond the traffic barrier, cars prowled the block for parking. "Maybe our friends came this far on foot," I said, "then were put into a car."

Brightening, Addison stood on hind legs to peek over the traffic barrier. "Yes! That must be it. Bright boy!"

"What are you so cheerful for?" said Emma. "If they were taken away in a car, they could be anywhere by now!"

"Then we'll *follow* them anywhere," Addison said pointedly. "Though I doubt they're terribly far. My old master had a townhouse not far from here, and I know this part of the city well. There are no major ports nor obvious points of exit from London nearby— but there *are* a few loop entrances. It's much more likely that they've been taken to one of those. Now lift me up!"

I did, and with my help he scrambled over the barrier and began to sniff around the other side. Within seconds he'd found our friends' scent trail again. "This way!" he said, pointing down the street after the wight, who'd gotten into the police car and was driving away.

"Looks like we're in for a walk," I said to Emma. "Think you can make it?"

"I'll manage," she said, "so as long as we find another loop within a few hours. Otherwise I may start sprouting gray hairs and crow's feet." She smiled, as if this were something to joke about.

"I won't let that happen," I said.

We jumped the barricade. I took one last look at the Underground station behind us.

"Do you see the hollow?" said Emma.

"No. I don't know where it is. And that worries me."

"Let's worry about one thing at a time," she said.

*   *   *

We walked as fast as Emma could manage, keeping to the side of the street still sunk in morning shadow, watching for police and following Addison's nose. We passed into an industrial area near the docks, the River Thames revealing itself darkly between the gaps in warehouses, then into a fancy shopping district where glittering stores were crowned with glassy townhouses. Over their roofs I caught glimpses of the dome of St. Paul's Cathedral, whole again, the sky around it clear and blue. The bombs had all been dropped and the bombers were long gone—shot down, scrapped, retired into museums where they gathered dust behind ropes, to be gawked at by schoolchildren for whom that war seemed as distant as the Crusades. To me it was, quite literally, yesterday. Hard to believe these were the same cratered, blacked-out streets through which we'd run for our lives only last night. They were unrecognizable now, shopping malls seemingly conjured from the ashes—and so were the people who walked them, heads down, glued to phones, clothed in logos. The present seemed suddenly strange to me, so trivial and distracted. I felt like one of those mythical heroes who fights his way back from the underworld only to realize that the world above is every bit as damned as the one below.

And then it hit me—*I was back*. I was in the present again, and I'd crossed into it without the intervention of Miss Peregrine . . . which was supposed to be impossible.

"Emma?" I said. "How did I get here?"

She kept her eyes trained on the street ahead, always scanning for trouble. "Where, London? On a train, silly."

"No." I lowered my voice. "I mean to *now*. You said Miss Peregrine was the only one who could send me back."

She turned to glance at me, eyes narrowing. "Yes," she said slowly. "She was."

"Or so you thought."

"No—she was, I'm sure of it. That's how it works."

"Then how did I get here?"

She looked lost. "I don't know, Jacob. Maybe . . . "

"There!" Addison said excitedly, and we broke off wondering to look. His body was rigid, pointing down the street we'd just turned onto. "I'm picking up dozens of peculiar scent trails now—dozens upon dozens—and they're fresh!"

"Which means what?" I said.

"Other kidnapped peculiars were brought this way, not just our friends," said Emma. "The wights' hideout must be close by."

"Close by *here*?" I said. The block was lined with fast food joints and tacky souvenir shops, and we stood framed in the neon-lit window of a greasy diner. "I guess I'd been imagining someplace . . . *eviller.*"

"Like a dungeon in some dank castle," Emma said, nodding.

"Or a concentration camp surrounded by guards and barbed-wire fences," I said.

"In the snow. Like Horace's drawing."

"We may find such a place yet," said Addison. "Remember, this is likely just the entrance to a loop."

Across the street, tourists were taking pictures of themselves in front of one of the city's iconic red phone boxes. Then they noticed us and snapped a picture in our direction.

"Hey!" Emma said. "No photos!"

People were beginning to stare. No longer surrounded by comic conventioneers, we stuck out like sore, bloody thumbs.

"Follow me," Addison hissed. "All the trails lead this way."

We hurried after him down the block.

"If only Millard were here," I said, "he could scout this place without being noticed."

"Or if Horace were here, he might remember a dream that would help us," Emma said.

"Or find us new clothes," I added.

"If we don't stop, I'll cry," Emma said.

We came to a jetty bustling with activity. Sun glinted off the water, a narrow inlet of the murky Thames, and clumps of tourists in visors and fanny packs waddled onto and off of several large boats, each offering more or less identical sightseeing tours of London.

Addison stopped. "They were brought here," he said. "It would appear they were put onto a boat."

We followed his nose through the crowd to an empty boat slip. The wights had indeed loaded our friends onto a boat, and now we needed to follow them—but in what? We walked around the jetty looking for a ride.

"This will never do," Emma grumbled. "These boats are too large and crowded. We need a small one—something we can pilot ourselves."

"Wait a moment," said Addison, his snout twitching. He trotted away, nose to the wooden boards. We followed him across the jetty and down a little unmarked ramp that was ignored by the tourists. It led to a lower dock, below the street, just at water level. There was no one around; it was deserted.

Here Addison stopped, wearing a look of deep concentration. "Peculiars have come this way."

"*Our* peculiars?" Emma said.

He sniffed the dock again and shook his head. "Not ours. But there are many trails here, new and old, strong and faded, all mixed together. This is an oft-used pathway."

Ahead of us, the dock narrowed and disappeared beneath the main jetty, where it was swallowed in shadows.

"Oft used by whom?" Emma said, peering anxiously into the dark. "I've never heard of any loop entrance underneath a dock in Wapping."

Addison had no answer. There was nothing to do but forge on and explore, so we did, passing nervously into the shadows. As our eyes adjusted, another jetty resolved into view—one altogether different from the sunny, pleasant one above us. The boards down here were green and rotting, broken in places. A scrum of squeaking rats scampered through a mound of discarded cans, then leapt a short distance from the dock into an ancient-looking skiff, bobbing in the dark water between wooden pylons slimed with moss.

"Well," Emma said, "I guess that would do in a pinch . . . "

"But it's filled with rats!" said Addison, aghast.

"It won't be for long," Emma said, igniting a small flame in her hand. "Rats don't much care for my company."

Since there didn't seem to be anyone to stop us, we crossed to the boat, hopscotching around the weakest-looking boards, and began to untie it from the dock.

"STOP!" came a booming voice from inside the boat.

Emma squealed, Addison yelped, and I nearly leapt out of my skin. A man who'd been sitting in the boat—how had we not seen him until now?!—rose slowly to his feet, straightening himself inch by inch until he towered over us. He was seven feet tall at least, his massive frame draped in a cloak and his face hidden beneath a dark hood.

"I'm—I'm so sorry!" Emma stammered. "It's—we thought this boat was—"

"Many have tried to steal from Sharon!" the man thundered. "Now their skulls make homes for sea creatures!"

"I swear we weren't trying to—"

"We'll just be going," squeaked Addison, backing away, "so sorry to bother you, milord."

"SILENCE!" the boatman roared, stepping onto the creaking

dock with one enormous stride. "Anyone who comes for my boat must PAY THE PRICE!"

I was completely terrified, and when Emma shouted "RUN!" I was already turning to go. We'd only gotten a few paces, though, when my foot crashed through a rotting board and I pitched face-first onto the dock. I tried to scramble up but my leg was thigh deep in the hole. I was stuck, and by the time Emma and Addison circled back to help me, it was too late. The boatman was upon us, looming overhead and laughing, his cavernous guffaws booming around us. It might have been a trick of the darkness, but I could've sworn I saw a rat tumble from the hood of his cloak, and another slip from his sleeve as he slowly raised his arm toward us.

"Get away from us, you maniac!" Emma shouted, clapping her hands to light a flame. Though the light she made did nothing to chase away the dark inside the boatman's hood—I suspected not even the sun could do that—it showed us what he held in his outstretched hand, which wasn't a knife, nor any weapon. It was a piece of paper, pinched between his thumb and a long, white forefinger.

He was offering it to me, bending low so I could reach it.

"Please," he said calmly. "Read it."

I hesitated. "What is it?"

"The price. And some other information regarding my services."

Quaking with fear, I reached up and took the paper. We all leaned in to read by the light of Emma's flame.

"IT'S THE DESTINATION, NOT THE JOURNEY"

SHARON'S RIVER TOURS.

OFFERING DAY TRIPS AND ROMANTIC
SUNSET CRUISES SINCE 1693

❀ PRICE. ❀

ONE GOLD
PIECE.

DISCRETION
GUARANTEED.

ASK ABOUT
OUR SPECIALS!

I looked up at the giant boatman. "So this is you?" I said uncertainly. "You're . . . Sharon?"

"In the flesh," he replied, his voice an oily slither that made my neck hairs stand on end.

"Good bird, man, you scared us half to death!" said Addison. "Was all that bluster and cackling really necessary?"

"My apologies. I was napping and you startled me."

"We startled *you*?"

"For a moment I thought you really were trying to steal my boat," he chuckled.

"Ha-ha!" Emma said, forcing a laugh. "No, we were just . . . making sure it was moored properly."

Sharon turned to examine the skiff, which was simply roped to one of the wooden pylons.

"And how do you find it?" he asked, the dull white crescent of a grin spreading beneath his hood.

"Totally . . . ship-shape," I said, finally jimmying my leg free from the hole. "Really good, um, mooring."

"Couldn't have tied a better knot myself," said Emma, helping me to my feet.

"By the way," said Addison. "The ones who *did* try . . . are they really all . . . ?" He glanced at the dark water and swallowed audibly.

"Never mind that," the boatman said. "Now you've woken me, and I am at your service. What can I do for you?"

"We need to hire your boat," Emma said firmly. "By ourselves."

"I can't allow that," Sharon said. "I always captain the boat."

"Ah, too bad then!" Addison said, turning eagerly to leave.

Emma caught him by the collar. "Wait!" she hissed. "We're not done here." She smiled pleasantly at the boatman. "So, we happen to know that a lot of peculiars come through this . . . "

She looked around, searching for the right word.

" . . . place. Is that because there's a loop entrance nearby?"

"I don't know what you mean," Sharon said flatly.

"Okay, yes, of course you can't just *admit* it. I completely understand. But you're in safe company with us. Obviously, *we're*—"

I elbowed her. "Emma, don't!"

"Why not? He's already seen the dog talk and me make fire. If we can't speak honestly . . . "

"But we don't know if *he* is," I said.

"Of course he is," she said, then turned to Sharon. "You are, aren't you?"

The boatman stared at us impassively.

"He is, isn't he?" Emma asked Addison. "Can't you smell it on him?"

"No, not clearly."

"Well, I suppose it doesn't matter, so long as he's not a wight." She gave Sharon a beady-eyed glare. "You're not, are you?"

"I am a businessman," he said evenly.

"Who's well accustomed to meeting talking dogs and girls who make fire with their hands," said Addison.

"In my line of work, one meets a wide variety of people."

"I'll cut to the chase," I said, shaking water off one foot, then the other. "We're looking for some friends of ours. We think they might've come this way within the last hour or so. Mostly kids, some adults. One was invisible, one could float . . . "

"They'd be hard to miss," Emma said. "They were being held at gunpoint by a gang of wights."

Sharon crossed his arms into a wide, black X. "As I said, all manner of people hire my boat, and each relies on my absolute discretion. I won't discuss my clientele."

"Is that so?" Emma said. "Excuse us just a moment."

She took me aside to whisper in my ear.

"If he doesn't start talking, I'm going to get really angry."

"Don't do anything reckless," I whispered back.

"Why? You believe that humbug about skulls and sea creatures?"

"Yes, actually. I know he's a slimebag, but—"

"Slimebag? He's practically admitted to doing business with wights! He might even *be* one!"

"—but he's a *useful* slimebag. I have a feeling he knows exactly where our friends were taken. It's just a matter of asking the right questions."

"Then have at it," she said crossly.

I turned to Sharon and said with a smile, "What can you tell me about your tours?"

He brightened immediately. "Finally, a subject I can speak freely about. I just happen to have some information right here . . . " He turned snappily and went to a nearby pylon. A shelf had been nailed onto it, and upon the shelf was displayed a skull dressed in old-time aviator garb—leather cap, goggles, a jaunty scarf. Gripped between its teeth were several pamphlets, and Sharon pulled one out and handed it to me. It was a cheesy tourist brochure that looked like it had been printed when my grandfather was a boy. I leafed through its pages as Sharon cleared his throat and spoke.

"Let's see now. Families enjoy the Famine 'n' Flames package . . . in the morning we go upriver to watch Viking siege engines catapult diseased sheep over the city walls, then have a nice boxed lunch and return in the evening via the Great Fire of 1666, which is a real treat after dark, with the flames reflecting on the water, very nice. Or if you've only a few hours to spare, we have a lovely gibbetting 'round Execution Dock—right at sunset, popular with honeymooners—in which some excellently foul-tongued pirates give colorful speeches before being put to the rope. For a small fee you can even have your photo taken with them!"

Inside the brochure were illustrations of smiling tourists enjoying the sights he'd described. The final page was a photo of one of Sharon's guests posing with a gang of surly pirates wielding knives and guns.

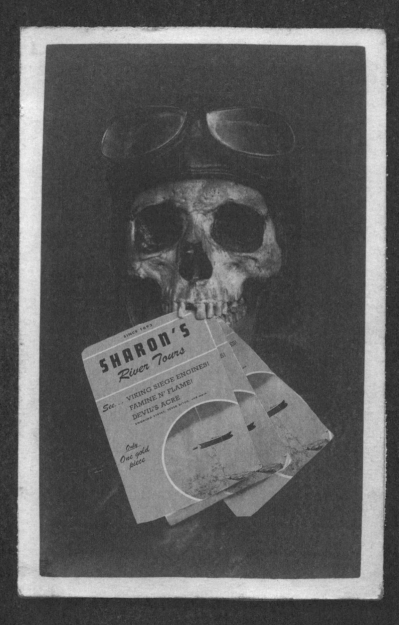

Another satisfied customer!

"Peculiars do this stuff for *fun*?" I marveled.

"This is a waste of time," Emma whispered, checking behind us anxiously. "I'll bet he's just running out the clock until the next patrol of wights arrives."

"I don't think so," I said. "Just wait . . . "

Sharon was plowing on as if he hadn't heard us. " . . . and you can see all the lunatics' heads arranged on pikes as we float beneath London Bridge! Lastly, there's our most requested excursion, which is a personal favorite of mine. But oh—never mind," he said coyly, waving his hand, "come to think of it, I doubt you'd be interested in Devil's Acre."

"Why not?" Emma said. "Too nice and pleasant?"

"Actually, it's rather a rough spot. Certainly no place for children . . . "

Emma stamped her foot and shook the whole rotting dock. "That's where our friends were taken, isn't it?" she shouted. "Isn't it!"

"Don't lose your temper, miss. Your safety is my highest concern."

"Quit winding us up and tell us what's there!"

"Well, if you insist . . . " Sharon made a sound like he was slipping into a warm bath and began rubbing his leathery hands together, as if just thinking about it brought him pleasure. "Nasty things," he said. "Dreadful things. Vile things. Anything you like, so long as what you like is nasty, dreadful, and vile. I've often dreamed of hanging up my oar pole and retiring there one day, perhaps to run the little abattoir on Oozing Street . . . "

"What name did you call it again?" said Addison.

"Devil's Acre," the boatman said wistfully.

Addison shuddered from tip to tail. "I know it," he said gravely. "It's a terrible place—the most depraved and dangerous slum in the whole long history of London. I've heard stories of peculiar animals brought there in cages and made to fight in blood-sport games.

Grimbears pitted against emu-raffes, chimpnoceri against flamingoats . . . parents against their own children! Forced to maim and kill one another for the entertainment of a few sick peculiars."

"Disgusting," Emma said. "What peculiar would participate in such a thing?"

Addison shook his head ruefully. "Outlaws . . . mercenaries . . . exiles . . . "

"But there *are* no outlaws in peculiardom!" said Emma. "Any peculiar convicted of a crime is brought by the home guard to a punishment loop!"

"How little you know of your own world," the boatman said.

"Criminals can't be jailed if they're never caught," Addison explained. "Not if they escape to a loop like that first—lawless, ungovernable."

"It sounds like Hell," I said. "Why would anyone go there voluntarily?"

"What's Hell for some," said the boatman, "is paradise for others. It's the last truly free place. Somewhere you can buy anything, sell anything . . . " He leaned toward me and lowered his voice. "Or *hide* anything."

"Like kidnapped ymbrynes and peculiar children?" I said. "Is that what you're getting at?"

"I said nothing of the sort," shrugged the boatman, busying himself with a rat plucked from the hem of his cloak. "Shoo there, Percy, Daddy's working."

While he placed the rat gently aside, I gathered Emma and Addison in a tight huddle. "What do you think?" I whispered. "Could this . . . *devil* place . . . really be where our friends were taken?"

"Well, they have to be keeping their prisoners inside a loop, and a pretty old one," said Emma. "Otherwise most of us would age forward and die after a day or two . . . "

"But what do the wights care if we die?" I said. "They just want to steal our souls."

"Maybe, but they can't let the ymbrynes die. They need them to re-create the 1908 event. Remember the wights' crazy plan?"

"All that stuff Golan was raving about. Immortality and ruling the world . . . "

"Yeah. So they've been kidnapping ymbrynes for months and need a place to hold them where they won't turn into dried fruit leather, right? Which means a pretty old loop. Eighty, a hundred years at least. And if Devil's Acre is really a lawless jungle of depravity . . . "

"It is," said Addison.

" . . . then it sounds like a perfect spot for wights to secret away their captives."

"Right in the heart of peculiar London, too," said Addison. "Right under everyone's noses. Clever little blighters . . . "

"Guess that settles it," I said.

Emma stepped smartly toward Sharon. "We'll take three tickets to that disgusting, horrible place you described, please."

"Be very, very certain that's what you want," said the boatman. "Innocent lambs like yourselves don't always return from Devil's Acre."

"We're sure," I said.

"Very good, then. But don't say I didn't warn you."

"Only thing is, we don't have three gold pieces," said Emma.

"Is that right?" Sharon tented his long fingers and let out a sigh that smelled like an opened tomb. "Normally I insist on payment up front, but I'm feeling generous this morning. I find your plucky optimism charming. You can owe me." And then he laughed, as if he knew we'd never live to repay him, and stepping aside he raised a cloaked arm toward his boat.

"Welcome aboard, children."

CHAPTER TWO

*S*haron made a big show of plucking six wriggling rats from his boat before we boarded—as if a pestilence-free journey were a luxury afforded only to Very Important Peculiars—and then he offered Emma his arm and helped her step from the dock. We were seated three abreast on a simple wooden bench. While Sharon was busy untying the mooring rope, I wondered whether trusting him was merely unwise or if it crossed the line into recklessness, like lying down for a nap in the middle of a road.

The trouble with the merely unwise/deeply stupid line is that you often don't know which side you're on until it's too late. By the time things have settled down enough for you to reflect, the button's been pushed, the plane's left the hangar, or in our case, the boat's left the dock—and as I watched Sharon shove us away from it with his foot, which was bare, and I noticed that his bare foot was not quite human-looking, with toes as long as mini hotdogs and thick yellow nails that curled like claws, I realized with sinking certainty which side of the line we were on, and also that it was too late to do much about it.

Sharon yanked the ignition cord on a dinky outboard motor and it coughed awake in a cloud of blue fumes. Tucking his considerable legs beneath him, he lowered into the puddle of black fabric his cloak made in the boat. He revved the puttering engine, then steered us out of the underjetty, through a forest of looming wood pylons and into warm sunlight. Then we were in a canal, a man-made tributary of the Thames walled on both sides by glassy buildings and bobbing with more boats than a toddler's tub at bath time—candy-red tugs and wide, flat barges and tour boats whose upper decks teemed with sightseers taking the air. Strangely, none of them trained their cameras at, nor seemed to even notice, the unusual craft that burbled past them, with an angel of death at the tiller, two blood-spattered children in the seat, and a dog in glasses peering over the side. Which was just as well. Had Sharon charmed his boat somehow so that only peculiars could see it? I decided to believe it was so, because there was nowhere to hide in it anyway, should we have needed to.

Looking it over in the full light of day, I noticed that the boat was extremely simple but for an intricately carved figurehead rising from its bow. The carving was shaped like a fat, scaly snake that curved upward in a gentle S, but where a head should've been was a giant eyeball, lidless and large as a melon, staring forever out before us.

"What is it?" I asked, running my hand over its polished surface.

"Yew wood," Sharon called over the motor's growl.

"I would what?"

"That's what it's made from."

"But what's it *for*?"

"To see with!" he replied testily.

Sharon pushed the motor harder—possibly just to drown out my questions—and as we picked up speed the bow lifted gently from the water. I took a deep breath, enjoying the sun and wind on my face, and Addison let his tongue hang out as he leaned over the side with his paws, looking as happy as I'd ever seen him.

What a beautiful day to go to Hell.

"So I've been thinking about how you got here," Emma said. "How you got back to the present."

"Okay," I said. "What do you think?"

"There's only one explanation that makes any sense—though not bloody much. When we were in the underground tunnels with all those wights, and we crossed back into the present, the reason you came with us instead of continuing on in eighteen-whatever-it-was, suddenly alone, was that Miss Peregrine was there somehow, nearby, and helped you cross without anyone knowing it."

"I don't know, Emma, that seems . . . " I hesitated, not wanting to be harsh. "You think she was hiding in the tunnel?"

"I'm saying it's possible. We've no idea where she was."

"The wights have her. Caul admitted it!"

"Since when do you believe anything the wights say?"

"You've got me there," I said. "But since Caul was boasting about having her, I figured he was probably telling the truth."

"Maybe . . . or he said it to crush our spirits and make us want to give up. He was trying to convince us to surrender to his soldiers, remember?"

"True," I said, frowning. My brain was starting to kink from all the possibilities. "Okay. Let's say for the sake of argument that Miss P was with us in the tunnel. Why would she have gone to the trouble of sending me back to the present as a captive of the wights? We were on our way to have our second souls sucked out. I would've been better off stuck in that loop."

For a moment Emma looked genuinely stumped. Then her face lit up and she said, "Unless you and I are *supposed* to rescue everyone else. Maybe it was all part of her plan."

"But how could she have known we would escape the wights?"

Emma cast a sidelong glance at Addison. "Maybe she had help," she whispered.

"Em, this hypothetical chain of events is getting *really* unlikely." I took a breath, choosing my words carefully. "I know you want to believe Miss Peregrine is out there somewhere, free, watching over us. I do, too . . . "

"I want that so badly, it hurts," she said.

"But if she were free, wouldn't she have contacted us somehow? And if *he* were involved," I said quietly, nodding toward

Addison, "wouldn't he have mentioned it by now?"

"Not if he's sworn to secrecy. Perhaps it's too dangerous to tell anyone, even us. If we knew Miss Peregrine's whereabouts, and someone *knew* we knew, we might break under torture . . . "

"And he wouldn't?" I said a little too loudly, and the dog looked up at us, his cheeks ballooning and tongue flapping ridiculously as the wind caught them. "Ho, there!" he cried. "I've counted fifty-six fish already, though one or two might've been bits of half-submerged rubbish. What are you two whispering about?"

"Oh, nothing," said Emma.

"Somehow I doubt that," he muttered, but his suspicion was quickly overwhelmed by his instincts, and a second later he yelped, "Fish!" and his attention lasered back to the water. "Fish . . . fish . . . rubbish . . . fish . . . "

Emma laughed darkly. "It's a completely mad idea, I know. But my brain is a hope-making engine."

"I'm so glad," I said. "Mine is a worst-case-scenario generator."

"We need each other, then."

"Yes. But we already knew that, I think."

The boat's steady heaving pushed us together and apart, together and apart.

"Sure you wouldn't rather go on the romantic cruise?" Sharon said. "It isn't too late."

"Very sure," I said. "We're on a mission."

"Then I suggest you open the box you're sitting on. You're going to need what's inside when we cross over."

We opened the bench's hinged top to find a large canvas tarp.

"What's this for?" I said.

"Cowering beneath," Sharon replied, and he turned the boat down an even narrower canal lined with new, expensive-looking condos. "I've been able to keep you hidden from view thus far, but the protection I can offer doesn't work inside the Acre—and unsavory characters tend to keep watch for easy prey 'round the entrance. And you are most certainly easy prey."

"I *knew* you were up to something," I said. "Not a single tourist so much as glanced at us."

"It's safer to watch historical atrocities being committed when the participants aren't able to watch you back," he said. "Can't have my customers being carried off by Viking raiders, can I? Imagine the user reviews!"

We were fast approaching a sort of tunnel—a bridged-over stretch of canal, perhaps a hundred feet long, atop which hulked a building like a warehouse or an old mill. From the far end shone a half circle of blue sky and sparkling water. Between here and there was only darkness. It looked as much like a loop entrance as anyplace I'd seen.

We heaved out the enormous tarp, which filled half the boat. Emma lay down beside me and we wriggled beneath it, drawing the edge up to our chins like bedsheets. As the boat glided beneath the bridge into shadow, Sharon cut the motor and hid it beneath another, smaller tarp. Then he stood and extended a collapsible staff, plunged it into the water until it touched bottom, and began poling us forward in long, silent strokes.

"By the way," Emma said, "what sort of 'unsavory characters' are we hiding from? Wights?"

"There's more evil in peculiardom than merely your hated wights," Sharon said, his voice echoing through the stone tunnel. "An opportunist disguised as a friend can be every bit as dangerous as an outright enemy."

Emma sighed. "Must you always be so vague?"

"Your heads!" he snapped. "You too, dog."

Addison snuffled beneath the tarp, and we pulled the edge over our faces. It was black and hot under the fabric, and it smelled overpoweringly of motor oil.

"Are you frightened?" Addison whispered in the dark.

"Not particularly," said Emma. "Are you, Jacob?"

"So much I might throw up. Addison?"

"Of course not," the dog said. "Fearfulness isn't a characteristic of my breed."

But then he snuggled right between Emma and me, and I could feel his whole body trembling.

*　　*　　*

Some changeovers are as fast and smooth as superhighways, but this one felt like slamming down a washboard road full of potholes, lurching around a hairpin turn, and then careening off a cliff—all in complete darkness. When it was finally over, my head was dizzy and pounding. I wondered what invisible mechanism made some changeovers harder than others. Maybe the journey was only as rough as the destination, and this one had felt like off-roading into a savage wilderness because that's precisely what we had done.

"We have arrived," Sharon announced.

"Is everyone okay?" I said, fumbling for Emma's hand.

"We must go back," Addison groaned. "I've left my kidneys on the other side."

"Do keep quiet until I find somewhere discreet to deposit you," Sharon said.

It's amazing how much more acute your hearing becomes the moment you can't use your eyes. As I lay quietly beneath the tarp, I was hypnotized by the sounds of a bygone world blooming around us. At first there was only the splash of Sharon's pole in the water, but soon it was complemented by other noises, all stirring together to paint an elaborate scene in my mind. That steady slap of wood against water belonged, I imagined, to the oars of a passing boat piled high with fish. I pictured the ladies I could hear shouting to one another as leaning from the windows of opposite-facing houses, trading gossip across the canal while tending lines of laundry. Ahead of us, children whooped with laughter as a dog barked, and distantly I could make out voices singing in time to the rhythm of hammers: "Hark to the clinking of hammers, hark to the driving of nails!" Before long I was imagining plucky chimneysweeps in top hats skipping down streets full of rough charm and people banding together to overcome their lot in life with a wink and a song.

I couldn't help it. All I knew about Victorian slums I'd learned from the campy musical version of *Oliver Twist*. When I was twelve I'd been in a community theater production of it; I was Orphan Number Five, if you must know, and had suffered such terrible stage fright on the night of the show that I faked a stomach flu and watched the whole thing from the wings, in costume, with a barf bucket between my legs.

Anyway, such was the scene in my head when I noticed a small hole in the tarp near my shoulder—chewed by rats, no doubt—and, shifting a little, I found I could peek through it. Within seconds, the happy, musical-inspired landscape I'd imagined melted away like a Salvador Dalí painting. The first horror to greet me were the houses that lined the canal, though calling them houses was generous. Nowhere in their sagging and rotted architecture could be found a single straight line. They slouched like a row of exhausted soldiers who'd fallen asleep at attention; it seemed the only thing keeping them from tipping straight into the water was the tightness with which they were packed—that and the mortar of black-and-green filth that smeared their lower thirds in thick, sludgy strata. On each of their rickety porches a coffinlike box stood on end, but only when I heard a loud grunt issue from one and saw something tumble into the water from beneath it did I realize what they were or that the slapping sounds I'd heard earlier hadn't come from oars but from outhouses, which were contributing to the very filth that held them up.

The women calling to one another from across the canal were leaning from opposite windows, just as I'd imagined, but they weren't hanging laundry and they certainly weren't trading gossip—at least, not anymore; now they were trading insults and issuing threats. One waved a broken bottle and laughed drunkenly while the other shouted epithets I could barely understand ("Yore nuffink but a stinkin' dollymop 'ood lay wi' the devil 'imself for a farthing!")—which was ironic, if I took her meaning correctly, because she was herself stripped to the waist and didn't seem to mind who noticed. Both stopped to whistle down at Sharon as we passed, but he ignored them.

Eager to wipe that image from my head, I managed to replace it with something even worse: ahead of us was a gang of kids swinging their feet from a rickety footbridge that spanned the canal. They were dangling a dog above the water by a rope tied around its hind legs, dipping the poor creature underwater and cackling when its desperate barks turned to bubbles. I resisted an urge to kick the tarp away and scream at them. At least Addison couldn't see; if he had, no amount of reasoning would've stopped him from going after them with teeth bared, blowing our cover.

"I see what you're up to," Sharon muttered at me. "If you want to have a look around just wait, we'll be through the worst of it in a tick."

"Are you peeking?" Emma whispered, poking me.

"Maybe," I said, still doing it.

The boatman shushed us. Drawing his pole from the water, he uncapped the handle to expose a short blade, then held it out to sever the boys' rope as we drifted by. The dog splashed into the water and paddled gratefully away, and howling with rage, the boys began to improvise projectiles to throw at us. Sharon pushed on, ignoring them as he had the ladies until a flying apple core missed his head by inches. Then he sighed, turned, and calmly pulled back the hood of his cloak—just enough so that the boys could see him, but I couldn't.

Whatever they saw must've scared them half to death, because all ran screaming from the bridge, one so fast he tripped and fell into the fetid water. Chuckling to himself, Sharon readjusted his hood before facing forward again.

"What's happened?" Emma said, alarmed. "What was that?"

"A Devil's Acre welcome," replied Sharon. "Now, if you care to see where we are, you may uncover your faces a bit, and I'll attempt to give you your gold coin's worth of tour-guiding with the time we have left."

We pulled the edge of the tarp down to our chins, and both Emma and Addison gasped—Emma, I think, at the sight, and Addison, judging from his wrinkled nose, at the smell. It was unreal, like a stew of raw sewage simmering all around us.

"You get used to it," Sharon said, reading my puckered face.

Emma gripped my hand and moaned, "Oh, it's *awful* . . ."

And it was. Now that I could see it with both eyes, the place looked even more hellish. The foundations of every house were decomposing into mush. Crazy wooden footbridges, some no wider than a board, crisscrossed the canal like a cat's cradle, and its stinking banks were heaped with trash and crawling with spectral forms at work sifting through it. The only colors were shades of black, yellow, and green, the flag of filth and decay, but black most of all. Black stained every surface, smeared every face, and striped the air in columns that rose from chimneys all around us—and, more ominously, from the smokestacks of factories in the distance, which announced themselves on the minute with industrial booms, deep and primal like war drums, so powerful they shook every window yet unbroken.

"This, friends, is Devil's Acre," Sharon began, his slithering voice just loud enough for us to hear. "Actual population seven thousand two hundred and six, official population zero. The city fathers, in their wisdom, refuse even to acknowledge its existence. The charming body of water in whose current we're currently drifting is called Fever Ditch, and the factory waste, night soil, and animal carcasses which flow perpetually into it are the source not only of its bewitching odor but also of disease outbreaks so regular you could set your watch to them and so spectacular that this entire area has been dubbed 'the Capital of Cholera.'

"And yet . . . " He raised a black-draped arm toward a young girl lowering a bucket into the water. "For many of these unfortunate souls, it serves as both sewer and spring."

"She isn't going to *drink* that!" Emma said, horrified.

"In a few days, once the heavy particles settle, she'll skim the clearest liquid from the top."

Emma recoiled. "No . . . "

"Yes. Terrible shame," Sharon said casually, then continued rattling off facts as if reciting from a book. "The citizenry's primary occupations are rubbish picking and luring strangers into the Acre to cosh them on the head and rob them. For amusement, they ingest whatever flammable liquids are at hand and sing badly at the top of their lungs. The area's main exports are smelted iron slag, bone meal, and misery. Notable landmarks include—"

"It isn't funny," Emma interrupted.

"Pardon me?"

"I said, it isn't funny! These people are suffering, and you're making jokes about it!"

"I am not making jokes," Sharon replied imperiously. "I'm providing you with valuable information that may save your life. But if you'd rather plunge into this jungle cocooned in ignorance . . . "

"We wouldn't," I said. "She's very sorry. Please keep going."

Emma shot me a disapproving look, and I disapproved right back at her. This was no time to take a stand on political correctness, even if Sharon sounded a bit heartless.

"Keep your voices down, for Hades' sake," Sharon said irritably. "Now, as I was saying. Notable landmarks include St. Rutledge's Foundlings' Prison, a forward-thinking institution which jails orphans before they've had the opportunity to commit any crimes, thereby saving society enormous cost and trouble; St. Barnabus's Asylum for Lunatics, Mountebanks, and the Criminally Mischievous, which operates on a voluntary, outpatient basis and is nearly always empty; and Smoking Street, which has been in flames for eighty-seven years due to an underground fire no one's bothered to extinguish. Ah," he said, pointing to a blackened clearing between houses on the bank. "Here's one end of it, which, as you can see, is burnt to a crisp."

Several men were at work in the clearing, hammering on a wooden frame—rebuilding one of the houses, I assumed—and when they saw us passing they stopped to shout hello to Sharon, who gave just a token wave back, as if slightly embarrassed.

"Friends of yours?" I asked.

"Distant relations," he muttered. "Gallows rigging is our family trade . . . "

"*What* rigging?" said Emma.

Before he could answer, the men had resumed work, singing loudly as they swung their hammers: "Hark to the clinking of hammers! Hark to the driving of nails! What fun to build a gallows, the cure for all that ails!"

If I hadn't been so horrified, I might've broken out laughing.

* * *

We coursed steadily down Fever Ditch. Like hands closing around us, it seemed to narrow with every stroke of Sharon's staff, sometimes so dramatically that the footbridges crossing it became unnecessary; you could practically leap across the water from roof to roof, the gray sky but a crack between them, suffocating all below in gloom. All the while, Sharon nattered on like a textbook come to life. In just a few minutes he'd managed to cover fashion trends in Devil's Acre (stolen wigs hung from belt loops were popular), its gross domestic product (firmly in the negative), and the history of its settlement (by enterprising maggot farmers in the early twelfth century). He was just launching into the highlights of its architecture when Addison, who'd been squirming next to me through it all, finally interrupted him.

"You seem to know every last fact about this hellhole with the exception of anything that would be remotely useful to us."

"Such as?" Sharon said, his patience thinning.

"Whom can we trust here?"

"Absolutely no one."

"How can we find the peculiars who live in this loop?" said Emma.

"You don't want to."

"Where are the wights holding our friends?" I asked.

"It's bad for business to know things like that," Sharon replied evenly.

"Then let us off this accursed boat and we'll set about finding them ourselves!" said Addison. "We're wasting precious time, and your endless monologuing is putting me to sleep. We hired a boatman, not a schoolmarm!"

Sharon harrumphed. "I should dump you into the Ditch for being so rude, but if I did, I'd never get the gold coins you owe me."

"Gold coins!" said Emma, fairly spitting with disgust. "What about the well-being of your fellow peculiars? What about *loyalty*?"

Sharon chuckled. "If I cared about things like that, I'd have been dead long ago."

"And wouldn't we all be better off," Emma muttered and looked away.

As we were talking, tendrils of fog had begun to curl around us. It was nothing like the gray mists of Cairnholm—this was greasy and yellow-brown, the color and consistency of squash soup. Its sudden appearance seemed to make Sharon uneasy, and as the view ahead dimmed, his head turned quickly from side to side, as if he were on the lookout for trouble—or searching for a spot to dump us.

"Drat, drat, *drat*," he muttered. "This is a bad sign."

"It's only fog," said Emma. "We're not afraid of fog."

"Neither am I," said Sharon, "but this isn't fog. It's *murk*, and it's man-made. Nasty things happen in the murk, and we must get out of it as quickly as we can."

He hissed at us to cover ourselves, and we did. I retreated to my peeking hole. Moments later a boat emerged from the murk and passed close-by going the opposite direction. A man was at the oars and a woman sat in the seat, and though Sharon said good morning they only stared back—and continued staring until they were well past us, and the murk had swallowed them up again. Grumbling under his breath, Sharon maneuvered us toward the left bank and a small dock I could just barely make out. But when we heard footsteps on the wooden planks and a low murmur of voices, Sharon leaned on his pole to turn us sharply away.

We zigzagged from bank to bank, looking for a place to land, but each time we got close, Sharon would see something he didn't like and turn away again. "Vultures," he muttered. "Vultures everywhere . . . "

I didn't see any myself until we passed beneath a sagging footbridge and a man crossing above us. As we drifted under him, the man stopped and looked down. He opened his mouth and drew a deep breath—about to yell for help, I thought—but rather than a voice, what came out of his mouth was a jet of heavy yellow smoke that shot toward us like water from a firehose.

I panicked and held my breath. What if it was poison gas? But Sharon wasn't covering his face or reaching for a mask—he was just muttering "Drat, drat, *drat*" while the man's breath swirled around us, merging with the murk and reducing our visibility to nothing. Within a few seconds the man, the bridge he stood on, and the banks on either side of us had all been blotted out.

I uncovered my head (no one could see us now anyway) and said quietly, "When you said this stuff was man-made, I thought you meant by smokestacks, not literally—"

"Oh, wow," Emma said, uncovering herself. "What's it for?"

"The vultures will murk an area to cloak their activities," Sharon said, "and to blind their prey. Fortunately for you, I am not easily preyed upon." And he drew his long staff from the water, passed it over our heads, and used it to tap the wooden eyeball at the bow of his boat. The eyeball began to glow like a fog lamp, piercing the murk before us. Then he returned his staff to the water and, leaning heavily on it, spun the boat in a slow circle, sweeping the water around us with his light.

"But if they're making this," said Emma, "then they're peculiar, aren't they? And if they're peculiar, perhaps they're friendly."

"The pure of heart don't end up as ditch pirates," said Sharon, and then he stopped the turning boat as our light fixed upon another approaching vessel. "Speak of the devil."

We could see them clearly enough, but for now all they would see of us was a glary bloom of light. It wasn't much of an advantage, but at least it allowed us to size them up before we had to retreat beneath the tarp. They were two men in a boat about twice the size of our own. The first man was operating a nearly silent outboard motor, and the second held a club.

"If they're so dangerous," I whispered, "why are we just waiting for them?"

"We're too deep inside the Acre to escape them now, and I can most likely talk us out of this."

"And if you can't?" said Emma.

"You may have to swim for it."

Emma glanced at the oily black water and said, "I'd rather die."

"That's your choice. Now, I recommend you disappear, children, and don't move a muscle under there."

We drew the tarp over our heads again. A moment later, a hearty voice called out, "Ho, there, boatman!"

"Ho, there," replied Sharon.

I heard oars drag the water, and then felt a jolt as the other boat knocked against ours.

"What's your business here?"

"Merely out for a pleasure cruise," Sharon said lightly.

"And a fine day for it!" the man replied, laughing.

The second man wasn't in the mood for jokes. "Wot's undah the rag?" he growled, his accent nearly impenetrable.

"What I carry on my boat is my own business."

"Innithin passes through Fever Ditch s'*our* business."

"Old ropes and bric-a-brac, if you must know," said Sharon. "Nothing of interest."

"Then you won't mind us having a look," said the first man.

"What about our arrangement? Haven't I paid you this month?"

"Hen't no arrangement nummore," said the second. "Wights are payin' five times the goin' rate fer nice plump feeders. Any as lets a feeder slip away . . . it's the pit, or worse."

"What could be worse than the pit?" said the first.

"I dun inten' t'fineout."

"Now gentlemen, be reasonable," said Sharon. "Perhaps it's time to renegotiate. I can offer terms competitive with anyone . . . "

Feeders. I shivered despite a clammy warmth building under the tarp from Emma's quickly heating hands. I hoped she wouldn't need to use them, but the men weren't budging, and I feared the boatman's blabber would stall them only so long. A fight would mean disaster, though. Even if we could take out the men in the boat, the vultures, as Sharon had said, were everywhere. I imagined a mob forming—coming after us in boats, firing on us from the banks, jumping onto us from the footbridges—and I began to freeze up with fear. I really, really did not want to find out what *feeders* meant.

But then I heard a hopeful sound—the clink of coins being exchanged, and the second man was saying, "Wy, 'ees *loaded*! I could retire to Spain wi' dis . . . "

But just as my hopes were rising, my stomach began to sink. A familiar old feeling crept into my belly, and I realized it had been building, slowly and gradually, for some time. It started as an itch, then become a dull ache, and now that ache was sharpening—the telltale tug of a nearby hollowgast.

But not just any hollow. *My* hollow.

The word popped into my head without warning or precedent. *Mine*. Or maybe I had it backward. Maybe *I* belonged to *it*.

Neither arrangement was any guarantee of safety. I expected it wanted to kill me just as badly as any hollow would, only something had temporarily plugged the urge. It was the same mysterious thing that had magnetized the hollow to me and tuned the compass needle inside me to it—and it was this needle that told me the hollow was close now and getting closer.

Just in time to get us caught, or killed, or kill us itself. I resolved then that should we make it safely to shore, my first order of business would be to get rid of it once and for all.

But where was it? If it was as close as it seemed to be, it would've been swimming toward us in the Ditch, and I definitely would've heard a creature with seven limbs doing the breaststroke. Then the needle shifted and dipped, and I knew—could see, almost—that it was *under* the water. Hollows did not, apparently, need to breathe often. A moment later there came a gentle *thunk* as it attached itself to the bottom of our boat. We all jumped at the sound, but only I knew what it was. I wished I could warn my friends, but I had to lie motionless, its body just inches away on the other side of the wooden boards we lay upon.

"What was that?" I heard the first man say.

"I didn't hear anything," Sharon lied.

Let go, I mouthed silently, hoping the hollow could hear. *Go away and leave us alone.* Instead, it began to make a grinding sound against the wood; I pictured it gnawing at the bottom of the boat with its long teeth.

"I heard'at plain as day," said the second man. "Boatman's tryin' to make us look like fools, Reg!"

"I think he is at that," said the first.

"I assure you, nothing could be further from the truth," said Sharon. "It's this damned defective boat of mine. Past due for a tune-up."

"Forget it, deal's off. Show us what you got."

"Or you could allow me to increase my offer," said Sharon. "We'll consider it a gratuity for all your kind understanding."

The men conferred in an undertone.

"If we let 'im go an' someone else catches 'im wi' feeders, it's the pit for us."

"Or worse."

Go away, go away, go AWAY, I begged the hollow in English.

Thud, thud, THUD, it answered, knocking against the hull.

"Pull back that rag!" demanded the first man.

"Sir, if you would wait just a moment—"

But the men were determined. Our boat rocked like someone was boarding it. There were shouts, then footfalls near our heads as a scuffle broke out.

There's no point hiding now, I thought, and the others seemed to agree. I saw Emma's glowing-hot fingers reach for the edge of the tarp.

"On three," she whispered. "Ready?"

"As a racehorse," Addison growled.

"Wait," I said, "first, you should know—under the boat, there's—"

And then the tarp was ripped away, and I never did finish that sentence.

*   *   *

What happened next happened fast. Addison bit the arm that had torn away the tarp and Emma made a swipe at its surprised owner, grazing the man's face with scalding fingers. He stumbled back howling and fell into the water. Sharon had been knocked down in the scuffle, and the second man was standing above him with his club raised. Addison leapt at him and grabbed hold of his leg. The man turned to shake off the dog, giving Sharon time to regain his feet and hit him in the stomach. The man doubled over and Sharon disarmed him with a tricky whirl of his staff.

The man decided to quit while he could and leapt back into his boat. Sharon tore away the canvas covering the outboard motor, yanked its ignition cord, and our boat sputtered to life just as a third came speeding out of the murk alongside us. Inside were three more men, one armed with an old-fashioned pistol that was leveled right at Emma.

I shouted at her to get down and tackled her just as it cracked and sent up a puff of white smoke. Then the man pointed it at Sharon, who let go of the throttle and put his hands up. And that would've been it for us, I think, had not a throat-full of strange words come gushing up and pouring out of me, loud and sure and foreign to my ears.

Sink their boat! Use your tongues to sink their boat!

In the half second it took everyone to turn and stare at me, the hollow had pushed off from our hull and flung its tongues at the other boat. They fired out of the water, whipped around the lip of its stern, and flipped the boat up and backward in a reverse somersault that launched all three men out.

The boat crashed upside down on two of them.

Sharon might've taken the opportunity to hit the throttle and get us out of there, but he stood frozen in shock, his hands still raised.

Which was fine. I wasn't done yet, anyhow.

That one, I said, looking at the gunman flailing in the water.

It seemed the hollow could hear me underwater because moments after I'd said it the man screamed, looked down, and was sucked under—gone, just like that—and immediately the water where he'd been bloomed red.

"I didn't say *eat* him!" I said in English.

"What are you waiting for?" Emma shouted at Sharon. "Go!"

"Right, right," the boatman stammered. Shaking off his stupor, he lowered his hands and leaned on the throttle. The motor whined and Sharon turned the rudder and spun us in a tight circle, tripping Emma, Addison, and me into a pile. The boat bucked and shot forward, and then we were speeding through whorls of murk, heading back the way we'd come.

Emma looked at me and I looked back, and though it was too loud to hear anything over the motor and the rush of blood in our ears, I thought I could read in her face both fear and exhilaration—a look that said, *You, Jacob Portman, are amazing and terrifying.* But when she finally spoke, I could make out only one word: *Where?*

Where, indeed. I'd hoped we could get away from the hollow while it was finishing off the Ditch pirate, but reading my gut now I knew it was still close, trailing behind us, most likely using one of its tongues as a towline.

Close, I mouthed back.

Her eyes brightened and she nodded once, sharply: *Good.*

I shook my head. Why wasn't she afraid? Why couldn't she see how dangerous it was? The hollow had tasted blood, and just left a meal half-finished behind us. Who knew what meanness still boiled inside it? But the way she looked at me. Just that crooked bit of smile gave me a surge, and I felt I could do anything.

We were coming up fast on the bridge and the murk-making peculiar. He was waiting for us, crouching and sighting us down the length of a rifle he'd rested on the bridge's handrail.

We ducked. I heard two shots. Looking up again, I saw that no one had been hit.

We were going under the bridge. In a moment we'd be out the other side and he'd have another shot at us. I couldn't let him take it.

I turned and shouted *Bridge!* in hollowspeak, and the creature seemed to know just what I meant. The two tongues that weren't holding on to our boat whipped upward, and with a wet slap each one wrapped around the bridge's flimsy supports. All three tongues unreeled triangularly until they were pulled taut, like elastic stretched to the limit. The hollow was forced up out of the water, tethered between boat and bridge like a starfish.

The boat slowed so quickly, it was like someone had thrown the emergency brake; we were all tossed forward onto the floor. The bridge groaned and rocked, and the peculiar taking aim at us stumbled and dropped his gun. I thought that surely either the bridge would give or the hollow would—it was squealing like a stuck pig, as if it might rip down the middle—but as the peculiar bent to snatch his gun, it seemed the bridge would hold, which meant I'd traded all our momentum and speed for nothing. Now we weren't even moving targets.

Let go! I screamed at the hollow, this time in its language.

It didn't—the thing would never leave me of its own accord. So I rushed to the back of the boat and bellied over the stern. There was one of its tongues, knotted around the rudder. Remembering how Emma's touch had once made a hollow's tongue release her ankle, I pulled her over and told her to burn the rudder. She did—nearly falling over the side to make the reach—and the hollow squealed and let go.

It was like releasing a slingshot. The hollow flew away and slammed into the bridge with a splintering crash; the whole tottering contraption buckled and went tumbling into the water. At the same time, the back of our boat dropped, and the motor, once again submerged, flung us forward. The sudden acceleration toppled us like bowling pins. Sharon managed to hold on to the rudder, and righting himself, he steered us sharply away from a collision course with the canal wall. We flew down the spine of the Ditch, a black V of water shooting out behind us.

We hunched low should any more bullets fly. We seemed to be out of immediate danger. The vultures were somewhere behind us, and I couldn't imagine how they'd catch us now.

Panting, Addison said, "That was the same creature we met in the Underground, wasn't it?"

I realized I'd been holding my breath and so let it out, then nodded. Emma looked at me, waiting for more, but I was still processing, every nerve jangling with the strangeness of what had just happened. This much I knew: this time I'd nearly had him. It was as if, with each encounter, I dove a little deeper into the hollowgast's nerve center. The words came easier, felt less foreign to my tongue, met less resistance from the hollow. Still, it was like a tiger onto which I'd managed to clap a dog leash. At any moment it might decide to turn and take a bite out of me, or any of us. And yet, for reasons beyond my understanding, it hadn't.

Maybe, I thought, with another attempt or two, I could really get my hands around it. And then—and then. My God, what a thought.

Then we'd be unstoppable.

I gazed back at the ghost of a bridge, dust and wood pulp spiraling in the air where the structure had stood only moments ago. In the wreckage below, I watched for a limb to break the surface, but there was only a lifeless swirl of trash. I tried to feel for it, but my gut was useless now, wrung out and empty. Then the mud-colored mist closed behind us and painted away the view.

Just when I needed a monster, it had gotten itself killed.

*　　*　　*

The boat nodded as Sharon eased the throttle and banked right, through the slowly clearing murk, toward a block of ghastly tenements.

They stood at the edge of the water in a vast unbroken wall, resembling not so much houses as the outermost boundary of a maze, scowling and fortresslike, with few points of entry. We drifted along at a crawl, searching for a way in. It was Emma who finally spotted one, though I had to squint to recognize it as more than just a trick of shadows.

To call it an alley would've been exaggerating. It was a slot canyon, narrow as a knife's edge, a shoulder's width from wall to wall and fifty times as high, its entrance marked by a moss-shagged ladder screwed flat to the bankside. I could see only a little distance in before the passage hid itself, curving away into sunless dark.

"Where does it go?" I asked.

"Where angels fear to tread," Sharon replied. "This wasn't the landing I'd have chosen for you, but our choices are limited now. Are you certain you wouldn't rather leave the Acre altogether? There's still time."

"*Quite* certain," Emma and Addison said simultaneously.

Me, I would've been happy to debate the matter—but it was too late to turn back now. *Get them back or die trying* was something I'd said in the past few days. Time to dive in.

"In that case, land ho," Sharon said dryly. He retrieved the mooring rope from under his seat, tossed it over the ladder, and pulled us toward the bank. "Everyone out, please. Do watch your step. Wait, allow me."

Sharon climbed the slippery, half-runged ladder with the nimbleness of someone who'd done it many times. Once at the top, he knelt on the bank and reached down to help each of us up in turn. Emma went first, then I handed up a nervous and wiggling Addison, and then, because I was proud and dumb, I climbed the ladder without taking Sharon's hand and nearly slipped off.

The moment we were all safely on land, Sharon was climbing back down the ladder. He'd left the motor idling.

"Just a minute," said Emma. "Where are you going?"

"Away from here!" Sharon replied, hopping from the ladder into his boat. "Would you mind tossing down that rope?"

"I will not! You must show us where to go first. We've no idea where we are!"

"I don't do land tours. I'm strictly a boat guide."

We exchanged looks of disbelief.

"Give us directions, at least!" I implored him.

"Or better yet, a map," said Addison.

"A map!" Sharon exclaimed, as if this were the silliest thing he'd ever heard. "There are more thief passageways, murder tunnels, and illegal dens in Devil's Acre than anywhere in the world. The place is unmappable! Now stop being childish and hand me down my rope."

"Not until you tell us something useful!" Emma said. "The name of someone we can ask for help—who won't try to sell us to the wights!"

Sharon broke out laughing.

Emma struck a defiant pose. "There must be *one.*"

Sharon bowed—"You're speaking to him!"—then climbed the ladder halfway and plucked his rope from Emma's hands. "Enough of this. Goodbye, children. I'm quite sure I'll never see you again."

And with that he stepped into his boat—and right into a puddle of ankle-deep water. He let out a girlish squeal and bent down to look. It seemed the gunshots that missed our heads had drilled a few holes in his hull, and the boat had sprung leaks.

"Look what you've done! My boat's shot all to pieces!"

Emma's eyes flashed. "What *we've* done?"

Sharon made a quick inspection and concluded the wounds were grave. "I am marooned!" he announced dramatically, then cut the motor, collapsed his long staff to the size of a baton, and climbed the ladder again. "I'm going find a craftsman qualified to repair my dinghy," he said, breezing past us, "and I won't have you following me."

We trailed him single file into the narrow passageway.

"And why not?" Emma shrilled.

"Because you're cursed! Bad luck!" Sharon waved his arm behind him as if shooing flies. "Begone!"

"What do you mean, *begone*?" She jogged a few paces and grabbed Sharon by his cloaked elbow. He spun around fast and yanked it away, and I thought for a moment his raised hand was about to strike her. I tensed, ready to leap at him, but his hand just hung there, a warning.

"I've run this route more times than I can count, and not once have I been attacked by Ditch pirates. Never have I been forced to abandon cover and use my petrol engine. And never, *ever* has my boat been damaged. You're more trouble than you're worth, plain and simple, and I want nothing more to do with you."

While he spoke, I glanced past him down the passage. My eyes were still adjusting to the dark, but what I could see was terrifying: winding and mazelike, it was lined with doorless doorways that gaped like missing teeth, and it was alive with sinister sounds—murmurs, scrapes, scurrying steps. Even now I could feel hungry eyes watching us, knives being drawn.

We couldn't be left here alone. The only thing to do was beg.

"We'll pay double what we promised," I said.

"And fix your boat," Addison chimed in.

"Never mind your bloody pocket change!" Sharon said. "Can't you see I'm ruined? How can I return to Devil's Acre? Do you think the vultures will ever let me be, now that my clients have killed two of them?"

"What did you want us to do?" Emma said. "We had to fight back!"

"Don't be facile. They would never have forced the issue if it wasn't for . . . for that . . . " Sharon looked at me, his voice falling to a whisper. "You might've mentioned earlier you were in league with *creatures of the night*!"

"Umm," I said awkwardly, "I wouldn't say 'in league with,' exactly . . . "

"There isn't much in this world I fear, but as a rule I keep my distance from soul-sucking monsters—and apparently you've got one following you like a bloodhound! I suppose it'll be along any minute?"

"Not likely," Addison said. "Don't you recall, some moments ago, when a bridge fell on its head?"

"Only a small one," Sharon said. "Now if you'll excuse me, I have to see a man about a boat." And with that he hurried away.

Before we could catch up to him he'd rounded a corner, and by the time we reached it he'd disappeared—vanished, perhaps, into one of those tunnels he'd mentioned. We stood turning circles, confounded and afraid.

"I can't believe he'd just abandon us like this!" I said.

"Neither can I," Addison replied coolly. "In fact, I don't think he has—I think he's negotiating." The dog cleared his throat, sat up on his hind legs, and addressed the rooftops in a booming voice. "Good sir! We mean to rescue our friends and our ymbrynes, and mark me, we will—and when we do, and they learn how you've aided us, they'll be *most* grateful."

He let that ring out for a moment, then went on.

"Never mind compassion! Fie on loyalty! If you're as intelligent and ambitious a fellow as I think you are, then you'll recognize an extraordinary opportunity for advancement when you see one. We are indebted to you already, but scrounging coins from children and animals is an awfully modest living compared to what having several ymbrynes in your debt could mean. Perhaps you'd enjoy having a loop all to yourself, your own personal playground with no other peculiars to spoil it! Anytime and anyplace you like: a lush summer isle in an age of abiding peace; some lowly pit in a time of plague. As you prefer."

"Could they really do that?" I whispered to Emma.

Emma shrugged.

"Imagine the possibilities!" Addison gushed.

His voice echoed away. We waited, listening.

Somewhere two people were arguing.

A hacking cough.

Something heavy was dragged down steps.

"Well, it was a nice speech," Emma sighed.

"Forget him, then," I said, peering into the passages that branched away left, right, and straight ahead. "Which way?"

We chose a passage at random—straight on—and started down it. We'd gone only ten paces when we heard a voice say, "I wouldn't go that way, if I were you. That's Cannibals' Alley, and it isn't just a cute nickname."

There was Sharon behind us, hands on his hips like a fitness coach. "My heart must be getting soft in my old age," he said. "Either that or my head."

"Does that mean you'll help us?" said Emma.

A light rain had begun to fall. Sharon looked up, letting a little splash his hidden face. "I know a lawyer here. First I want you to sign a contract laying out what you owe me."

"Fine, fine," said Emma. "But you'll help us?"

"Then I've got to see about getting my boat fixed."

"And *then*?"

"Then I'll help you, yes. Though I can't promise any results, and I want to state at the outset that I think you're all fools."

We couldn't quite bring ourselves to thank him, given what he'd put us through.

"Now stay close, and follow every instruction I give you to the letter. You killed two vultures today, and they'll be hunting you, mark my words."

We readily agreed.

"If they catch you, you don't know me. Never saw me."

We nodded like bobbleheads.

"And whatever you do, never, *never* touch so much as a drop of ambrosia, or on my eyes, you'll never leave this place."

"I don't know what that is," I said, and from their expressions I saw that Emma and Addison were likewise in the dark.

"You'll find out," Sharon said ominously, and with a swish of his cloak he turned and plunged into the maze.

CHAPTER THREE

*J*ust before a cow is put to the hammer in a modern slaughterhouse, it is prodded through a winding maze. The tight curves and blind corners prevent the animal from seeing more than a short distance ahead, so it doesn't realize until the last few steps, when the maze abruptly narrows and a metal collar clamps tight around its neck, where the journey has taken it. But as the three of us hurried after Sharon into the heart of Devil's Acre, I felt sure I knew what was coming, if not when nor how. With each step and each turn, we threaded deeper inside a knot, one I feared we'd never work apart.

The fetid air did not move, its only outlet an uneven crack of sky high above our heads. The bulged and slumping walls were so narrow that we had to go shoulder-first in places, the tight spots greased black by the clothes of those who'd gone before. There was nothing natural here, nothing green, nothing living at all save scurrying vermin and the bloodshot-eyed revenants who lurked behind doorways and under grates in the street, and who surely would've jumped at us if not for our towering, black-clad guide. We were chasing Death himself into the pit of Hell.

We turned and turned again. Every passage looked just like the one before it. There were no signs, no markers. Either Sharon was navigating by some brilliant feat of memory, or completely at random, trying to throw off any Ditch pirates who might've been pursuing us.

"Do you really know where we're going?" Emma asked him.

"Of course I do!" Sharon barked, bombing around a corner

without looking back. Then he stopped, doubled back, and stepped down through a doorway sunk half below street level. Inside was a dank cellar, just five feet high and lit by the merest breath of sallow gray light. We ran hunched along a subterranean corridor, discarded animal bones underfoot, the ceiling brushing our heads, past things I tried not to see—a slumped figure in a corner, sleepers shivering on miserable mats of straw, a boy in rags lying on the ground with a beggar's pail bangled around one arm. At its far end the passage widened into a room, and in the light of a few grimed windows there knelt a pair of miserable washerwomen, scrubbing laundry in a stinking pool of Ditch water.

Then we mounted more steps and went out, thank God, into a walled courtyard common to the backs of several buildings. In some other reality it might've contained a happy patch of grass or a little gazebo, but this was Devil's Acre, and it was a dump and a pigsty. Waves of fly-blown trash tossed from windows crested against the walls, and in the center, staked crookedly in the mud, was a wooden pen in which a skinny boy stood guarding an even skinnier pig—just one. By a mud-brick wall a woman sat smoking and reading a news-paper while a young girl stood behind her, picking nits from her hair. The woman and girl took no notice as we trooped past, but the boy leaned the tines of a pitchfork at us. When it was clear we had no designs on his pig, he sank into an exhausted squat.

Emma stopped in the middle of the yard to look up at lines of laundry strung between roof gutters. She pointed out again that our bloodstained clothes made us look like participants in a murder, and suggested we should change. Sharon replied that murderers were hardly outlandish here and urged her on, but she hung back, arguing that a wight in the Underground had seen our bloodstained clothes and radioed his comrades about us; they made us too easy to pick out of a crowd. Really, I think it was more that she felt uncomfortable in a blouse now stiff with another person's blood. I did, too—and if we found our friends again, I didn't want them to see us like this.

Sharon grudgingly assented. He'd been leading us toward a fence at the edge of the yard but now pivoted and took us into one of the buildings. We climbed two, three, four flights of stairs, until even Addison was wheezing, then followed Sharon through an open door into a small, squalid room. A gash in the ceiling had let in rain and warped the landing like ripples in a pond. Black mold veined the walls. At a table by a smoky window, two women and a girl were sweating over foot-powered sewing machines.

"We need some clothes," Sharon said, addressing the women in a stentorian basso that shook the thin walls.

Their pale faces looked up. One of the women picked up a sewing needle and gripped it like a weapon. "Please," she said.

Sharon reached up and pulled back the hood of his cloak a little, so that only the seamstresses could see his face. They gasped, then whimpered and fainted forward onto the table.

"Was that really necessary?" I said.

"Not strictly," Sharon replied, replacing his hood. "But it was expedient."

The seamstresses had been assembling simple shirts and dresses from scraps of cloth. The rags they worked with were heaped around the floor, and the results, which had more patches and seams than Frankenstein's monster, were hung on a line out the window.

As Emma reeled them in, my gaze crawled around the room. It was clearly more than just a workspace: the women lived here, too. There was a bed nailed together from scrap wood. I peered into a dented pot that hung in the hearth and saw the makings of starvation soup, fish skin and withered cabbage leaves. Their half-hearted attempts at decorating—a sprig of dried flowers, a horseshoe nailed to the mantel, a framed portrait of Queen Victoria—were somehow sadder than nothing at all.

Despair was tangible here, weighting down everything, the very air. I'd never been confronted with such pure misery. Could peculiars really be living these discarded lives? As Sharon pulled in an armful of shirts through the window, I asked him. He seemed almost offended by the idea. "Peculiars would never allow themselves to be so reduced. These are common slum dwellers, trapped in an endless repetition of the day this loop was made. Normals occupy the Acre's festering edges—but its heart belongs to us."

They were normals. Not only that, but loop-trapped normals, like the ones on Cairnholm whom the crueler kids would torment during games of Raid the Village. As much a part of the background scenery as the sea or the cliffs, I told myself. But somehow, looking at the women's weathered faces buried in rags, I felt no less terrible about stealing from them.

"I'm sure we'll know the peculiars when we see them," Emma said, sorting through a pile of dirty blouses.

"One always does," said Addison. "Subtlety has never been our kind's strength."

I slipped out of my bloody shirt and traded it for the least filthy alternative I could find, the kind of garment you'd be issued at a prison camp: collarless and striped, its sleeves of unequal length, patched together from cloth rougher than sandpaper. But it fit me, and with the addition of a simple black coat I found tossed over a chair back, I now looked like someone who might plausibly be from this place.

We turned our backs while Emma changed into a sacklike dress that pooled around her feet. "It'll be impossible to run in this," she grumbled. Plucking a pair of scissors from the seamstresses' table, she began to alter it with all the care of a butcher, ripping and jabbing until she'd sliced off the bottom at the knee.

"There." She admired her rough handiwork in a mirror. "A bit raggedy, but . . . "

Without thinking I said, "Horace can make you one better." Somehow I'd forgotten that our friends weren't just waiting for us in the next room. "I mean . . . if we see them again . . . "

"Don't," Emma said. For an instant she looked so sad, absolutely lost in it—and then she turned away, put down the scissors, and moved purposefully toward the door. When she turned to face us again, her expression had gone hard. "Come on. We've wasted enough time here as it is."

She had this amazing capacity to turn sadness into anger and anger into action, which meant nothing ever kept her down for long. And then Addison and I—and Sharon, who I suspect hadn't quite known whom he was dealing with until now—were following her out the door and down the stairs.

* * *

The whole of Devil's Acre—the peculiar heart of it, anyway—was only ten or twenty blocks square. After coming down from the workhouse we pried loose a board from a fence and squeezed into a suffocating passageway. It led to another that was slightly less suffocating, and that led to one a bit wider still, and that to one wide enough that Emma and I could walk side by side. On they widened, like arteries relaxing after a heart attack, until we came to something that might properly have been called a street, with red bricks running down the middle and sidewalks paving the edges.

"Fall back," Emma muttered. We shrank behind a corner and

peeked out like commandos, our heads stacked.

"What do you think you're doing?" Sharon said. He was still in the street and seemed more worried about being embarrassed by us than being killed.

"Looking for ambush points and escape routes," Emma said.

"No one's ambushing anyone," Sharon replied. "The pirates only operate in no man's land. They won't come after us here—this is Louche Lane."

There was, in fact, a street sign to that effect—the first I'd seen in all of Devil's Acre. *Louche Lane*, it read in fancy handwritten script. *Piracy discouraged*.

"Discouraged?" I said. "Then what's murder? Frowned upon?"

"I believe murder is 'tolerated with reservations.'"

"Is *anything* illegal here?" Addison asked.

"Library late fines are stiff. Ten lashes a day, and that's just for paperbacks."

"There's a library?"

"Two. Though one won't lend because all the books are bound in human skin and quite valuable."

We shuffled out from behind the wall and cast a somewhat baffled look around. In no man's land I'd anticipated death at every turn, but Louche Lane, from all appearances, was a haven of civic order. The street was lined with neat little shops, and the shops had signs and display windows and apartments on the upper floors. There was not a caved roof or a broken pane of glass in sight. There were people on the street, too, and they lingered, ambling along in singles and pairs, pausing now and then to duck into a shop or look in a window. Their clothes weren't rags. Their faces were clean. Maybe everything here wasn't new and sparkling, but the weathered surfaces and patched paint gave it all a handmade, worn-around-the-edges look that was quaint, even charming. My mother, if she'd seen Louche Lane in one of those thumbed-through-but-never-read travel magazines that papered our coffee table at home, would've crooned about its cuteness and complained that she and my dad had never taken a real European vacation—*Oh, Frank, let's go.*

Emma seemed palpably disappointed. "I was expecting something more sinister."

"Me too," I said. "Where are all the murder dens and bloodsport arenas?"

"I don't know what sort of business you think people get up to around here," Sharon said, "but I've never heard of a murder den. As for bloodsport arenas, there's only the one—Derek's, down Oozing Street. Good chap, Derek. Owes me a fiver . . . "

"And the wights?" said Emma. "What about our kidnapped friends?"

"Keep your voice down," Sharon hissed. "As soon as I take care of my own business, we'll find someone who can help you. Until then, don't repeat that to anyone."

Emma got in Sharon's face. "Then don't make me repeat *this*. While we appreciate your help and expertise, our friends' lives have been given an expiration date. I won't stall and dawdle about simply to avoid ruffling some feathers."

Sharon looked down at her, quiet for a moment. Then he said, "We all have an expiration date. If I were you, I wouldn't be in such a hurry to find out what it is."

We set off to find Sharon's lawyer. He quickly became frustrated. "I could've sworn his office was along this street," he said, turning on his heel. "Though it's been years since I've been to see him. Perhaps he's moved."

Sharon decided to go looking on his own and told us to stay put. "I'll be back in a few minutes. Don't speak to anyone."

He strode away, leaving us alone. We clustered awkwardly on the sidewalk, unsure what to do with ourselves. People stared as they passed by.

"He really had us going, didn't he?" said Emma. "He made this place sound like a hotbed of criminality, but it looks like any other loop to me. In fact, the people here look more normal than any peculiars I've ever seen. It's as if they've had every distinguishing characteristic vacuumed out of them. It's downright boring."

"You must be joking," said Addison. "I've never seen anyplace so vile or disgusting."

We both looked at him in surprise.

"How's that?" said Emma. "All that's here are little shops."

"Yes, but look what they're selling."

We hadn't until now. Just behind us was a display window, and in it stood a well-dressed man with mournful eyes and a cascading beard. When he saw that he had our attention, he nodded slightly, held up a pocketwatch, and touched a button on its side. The moment he pressed it he froze, and his image seemed to blur. A few seconds later, he moved without moving—disappearing and then reappearing instantaneously in the opposite corner of the window.

"Wow," I said. "That's quite a trick!"

He did it a second time, teleporting back to the other corner. While I stood mesmerized, Emma and Addison moved on to the next shop's window. I joined them and found a similar display, only standing behind the glass here was a woman in a black dress, a long string of beads dangling from one hand.

When she saw that we were looking, she closed her eyes and stretched her arms like a sleepwalker. She began to pass the beads slowly through her fingers, turning each one. My eyes were so locked on the beads that it took me a few seconds to realize something was happening to her face: it was changing, subtly, with each bead she turned. At the turn of one bead, I watched the pallor of her skin lighten. At the next, her lips thinned. Then her hair reddened ever so slightly. The cumulative effect, over the course of several dozen beads, was that her face became entirely different, morphing from that of a dark, round-featured grandmother to a young, sharp-nosed redhead. It was both enthralling and unsettling.

When the show was over, I turned to Addison. "I don't under-stand," I said. "What are they selling?"

Before he could answer, a preteen boy came hustling up to us and forced a pair of cards into my hand. "Two for one, today only!" he crowed. "No reasonable offer refused!"

I turned the cards over in my hand. One had the stopwatch man's photo on it, and on the back it read *J. Edwin Bragg, bi-locationalist*. The other was a photo of the bead lady in a trance, and it read *G. Fünke, woman of a thousand faces*.

"Shoo, we're not buying," Emma said, and the boy scowled at her and scurried off.

"Now do you see what they're selling?" said Addison.

I cast my eyes down the street. There were people like the stopwatch man and bead lady in almost every shop window along Louche Lane—peculiars, ready to put on a show if you so much as glanced in their direction.

I hazarded a guess. "They're selling . . . themselves?"

"Like a dim bulb flickering to life," said Addison.

"And that's bad?" I said, guessing again.

"Yes," Addison said sharply. "It's outlawed throughout peculiardom, and for good reason."

"One's peculiarity is a sacred gift," Emma said. "To sell it cheapens what is most special about us."

It sounded like she was parroting a platitude that had been drilled into her from an early age.

"Huh," I said. "Okay."

"You aren't convinced," said Addison.

"I guess I don't see what the harm would be. If I need the services of an invisible person, and that invisible person needs money, why shouldn't we trade?"

"But you have strong morals, and that sets you apart from ninety-nine percent of humanity," said Emma. "What if a bad person—or even a below-averagely-moraled person—wanted to buy the services of the invisible peculiar?"

"The invisible peculiar should say no."

"But it isn't always so black and white," Emma said, "and selling yourself erodes your moral compass. Pretty soon you're dipping into the wrong side of that gray area without knowing it, doing things you'd never do if you weren't being paid to do them. And if someone were desperate enough, they might sell themselves to anyone, no matter what the other's intentions."

"To a wight, for instance," Addison added pointedly.

"Okay, yeah, that would be bad," I said. "But do you really think a peculiar would do that?"

"Don't be daft!" said Addison. "Just look at the state of this place. Probably the only loop in Europe that hasn't been laid waste to by the wights! And why do you think that is? Because it's been extremely useful, I am sure, to have an entire population of perfectly willing turncoats and informants waiting to do your bidding."

"Maybe you should keep your voice down," I said.

"It makes sense," Emma said. "They must have infiltrated our loops with peculiar informants. How else could they have known so much? Loop entrances, defenses, weak spots . . . only with help from people like this." She cast a venomous look around, her expression that of someone who'd just drunk curdled milk.

"No reasonable offer refused, indeed," Addison snarled. "Traitors, every one of them. Ought to be hanged!"

"What's the matter, hon? Having a bad day?"

We turned to find a woman standing behind us. (How long had she been there? What had she heard?) She was dressed in sharp and businesslike 1950s style—knee-length skirt and short black pumps—and puffed lazily at a cigarette. Her hair was teased up in a beehive and her accent was as flat and American as the Midwestern plains.

"I'm Lorraine," she said, "and you're new in town."

"We're waiting for someone," said Emma. "We're . . . on holiday."

"Say no more!" said Lorraine. "I'm on vacation myself. Have been for the last fifty years." She laughed, showing lipstick-stained teeth. "You just let me know if I can help you with anything. Lorraine's got the best selection on Louche Lane, and that's an actual fact."

"No, thanks," I said.

"Don't worry, hon. They won't bite."

"We're not interested."

Lorraine shrugged. "I was just being friendly. You looked a

little lost, is all."

She started to leave, but something she'd said had piqued Emma's interest.

"Selection of what?"

Lorraine turned back and flashed a greasy smile. "Old ones, young ones. All sorts of talents. Some of my customers just want a show, and that's fine, but others have specific needs. We make sure everyone leaves satisfied."

"The boy said no thank you," Addison said gruffly, and he seemed about to tell the woman off when Emma stepped in front of him and said, "I'd like to see."

"You what?" I said.

"I want to see," Emma said, an edge creeping into her voice. "Show me."

"Serious inquiries only," said Lorraine.

"Oh, I'm very serious."

I didn't know what Emma was up to, but I trusted her enough to go with it.

"What about them?" Lorraine said, casting an uncertain gaze at Addison and me. "They always so rude?"

"Yes. But they're all right."

Lorraine squinted at us as if imagining what it might take to forcibly eject us from her place, should the need arise.

"What can you do?" she said to me. "Anything?"

Emma cleared her throat, then bugged her eyes at me. I knew right away what she was telegraphing: *Lie!*

"I used to be able to levitate pencils and things," I said, "but now I can't even get one to stand on end. I think I'm . . . out of order, or something."

"Happens to the best of 'em." She looked to Addison. "And you?"

Addison rolled his eyes. "I'm a talking dog?"

"And that's all you do, talk?"

"Sometimes it seems that way," I couldn't resist saying.

"I don't know whom to feel more insulted by," said Addison.

Lorraine took a final puff of her cigarette and flicked it away. "All right, sugars. Follow me."

She started to walk away. We hung behind a moment and conferred in a whisper.

"What about Sharon?" I said. "He told us to wait here."

"This will only take a minute," Emma said. "And I have a hunch she knows a lot more about where the wights are hiding than Sharon does."

"And you think she's just going to volunteer such information?" said Addison.

"We'll see," Emma said, and she turned to follow Lorraine.

*　　*　　*

Lorraine's place had no window and no sign, just a blank door with a silver bell on a pull chain. Lorraine rang the bell. We waited while a series of deadbolts were slid from the inside, and then the door opened a crack. An eye glinted at us from the shadows.

"Fresh meat?" said a man's voice.

"Customers," Lorraine replied. "Let us in."

The eye disappeared and the door opened the rest of the way. We came into a formal entrance hall, where the doorman waited to look us over. He wore a massive overcoat with a high collar and a wide-brimmed fedora, the hat tilted so low that all we could see of his face were two pinprick eyes and the tip of his nose. He stood blocking our way, staring us down.

"Well?" said Lorraine.

The man seemed to decide we weren't a threat. "Okay," he said, stepping aside. He closed and locked the door behind us, then trailed after as Lorraine showed us down a long hallway.

We came into a dim parlor flickering with oil lamps. It was a sleazy place with delusions of grandeur: the walls were trimmed with gold scrollwork and velvet drapes, the domed ceiling was painted with tanned and tunicked Greek gods, and marble columns framed the entrance to the hall.

Lorraine nodded to the doorman. "Thank you, Carlos."

Carlos glided away to the back of the room. Lorraine walked to a curtained wall and pulled a cord, and the fabric slid aside to reveal a wide panel of sturdy glass. We stepped forward to look, and through it saw another room. It was very much like the one we were standing in, but smaller, and people were lazing about on chairs and sofas, some reading while others napped.

I counted eight of them. A few were older, graying at the temples. Two, a boy and a girl, were under the age of ten. They were all, I realized, prisoners.

Addison started to ask a question, but Lorraine gestured impatiently. "Questions after, please." She strode to the glass, picked up a tube connected umbilically to the wall below it, and spoke into one end. "Number thirteen!"

On the other side of the glass, the youngest boy stood and shuffled forward. His hands and legs were chained, and he was the only peculiar wearing anything resembling prisoner's garb: a striped suit and cap with the number 13 stitched boldly onto them. Though he couldn't have been older than ten, he had a man's facial hair: a bushy, triangular goatee and eyebrows like jungle caterpillars, the eyes below them cold and appraising.

"Why is he chained like that?" I said. "Is he dangerous?"

"You'll see," Lorraine said.

The boy closed his eyes. He seemed to be concentrating. A moment later, hair began to emerge from the brim of his cap, creeping down his forehead. His goatee grew, too, twisting into a clump, then rising and swaying like a charmed snake.

"Heavenly herons," said Addison. "How marvelously strange."

"Watch closely now," said Lorraine, grinning.

Number thirteen raised his shackled hands. The pointed end of his charmed goatee aimed itself at the lock, sniffed around the keyhole, and wriggled inside. The boy opened his eyes and stared ahead, expressionless. After ten or so seconds, the twisted goatee stiffened and began to vibrate, making a high musical note we could hear through the glass.

The padlock opened and the chains fell away from his wrists.

He bowed slightly. I stifled an urge to applaud.

"He can open any lock in the world," Lorraine said with a hint of pride.

The boy returned to his chair and magazine.

Lorraine covered the tube with her hand. "He's one of a kind, and so are the rest. One's a thought reader, very adept. Another can reach through walls up to her shoulder. That's more useful than it sounds, believe me. The little girl here flies if she's had enough grape soda."

"Is that right," Addison said thickly.

"She'd be happy to demonstrate," said Lorraine, and speaking into the tube, she summoned the girl to the window.

"It's not necessary," Emma said through clenched teeth.

"It's their job," said Lorraine. "Five, come forward!"

The little girl went to a table stocked with bottles, selected one filled with purple liquid, and took a long drink. When she'd drained it, she set down the bottle, let out a dainty hiccup, and went to stand by a cane-backed chair. A moment later she hiccupped again and her feet began to lift off the ground, pivoting upward while her head remained level. By the third hiccup, her feet had risen ninety degrees and she lay flat on her back in the air, her only support the top of the chair beneath her neck.

I think Lorraine expected more of a reaction from us, but—though impressed—we were a study in silence. "Tough crowd," she said and dismissed the girl.

"Now," Lorraine said, hanging up the tube and turning to face us. "If none of that was your cup of tea, I have lending agreements with other stables. By no means are your choices limited to what you see here."

"Stables," Emma said. Her voice was flat, but I could tell she was boiling just below the surface. "So you admit you treat them like animals?"

Lorraine studied Emma for a moment. Her eyes flitted to the man in the overcoat standing guard in the back. "Course not," she said. "These are high-performance assets. They're well fed, well rested, trained to perform under pressure, and pure as the driven snow. Most have never touched so much as a drop of ambro—and I've got the papers to prove it in my office. Or you could just ask them. Numbers thirteen and six!" she shouted into the speaking tube. "Come tell these people how you like it here."

The little boy and girl got up and shuffled to the window. The boy picked up the speaking tube. "We like it here very much," he said robotically. "Mam treats us real nice."

He handed the tube to the girl. "We like to do our work. We . . . " She paused, trying to recall something learned and forgotten. "We like our work," she mumbled.

Lorraine dismissed them irritably. "And there you have it. Now, I can let you test drive one or two more, but beyond that I'll need some kind of down payment."

"I'd like to see those papers," Emma said, glancing back at the overcoat man. "The ones in your office." Her hands, clenched at her sides, were starting to go red. I could see we needed to leave before things turned ugly. Whatever information this woman might've had wasn't worth the fight, and rescuing all these kids . . . well, as callous as it sounded, we had our own kids to rescue first.

"Actually, that won't be necessary," I said, then leaned in to Emma and whispered, "we'll come back to help them. We have to prioritize."

"The papers," she said, ignoring me.

"No problem," Lorraine replied. "Step into my office and let's talk turkey."

And then Emma was going and there was no unsuspicious way to stop her.

Lorraine's office was a desk and chair crammed into a walkin closet. She had only just closed the door behind us when Emma sprang at her, pushing her hard against it. Lorraine swore and shouted for Carlos but went quiet when Emma held a hand to her face that glowed hot as an oven coil. On Lorraine's blouse, two blackened handprints smoked where Emma had pushed her.

There was a thump on the door and a grunt from the other side.

"Tell him you're fine," Emma said, her voice low and flinty.

"I'm fine!" Lorraine said stiffly.

The door rattled against her back.

"Tell him again."

Lorraine, more convincing now: "Get lost! I'm doing business!"

Another grunt, then receding footsteps.

"You're being very stupid," Lorraine said. "No one's ever stolen from me and lived."

"We don't want money," Emma said. "You're going to answer some questions."

"About what?"

"Those people out there. You think you own them?"

Lorraine's brow furrowed. "What's this about?"

"Those people. Those children. You bought them—do you think you own them?"

"I never bought anyone."

"You bought them and now you're selling them. You're a slaver."

"That isn't how it works. They came to me willingly. I'm their agent."

"You're their pimp," Emma spat.

"Without me they'd have starved. Or been taken."

"Taken by who?"

"You know who."

"I want to hear you say it."

The woman laughed. "That's not a good idea."

"Yeah?" I said, taking a step forward. "Why not?"

"They have ears everywhere, and they don't like being talked about."

"I've killed wights," I said. "I'm not scared of them."

"Then you're an idiot."

"Shall I bite her?" said Addison. "I'd really like to. Just a little."

"What happens when they take people?" I said, ignoring him.

"No one knows," she said. "I've tried to find out, but . . . "

"I'll bet you tried *very* hard," Emma said.

"They come in here sometimes," Lorraine said. "To shop."

"Shop," Addison said. "That's a nice word for it."

"To use my people." She looked around. Her voice dropped to a whisper. "I hate it. You never know how many they're going to want or for how long. But you give them what they ask for. I'd complain, but . . . you don't complain."

"Bet you don't complain about what they pay," Emma said contemptuously.

"It's not hardly enough for what they put 'em through. I try to hide the little ones when I hear they're coming. They bring 'em back roughed up, memories blanked out. I say, 'Where'd you go? What'd they make you do?' But the kids don't remember zip." She shook her head. "They get these nightmares, though. Nasty ones. It's hard to sell 'em after that."

"I oughta sell *you*," Emma said, livid, trembling. "Not that anyone would pay half a farthing."

I stuffed my fists into my pockets to stop them from flying at

Lorraine. There was more to be gotten from her. "What about the peculiars they kidnap from other loops?" I asked.

"They bring them through in trucks. Used to be a rare thing. Lately it's been all the time."

"Did one come through earlier today?" I said.

"A couple of hours ago," she said. "They had guards with guns all over the place, blocking the street. Made a big production of it."

"They don't usually?"

"Not usually. Guess they feel safe here. This delivery must've been important."

It was them, I thought. A trill of excitement shot through me—but was immediately stifled by Addison lunging at Lorraine. "I'm sure they feel *quite* safe here," he snarled, "among such perfect traitors!"

I snatched his collar and held him back. "Calm down!"

Addison struggled against me, and I thought for a moment he might snap at my hand, but then he relaxed.

"We do what we have to to survive," Lorraine hissed.

"So do we," said Emma. "Now tell us where those trucks go, and if you lie, or it turns out to be a trap, I'll come back and melt your nostrils shut." She held one burning finger just beyond the tip of Lorraine's nose. "Agreed?"

I could almost imagine Emma doing it. She was tapping into a deep well of hatred I'd never seen fully revealed before, and as useful as it was in situations like this, it was a little scary, too. I didn't like to think what she might be capable of, given the proper motivation.

"They go to their part of the Acre," Lorraine said, turning her head away from Emma's hot finger. "Over the bridge."

"What bridge?" said Emma, holding it closer.

"At the top end of Smoking Street. Don't bother trying to cross, though, unless you want your head to end up on a pike."

I reckoned that was all we were going to get out of Lorraine. Now we had to figure out what to do with her. Addison wanted to bite her. Emma wanted to trace an *S* on her forehead with her white-hot finger, branding her for life as a slaver. I talked them out of doing either, and instead we gagged her with a sash cord from the curtains and tied her to a leg of the desk. We were about to leave her like that when I thought of one last thing I wanted to know.

"The peculiars they kidnap. What happens to them?"

"Mrrrf!"

I pulled down her gag.

"None have escaped to tell," she said. "But there are rumors."

"About?"

"Something worse than death." She gave us a smile dripping with slime. "I guess you'll just have to find out, won't you?"

* * *

The moment we opened the office door, the man in the overcoat charged at us from across the parlor, something heavy raised in his hand. Before he could reach us, a muffled shout of alarm sounded from the office and he stopped, changing course to see about Lorraine. When he'd crossed the office threshold, Emma slammed the door behind him and melted the handle into useless slag.

That bought us a minute or two.

Addison and I bolted for the exit. Halfway there, I realized Emma hadn't followed. She was banging on the window of the enslaved peculiars' quarters.

"We can help you escape! Show me where the door is!"

They turned sluggishly to stare, splayed on their chaises and daybeds.

"Throw something to break the glass!" Emma said. "Be quick!"

None moved. They seemed confused. Perhaps they didn't believe rescue was really possible—or perhaps they didn't want to be rescued.

"Emma, we can't wait," I said, tugging at her arm.

She wouldn't give up. "Please!" she cried into the tube. "At least send out the children!"

Full-throated shouts from inside the office. The door shook on its hinges. Frustrated, Emma slammed the glass with her fist.

"What's the matter with them?"

Rattled stares. The little boy and girl began to cry.

Addison tugged the hem of Emma's dress with his teeth. "We must go!"

Emma let the speaking tube fall and turned away bitterly.

We hit the door running and burst out onto the sidewalk. A thick yellow murk had blown in, bundling everything in gauze and hiding one side of the street from the other. By the time we'd sprinted to the end of the block we could hear Lorraine bellowing behind us but couldn't see her; we turned one corner and then another until it seemed we'd lost her. On a deserted street by a boarded-up storefront, we stopped to catch our breaths.

"It's called Stockholm syndrome," I said. "When people start to sympathize with their captors."

"I think they were just scared," said Addison. "Where would they have run to? This whole place is a prison."

"You're both wrong," Emma said. "They were drugged."

"You sound pretty sure," I said.

She pushed back hair that had fallen over her eyes. "When I was working in the circus, after I'd run away from home, a woman approached me after one of my fire-eating shows. She said she knew what I was—knew others like me—and that I could make a lot more money if I went and worked for her." Emma gazed out at the street, her cheeks flushed from the sprint. "I told her I didn't want to go. She kept insisting. When she finally left she was angry. That night I woke up in the back of a wagon with my mouth gagged and hands cuffed. I couldn't move, couldn't think straight. It was Miss Peregrine who rescued me. If she hadn't found me when they stopped to reshoe their horse the next day"—Emma nodded behind us, to where we'd come from—"I might have ended up like them."

"You never told me that," I said quietly.

"It's not something I like to talk about."

"I'm very sorry that happened to you," said Addison. "Was that woman back there—was she the one who kidnapped you?"

Emma thought for a moment.

"It happened such a long time ago. I've blocked out the worst of it, including my abductor's face. But I know this. If you'd left me alone with that woman, I'm not sure I could've stopped myself from taking her life."

"We've all got demons to slay," I said.

I leaned against a boarded window, a sudden wave of exhaustion breaking over me. How long had we been awake? How many hours since Caul had revealed himself? It seemed like days ago, though it couldn't have been more than ten or twelve hours. Every moment since had been a war, a nightmare of struggle and terror without end. I could feel my body inching toward collapse. Panic was the only thing keeping me upright, and whenever it began to fade, I did, too.

For the merest fraction of a second, I allowed my eyes to close. Even in that slim black parenthesis, horrors awaited me. A specter of eternal death, crouched and feeding upon the body of my grandfather, its eyes weeping oil. Those same eyes planted with the twin stalks of garden shears, howling as it sank into a boggy grave. Its master's face contorted in pain, tumbling backward into a void, gutshot, screaming. I had slain my demons already, but the victories were fleeting; others had risen up quickly to replace them.

My eyes flew open at the sound of footsteps behind me, on the other side of the boarded-up window. I hopped away and turned. Though the store looked abandoned, someone was inside, and they were coming out.

There it was: panic. I was awake again. The others had heard the noise, too. Acting on collective instinct, we ducked behind a stack of firewood nearby. Through the logs I peeked at the storefront, reading the faded sign that hung above the door.

Munday, Dyson and Strype, attnys at law. Hated and feared since 1666.

A bolt slid and slowly the door opened. A familiar black hood appeared: Sharon. He looked around, judged the coast clear, then slipped out and locked the door behind him. As he hurried away in the direction of Louche Lane, we consulted in whispers about whether to go after him. Did we need him anymore? Could he be trusted? Maybe and maybe. What had he been doing in that shuttered storefront? Was this the lawyer he'd talked about seeing? Why the sneaking?

Too many questions, too many uncertainties about him. We decided we could make it on our own. We stayed put and watched as he turned ghostly in the murk and was gone.

*   *   *

We set out to find Smoking Street and the wights' bridge. Not wanting to risk another unpredictable encounter, we resolved to search without asking for directions. That became easier once we discovered the Acre's street signs, which were concealed in the most inconvenient places—behind public benches at knee height, dangling from the tops of lampposts, inscribed into worn cobblestones underfoot—but even with their help, we took as many wrong turns as right. It seemed the Acre had been designed to drive those trapped inside it mad. There were streets that ended at blank walls only to begin again elsewhere. Streets that curved so sharply they spiraled back on themselves. Streets with no name—or two or three. None were as tidy or tended to as Louche Lane, where it was clear a special effort had been made to create a pleasing environment for shoppers in the market for peculiar flesh—the idea of which, now that I'd seen Lorraine's wares and heard Emma's story, turned my stomach.

As we wandered, I began to get a handle on the Acre's unique geography, learning the blocks less by their names than by their character. Each street was distinct, the shops along them grouped according to type. Doleful Street boasted two undertakers, a medium, a carpenter who worked exclusively with "repurposed coffinwood," a troupe of professional funeral-wailers who did weekend duty as a barbershop quartet, and a tax accountant. Oozing Street was oddly cheerful, with flower boxes hanging from windowsills and houses painted bright colors; even the slaughterhouse that anchored it was an inviting robin's-egg blue, and I resisted an odd impulse to go inside and ask for a tour. Periwinkle Street, on the other hand, was a cesspit. There was an open sewer running down its center, a thriving population of aggressive flies, and sidewalks that overflowed with putrefying vegetables, the property of a cut-rate greengrocer whose sign claimed he could turn them fresh again with a kiss.

Attenuated Avenue was just fifty feet long and had only one business: two men selling snacks from a basket on a sled. Children crowded around, clamoring for handouts, and Addison veered off to snuffle around their feet for droppings. I was about to call after him when one of the men shouted, "Cat's meat! Boiled cat's meat here!" He came scurrying back on his own, tail tucked between his legs, whimpering, "I shall never eat again, never, never again . . . "

We approached Smoking Street from Upper Smudge. The closer we got, the more the block seemed to wither, its storefronts abandoned, its sidewalks emptying, the pavement blackening with currents of ash that blew around our feet, as if the street itself had been infected by some creeping death. At the end it curved sharply to the right, and just before the bend was an old wooden house with an equally old man guarding its stoop. He swept at the ash with a stubbly broom, but it piled up faster than he could ever hope to collect it.

I asked him why he bothered. He looked up suddenly, hugging the broom to his chest as if afraid I'd steal it. His feet were bare and black and his pants were sooty to the knee. "Someone's got to," he said. "Can't let the place go to hell."

As we passed he returned grimly to his task, though his arthritic hands could hardly close around the stick. There was something almost regal about him, I thought; a defiance I admired. He was a holdout who refused to give up his post. The last watchman at the end of the world.

Turning with the road, we moved through a zone of buildings that shed their skins as we walked: first the paint was singed away, and farther along the windows had blackened and burst; next, the roofs were caving and the walls coming down, and finally, as we came to the junction with Smoking Street, only their bones were left—a chaos of timbers charred and leaning, embers glowing in the ash like tiny hearts beating their last. We stood and looked around, thunderstruck. Sulfurous smoke rose from deep cracks that fissured the pavement. Fire-stripped trees loomed like scarecrows over the ruins. Drifts of ash flowed down the street, a foot deep in places. It was as close to Hell as I ever intend to find myself.

"So this is the wights' front driveway," said Addison. "How fitting."

"It's unreal," I said, unbuttoning my coat. Sauna-like warmth rose all around, radiating through the soles of my shoes. "What did Sharon say happened here?"

"Underground fire," Emma said. "They can burn for years. Notoriously difficult to extinguish."

There was a sound like a giant can of soda being opened, and a tall prong of orange flame shot up from a seam in the pavement not ten feet away. We started and jumped and then had to collect ourselves.

"Let's not spend one minute longer here than we need to," said Emma. "Which way?"

There was only left and right to choose from. We knew that Smoking Street terminated at the Ditch on one end and at the wights' bridge on the other, but we didn't know which way was which, and between the smoke, the fog, and the wind-blown ash, we couldn't see far in either direction. Choosing at random could mean a dangerous detour and a waste of time.

We were getting desperate when we heard a warbling tune drifting toward us through the fog. We scuttled off the road to hide among the carbonized ribs of a house. As the singers approached, their voices growing louder, we could make out the words to their strange song:

> The night before the thief was stretched,
>   the hangman came around
> I've come, he said, before you're dead,
>   a warning to expound
> I'll strangle your neck and send you to heck
>   and cut off your arm and do you some harm
>   and flay your hide and give you a riiiiiiiide . . .

Here they all paused for breath, then finished with: "SIX FEET UNDER THE GROUND!"

Long before they emerged from the fog, I knew whose voices they were. The figures took form in black overalls and sturdy black boots, tool bags swinging gaily at their sides. Even after a hard day's work, the indomitable gallows riggers were still singing at the top of their lungs.

"Bless their tuneless souls," Emma said, laughing softly.

Earlier we'd seen them working at the Ditch end of Smoking Street, so it seemed reasonable to assume that's where they were coming from—which meant they were walking in the direction of the bridge. We waited for the men to pass and disappear again into the fog before venturing back onto the road to follow.

We shuffled through reefs of ash that blackened everything—the cuffs of my pants, Emma's shoes and bare ankles, the full height of Addison's legs. Somewhere in the distance the riggers took up another song, their voices echoing weirdly through the burned landscape. Nothing around us but ruin. Now and then we heard a sharp *whoosh*, quickly followed by a spout of flame bursting from the ground. None erupted as close as the first one. We were lucky—getting roasted alive here would've been easy.

Out of nowhere a wind kicked up, sending ash and hot cinders skyward in a black blizzard. We turned and covered our faces in an effort to breathe. I pulled my shirt collar over my mouth, but it didn't help much and I started to cough. Emma took Addison into her arms, but then she started to choke. I tore off my coat and threw it over their heads. Emma's coughing quieted and I heard Addison's muffled voice say "Thank you!" beneath the fabric.

It was all we could do to huddle there and wait for the ash storm to end. I had my eyes closed when I heard something move nearby, and peeking through slit fingers I saw something that even here, amidst all I'd witnessed in Devil's Acre, startled me: a man strolling casual as could be, a handkerchief pressed to his mouth but otherwise unperturbed. He had no trouble navigating the dark because beams of strong white light were shooting from each of his eye sockets.

"Evening!" he called out, swinging his sight-beams toward me and tipping his hat. I tried to reply but my mouth filled with ash and then so did my eyes, and when I reopened them he was gone.

As the wind began to die, we coughed and spat and rubbed our eyes until we could function again. Emma set Addison on the ground. "If we're not careful, this loop will kill us before the wights do," he said. Emma handed me back my coat and hugged me hard until the air cleared. She had a way of wrapping her arms around me and nudging her head into the hollow of my chest so that no gaps were left between us, and I wanted badly to kiss her, even here, covered in soot from head to toe.

Addison cleared his throat. "I hate to interrupt, but we really should be getting on."

We unhooked our limbs, slightly embarrassed, and continued walking. Soon pale figures appeared in the fog ahead. They were milling in the street, crossing between shacks that encrusted the roadside. We hesitated, nervous about who they might be, but there was no other way forward.

"Chin up, back straight," Emma said. "Try to look scary."

We closed ranks and walked into their midst. They were shifty eyed and wild looking. Soot-stained all over. Dressed in scavenged castoffs. I scowled, doing my best impression of a dangerous person. They shied away like beaten dogs.

Here was a kind of shantytown. Low-slung huts made from fire-proof scrap metal, tin roofs weighed down with boulders and tree stumps, canvas flaps for doors if they had doors at all. A fungal smear of life overgrowing the bones of a burned civilization; hardly there at all.

Chickens ran in the street. A man knelt by a smoking hole in the road, cooking eggs in its blistering heat.

"Don't get too close," Addison muttered. "They look ill."

I thought so, too. It was the limping way they carried themselves, their glassy stares. Several wore crude masks or sacks over their heads with only slits for eyes, as if to hide faces chewed by disease, or to slow a disease's transmission.

"Who are they?" I asked.

"No idea," said Emma, "and I'm not about to ask."

"My guess is they're welcome nowhere else," Addison said. "Untouchables, plague carriers, criminals whose offenses are considered unforgivable even in Devil's Acre. Those who escaped the noose settled here, at the very bottom, the absolute edge of peculiar society. Exiled from the outcasts of outcasts."

"If this is the edge," said Emma, "then the wights can't be far away."

"Are we sure these people are peculiar?" I asked. There seemed to be nothing unique about them, aside from their wretchedness. Maybe it was pride, but I didn't believe a community of peculiars, however degraded, would allow themselves to live in such medieval squalor.

"Don't know, don't care," Emma replied. "Just walk."

We kept our heads down and our eyes forward, feigning disinterest in hopes that these people would return the favor. Most stayed away, but a few trailed us, begging.

"Anything, anything. A dropper, a vial," said one, gesturing to his eyes.

"Please," implored another. "We haven't had a kick in days."

Their cheeks were pocked and scarred, like they'd been crying tears of acid. I could hardly look at them.

"Whatever you want, we haven't got it," said Emma, shooing them away.

The beggars dropped back and stood in the road, watching us darkly. Another called out in a high, fraying voice. "You there! Boy!"

"Ignore him," Emma muttered.

I side-eyed him without turning my head. He was squatting against a wall, in rags, pointing at me with a trembling hand.

"You him? Boy! You're him, aincha?" He wore an eyepatch over glasses and flipped it up to study me. "Yeahhhhh." He whistled low, then flashed a black-gummed smile. "They been *waitin'* for you."

"Who has?"

I couldn't take it anymore. I stopped in front of him. Emma sighed impatiently.

The beggar's smile grew wider, crazier. "The dust-mothers and knot-blowers! The damned librarians and blessed cartographers! Anyone who's everyone!" He raised his arms and bowed in mocking worship, and I got a whiff of ripe funk. "Waitin' a *lonnnnnng* time."

"For what?"

"Come on," said Emma, "he's obviously a lunatic."

"The big show, the big show," said the beggar, his voice rising and falling like a carnival barker's. "The biggest and best and most and last! It's *allllllll*most here . . . "

A weird chill rattled through me. "I don't know you, and you sure as hell don't know me." I turned and walked away.

"Sure I do," I heard him say. "You're the boy who talks to hollows."

I froze. Emma and Addison turned to gape at me.

I ran back, confronting him. "Who are you?" I shouted in his face. "Who told you that?"

But he just laughed and laughed, and I could get nothing more out of him.

We slipped away just as a crowd began to gather.

"Don't look back," Addison warned.

"Forget him," said Emma. "He's a madman."

I think we all knew he was more than that—but that's all we knew. We walked fast in paranoid silence, our brains humming with unanswerable questions. No one mentioned the beggar's bizarre pronouncements, for which I was grateful. I had no clue what they meant and was too exhausted to speculate, and I could tell from their dragging feet that Emma and Addison were flagging, too. We didn't talk about that, either. Exhaustion was our new enemy, and to name it would only have empowered it more.

We strained to see any sign of the wights' bridge as the road ahead sloped downward into an obscuring bowl of fog. It occurred to me that Lorraine might've lied to us. Maybe there was no bridge. Maybe she'd sent us into this pit hoping its denizens would eat us alive. If only we had brought her with us, then we could've have forced her to—

"There it is!" Addison cried, his body forming an arrow that pointed straight ahead.

We struggled to see what he saw—even with his glasses, Addison's vision was sharper than ours—and after a dozen paces we could make out, just dimly, how the road narrowed and then arched over some sort of chasm.

"The bridge!" Emma cried.

We broke into a run, exhaustion momentarily forgotten, our feet sending up puffs of black dust. A minute later when we stopped for breath, the view had cleared. A shroud of greenish mist hung over the chasm. Looming faintly beyond was a long wall of white stone, and beyond that, a high pale tower, the top of which was lost among low clouds.

That was it: the wights' fortress. There was an unsettling

blankness about it, like a face with its features wiped clean. There was a wrongness about its placement, too—its great white edifice and clean lines contrasting bizarrely with the burned-over waste of Smoking Street, like a suburban shopping center plopped in the midst of the Battle of Agincourt. Just looking at it charged me with dread and purpose, as if I could feel all the disparate strands of my silly and scattered life converging toward a single point, unseen behind those walls. That's where it was: the thing I was supposed to do—or die trying. The debt I had to pay. The thing for which all the joys and terrors of my life thus far had been a prelude. If everything happens for a reason, my reason was on the other side.

Beside me, Emma was laughing. I gave her a baffled look and she composed herself.

"*That's* where they've been hiding?" she said by way of explanation.

"It would seem so," Addison said. "Do you find that humorous?"

"Nearly all my life I've hated and feared the wights. Across all those years, I can't tell you how many times I've imagined the moment we'd finally find their lair, their den. I'd expected at the very least a foreboding castle. Walls dripping with blood. A lake of boiling oil. But no."

"So you're disappointed?" I said.

"I am, a bit." She pointed accusingly at the fortress. "Is that the best they can do?"

"I'm disappointed, too," said Addison. "I hoped at least we'd have an army alongside us. But from the looks of it, perhaps we won't need one."

"I doubt that," I said. "Anything could be waiting for us on the other side of that wall."

"Then we'll be *ready* for anything," Emma said. "What could they throw at us that we haven't faced already? We've survived bullets, bombing, hollow attacks. . . . The point is, we're finally here, and after all these years of them ambushing *us*, we're finally bringing some fight to *them*."

"I'm sure they're quaking in their boots," I said.

"I'm going to find Caul," Emma went on. "I'm going to find him and make him weep for his mother. I'm going to make him beg for his worthless life, and then I'm going to put both hands around his neck and squeeze until his head melts off . . . "

"Let's not get ahead of ourselves," I said. "I'm sure there's a lot standing between us and him. There'll be wights everywhere. And armed guards probably."

"Maybe even hollows," Addison said.

"Definitely hollows," said Emma. She sounded vaguely excited by the idea.

"Point being," I said, "I don't think we should storm the gates without knowing more about what's waiting for us on the other side. We may only have one chance at this, and I don't want to throw it away."

"Okay," said Emma. "What do you suggest?"

"That we find a way to sneak Addison inside. He's the least likely to be noticed, small enough to hide almost anywhere, and he's got the best nose. He could do recon, then sneak out again and tell us what he found. That is, if he's up for it."

"And if I don't return?" said Addison.

"Then we'll come after you," I said.

The dog took a moment to consider—but only a moment. "I accept, on one condition."

"Name it," I said.

"In the tales that are told about us after our victory, I should like to be known as Addison the Intrepid."

"And so you shall," said Emma.

"Make that Extremely Intrepid," Addison said. "And handsome."

"Done," I said.

"Excellent," said Addison. "Time to have at it, then. Nearly everyone we care about in the world is on the other side of that bridge. Every minute I spend on this side is a minute wasted."

We would accompany Addison as far as the bridge, then wait nearby for his return. We began to jog downhill, the going easy, the shantytown around us growing denser as we advanced. The gaps between shacks closed until none remained, the whole of it blurring past in an unbroken patchwork of rust-eaten metal. Then abruptly the shacks and lean-tos came to an end, and for a hundred yards Smoking Street returned to a wilderness of caved walls and blackened timbers—a buffer zone of sorts, perhaps enforced by the wights. At last we came to the bridge, the mouth of it bearded by a scrum of people, a few dozen in all. While we were still too far away to register the state of their clothes, Addison said, "Look, an encamped army laying siege to the fortress! I knew we wouldn't be the only ones to take up the fight . . . "

Upon closer inspection, however, these were anything but soldiers. With a disappointed *humph* Addison's bright little hope winked out.

"They're not laying siege," I said. "They're just . . . laying."

The wretchedest shantytowners we'd seen yet, they were slumped in the ashes, arranged in postures of such listless torpor that for a moment I mistook even the ones who were sitting upright for dead. Their hair and bodies were blacked with ash and grease, and their faces so afflicted with pits and scars that I wondered if they were lepers. As we picked our way between them a few looked up weakly, but if they were waiting for something, it wasn't us, and their heads slumped down again. The only one standing was a boy in a flap-eared hunting cap who prowled between the sleepers, rifling their pockets. Those he woke swatted at him but didn't bother giving chase. They had nothing worth stealing anyway.

We were nearly past when one called out: "You'll die!"

Emma stopped and turned, defiant. "What was that?"

"You'll die."

The man who spoke lounged on a sheet of cardboard, his yellow eyes peeping through a burrow of black hair. "No one crosses their bridge without permission."

"We mean to cross it anyway. So if you know something we should beware of, speak now!"

The lounger stifled a laugh. The rest were silent.

Emma looked them over. "None of you will help us?"

One man started to say, "Be careful to—" but as soon as he'd begun, another man hushed him.

"Let them go, and in a few days we'll have their drippings!"

A moan of agonized desire went up among the shantytowners.

"Oh, what I wouldn't give for a vial of that," said a woman by my feet.

"For just a drop, a drop!" sang a man, bouncing on his haunches. "A drop o' their drippings!"

"Stop, it's torture!" another whimpered. "Don't even mention it!"

"To hell with all of you!" Emma shouted. "Let's get you across, Addison the Intrepid."

And we turned away in disgust.

*   *   *

The bridge was narrow, arched in the middle, and built from marble so clean that even ash from the street seemed wary of trespassing on it. Addison stopped us just shy of the edge. "Wait, there's something here," he said, and we stood by nervously while he closed his eyes and sniffed the air like a clairvoyant reading a crystal ball.

"We need to cross *now*—we're exposed out here," Emma muttered, but Addison was elsewhere; besides, it really didn't seem like we were in much danger. No one was on the bridge, nor was anyone guarding the barred gate on the other side. The top of the long white wall, where you might expect to see men posted with rifles and bin-oculars, was similarly empty. Other than its walls, the fortress's sole defense seemed to be the chasm that curved around it like a moat, at the bottom of which churned a boiling river that released the sulfu-rous green steam which hung all around us. The bridge was the only way across that I could see.

"Still disappointed?" I asked Emma.

"Downright insulted," she replied. "It's like they're not even trying to keep us out."

"Yeah, that's what worries me."

Addison gasped and his eyes sprang open. They shone, electric.

"What is it?" Emma said, breathless.

"It's only the faintest of traces, but I'd know Balenciaga Wren's scent anywhere."

"And the others?"

Addison sniffed again. "There were more of our kind with her. I can't say who, precisely, or how many. The trail goes quite mud-dy. Many peculiars have come this way recently—and I don't mean them," he said, looking banefully at the squatters behind us. "Their peculiar essence is weak, almost nonexistent."

"Then that woman we interrogated was telling the truth," I said. "This is where the wights bring their captives. Our friends were here."

Ever since they'd been taken, an awful suffocating hopelessness had been tightening around my heart, but its grip loosened now, slightly. For the first time in hours, we were running on more than just hope and guesswork. We had tracked our friends across hostile territory all the way to the wights' doorstep. That in itself was a small victory, and it made me feel, if only for a moment, like any-thing was possible.

"Then it's even stranger that no one's guarding this place," Emma said darkly. "I don't like this at all."

"I don't either," I said. "But I don't see any other way across."

"I might as well get it over with," said Addison.

"We'll come with you as far as we can," said Emma.

"I appreciate that," Addison replied, sounding somewhat less than extremely intrepid.

The bridge could be sprinted across in under a minute, I guessed, but why run? *Because*, I thought, a line from Tolkien materializing in my head, *one does not simply walk into Mordor.*

We started across at a brisk pace, murmurs and muted laughs following us. I glanced back at the squatters. Certain we were about to meet some grisly end, they were shifting around, angling for good views. All they needed was popcorn. I wanted to go back and pitch every last one into the boiling river.

In a few days we'll have their drippings. I didn't know what that meant and hoped I never would.

The bridge steepened. An encroaching paranoia was making my heart beat double time. I felt sure something was about to swoop down and we'd have nowhere to run. I felt like a mouse scurrying toward a trap.

In whispers we reviewed our plan: get Addison through the gate, then fall back to the shantytown and find somewhere unobtrusive to wait. If he hadn't returned within three hours, Emma and I would find a way in.

We were coming to the crest of the bridge, beyond which I'd be able to see a small section of the downslope that till now had been hidden. And then the lampposts shouted:

"Stop!"

"Who goes there!"

"None shall pass!"

We stopped and gaped at them, stunned to realize they weren't lampposts at all but desiccated heads impaled on long pikes. They were horrible, skin drawn and gray, tongues lolling—and yet, despite not being attached to throats, three of the heads had spoken to us. There were eight altogether, mounted in pairs on either side of the bridge.

Only Addison seemed unsurprised. "Don't tell me you've never seen a bridge head," he said.

"Go no further!" said the head on our left. "Almost certain death awaits those who cross without permission!"

"Perhaps you should say *certain* death," said the head on our right. "*Almost* sounds wishy-washy."

"We have permission," I said, improvising a lie. "I'm a wight, and I'm delivering these two captured peculiars to Caul."

"No one told *us*," the head on the left said irritably.

"Do they look captured to you, Richard?" said the one on the right.

"I couldn't tell you," said the left. "Ravens pecked out my eyes weeks ago."

"Yours, too?" said the right. "Pity."

"He don't sound like any wight *I* know," said the left. "What's your name, sirrah?"

"Smith," I said.

"Ha! We don't have a Smith!" said the right.

"I just joined up."

"Nice try. No, I don't think we'll let you through."

"And who's going to stop us?" I said.

"Obviously not us," said the left. "We're just here to forebode."

"And to inform," said the right. "Did you know I took a degree in museum studies? I never wanted to be a bridge head . . . "

"No one *wants* to be a bridge head," snapped the left. "No child grows up dreaming of becoming a bloody bridge head, foreboding at people all day and having your eyes pecked out by ravens. But life doesn't always scatter roses at your feet, does it?"

"Let's go," muttered Emma. "All they can do is natter at us."

We ignored them and continued up the bridge, each head warning us in turn as we passed.

"Step no further!" shouted the fourth.

"Continue at your peril!" wailed the fifth.

"I don't think they're listening," said the sixth.

"Oh, well," said the seventh airily. "Don't say we didn't warn you."

The eighth only stuck out his fat green tongue at us. Then we were beyond them and cresting the bridge, and there it came to a sudden end—a yawning, twenty-foot gap in the place where stone should've been, and I nearly stepped into it. Emma caught me as I reeled backward, arms pinwheeling.

"They didn't finish the damned bridge!" I said, my cheeks flushing with adrenaline and embarrassment. I could hear the heads laughing at me, and behind them, the road squatters.

If we'd been going at a run, we wouldn't have stopped in time and would've pitched right over the edge.

"Are you all right?" Emma asked me.

"I'm fine," I said, "but *we're* not. How are we supposed to get Addison across now?"

"This *is* vexing," said Addison, pacing along the edge. "I don't suppose we could jump?"

"No chance," I said. "It'd be way too far, even at a full run. Even with a pole vault."

"Huh," said Emma. She looked behind us. "You just gave me an idea. I'll be right back."

Addison and I watched as she marched down the bridge. At the first head she came to, she stopped, wrapped her hands around the pike it was impaled on, and pulled.

The pike came out with ease. As the head protested loudly, she laid it on the ground, planted her foot on its face, and gave a mighty yank. The pike slid free of the head, which went rolling off down the bridge, howling with rage. Emma returned triumphant, stood the pike at the edge of the gap, and let it fall across with a loud metallic clang.

Emma looked at it and frowned. "Well, it isn't London Bridge." Twenty feet long by one inch wide and slightly bowed in the middle, it looked like something a circus acrobat might balance on.

"Let's get a few more," I suggested.

We ran back and forth, prying up pikes and laying them across the gap. The heads spat and swore and issued empty threats. When the last of them had been pried off and rolled away, we'd made a small metal bridge, roughly a foot wide, slippery with head goo and rattling in the ashy breeze.

"For England!" Addison said, and he shimmied haltingly onto the pikes.

"For Miss Peregrine," I said, following him.

"For the love of birds, just go," said Emma, and she stepped on behind me.

Addison slowed us down badly. His little legs kept slipping between the pikes, which made the pikes roll like axles and gave me awful stomach flutters. I tried focusing on where to place my feet without seeing past them into the chasm, but it was impossible; the boiling river attracted my eyes like a magnet, and I found myself wondering whether we were high enough for the fall alone to kill me or whether I'd survive long enough to feel myself cooking to death. Addison, meanwhile, had given up trying to walk altogether and instead laid down, whereupon he began to push himself along the pikes like a slug. In this way we proceeded, inch by undignified inch, to just beyond the halfway point—and then my flutters sharpened and gave way to something else: a knot in my stomach that I'd come to know all too well.

Hollow. I tried to say it aloud but my mouth had gone dry; by the time I'd swallowed and got the word out, the feeling had multiplied tenfold.

"What dreadful luck," Addison said. "Is it ahead of us or behind?"

I couldn't tell right away and had to poke around the feeling for a moment before I could pin it down.

"Jacob! Ahead or behind?" Emma shouted in my ear.

Ahead. My gut-compass was certain, but it made no sense: the downward slope of the bridge was now visible all the way to the gate, and the whole length was deserted. There was nothing there.

"I don't know!" I said.

"Then keep going!" Emma replied.

We were closer to the far side of the gap than the near; we'd be off the pikes faster if we continued forward. I shoved down my fear, bent and scooped up Addison, and started to run, slipping and wobbling on the unsteady pikes. The hollow felt close enough to touch, and I could hear it now, grunting toward us from some unseen place ahead. My eyes followed the sound to a spot in front of us but below our feet—on the cut-away face of the bridge, where several tall, narrow apertures had been carved into the stone.

There. The bridge was hollow, and a hollow was inside the bridge. Though its body would never fit through the openings in the stone, its tongues easily could.

I'd made it across the pikes and onto solid bridge when I heard Emma cry out. I dropped Addison and spun to see her behind me, one of the hollow's tongues wrapped around her waist and whisking her into the air.

She screamed my name and I screamed hers. The tongue flipped her upside down and shook her. She screamed again. There was no worse sound.

Another of its tongues slapped the underside of the pikes and our makeshift bridge went flying, clattering apart and plunging like matchsticks into the chasm below. Then the second tongue went for Addison, and the third punched me in the chest.

I fell to the ground, the wind knocked out of me. While I struggled for a breath, the tongue slithered around my waist and scooped me into the air. The other had Addison by his hind legs. In a moment, all three of us were dangling upside down.

Blood rushed to my head, darkening my vision. I could hear Addison barking and nipping at the tongue.

"Don't, it'll drop you!" I shouted, but he kept on.

Emma was helpless, too; if she burned the tongue around her waist, the hollow would drop her.

"Talk to it, Jacob!" she shouted. "Make it stop!"

I twisted to see the narrow openings through which its tongues had squeezed. Its teeth gnawed at the stone slats. Its black eyes bulged hungrily. We hung like fruit on thick black vines, the chasm yawning below.

I tried to speak its language. "SET US DOWN!" I shouted—but what came out was English.

"Again!" Addison said.

I shut my eyes and imagined the hollow doing as I asked, then tried again.

"Put us down on the bridge!"

More English. This wasn't the hollow I'd come to know, the one I'd communed with for hours while it was frozen in ice. This was a new one, a stranger, and my connection with it was thin and weak. It seemed to sense that I was fumbling for a key to its brain, and it hauled us suddenly upward, as if winding up to fling us into the chasm. I had to connect, somehow, *now*—

"STOP!" I screamed, my throat raw—and this time, out came the guttural scratch of hollowspeak.

We jolted to a stop in midair. For a moment we just hung there, swinging like laundry in a breeze. My words had done something but not enough. I'd merely confused it.

"Can't breathe," Emma croaked. The tongue around her was squeezing too hard, and her face was turning purple.

"Put us down on the bridge," I said—in Hollow again!—the words clawing at my throat as they came. Every burst of hollow-speak felt like I was coughing up staples.

The hollow made an uncertain rattle. For an optimistic

moment I thought it might actually do as I'd asked. Then it snapped me up and down as fast and hard as you'd shake out a towel.

Everything blurred and briefly went black. When I came to, my tongue was numb and I tasted blood.

"Tell it to put us down!" Addison was shouting. But now I could hardly speak at all.

"Ahm twying," I mumbled. I coughed, spitting out a mouthful of blood. "Puhh uff dow," I said, in broken-tongued English. "Puhh uff—"

I stopped, reoriented my brain. Took a deep breath.

"Put us down on the bridge," I said in crisp hollowspeak.

I repeated it three more times, hoping it might slip into some furrow of the hollow's reptilian brain. "Put us down on the bridge. Put us down on the bridge. Put us down on the—"

It gave a sudden bone-rattling roar of frustration, pulled me to the openings in the bridge where it was imprisoned, and roared again, flecks of black spittle spraying my face. Then it hauled all three of us up and hurled us back the way we'd come.

We tumbled through the air for what felt like too long—we were falling now, I was sure of it, arcing downward to our doom—and then my shoulder connected with the hard stone of the bridge, and we slid and skidded all the way down its slope to the bottom.

*   *   *

We were, miraculously, alive—banged up but conscious, our limbs still connected to our bodies. We'd tumbled down the smooth marble bridge, scattering the pile of heads at the bottom as we rolled to a stop. They were all around now, taunting us as we collected ourselves.

"Welcome back!" said the one nearest me. "We quite enjoyed your screams of terror. What powerful lungs you have!"

"Why didn't you tell us a hollow was hiding in the damned

bridge?" I said, rocking myself up to a sitting position. Pains flared all over my body, from scraped hands, scuffed knees, and a throbbing shoulder that was likely dislocated.

"Where's the fun in that? Surprises are much better."

"Tickles must've taken a fancy to you," said another. "He chewed the legs off his last visitor!"

"That's nothing," said a head with a shiny hoop earring like a pirate. "Once I saw him tie a rope around a peculiar, lower him into the river for five minutes, then reel him up and eat him."

"Peculiar al dente," the third said, impressed. "Our Tickles is a gourmand."

Not quite ready to stand, I scooted over a few feet to Emma and Addison. While she sat rubbing her head, he tested his weight on an injured paw.

"You okay?" I asked.

"I knocked my head pretty good," Emma replied, wincing as I parted her hair to examine a trickle of blood.

Addison held up a limp paw. "I fear it's broken. I don't suppose you could've asked the beast to set us down gently."

"Very funny," I said. "Come to think of it, why didn't I just tell it kill to all the wights and rescue our friends, too?"

"Actually, I was wondering the same thing," said Emma.

"I'm *joking.*"

"Well, I'm not," she said. I dabbed at her wound with my shirt cuff. She drew a sharp breath and pushed my hand away. "What happened back there?"

"I think the hollow understood me, but I couldn't make it obey. I don't have a connection with that hollow like I do—did—with the other one."

That beast was dead, crushed under a bridge and probably drowned, and now I was a little sorry about it.

"How did you connect with the first one?" asked Addison.

I quickly recounted how I'd found it frozen in ice up to its eyeballs, and after a night spent in strangely intimate, hand-atop-head communion I had, apparently, managed to safe-crack some vital part of its neurology.

"If you had no connection with the bridge hollow," said Addison, "why did it spare our lives?"

"Maybe I confused it?"

"You need to get better at this," Emma said bluntly. "We have to get Addison across."

"Better? What am I supposed to do, take lessons? That thing will kill us the next time we get near it. We'll have to find another way across."

"Jacob, there *is* no other way." Emma raked a veil of mussed hair away from her face and held me with her eyes. "*You're* the way."

I was launching into a creaky rebuttal when I felt a sharp pain in my backside and leapt yelping to my feet. One of the heads had bitten me on the ass.

"Hey!" I shouted, rubbing the spot.

"Stick us back on our pikes like you found us, vandal!" it said.

I punted it as hard as I could and it tumbled away into the crowd of squatters. All the heads began to shout and curse us, rolling about grotesquely with the action of their jaws. I cursed back and kicked ash in their horrible leathery faces until they were all spitting and choking. And then something small and round came sailing through the air and hit me wetly in the back.

A rotten apple. I spun to face the squatters. "Who threw that?"

They laughed like stoners, low and snickering.

"Go back where you came from!" one of them yelled.

I was starting to think that wasn't a bad idea.

"How dare they," Addison snarled.

"Forget it," I said to him, my anger already fading. "Let's just—"

"How *dare* you!" Addison shouted, livid, rising up to address

them on hind legs. "Are you not peculiar? Have you no shame? We're trying to help you!"

"Give us a vial or get stuffed!" said a ragged woman.

Addison trembled with outrage. "We're trying to help you," he said again, "and here you are—*here you are!*—while our people are being murdered, our loops torn out root and branch, sleeping before the enemy's gate! You should be flinging yourselves at it!" He pointed his wounded paw at them. "You are all traitors, and I swear one day I shall see you dragged before the Council of Ymbrynes and punished!"

"Okay, okay, don't waste all your energy on them," Emma said, wobbling to her feet. Then a rotten head of cabbage bounced off her shoulder and fell *splat* to the ground.

She lost it.

"All right, someone's gonna get their face melted!" she yelled, waving a flaming hand at the squatters.

During Addison's speech, a group had been muttering in a conspiratorial huddle, and now they came forward holding blunt weapons. A sawed branch. A length of pipe. The scene was turning ugly fast.

"We're tired of you," a bruised man said in a lazy drawl. "We're puttin' you in the river."

"I'd like to see that," Emma said.

"I wouldn't," I said. "I think we should go."

There were six of them, three of us, and we were in rough shape: Addison was limping, Emma had blood running down her face, and thanks to my injured shoulder I could hardly lift my right arm. Meanwhile, the men were spreading apart and closing in. They meant to drive us into the chasm.

Emma looked back at the bridge and then at me. "Come on. I know you can get us across. One more try."

"I can't, Em. I *can't*. I'm not messing around."

And I wasn't. I didn't have it in me to control that hollow—not yet, at least—and I knew it.

"If the boy says he can't do it, I'm not inclined to disbelieve him," Addison said. "We must find another way out of this."

Emma huffed. "Like what?" She looked at Addison. "Can you run?" She looked at me. "Can you fight?"

The answer to both was no. I took her point: our options were winnowing fast.

"At times like this," Addison said imperiously, "my kind don't fight. We orate!" Facing the men, he called out in a booming voice, "Fellow peculiars, be reasonable! Allow me a few words!"

They paid him no attention. As they continued closing off our escape routes, we backed toward the bridge, Emma crafting the largest fireball she could muster while Addison yammered about how the animals of the forest live in harmony, so why can't we? "Consider the simple hedgehog, and his neighbor, the opossum . . . do they waste their energy trying to throw one another into chasms when they face a common enemy, the winter? No!"

"He's gone completely crackers," Emma said. "Shut your gob and bite one of them!"

I looked around for something to fight with. The only hard objects within reach were the heads. I picked one up by the last wisps of its hair.

"Is there another way across?" I shouted into its face. "Quick, or I'm throwing you into the river!"

"Go to Hell!" it spat, then snapped at me with its teeth.

I flung it at the men—awkwardly, with my left arm. It fell short. I rooted around for another head, picked it up, and repeated my question.

"Sure there is," the head sneered. "In the back of a prizzo van! Though if I were you I'd take my chances with the bridge hollow . . . "

"What's a prizzo van? Tell me or I'll fling you, too!"

"You're about to get hit by one," it replied, and then three gunshots rang out in the distance—*bam, bam, bam,* slow and measured, like a warning. Immediately the men who'd been coming at us stopped, and everyone turned to look down the road.

Half drawn through a cloud of swirling ash, something large and boxy was rumbling toward us. Then came the growl of a big engine downshifting, and out of the black appeared a truck. It was a modern machine of military issue, all rivets and reinforcements and tires half a man high. The back was a windowless cube, and two flak-jacketed, machine-gun-armed wights stood guard along its running boards.

The moment it appeared, the squatters went into a kind of frenzy, laughing and gasping for joy, waving their arms and clasping their hands like marooned shipwreck survivors flagging down a passing plane—and just like that, we were forgotten. A golden opportunity had smacked into us, and we weren't about to waste it. I tossed aside the head, scooped Addison into the crook of my left arm, and scrambled out of the road after Emma. We could've kept going—cut away from Smoking Street and retreated to some safer quarter of Devil's Acre—but here, finally, was our enemy in the flesh, and whatever was happening or about to happen was clearly of importance. We stopped not far off the roadside, barely hidden behind a knot of charred trees, and watched.

The truck slowed and the crowd swarmed it, groveling and begging—for *vials*, for *suulie* and *ambro* and *just a taste, just a little, please sir*, disgusting in their worship of these butchers, pawing at the soldiers' clothes and shoes and getting steel-toed kicks in return. I thought surely the wights would start shooting, or gun the engine and crush those foolish enough to stand between them and the bridge. Instead the truck stopped and the wights began to shout instructions. *Form a line, right over here, keep orderly or you'll get nothing!* The crowd fell into formation like destitutes in a bread line, cowed and fidgeting in anticipation of what they were about to receive.

Without warning, Addison began to struggle to be set down. I asked him what was the matter, but he only whimpered and struggled harder, a desperate look on his face like he'd just caught a major scent trail. Emma pinched him and he snapped out of it long enough to say, "It's her, it's her—it's Miss Wren," and I realized that *prizzo van* was short for prison van, and that the cargo in the back of the wights' enormous vehicle was almost certainly human.

Then Addison bit me. I yelped and let him go, and in an instant he was scrambling away. Emma swore and I said, "Addison, don't!" But it was useless; he was operating on instinct, the irrepressible reflex of a loyal dog trying to protect his master. I dove for him and missed—he was surprisingly speedy for a creature with just three working legs—and then Emma hauled me up and together we were after him, out of our hiding place and into the road.

There was a moment, a fleeting instant, when I thought we could catch him, that the soldiers were too mobbed and the crowd too preoccupied to notice us. And it might've happened but for the shift that came over Emma halfway across the road, when she spied the doors at the back of the truck. *Doors with locks that could be melted. Doors that could be flung open*, she must've thought—I could read it in the hope dawning on her face—and she passed Addison without even reaching for him and clambered onto the truck's bumper.

Shouts from the guards. I grabbed for Addison but he slid away, under the truck. Emma was starting to melt the handle of one door when the first guard swung his gun like a baseball bat. It hit her in the side and she tumbled to the ground. I ran at the guard, ready to do to him whatever I could with my one good arm, but my legs were kicked out from under me and I crashed down onto my hurt shoulder, a thunderbolt of pain surging through me.

Hearing the guard scream I looked up, saw him unarmed and waving an injured hand, and then he was tripping away into the mad swim of churning bodies. The squatters swarmed him, not just begging but demanding, threatening, crazed—and now, somewhere, one of them had his weapon. Looking panicked, he waved to the other wight with a two-hands-over-the-head *get me out of here!*

I struggled to my feet and ran for Emma. The other guard dove into the crowd, firing into the air until he could pull out his comrade and get back to the truck. The moment their feet hit the running boards, they slapped the side of the truck and the engine roared. I reached Emma just as it took off for the bridge, its monster tires spitting gravel and ash.

I clasped her arm to reassure myself she was still whole. "You're bleeding," I said, "a lot," which was a clunky statement of fact but also the best I could articulate how awful it felt to see her hurt— limping, a gash on her scalp leaking blood into her hair.

"Where's Addison?" she said. But before "I don't know" had left my lips, she interrupted—"We've got to go after it. This may be our only chance!"

We looked up as the truck was reaching the bridge and saw the guard gun down two squatters chasing after it. As they fell writhing to the dirt, I knew she was wrong: there was no chasing down the truck, no getting across the bridge. It was hopeless—and now the squatters knew it. As their comrades fell, I could feel their desperation turn to rage, and in what seemed an instant that rage turned on us.

We tried to run but found ourselves blocked on all sides. The mob was shouting that we'd "ruined it," that "they'd cut us off now," that we deserved to die. Blows started raining down on us—slaps, punches, hands tearing at our hair and clothes. I tried to protect Emma but she ended up protecting me, for a few moments at least, swinging her hands around, burning whomever she could. Even her fire wasn't enough to get them away from us, and the hits kept coming until we were on our knees, then balled up on the ground, arms protecting our faces, pain coming from every direction.

I was almost sure I was dying, or dreaming, because I heard at that moment singing—a loud, peppy chorus of "Hark to the driving of hammers, hark to the driving of nails!"—but with each line came a smattering of fleshy thuds and corresponding yelps: "What *(SMACK!)* to build a gallows, the *(THWACK!)* for all that ails!"

After a few lines and a few thwacks, the blows stopped raining down and the mob backed away, wary and grumbling. I saw dimly, through a haze of blood and grit, five brawny gallows riggers, tool belts hung from their waists and hammers raised in their hands. They'd cut a wedge through the crowd, and now they circled us, looking down doubtfully as if we were some strange species of fish they hadn't been expecting to find in their nets.

"Is this them?" I heard one of them say. "They don't look so good, cousin."

"Of course it's them!" said another, his voice like a foghorn, deep and familiar.

"It's Sharon!" Emma cried.

I could move my hand just enough to wipe one eye clear of blood. There he stood, all seven black-cloaked feet of him. I felt myself laugh, or try to; I'd never been so glad to see someone so ugly. He was digging something out of his pocket—little glass vials—and raised them above his head shouting, "I'VE GOT WHAT YOU WANT RIGHT HERE, YOU SICK MONKEYS! GO TAKE THEM AND LEAVE THESE CHILDREN BE!"

He turned and threw the vials down the road. The mob flooded after them, gasping and shouting, ready to tear one another apart to get them. And then it was just the riggers, slightly rumpled from the melee but unscathed, tucking their hammers back into their belts. Sharon, striding toward us with one snow-white hand outstretched, was saying, "What were you thinking, wandering off like that? I was worried sick!"

"It's true," said one of the riggers. "He was beside himself. Had us looking everywhere for you."

I tried sitting up but couldn't. Sharon was right over top of us, peering down like he was examining roadkill.

"Are you whole? Can you walk? What in the devil's name have these reprobates done to you?" His tone was somewhere between angry drill sergeant and concerned father.

"Jacob's hurt," I heard Emma say, her voice cracking. "So are you," I tried to say but couldn't get my tongue straight. It seemed she was right: my head felt heavy as stone, and my vision was a failing satellite signal, good one moment, gone the next. I was being lifted, carried in Sharon's arms—he was much stronger than he looked— and I had a sudden flashing thought, which I tried to say aloud:

Where's Addison?

I was all mush-mouthed but somehow he understood me, and turning my head toward the bridge, he said, "There."

In the distance, the truck seemed to be floating in midair. Was my concussed brain playing tricks?

No. I could see it now: the truck was being lifted across the gap by the hollow's tongues.

But where's Addison?

"There," Sharon repeated. "Underneath."

Two hind legs and a small brown body dangled from the truck's underside. Addison had clamped onto some part of its undercarriage with his teeth and caught a ride, the clever devil. And as the tongues deposited the truck on the far side of the bridge, I thought, *Godspeed, intrepid little dog. You may be the best hope we've got.*

And then I was fading, fading, the world irising toward night.

CHAPTER FOUR

*T*urbulent dreams, dreams in strange languages, dreams of home, of death. Odd bits of nonsense that spooled out in flickers of consciousness, swimmy and unreliable, inventions of my concussed brain. A faceless woman blowing dust into my eyes. A sensation of being immersed in warm water. Emma's voice assuring me everything would be okay, they're friends, we're safe. Then deep and dreamless dark for unknown hours.

The next time I woke, I wasn't dreaming and I knew it. I was tucked into a bed in a small room. Weak light spilled from behind a drawn window shade. So, daytime. But what day?

I was in a nightgown, not my old, blood-stained clothes, and my eyes were clear of grit. Someone had been taking care of me. Also: though I was bone-tired, I felt little pain. My shoulder had stopped aching, and so had my head. I wasn't sure what that meant.

I tried sitting up. I had to stop halfway and rest on my elbows. A glass pitcher of water stood on a night table by the bedside. In one corner of the room was a hulking wooden wardrobe. In the other— I blinked and rubbed my eyes, making sure—yes, there was a man sleeping in a chair. My mind was moving so sluggishly that I wasn't even startled; I merely thought, *that's odd*. And he was: so odd-looking, in fact, that I struggled briefly to understand what I was seeing. He seemed a man composed of halves: half his hair was slicked down while the other half was cowlicked all over the place; half his face was scraggly beard and the other half clean-shaven. Even his clothes (pants, rumpled sweater, ruffled Elizabethan collar) were half modern, half archaic.

"Hello?" I said uncertainly.

The man shouted, startling so badly that he fell out of his chair and landed on the floor in a clatter. "Oh, my! Oh, goodness!" He climbed back into the chair, eyes wide and hands aflutter. "You're awake!"

"Sorry, I didn't mean to scare you . . . "

"Ah, no, it was my fault entirely," he said, smoothing his clothes and straightening his ruffled collar. "Please don't tell anyone I fell asleep watching you!"

"Who are you?" I asked. "Where am I?" My mind was clearing fast, and as it did it filled with questions. "And where's Emma?"

"Right, yes!" the man said, looking flustered. "I might not be the best-equipped member of the household to answer . . . *questions* . . . "

He whispered the word, eyebrows raised, as if questions were forbidden. "But!" He pointed at me. "*You're* Jacob." He pointed at himself. "*I'm* Nim." He made a whirling motion with his hand. "And *this* is Mr. Bentham's house. He's very eager to meet you. In fact, I'm to notify him as soon as you're awake."

I squirmed up from my elbows to sit fully upright, the effort of which nearly exhausted me. "I don't care about any of that. I want to see Emma."

"Of course! Your friend . . ."

He flapped his hands like little wings while his eyes darted from side to side, as if he might find Emma in a corner of the room.

"I want to see her. Now!"

"My name's Nim!" he squeaked. "And I'm to notify—yes, under *strict* instructions . . . "

A panicky thought flew into my head—that Sharon, mercenary that he was, had rescued us from the mob only to sell us for spare parts.

"EMMA!" I managed to shout. "WHERE ARE YOU?"

Nim went blank and plopped into the chair—I'd scared him silly, I think.

A moment later feet came pounding down the hall. A man in a white coat burst into the room. "You're awake!" he exclaimed. I could only assume he was a doctor.

"I want to see Emma!" I said. I tried to swing my legs out of the bed, but they felt heavy as logs.

The doctor rushed to my side and pushed me back toward the sheets. "Don't exert yourself, you're still recovering!"

The doctor ordered Nim to go find Mr. Bentham. Nim ran out, bouncing off the doorjamb and flopping into the hall. And then Emma was at the door, out of breath and beaming, her hair spilling down a clean white dress.

"Jacob?"

At the sight of her, a burst of strength coursed through me and I sat up, pushing the doctor aside.

"Emma!"

"You're awake!" she said, running to me.

"Careful with him, he's delicate!" the doctor warned.

Checking herself, Emma gave me the gentlest of hugs, then sat

on the edge of the bed next to me. "I'm sorry I wasn't here when you woke up. They said you'd be out for hours more . . . "

"It's okay," I said. "But where are we? How long have we been here?"

Emma glanced at the doctor. He was writing in a small notebook but obviously listening. Emma turned her back to him and lowered her voice. "We're at a rich man's house in Devil's Acre. Someplace hidden. Sharon brought us here a day, day and a half ago."

"Is that all?" I said, studying Emma's face. Her skin was perfectly smooth, her cuts faded to thin white lines. "You look almost healed!"

"I only had a few nicks and bumps . . . "

"No way," I said. "I remember what happened out there."

"You had a broken rib and a torn shoulder," the doctor interjected.

"They have a woman here," Emma said. "A healer. Her body produces a powerful dust . . . "

"And a double concussion," said the doctor. "Nothing we couldn't handle in the end. But you, boy—you were nearly dead when you arrived."

I patted my chest, my stomach, all the places I'd been pummeled. No pain. I lifted my right arm and rotated the shoulder. No problem. "It feels like I've got a new arm," I said, marveling.

"You're lucky you didn't need a new head," came another voice—Sharon, ducking to fit his full height through the doorway. "In fact, it's a shame they *didn't* give you one, because apparently the one you've got now is full of sawdust. Disappearing like that, running off without a clue where you were going—and after all my warnings about the Acre! What were you *thinking*?" He towered over Emma and me, wagging his long white finger.

I grinned at him. "Hello, Sharon. Nice to see you again."

"Yes, ha-ha, it's all smiles now that everything's rosy, but you nearly got yourselves killed out there!"

"We were lucky," Emma said.

"Yes—lucky *I* was there! Lucky my gallows-rigging cousins were available that evening and I was able to catch them before they'd had too much Ditch lager at the Cradle and Coffin! They don't work for free, by the way. I'm adding their services to your tab, along with my damaged boat!"

"Fine, fine!" I said. "Settle down, okay?"

"What were you thinking?" he said again, his awful breath settling over us like a cloud.

And then it came back to me, what I'd been thinking, and I kind of lost it. "That you were an untrustworthy lout!" I fired back. "That it's only about money with you, and you probably would have sold us into slavery the first chance you got! Yeah," I said, "we looked into it. We know all about the shady things you peculiars get up to around here, and if you think for a minute we believe that *you*"—I pointed at Sharon—"or *any* of you"—I pointed at the doctor—"are helping us purely out of kindness, you're nuts! So either tell us what you want with us or let us go, because we've . . . we've got . . . "

A sudden, crashing wave of exhaustion. My vision unfocused.

"Got better things to . . . "

I shook my head, tried standing up, but the room had begun to spin. Emma held my arms and the doctor pushed me back gently onto my pillow. "We're helping you because Mr. Bentham asked us to," he said tersely. "What he wants with you, well, you'll have to ask him yourself."

"Like I keep saying, Mister whoever can kiss my *mmmff*—"

Emma clapped a hand over my mouth. "Jacob's not feeling himself at the moment," she said. "I'm sure what he meant to say was, thanks for saving us. We're in your debt."

"That, too," I mumbled through her fingers.

I was angry and scared, but also genuinely happy to be alive—

and to see Emma whole and healed. When I thought about that, all the fight leaked out of me and I was filled with simple gratitude. I closed my eyes to stop the room from spinning and listened to them whisper about me.

"He's a problem," said the doctor. "He can't be allowed to meet Mr. Bentham like this."

"His brain is addled," Sharon said. "If the girl and I could just talk with him in private, I'm sure he could be brought around. Might we have the room to ourselves?"

Reluctantly, the doctor left. When he was gone, I opened my eyes again and focused on Emma, looking down at me.

"Where's Addison?" I asked.

"He got across," she said.

"Right," I said, remembering. "Have you heard from him? Has he come back yet?"

"No," she said quietly. "Not yet."

I considered what that might mean—what might have happened to him—but I couldn't bear the thought. "We promised to go after him," I said. "If he can get across, so can we."

"That bridge hollow might not have cared about a dog getting across," Sharon butted in, "but you he'd peel off and toss right into the boil."

"Go away," I said to him. "I want to talk to Emma in private."

"Why? So you can climb out the window and run away again?"

"We're not going anywhere," Emma said. "Jacob can't even get out of bed."

Sharon wasn't swayed. "I'll go to the corner and mind my own business," he said. "That's my best offer." He went and perched himself on Nim's one-armed chair and began to whistle and clean his fingernails.

Emma helped me sit up, and we pressed our foreheads together and spoke in whispers. For a moment I was so overwhelmed by her closeness that all the questions flooding my brain vanished, and there was only her hand touching my face, brushing my cheek, my jaw.

"You had me so frightened," Emma said. "I really thought I'd lost you."

"I'm fine," I said. I knew I hadn't been, but it embarrassed me to be worried over.

"You weren't. Not at all. You should apologize to the doctor."

"I know. I was just freaked out. And I'm sorry if I scared you."

She nodded and then looked away. Her eyes drifted briefly to the wall, and when they returned, a new hardness glittered in them.

"I like to think I'm strong," she said. "That the reason I'm free right now instead of Bronwyn or Millard or Enoch is that I'm strong enough to be depended upon. That's always been me—the one who could take anything. Like there's a pain sensor inside me that's not switched on. I can block out awful things and get on with it, do what needs doing." Her hand found mine atop the sheets. Our fingers knotted together, automatic. "But when I think about you—how you looked when they pulled you off the ground, after those people . . . "

She let out a shaky breath and shook her head, as if chasing away the memory. "I just break."

"Me, too," I said, remembering the pain I felt whenever I saw Emma hurt, the terror that gripped me every time she was in danger. "Me, too." I squeezed her hand and searched for something more to say, but she spoke first.

"I need you to promise me something."

"Anything," I said.

"I need you not to die."

I cracked a smile. Emma didn't. "You can't," she said. "If I lose you, the rest isn't worth a damn."

I slid my arms around her, pulled her tight against me. "I'll do my best."

"That's not good enough," she whispered. "Promise me."

"Okay. I won't die."

"Say, 'I promise.'"

"I promise. You say it, too."

"I promise," she said.

"Ahh," Sharon said airily from the corner, "the sweet lies lovers tell . . . "

We broke apart. "You're not supposed to be listening!" I said.

"That was long enough," he said, dragging his chair loudly across the floor and planting it next to the bed. "We have important things to discuss. Namely, the apology you owe me."

"For what?" I said, irritated.

"Impugning my character and reputation."

"Every word was true," I said. "This loop *is* full of scumbags and creeps, and you *are* a money-driven lout."

"With not an ounce of sympathy for the plight of his own people," Emma added. "Though, again, thank you for saving us."

"Around here you learn to look out for number one," Sharon said. "Everyone's got a story. A plight. Everyone wants something from you, and they're almost always lying. So yes, I remain unapologetically self-directed and profit motivated. But I deeply resent your suggestion that I would have dealings of any kind with someone who trades in peculiar flesh. Just because I'm a capitalist doesn't mean I'm a black-hearted bastard."

"And how could we have known that?" I said. "We had to beg and bribe you not to abandon us at the dock, remember?"

He shrugged. "That was before I realized who you are."

I glanced at Emma, then pointed to my chest. "Who *I* am?"

"You, my boy. Mr. Bentham's been waiting a long time to speak to you. Since the day I first hung my shingle as a boatman— forty-odd years ago. Bentham ensured me safe passage in and out of the Acre if I promised to keep an eye out for you while I did it. I was to bring you to see him. And now, finally, I've kept my end of the bargain."

"You must have me confused with someone else," I said. "I'm nobody."

"He said you'd be able to speak to hollowgast. How many peculiars do you know who can do that?"

"But he's only sixteen," Emma said. "*Really* sixteen. So how can—"

"That's why it took me a while to put it all together," said Sharon. "I had to go see Mr. Bentham about it personally, which is where I was when you two ran away. You don't fit the description, see. All these years I've been keeping watch for an old man."

"An old man," I said.

"Right."

"Who can talk to hollows."

"As I said."

Emma tightened her grip on my hand and we exchanged a look—*no, it couldn't be*—and then I swung my legs out of bed, charged with new energy. "I want to talk to this Bentham guy. Right now."

"He'll see you when he's ready," Sharon said.

"No," I said. "*Now.*"

As it happened, at that very moment there was a knock at the door. Sharon opened it to find Nim. "Mr. Bentham will meet our guests for tea in one hour," he said, "in the library."

"We can't wait an hour," I said. "We've wasted too much time here already."

At this, Nim went a bit red and puffed out his cheeks. "Wasted?"

"What Jacob meant," Emma said, "is that we have another pressing engagement elsewhere in the Acre that we're already late for."

"Mr. Bentham insists upon meeting you properly," Nim said. "As he always says, the day there's no time for manners, the world's lost to us anyway. Speaking of which, I'm to make sure you're dressed appropriately." He went to the wardrobe and swung open its heavy doors. Inside were several racks of clothes. "You may choose what you like."

Emma pulled out a frilly dress and curled her lip. "This feels so wrong. Playing dress-up and having tea while our friends and ymbrynes are forced to endure bird knows what."

"We're doing it for them," I said. "We only have to play along till Bentham tells us what he knows. It could be important."

"Or he could just be a lonely old man."

"Don't talk about Mr. Bentham that way," Nim said, his face puckering. "Mr. Bentham is a saint, a giant among men!"

"Oh calm down," Sharon said. He went to the window and pulled open the blinds, allowing a weak, pea-soup daylight to dribble into the room. "Up and at 'em!" he said to us. "You two have a date."

I threw back my covers and Emma helped me out of bed. To my surprise, my legs took my weight. I glanced out the window at an empty street enveloped in yellow murk, and then, with Emma holding my arm, went to the wardrobe to pick out a change of clothes. I found an outfit on a hanger tagged with my name.

"Can we have some privacy to change, please?" I said.

Sharon looked at Nim and shrugged. Nim's hands flapped. "It wouldn't be proper!"

"Ahh, they're fine," Sharon said, waving his hand. "No monkey business, all right?"

Emma turned beet red. "I wouldn't have any idea what you mean."

"Sure you wouldn't." He shooed Nim out of the room, then paused at the doorway. "I can trust you not to run away again?"

"Why would we?" I said. "We want to meet Mr. Bentham."

"We're not going anywhere," Emma said. "But why are *you* still here?"

"Mr. Bentham asked me to keep an eye on you."

I wondered if that meant Sharon would stop us if we tried to leave.

"Must be a pretty big favor you owed him," I said.

"Massive," he replied. "I owe the man my life." And bending himself nearly in half, he squeezed out into the hallway.

*　　*　　*

"You change clothes in there," Emma said, nodding toward a small connecting bathroom. "I'll change in here. And no peeking until I knock!"

"Ok*ayyy*," I said, exaggerating my disappointment in order to hide it. While seeing Emma in her underwear was an undeniably appealing prospect, all the life-threatening peril we'd endured lately had put that part of my teenage brain into a kind of deep freeze. A few more serious kisses, though, and my baser instincts might start to reassert themselves.

But anyway.

I shut myself in the bathroom, all gleaming white tile and heavy iron fixtures, and leaned over the sink to examine myself in a silvered mirror.

I was a mess.

My face was puffy and crosshatched with angry pink lines, which were healing quickly but still there, reminders of every blow I'd suffered. My torso was a geography of bruises, painless but ugly. Blood was caked into the hard-to-clean folds of my ears. The sight of it made me dizzy, and I had to grip the sink to stay upright. I had a sudden nasty flashback: fists and feet thrashing at me, the ground rushing up.

No one had ever tried to kill me with bare hands before. That was something new, much different than being hunted by hollows, which ran on instinct. Different, too, than being shot at: bullets were a quick, impersonal way to kill. Using your hands, though—that took work. It required hate. It was a strange and sour thing to know that such hatred had been directed at me. That peculiars who didn't even know my name had, in a moment of collective madness, hated me enough to try to beat out my life with their fists. I felt shamed by it, dehumanized somehow, though I couldn't exactly understand why. It was something I'd have to reckon with, if one day I ever had the luxury of time to reckon with such things.

I turned on the tap to wash my face. The pipes shuddered and groaned, but after a big orchestral flourish, they produced only a hiccup of brown water. This Bentham fellow might've been rich, but no amount of luxury could cocoon him from the reality of the hellish place where he lived.

How had he ended up here?

More intriguing still: how did the man know, or know about, my grandfather? Surely that's who Sharon had been referring to when he said Bentham was looking for an old man who could speak to hollows. Perhaps my grandfather had met Bentham during his war years, after he'd left Miss Peregrine's house but before he'd come to America. It was a defining period of his life which he'd spoken about only rarely, and never in detail. Despite all I'd learned about my grandfather in the past few months, in many respects he remained a mystery to me. Now that he was gone, I thought sadly, perhaps it would always be so.

I put on the clothes Bentham had given me, a preppy-looking blue shirt and gray wool sweater combo with simple black pants. It all fit perfectly, as if they'd known I was coming. As I was slipping into a pair of brown leather oxford shoes, Emma knocked on the door.

"How're you faring in there?"

I opened the door to a blast of yellow. Emma looked miserable in an enormous canary-colored dress with poufy sleeves and a hem that swam around her feet.

She sighed. "It was the lesser of many sartorial evils, I assure you."

"You look like Big Bird," I said, following her out of the bathroom, "and I look like Mr. Rogers. This Bentham is a cruel man."

Both references were lost on her. Ignoring me, she crossed to the window and looked out.

"Yes. Good."

"What's good?" I said.

"This ledge. It's the size of Cornwall, and there are handholds everywhere. Safer than a jungle gym."

"And why would we care about the safety of the ledge?" I asked, joining her at the window.

"Because Sharon's watching the hall, so obviously we can't go out that way."

Sometimes it seemed like Emma had whole conversations with me inside her head—ones I wasn't privy to—and then she'd get frustrated that I was confused when she finally let me in on them. Her brain worked so quickly that once in a while it got ahead of itself.

"We can't go anywhere," I said. "We've got to meet Bentham."

"And we will, but I'll be hanged if I'm spending the next hour twiddling my thumbs in this room. Saintly Mr. Bentham is an exile living in Devil's Acre, which means he's likely a dangerous lowlife with a sordid past. I want to have a look 'round his house and see what we can find out. We'll be back before anyone notices we're gone. Word of honor."

"Ah, good, a stealth operation. We're dressed perfectly, then."

"Very funny."

I was in hard-soled shoes that made every footstep sound like a hammer blow, she was in a dress yellower than a hazard sign, and I'd only recently found the energy to stand on my own two feet—and yet I agreed. She was often right about these things, and I had come to depend on her instincts.

"If someone spots us, so be it," she said. "The man's waited eons to meet you, apparently. He's not going to kick us out now for giving ourselves a little tour."

She opened the window and climbed onto the ledge. I stuck my head out cautiously. We were two stories above an empty street in the "good" section of Devil's Acre. I recognized a stack of firewood: it was where we'd been hiding when Sharon exited the abandoned-looking storefront. Directly below us was the law office of Munday, Dyson, and Strype. There was no such firm, of course. It was a front, a secret entrance to Bentham's house.

Emma offered her hand to me. "I know you're not a great fan of heights, but I won't let you fall."

After being dangled above a boiling river by a hollow, this little drop didn't seem so frightening. And Emma was right—the ledge was wide, and decorative knobs and gargoyle faces protruded everywhere from the masonry, making natural handholds. I climbed out, grabbed on, and shimmied along after her.

When the ledge turned a corner, and we felt fairly certain that we were paralleling a hallway out of Sharon's view, we tried opening a window.

It was locked. We shimmied on and tried the next one, but it, too, was locked—as were the third, fourth, and fifth windows.

"We're running out of building," I said. "What if none of them open?"

"This next one will," Emma said.

"How do you know?"

"I'm clairvoyant." And with that she kicked it, sending shattered glass into the room and tinkling down the front of the building.

"No, you're a hoodlum," I said.

Emma grinned at me and then knocked the last few shards from the frame with the flat of her hand.

She stepped through the opening. I followed, somewhat reluctantly, into a dark and cavernous room. It took a moment for our eyes to adjust. The only light came from the window shade we'd just broken, its puny glow revealing the edge of a packrat's paradise.

Wooden crates and boxes climbed to the ceiling in teetering stacks, leaving only a small aisle between them.

"I get the feeling Bentham doesn't like to throw things away," Emma said.

In reply, I released a rapid-fire triple sneeze. The air was swimming with dust. Emma blessed me and lit a flame in her hand, which she held up to the nearest crate. It was labeled *Rm. AM-157*.

"What do you think is in them?" I said.

"We'd need a crowbar to find out," said Emma. "These are sturdy."

"I thought you were clairvoyant."

She made a face at me.

Lacking a crowbar, we ventured farther into the room, Emma enlarging her flame as we left the petering window light behind. The narrow path between the boxes led through an arched door and into another room, which was equally dark and nearly as cluttered. Instead of crates, it was crammed with bulky objects hidden beneath white dust covers. Emma was about to pull one away, but before she could I caught her arm.

"What's wrong?" she said, annoyed.

"There might be something awful under there."

"Yes, exactly," she said, and tore away the cover, which scared up a cyclone of dust.

When the air cleared, we saw ourselves reflected dimly in a glass-topped case of the sort you find in museums, waist high and about four feet square. Inside, neatly arranged and labeled, were a carved coconut husk, a whale vertebra fashioned into a comb, a small stone axe, and a few other items, the usefulness of which wasn't immediately obvious. A placard on the glass read *Housewares Used by Peculiars on the Island of Espiritu Santo, New Hebrides, South Pacific Region, circa 1750.*

"Huh," Emma said.

"Weird," I replied.

She replaced the dust cover, even though there was little use in covering our tracks—it wasn't as if we could unbreak the window—and we moved slowly through the room, uncovering other objects at random. All were museum displays of one type or another. The contents bore little relation to one another save that they had once been owned or used by peculiars. One contained a selection of brightly colored silks worn by peculiars in the Far East, circa 1800. Another displayed what appeared at first glance to be a wide cross-section of tree trunk but upon closer inspection was in fact a door with iron hinges and a knob made from a tree knot. Its placard read *Entrance to a Peculiar Home in the Great Hibernian Wilderness, circa 1530.*

"Wow," Emma said, leaning in for a closer look. "I never knew there were so many of us in the world."

"Or used to be," I said. "I wonder if they're still out there."

The last display we looked at was labeled *Weaponry of the Hittite Peculiars, Kaymakli Underground City, no date.* Bafflingly, all we could see inside were dead beetles and butterflies.

Emma swung her flame around to look at me. "I think we've established that Bentham's a history buff. Ready to move on?"

We hurried through two more rooms filled with dust-covered display cases, then arrived at a utilitarian staircase, which we climbed to the next floor. The landing door opened onto a long and lushly carpeted hallway. It seemed to go on forever, its regularly spaced doors and repeating wallpaper creating a dizzying impression of endlessness.

We walked along peeking into rooms. They were furnished identically, laid out identically, wallpapered identically: each had a bed, a night table, and a wardrobe, just like the room I'd recuperated in. A pattern of red poppy vines curled across the wallpaper and continued through the carpeting in hypnotic waves, making the whole place seem like it was being slowly reclaimed by nature. In fact, the rooms would've been entirely indistinguishable had it not been for the small brass plaques nailed to the doors, which gave each a unique name. All were exotic sounding: *The Alps Room*, *The Gobi Room*, *The Amazon Room*.

Perhaps fifty rooms lined the hallway, and we were halfway down its length—hurrying now, certain there was nothing of use to be discovered here—when a blast of air rolled over us that was so cold it prickled my skin.

"Whoo!" I said, hugging myself. "Where'd that come from?"

"Could be someone left a window open?" Emma said.

"But it's not cold outside," I said, and she shrugged.

We continued down the hall, the air chilling more the farther we went. Finally, we turned a corner and came to a section of hall where icicles had formed on the ceiling and frost glistened on the carpet. The cold seemed to be emanating from one room in particular, and we stood before it watching flakes of snow waft, one by one, from the crack beneath its door.

"That is very strange," I said, shivering.

"Definitely unusual," Emma agreed, "even by my standards."

I stepped forward, my feet crunching on the snowy carpet, to examine the plaque on the door. It read: *The Siberia Room*.

I looked at Emma. She looked at me.

"It's probably just a hyperactive air conditioner," she said.

"Let's open it and find out," I said. I reached for the knob and tried it, but it wouldn't turn. "It's locked."

Emma put her hand on the knob and kept it there for several seconds. It began to drip water as ice melted from inside it.

"Not locked," she said. "Frozen."

She twisted the knob and pushed the door, but it opened only an inch; snow was piled up on the other side. We put our shoulders to its surface and, on the count of three, shoved. The door flung open and a gust of arctic air slapped us. Snow flurried everywhere, into our eyes, into the hall behind us.

Shielding our faces, we peered inside. It was furnished like the other rooms—bed, wardrobe, night table—but here were indistinct humps of white buried under deep-piled snow.

"What *is* this?" I said, shouting to be heard above the wind's howl. "Another loop?"

"It can't be!" Emma shouted back. "We're already in one!"

Leaning into the wind, we stepped inside for a closer look. I'd thought that the snow and ice were coming through an open window, but then the flurry abated and I saw there was no window at all, not even a wall at the far end of the room. Ice-coated walls stood on either side of us, a ceiling above us, and probably a carpet was somewhere below our feet, but where a fourth wall should've been the room gave way to an ice cave, and beyond that to open air, open ground, and an endless vista of white snow and black rocks.

This was, as near as I could tell, Siberia.

A single track of shoveled snow led through the room and into the whiteness beyond. We shuffled down the path, out of the room and into the cave, marveling at everything around us. Giant spikes of ice rose from the floor and hung from the ceiling like a forest of white trees.

Emma was hard to impress—she was nearly a hundred years old and had seen a lifetime's worth of peculiar things—but this place seemed to fill her with genuine wonder.

"This is astonishing!" she said, bending to scoop up a handful of snow. She tossed it at me, laughing. "Isn't it astonishing?"

"It is," I said through chattering teeth, "but what's it doing here?"

We threaded between the giant icicles and emerged into the open. Looking back, I could no longer see the room at all; it was perfectly camouflaged inside the cave.

Emma hurried ahead, then turned back and said, "Over here!" in an urgent voice.

I shuffled through deepening snow to her side. The landscape was bizarre. Before us was a white, flat field, past which the ground fell away in deep, undulating folds, like crevasses.

"We're not alone," said Emma, and pointed to a detail I'd missed. A man was standing at the edge of a crevasse, peering down into it.

"What's he doing?" I said, more or less rhetorically.

"Looking for something, it would seem."

We watched him walk slowly along the crevasse, always staring down. After about a minute, I realized I was so cold that I could no longer feel my face. A gust of snowy wind blew up and blanked the scene.

When it died down a moment later, the man was staring right at us.

Emma stiffened. "Uh-oh."

"Do you think he sees us?"

Emma looked down at her bright yellow dress. "Yes."

We stood there for a moment, our eyes locked on the man as he stared at us across the white wasteland—and then he took off running in our direction. He was hundreds of yards away through deep snow and a landscape of undulating fissures. It was unclear whether he meant us harm, but we were in a place we weren't supposed to be and it seemed like the best thing to do was leave—a decision that was soundly reinforced by a howl, the likes of which I'd heard only once before, in the Gypsies' camp.

A bear.

A quick look over our shoulders confirmed it: a giant black bear had clawed its way up from one of the crevasses to join the man on the snow, and *they were both coming after us*, the bear clearing ground much more quickly than the man.

"BEAR!" I shouted, redundantly.

I tried to run but my frozen feet refused to cooperate. Seemingly impervious to the cold, Emma grabbed my arm and swept me along. We lurched back into the cave, stumbled through the room, and tripped out the door, around which a penumbra of blowing snow was filling the hallway. I pulled the door shut behind us—as if that would stop a bear—and we retraced our steps down the long hall, down the stairs, and back into Bentham's dead museum to hide ourselves among his white-draped phantoms.

*   *   *

We hid between a wall and a hulking dust-sheeted monolith in the farthest corner we could find, straitjacketing ourselves into a space so narrow that we could not turn to face each other, the cold we'd run from settling firmly into our bones. We stood silent and shivering, stiff as mannequins, the snow on our clothes melting into puddles at our feet. Emma's left hand took my right—it was all the warmth and meaning we could trade. We were developing a language that was entirely untranslatable into words, a special vocabulary of gestures and glances and touches and increasingly deep kisses that was growing richer, more intense, more complex by the hour. It was fascinating and essential and in moments like this, made me just a little less cold and a little less scared than I might've been otherwise.

When, after a few minutes, no bears showed up to eat us, we dared to exchange whispers.

"Was that a loop we were in?" I asked. "A loop within a loop?"

"I don't know what that was," Emma replied.

"Siberia. That's what the door said."

"If that was Siberia, then the room it was in was some kind of portal, not a loop. And portals don't exist, of course."

"Of course," I replied, though it wouldn't have been so strange to believe, in a world where time loops existed, that portals did, too.

"What if it was just a really old loop?" I suggested. "Like ice-age old, ten or fifteen thousand years? Devil's Acre might've looked like that back then."

"I don't think there are any loops that ancient," Emma said.

My teeth chattered. "I can't stop shaking." I said.

Emma pressed her side to mine and rubbed my back with her warm hand.

"If I could make a portal to anywhere," I said, "Siberia would not be high on my list of choices."

"Where would you go, then?"

"Hm. Hawaii, maybe? Though I guess that's boring. Everyone would say Hawaii."

"Not me."

"Where would you go?"

"The place you're from," Emma said. "In Florida."

"Why on earth would you want to go there?"

"I think it'd be interesting to see where you grew up."

"That's sweet," I said. "There's not much to it, though. It's really quiet."

She leaned her head on my shoulder and exhaled a warm breath

down my arm. "Sounds like heaven."

"You've got snow in your hair," I said, but it melted when I tried to brush it out. I shook the cold water from my hand onto the floor—and that's when I noticed our footprints. We'd left a trail of melting snow that probably led right to our hiding spot.

"What dimwits we are," I said, pointing out the tracks. "We should've left our shoes behind!"

"It's okay," said Emma. "If they haven't tracked us by now, they probably—"

Loud, clonking footsteps echoed from across the room, accompanied by the sound of a large animal breathing.

"Back to the window, quick as you can," Emma hissed, and we wormed out of our hiding spot.

I tried to run but slipped in a puddle. I grabbed the closest thing at hand, which happened to be the sheet covering the large object we'd been hiding behind. The sheet came ripping away, uncovering another display case with a resounding *zzzzzwit!* and landing me on the floor in a pile of rumpled canvas.

When I looked up, the first thing I saw was a girl—not Emma, who was standing above me, but past her, inside the case, behind the glass. She had a perfectly angelic face and a ruffled dress and a bow in her hair, and she stared glassily at nothing in what seemed the permanent rictus of a taxidermied human being.

I freaked. Emma turned to see what I was freaking out about, and then *she* freaked.

She dragged me to my feet and we ran.

I'd forgotten all about the guy chasing us, the bear, Siberia. I just wanted to get out of that room, away from the stuffed girl, and far away from any possibility that Emma and I might end up like her, dead and encased behind glass. Now I knew all I needed to know about this Bentham guy—he was some kind of twisted collector, and I was sure that if we looked under more dust covers, we'd find more specimens like the girl.

We sped around a corner only to find, towering before us, a terrifying ten-foot mountain of fur and claws. We screamed, tried too late to stop running, and slid into a pile at the bear's feet. There we cowered, waiting to die. Hot, stinking breath rolled over us. Something wet and rough mopped the side of my face.

I'd been licked by a bear. I'd been licked by a bear, and someone was *laughing*.

"Calm yourself, he won't bite!" the someone said, and I uncovered my face to see a long furry nose and big brown eyes staring down at me.

Had the bear spoken? Do bears talk about themselves in the third person?

"His name's PT," the someone continued, "and he's my bodyguard. He's quite friendly, provided you stay on my good side. PT, sit!"

PT sat, then began licking his paw instead of my face. I flipped myself right side up, wiped the slobber from my cheek, and finally saw the owner of the voice. He was an older man—a gentleman—and he wore a subtle smirk that complemented his killer outfit: top hat, cane, gloves, and a high white collar that rose from the top of his dark jacket.

He bowed slightly and tipped his hat. "Myron Bentham, at your service."

"Back away slowly," Emma whispered in my ear, and we stood up together and side-stepped out of the bear's reach. "We don't want any trouble, mister. Just let us go and no one gets hurt."

Bentham spread his arms and smiled. "You're free to leave anytime you like. But that would be such a disappointment. You've only just arrived, and we have so much to talk about."

"Yeah?" I said. "Maybe you can start by explaining that girl in the case over there!"

"And the Siberia Room!" said Emma.

"You're upset, you're cold, and you're wet. Wouldn't you rather discuss all this over a pot of hot tea?"

Yes, but I wasn't going to say so.

"We're not going anywhere with you until we know what's happening here," said Emma.

"Very well," Bentham replied, not losing an ounce of his good humor. "That was my assistant you surprised in the Siberia Room—which, as you likely gathered, leads to a time loop in Siberia."

"But that's impossible," said Emma. "Siberia is thousands of miles away."

"Three thousand four hundred and eighty-nine," he replied. "But making interloop travel possible has been my life's work." He turned to me. "As for the case you uncovered, that's Sophronia Winstead. She was the first peculiar child born to the royal family of England. Fascinating life she led, if a bit tragic in the end. I have all sorts of notable peculiars here in my *peculiarium*—well known and unknown, famous and infamous—any or all of which I'm happy to show you. I have nothing to hide."

"He's a psycho," I muttered to Emma. "He just wants to stuff us and add us to his collection!"

Bentham laughed. (His hearing, apparently, was very sharp.) "They're only wax models, my boy. I am a collector and a preservationist, yes—but not of humans. Do you really think I waited so long to meet you, only to pull out your insides and lock you in a cabinet?"

"I've heard of stranger hobbies," I said, thinking of Enoch and his army of homunculi. "What is it you want with us?"

"All in good time," he said. "Let's get you warm and dry first. Then, tea. Then—"

"I don't mean to be rude," Emma cut in, "but we've spent too much time here already. Our friends—"

"Are all right, for the moment," Bentham said. "I've looked into the matter, and it isn't as close to midnight for them as you might imagine."

"How do you know?" Emma said quickly. "What do you mean, it isn't close—"

"What do you mean, looked into it?" I said, talking over her.

"All in good time," Bentham repeated. "I know it's difficult, but you must be patient. There's too much to tell all at once, and in such a sorry state." He stretched out an arm toward us. "Look. You're shivering."

"Fine, then," I said. "Let's have tea."

"Excellent!" said Bentham. He rapped his cane twice on the floor. "PT, come!"

The bear grunted in an agreeable sort of way, stood on its hind legs, and walked—waddling like a stubby-legged fat person—to where Bentham stood. Upon reaching him, the animal bent down and scooped him into the air, carrying him like a baby, one paw supporting his back and the other his legs.

"I know it's an unconventional way to travel," Bentham said over PT's bushy shoulder, "but I tire easily." He pointed ahead of them with his cane and said, "PT, library!"

Emma and I watched in amazement as PT began to walk away with Mr. Bentham.

You don't see that every day, I thought. Which was true of nearly everything I'd seen that day.

"PT, stop!" Bentham commanded.

The bear stopped. Bentham waved to us.

"Are you coming?"

We'd been staring.

"Sorry," Emma said, and we ran to catch up.

*　　*　　*

We wended our way through the maze after Bentham and his bear.

"Is your bear peculiar?" I asked.

"Yes, he's a grimbear," said Bentham, rubbing PT's shoulder affectionately. "They are the preferred companion of ymbrynes in Russia and Finland, and grimbear-taming is an old and respected art among peculiars there. They're strong enough to fight off a hollow-gast yet gentle enough to care for a child, they're warmer than electric blankets on winter nights, and they make fearsome protectors, as you'll see here . . . PT, left!"

As Bentham extolled the virtues of grimbears, we came into a small anteroom. Under a glass canopy in the middle of the room were three ladies and, towering over them, a giant, vicious-looking bear. My breath caught for a moment before I realized they were motionless, another of Bentham's displays.

"That's Miss Waxwing, Miss Troupial, and Miss Grebe," Bentham said, "and their grim, Alexi."

The grimbear, on second look, appeared to be protecting the wax ymbrynes. The ladies were posed calmly around it while the bear was raised on its hind legs, frozen in midroar while swiping its paw at an enemy. Its other paw rested almost sweetly on one of the ymbrynes' shoulders, and her fingers were hooked around one of its long nails, as if to demonstrate her casual mastery over such a fearsome creature.

"Alexi was PT's great-uncle," Bentham said. "Say hello to your uncle, PT!"

PT grunted.

"If only you could do that with hollows," Emma whispered to me.

"How long does it take to train a grimbear?" I asked Bentham.

"Years," he replied. "Grims are naturally very independent."

"Years," I whispered to Emma.

Emma rolled her eyes. "And is Alexi made of wax, too?" she said to Bentham.

"Oh no, he's taxidermy."

Apparently Bentham's aversion to stuffing peculiar folk did not extend to peculiar animals. If Addison were here, I thought, there'd be fireworks.

I shivered. Emma ran a warm hand up my back. Bentham noticed, too, and said, "Forgive me! I so seldom have visitors that I can't help showing off my collection when they come. Now, I keep promising tea, and tea there shall be!"

Bentham pointed his cane and PT resumed walking. We followed them out of the dust-sheeted artifact storerooms through other parts of the house. It was in many ways the home of an average rich man—there was a marble-columned entry hall, a formal dining room with tapestried walls and seating for dozens, wings whose sole purpose seemed to be the display of tastefully arranged furnishings. But in each room, alongside everything else, were always a few objects from Bentham's peculiar collection.

"Fifteenth-century Spain," he said, indicating a gleaming suit of armor standing in a hall. "Had it made new. Fits me like a glove!"

At last we came to the library—the most beautiful I'd ever seen. Bentham told PT to set him down, brushed fur from his jacket, and showed us in. The room was three stories high at least, with shelves rising to dizzying heights above us. An array of staircases, catwalks, and rolling ladders had been constructed to reach them.

"I confess I haven't read them all," Bentham said, "but I'm working on it."

He ushered us toward a battalion of couches surrounding a flaming hearth whose warmth filled the room. Waiting by the fire were Sharon and Nim. "Call *me* an untrustworthy lout!" Sharon hissed, but before he berated me further Bentham shooed him away to fetch us blankets. We were under the protection of the master's good graces, and Sharon's tongue-lashing would have to wait.

Within a minute we were seated on a couch and wrapped in blankets. Nim fluttered around preparing tea on gilded trays, and PT, curled before the flames, was fast settling into a state of hibernation. I tried to resist the feeling of cozy contentedness that was beginning to settle over me and focus on our unfinished business—the big questions and seemingly intractable problems. Our friends and ymbrynes. The absurd and hopeless task we had assigned ourselves. It was enough to crush me if I thought about it all at once. So I asked Nim for three lumps of sugar and enough cream to turn the tea white, then downed it in three gulps and asked for more.

Sharon had retreated to a corner, where he could sulk but still overhear our conversation.

Emma was eager to dispense with the formalities. "So," she said. "Can we talk now?"

Bentham ignored her. He was sitting across from us but staring at me, the oddest little grin on his face.

"What?" I said, wiping a dribble of tea from my chin.

"It's uncanny," he replied. "You're the spitting image."

"Of who?"

"Of your grandfather, of course."

I lowered my teacup. "You knew him?"

"I did. He was a friend to me, long ago, when I badly needed one."

I glanced at Emma. She'd gone a bit pale and was clenching her teacup.

"He died a few months ago," I said.

"Yes. I was very sorry to hear it," Bentham said. "And surprised, to be honest, that he held out as long as he did. I assumed he'd been killed years ago. He had so many enemies—but he was exceedingly talented, your grandfather."

"What was the nature of your friendship, exactly?" said Emma, her tone like a police interrogator's.

"And you must be Emma Bloom," Bentham said, finally looking at her. "I've heard a great deal about you."

She seemed surprised. "You have?"

"Oh, yes. Abraham was very fond of you."

"That's news to me," she said, blushing.

"You're even prettier than he said you were."

She clenched her jaw. "Thank you," she said flatly. "How did you know him?"

Bentham's smile wilted. "Down to business, then."

"If you wouldn't mind."

"Not at all," he said, though his demeanor had cooled by a few degrees. "Now, you asked me before about the Siberia Room, and I know, Miss Bloom, that you were unsatisfied with the answer I gave."

"Yes, but I'm—we are—more interested in Jacob's grandfather, and why you brought us here."

"They are related, I promise. That room, and this house generally, is the place to begin."

"Okay," I said. "Tell us about the house."

Bentham took a breath and steepled his fingers against his lips for a moment, thinking. Then he said, "This house is filled with priceless artifacts I've brought back over a lifetime of expeditions, but none are more valuable than the house itself. It is a machine, a device of my own invention. I call it the Panloopticon."

"Mr. Bentham's a genius," Nim said, laying a plate of sandwiches before us. "Sandwich, Mr. Bentham?"

Bentham waved him away. "But even that is not quite bed-rock," he continued. "My story begins long before this house was built, when I was a lad about your age, Jacob. My brother and I fancied ourselves explorers. We pored over the maps of Perplexus Anomalous and dreamed of visiting all the loops he'd discovered. Of finding new ones, and visiting them not just once, but again and again. In this way we hoped to make peculiardom great again." He leaned forward. "Do you understand what I mean?"

I frowned. "Make it great . . . with maps?"

"No, not just with maps. Ask yourself: what makes us weak, as a people?"

"Wights?" Emma guessed.

"Hollows?" I said.

"Before either of them existed," Bentham prodded.

Emma said, "Persecution by normals?"

"No. That is just a symptom of our weakness. What makes us weak is *geography*. There are, by my rough estimate, some ten thousand peculiars in the world today. We know there must be, just as we know there must be other planets in the universe that harbor intelligent life. It is mathematically mandatory." He smiled and sipped his tea. "Now just imagine ten thousand peculiars, all with astounding talents, all in one place and united by a common cause. They'd be a power to be reckoned with, no?"

"I suppose so," Emma said.

"Most definitely so," Bentham said. "But we are splintered by geography into hundreds of weak subunits—ten peculiars here, twelve there—because it is extraordinarily difficult to travel from a loop in the Australian outback, for example, to a loop in the horn of Africa. There are not only the inherent dangers of normals and the natural world to consider, but the dangers of aging forward during a long journey. The tyranny of geography precludes all but the most cursory visits between distant loops, even in this modern era of air travel."

He paused for a moment before continuing, his eyes scanning the room.

"Now then. Imagine there was a link between that loop in Australia and the one in Africa. Suddenly those two populations could develop a relationship. Trade with each other. Learn from each other. Band together to defend each other in times of crisis. All sorts of exciting possibilities arise which were previously impossible. And gradually, as more and more such connections are made, the peculiar world is transformed from a collection of far-flung tribes hiding in isolated loops to a mighty nation, united and strong!"

Bentham had grown increasingly animated as he spoke, and at this last bit he'd raised his hands and spread his fingers like he was grasping for an invisible pull-up bar.

"Hence the machine?" I ventured.

"Hence the machine," he said, lowering his hands. "We'd been searching, my brother and I, for an easier way to explore the peculiar world, and instead we hit upon a way to unite it. The Panloopticon was to be the savior of our people, an invention that would change the nature of peculiar society forever. It works like this: you begin here, in the house, with a small piece of the machine called a shuttle. It fits in your hand," he said, opening his palm. "You take it with you, out of the house, out of the loop, and then across the present to another loop, which could be on the other side of the world or the next village over. And when you return here, the shuttle will have collected and brought back the DNA-like signature of that other loop, which can be used to grow a second entrance to it—here, inside this house."

"In that hallway upstairs," Emma guessed. "With all the doors and little plaques."

"Exactly," said Bentham. "Every one of those rooms is a loop entrance that my brother and I, over the course of many years, harvested and brought back. With the Panloopticon, the initial, arduous trek of first contact has to be made only once, and every return trip thereafter is instantaneous."

"Like laying telegraph lines," Emma said.

"Just so," said Bentham. "And in that way, theoretically, the house becomes a central repository for all loops everywhere."

I thought about that. About how hard it had been to reach Miss Peregrine's loop the first time. What if instead of having to go all the way to a little island off the coast of Wales, I could've entered Miss Peregrine's loop from my closet in Englewood? I could have lived both lives—at home with my parents, and here, with my friends and Emma.

Except. If that had existed, Grandpa Portman and Emma never would've had to break up. Which was a sentence so strange it gave me the tailbone-tingling willies.

Bentham stopped and sipped his tea. "Cold," he said, and set it down.

Emma peeled off her blanket, got up, crossed the floor to Bentham's couch, and dipped the tip of her index finger in his tea. In a moment it was boiling again.

He grinned at her. "Fantastic," he said.

She removed her finger. "One question."

"I'll bet I know what it is," Bentham said.

"Okay. What is it?"

"If such a wonderful thing really exists, why haven't you heard about it before now?"

"That's it," she said, and returned to sit next to me.

"You never heard about it—no one did—because of the unfortunate trouble with my brother." Bentham's expression darkened. "The machine was born with his help, but ultimately he was its downfall as well. Ultimately, the Panloopticon was never used as a tool to unite our people, as it was intended, but for quite the opposite purpose. The trouble began when we realized that the task of visiting every loop in the world so that we might re-create their entrances here was laughable at best—so far beyond our abilities that it bordered on delusional. We needed help, and a great deal of it. Luckily, my brother was such a charismatic and convincing fellow that recruiting all the help we needed proved easy. Before long we had a small army of young, idealistic peculiars willing to risk life and limb to help us achieve our dream. What I didn't realize at the time was that my brother had a different dream than I did—a hidden agenda."

With some effort, Bentham stood up. "There is a legend," he said. "You might know it, Miss Bloom." Tapping with his cane, he moved across the floor to the shelves and pulled down a small book. "It's the tale of a lost loop. A kind of afterworld where our peculiar souls are stored after we die."

"Abaton," Emma said. "Sure, I've heard of it. But it's just a legend."

"Perhaps you can tell the tale," he said, "for the benefit of our neophyte friend."

Bentham hobbled back to the couches and handed me the book. It was slim and green and so old it crumbled around the edges. On the front was printed *Tales of the Peculiar*.

"I've read this!" I said. "Part of it, at least."

"This edition is nearly six hundred years old," said Bentham. "It was the last to contain the story Miss Bloom is about to recount, because it was regarded as dangerous. For a time it was a criminal act simply to tell it, and thus the book you hold is the only volume in the history of peculiardom ever to have been banned."

I opened the book. Every page was handwritten in ornate, superhumanly neat script, and every margin was crowded with illustrations.

"It's been a long time since I heard it," Emma said tentatively.

"I'll help you along," Bentham said, lowering himself gently onto the couch. "Go on."

"Well," Emma began, "the legend goes that back in the old days—the really, really, thousands-of-years-ago old days—there was a special loop peculiars went to when they died."

"Peculiar Heaven," I said.

"Not quite. We didn't stay there for all eternity or anything. It was more like a . . . library." She seemed uncertain of her word choice, and looked to Bentham. "Right?"

"Yes," he said, nodding. "It was thought that peculiar souls were a precious thing in limited supply, and it would be a waste to take them with us to the grave. Instead, at the end of our lives we were to make a pilgrimage to the library, where our souls would be deposited for future use by others. Even in spiritual matters, we peculiars have always been frugal-minded."

"The first law of thermodynamics," I said.

He looked at me blankly.

"Matter can neither be created nor destroyed. Or souls, in this case." (Sometimes I surprise myself with the things I remember from school.)

"The principle is similar, I suppose," said Bentham. "The ancients believed that only a certain number of peculiar souls were available to humanity, and that when a peculiar was born, he or she checked one out, as you or I might borrow a book from a library." He gestured at the stacks around us. "But when your life—your borrowing term—was over, the soul had to be returned."

Bentham gestured to Emma. "Please go on."

"So," Emma said, "there was this library. I always imagined it filled with beautiful, glowing books, each containing a peculiar soul. For thousands of years people checked out souls and returned them just before they died, and everything was rosy. Then one day someone figured out that you could break in to the library, even if you weren't about to die. And he did break in—and then robbed the place. He stole the most powerful souls he could find and used them to wreak havoc." Emma looked at Bentham. "Right?"

"Factually correct, if a bit artless in the telling," Bentham said.

"Used them?" I said. "How?"

"By combining their powers with his own," Bentham explained. "Eventually the library's guardians killed the rogue, took back the stolen souls, and set things aright. But the genie was out of the bottle, so to speak. The knowledge that the library could be breached became a poison that spread throughout our society. Whoever controlled the library could dominate all peculiardom, and before long more souls were stolen. There dawned a dark time, in which the power-mad waged epic battles against one another for control of Abaton and the Library of Souls. Many lives were lost. The land was scorched. Famine and pestilence reigned while peculiars with power beyond imagination murdered one another with floods and lightning bolts. This is where normals got their tales of gods fighting for supremacy in the sky. Their *Clash of the Titans* was our battle for the Library of Souls."

"I thought you said this story wasn't real," I said.

"I'm getting to that," Bentham said, then turned to Nim, who was hovering nearby. "You can go, Nim. We don't need any more tea."

"Sorry, sir, didn't mean to eavesdrop, sir, but this is my favorite part."

"Then sit!"

Nim dropped cross-legged to the floor and propped his chin on his hands.

"As I was saying. For a short but terrible time, destruction and misery befell our people. Control of the library changed hands often, accompanied by immense bloodletting. Then one day it stopped. The self-declared king of Abaton had been killed in battle, and the one who killed him was on his way to claim the library for himself— but he never found it. Overnight, the loop had disappeared."

"Disappeared?" I said.

"There one day, gone the next," said Emma.

"Poof," said Nim.

"According to legend, the Library of Souls was located in the hills of the ancient city of Abaton. But when the would-be king arrived to claim his prize, the library was gone. So was the town. Gone as if they'd never been there at all, a smooth green meadow in their place."

"That's crazy," I said.

"There's nothing to it, though," Emma said. "It's just an old tale."

"*The Legend of the Lost Loop*," I said, reading the page that the book in my hands was open to.

"We may never know for certain if Abaton is a real place," Bentham said, his lips spreading into a sphinx's smile. "That's what makes it a legend. But like rumors of buried treasure, the legendariness of the story has not stopped people, over the centuries, from searching for it. It is said that Perplexus Anomalous himself committed years to the hunt for the lost loop of Abaton—which is how he began to discover so many of the loops that appear on his famous maps."

"I didn't know that," said Emma. "I suppose something good came of it, then."

"And something very bad," Bentham added. "My brother, too, believed the story. Foolishly, I forgave him this frailty—and I ignored it, realizing too late how completely it drove him. By then, my charismatic brother had convinced our small army of young recruits that it was true. Abaton was real. The Library of Souls was discoverable. Perplexus had gotten so close, he told them, and all that was left to do was to complete his work. Then the vast and dangerous power contained in the library could belong to us. To them.

"I waited too long, and this idea became a cancer. They searched and searched for the lost loop, mounting expedition after expedition, each failure only fueling their zeal. The goal of uniting peculiardom was forgotten. All along, my brother had cared only about ruling it, like the would-be peculiar gods of old. And when I tried to challenge him and regain control of the machine I'd built, he smeared me as a traitor, turned the others against me, and locked me in a cell."

Bentham had been squeezing the crook of his cane like a neck he wished he could wring, but now he looked up, his face gaunt as a death mask. "Perhaps by now you've guessed his name."

My eyes snapped to Emma. Hers were wide as moons. We said it together:

"Caul."

Bentham nodded. "His real name is Jack."

Emma leaned forward. "Then your sister is . . . "

"My sister is Alma Peregrine," he said.

*　　*　　*

We gaped at Bentham, thunderstruck. Could the man before us really be Miss Peregrine's brother? I'd known she had two—she'd mentioned them once or twice, even shown me a picture of them as boys. She told me the story, too, of how their quest for immortality led to the disaster in 1908 that turned them and their followers into hollowgast and, later, the wights we knew and feared. But she'd never mentioned either brother by name, and her story bore little resemblance to the one Bentham had just laid out.

"If what you say is true," I said, "then you must be a wight."

Nim's mouth fell open. "Mr. Bentham is *not*." He was ready to stand and defend his master's honor when Bentham waved him off.

"It's all right, Nim. They've only heard Alma's version of things. But there are gaps in her knowledge."

"I don't hear you denying it," said Emma.

"I'm not a wight," Bentham said sharply. He was also not accustomed to being questioned by the likes of us, and his pride was beginning to poke through his genteel veneer.

"Then would you mind if we checked," I said, "just so we can be sure . . . "

"Not at all," Bentham said. He pushed himself up with his

cane and hobbled into the no-man's-land between our couches. PT raised his head, idly curious, while Nim turned his back, angry that his master should have to endure such humiliations.

We met Bentham on the carpet. He bent down a little so we wouldn't have to stand on our tiptoes—he was surprisingly tall—and waited while we searched the whites of his eyes for signs of contact lenses or other fakery. His pupils were terribly bloodshot, as if he hadn't slept in days, but otherwise unsuspicious.

We stepped back. "Okay, you're not a wight," I said. "But that means you can't be Caul's brother."

"I'm afraid the set of assumptions you are working from is erroneous," he said. "I was responsible for my brother and his followers becoming hollowgast, but I never became one myself."

"*You* made the hollows?" Emma said. "Why?!"

Bentham turned and gazed into the fire. "It was a terrible mistake. An accident." We waited for him to explain. It seemed to cost him real effort to drag up the story from wherever he'd hidden it away. "It was my fault for letting things go on as long as they did," he said heavily. "I kept telling myself that my brother wasn't as dangerous as he seemed. It was only after he imprisoned me, and it was too late to act, that I realized how wrong I'd been."

He stepped closer to the warmth of the fire and knelt down to stroke the bear's wide belly, letting his fingers get lost in PT's fur. "I knew Jack had to be stopped, and not simply for my own sake—nor because there was any danger he'd ever find the Library of Souls. No, it was clear his ambitions had grown beyond that. For months he'd been molding our recruits into the foot soldiers of a dangerous political movement. He cast himself as an underdog fighting to wrest control of our society from what he called 'the infantilizing influence of ymbrynes.'"

"Ymbrynes are the reason our society still exists," Emma said bitterly.

"Yes," Bentham said, "but you see, my brother was terribly

jealous. From the time we were boys, Jack envied our sister's power and status. Our inborn abilities were puny compared to hers. By her third birthday the elder ymbrynes who cared for us knew Alma was a great talent. People made such a fuss over her, and it drove Jack mad. When she was a baby he would pinch her just to see her cry. When she practiced turning into a bird, he would chase her and pluck her feathers."

I saw an angry flame curl up from one of Emma's fingers, which she extinguished in her tea.

"That ugliness only deepened over time," Bentham said. "Jack was able to harness and exploit the same poisonous envy latent in some of our fellow peculiars. He held meetings and made speeches, rallying malcontents to his cause. Devil's Acre was fertile ground, since many of the peculiars here were exiles, alienated from and hostile to the ymbrynic matriarchy."

"The Claywings," Emma said. "Before the wights became wights, that's what they called themselves. Miss Peregrine taught us a little about them."

"'We don't need their wings!' Jack used to preach. 'We'll grow wings of our own!' He meant this metaphorically, of course, but they used to march around wearing fake wings as a symbol of their movement." Bentham stood up and motioned us toward the bookshelves. "Look here. I still have a photo or two from those days. A few he wasn't able to destroy." He pulled down an album from a shelf and turned to a picture of a large crowd listening to a man speak. "Ah, here's Jack giving one of his hateful speeches."

The crowd, almost exclusively male, wore big sturdy hats and were packed thirty deep, balancing on boxes and clinging to fence tops to hear what Caul had to say.

Bentham turned the page and showed us another photo, this one of two hale young men in suits and hats, one grinning earnestly, the other expressionless. "That's me on the left, Jack on the right," Bentham said. "Jack smiled only when he was trying to get something out of you."

Lastly, he turned to a photo of a boy with a pair of large owlish wings that spread from behind his shoulders. He was slouched on a pedestal and regarded the camera with quiet contempt, one eye hidden behind his cocked hat. Printed across the bottom were the words *We don't need their wings*.

"One of Jack's recruiting posters," Bentham explained.

WE DON'T NEED THEIR WINGS

Bentham held the second photo closer, studying his brother's face. "There had always been a darkness in him," he said, "but I refused to see it. Alma's vision was sharper—she pushed Jack away early. But Jack and I were close in age and in mentality, or so I thought. We were chums, thick as thieves. But he hid his true self from me. I didn't see him for what he was until the day I said, 'Jack, you have stop this,' and he had me beaten and thrown into a lightless hole to die. By then it was too late."

Bentham looked up, his eyes reflecting the fire's glow. "It's quite something to realize you mean less than nothing to your own brother." He was quiet for a moment, tangled in an awful memory.

"But you didn't die," said Emma. "You turned them into hollows."

"Yes."

"How?"

"I tricked them."

"Into becoming horrible monsters?" I said.

"I never meant to turn them into monsters. I meant only to get rid of them." He returned stiffly to the couch and lowered himself onto the cushions. "I was starving, near death when it came to me: the perfect story with which to ensnare my brother. A lie as old as humanity itself. The fountain of youth. With my finger I scratched it into the dirt of my cell floor: the steps of an obscure loop manipulation technique that could reverse, and forever eliminate, the dangers of aging forward. Or so it seemed. In reality, that was just a side effect of what the steps truly described, which was an arcane and largely forgotten procedure to collapse loops, quickly and permanently, in an emergency."

I pictured the "autodestruct" button of sci fi cliché. A super nova in miniature; stars winking out.

"I never expected my trick to work so well," Bentham said. "A member of the movement whose sympathy I had earned circulated my technique as his own, and Jack believed it. He led his followers to a distant loop to enact the procedure—and there, I hoped, they would slam the door behind themselves forever."

"But that's not what happened," said Emma.

"Is that when half of Siberia got blown up?" I asked.

"The reaction was so strong, it lasted a day and a night," said Bentham. "There are photos of it, and of the aftermath . . . "

He nodded at the album on the floor, then waited while we found the pictures. One, taken at night in some indistinct wilderness, was striped by a jet of vertical flame, a massive but distant release of white-hot energy that lit the night like a skyscraper-sized Roman candle. The other was a ruined village made up of rubble and cracked houses and trees raked clean of bark. Just looking at it, I could almost hear a lonely wind blowing; the palpable silence of a place robbed suddenly of life.

Bentham shook his head. "Never in my wildest dreams did I imagine what would crawl out of that collapsed loop," he said. "For a brief time afterward, things were quiet. Released from confinement, I began to recover. I regained control of my machine. It seemed my brother's dark age had drawn to a close—but it was only beginning."

"That was the start of the Hollow Wars," Emma said.

"Soon we began to hear stories about creatures made of shadow. They were emerging from the ruined forests to feed on peculiars—and normals, and animals, and anything that would fit between their jaws."

"Once I saw one eat a car," Nim said.

I said, "A car?"

"I was inside it," he replied.

We waited for him to elaborate.

"And?" said Emma.

"I got away," he said, shrugging. "The steering column got stuck in its throat."

"May I continue?" said Bentham.

"Of course, sir. My apologies."

"As I was saying, there wasn't much that would stop these new abominations, save the odd steering column—and loop entrances. Luckily, we had plenty of those. So most of us dealt with the hollowgast problem by staying put in our loops, venturing out only when we had no choice. The hollows didn't end our lives, but they made them vastly more difficult, isolated, and dangerous."

"What about the wights?" I asked.

"I imagine he's coming to that," said Emma.

"I am," said Bentham. "Five years after encountering my first hollowgast, I met my first wight. There was a knock at my door after midnight. I was in my house, safe inside my loop—or so I thought. But when I opened the door, there stood my brother Jack, a bit worse for wear but looking like his old self—save his dead eyes, which were blank as unmarked paper."

Emma and I had folded ourselves into cross-legged positions and were now leaning toward Bentham, hanging on his every word. Bentham stared over our heads with haunted eyes.

"He'd consumed enough peculiars to fill his hollow soul and turn himself into something that resembled my brother—but wasn't, quite. What little humanity he'd clung to through the years was gone completely, leaked away with the color in his eyes. A wight is to the peculiar he once was as a thing copied many times is to its original. Detail is lost, and color . . . "

"What about memory?" I asked.

"Jack retained his. A pity: otherwise he might've forgotten all about Abaton and the Library of Souls. And what I'd done to him."

"How did he find out it was you?" Emma asked.

"Chalk it up to brotherly intuition. And then one day, when he had nothing better to do, he tortured me until I confessed to it." Bentham nodded at his legs. "Never quite healed properly, as you can see."

"But he didn't kill you," I said.

"Wights are pragmatic creatures, and revenge is not a great motivator," Bentham said. "Jack was more obsessed than ever with finding Abaton, but to do it he needed my machine—and me to operate it. I became his prisoner and his slave, and Devil's Acre the secret headquarters for a small but influential contingent of wights bent on finding and cracking open the Library of Souls. Which is, you'll have guessed by now, their ultimate goal."

"I thought they wanted to re-create the reaction that turned them into hollows," I said, "only bigger and better. '*Do it right this time*,'" I said, making air quotes.

Bentham frowned. "Where did you hear that?"

"A wight told us just before he died," Emma said. "He said that's why they needed all the ymbrynes. To make the reaction more powerful."

"Utter nonsense," Bentham said. "Probably just a cover story to throw you off the scent. Though it's possible the wight who told you this lie believed it. Only Jack's innermost circle knew about the search for Abaton."

"But if they didn't need the ymbrynes for their reaction," I said, "then why'd they go to all the trouble of kidnapping them?"

"Because the lost loop of Abaton isn't just lost," said Bentham. "According to legend, before it was lost it was also locked—and it was ymbrynes who locked it. Twelve of them, to be exact, who came together from twelve far-flung corners of peculiardom. To open Abaton again, if you can manage to find it, would require those same twelve ymbrynes, or their successors. So it's no surprise that my brother has kidnapped precisely twelve ymbrynes, whom he spent many years hunting and tracking."

"I knew it," I said. "It had to be something more than just re-creating the reaction that turned them into hollows."

"Then he's found it," Emma said. "Caul wouldn't have pulled the trigger and kidnapped the ymbrynes if he didn't know where Abaton was."

"I thought you said it was legendary," I said. "Now you're talking like it's a real. Which is it?"

"The official position of the Council of Ymbrynes is that the Library of Souls is nothing but a story," Bentham said.

"I don't care what the council says," said Emma. "What do *you* say?"

"My opinions are my own," he said evasively. "But if the library is real, and Jack manages to find and open it, he still won't be able to steal its souls. He doesn't know it, but there's a third element he needs, a third key."

"And what's that?" I said.

"No one can take the soul jars. To most everyone they would be invisible and intangible. Even ymbrynes can't touch them. In the stories, only special adepts called librarians can see and handle them—and a librarian hasn't been born for a thousand years. If the library exists, all Jack would find there are empty shelves."

"Well, that's a relief," I said.

"Yes and no," said Emma. "What's he going to do when he figures out the ymbrynes he spent so long hunting are useless to him? He'll go mad!"

"That's what I worry about most," Bentham said. "Jack has a bad temper, and when the dream he's nurtured for so long dies . . . "

I tried to imagine what that could mean—all the tortures a man like Caul might be capable of—but my mind recoiled from the idea. It seemed the same horrors had broadcast themselves to Emma, because what she said next was sharp and charged with anger.

"We're going to get them back."

"We share a common goal," Bentham said. "To destroy my brother and his kind, and to save my sister and hers. Together, I believe we can do both."

He looked so small in that moment, sunk into the massive couch, cane leaning against his rickety legs, that I nearly laughed.

"How?" I said. "We'd need an army."

"Incorrect," he replied. "The wights could easily repel an army. Luckily, we have something even better." He looked at Emma and me, his lips curling into a smile. "We have the both of you. And luckily for you, you have me." Bentham leaned on his cane and rose slowly to his feet. "We have to get you inside their fortress."

"It seems pretty impenetrable," I said.

"That's because it is, conventionally speaking," Bentham replied. "In the years when Devil's Acre was a prison loop, it was designed to hold the worst of the worst. After the wights returned here, they adopted it as their home—and what had been an inescapable prison became their impenetrable fortress."

"But you have a way in," Emma guessed.

"I might, if you can help me," Bentham said. "When Jack and his wights came, they stole the heart of my Panlooptical. They forced me to break my own machine, to copy its loops and re-create them inside their fortress so that they could continue their work in a more protected location."

"So there's . . . *another* one?" I said.

Bentham nodded. "Mine is the original and theirs is the copy," he said. "The two are linked, and there are doorways in each that lead to the other."

Emma sat up straight. "You mean, we can use your machine to get inside theirs?"

"Correct."

"Then why haven't you?" I said. "Why didn't you do it years ago?"

"Jack broke my machine so irrevocably that I thought it could never be fixed," Bentham said. "For years, only one room has remained functional: the one that leads to Siberia. But though we've searched and searched, we haven't found a way through it into Jack's machine."

I remembered the man we'd seen peering into the crevasse— looking for a door, it seemed, deep in the snow.

"We need to open other doors, other rooms," Bentham said, "but to do that I need an adequate replacement for the part Jack stole—the dynamo at the heart of my Panloopticon. I've long sus- pected there's something that might work—a very powerful, very dangerous item—but though it exists right here in Devil's Acre, get- ting one has never been possible for me. Until now."

He turned to me.

"My boy, I need you to bring me a hollowgast."

*　　*　　*

I agreed to, of course. I would've said yes to almost anything then if I thought it might help free our friends. It occurred to me only after I'd said it, though, and Bentham had clapped his hands around mine and shook them, that I had no idea where to *get* a hollowgast. I was sure there were plenty inside the wights' fortress, but we'd already established that there was no getting inside. That's when Sharon stepped out of the shadows that had been growing at the edges of the room to give us a bit of good news.

"Remember your friend who got smashed by a falling bridge?" he said. "Turns out he's not quite dead. They pulled him out of the Ditch a few hours ago."

"They?" I said.

"The pirates. They've got him chained and caged down the end of Oozing Street. He's causing quite a stir, I hear."

"That's it, then," Emma said, tensing with excitement. "We'll steal the hollow and bring him back here, restart Mr. Bentham's machine, open a door to the wights' fortress, and get our friends back."

"Simple!" Sharon said, and he let out a barking laugh. "Except for that last part."

"And the first," I said.

Emma stepped close to me. "Sorry, love. I volunteered your services without asking. Think you can handle that hollow?"

I wasn't sure. True, I'd been able to make it perform a few spectacular moves in Fever Ditch, but bringing it to heel like a puppy and leading it all the way back to Bentham's house was asking a great deal of my rudimentary hollow-taming skills. My confidence, too, was at an all-time low after my last disastrous encounter. But everything hinged on me being able to do it.

"Of course I can handle it," I took too long to say. "When can we go?"

Bentham clapped his hands. "That's the spirit!"

Emma's gaze lingered on my face. She could tell I was faking.

"You can leave as soon as you're ready," Bentham said. "Sharon will be your guide."

"We shouldn't wait," Sharon said. "Once the locals have had their fun with that hollow, I reckon they'll kill it."

Emma picked at the front of her poufy dress. "In that case, I think we should change."

"Naturally," said Bentham, and he sent Nim to find us clothes more befitting our errand. He returned a minute later with thick-soled boots and modern work pants and jackets: black, waterproof, and with a bit of stretch to them.

We retreated to separate rooms to change and then met in a hallway, just Emma and me dressed in our adventure clothes. Rough and shapeless, they made Emma look slightly mannish (though not in a bad way), but she didn't grumble—she just tied back her hair, snapped her head to attention, and saluted me. "Sergeant Bloom, reporting for duty."

"Purdiest soldier I ever did see," I said, drawling out a terrible John Wayne impression.

There was a direct correlation between how nervous I was and how many dumb jokes I made. And right now I was practically quaking, my stomach a leaky faucet dripping acid all over my insides. "You really think we can do this?" I said.

"I do," she said.

"You never doubt, ever?"

Emma shook her head. "Doubt is the pinprick in the life raft."

She stepped close and we hugged. I could feel her trembling ever so slightly. She wasn't bulletproof. I knew then that my shaky faith in myself was starting to dig a hole in hers, and Emma's confidence was what held everything together. It was the life raft.

I'd come to regard her faith in me as somewhat reckless. She seemed to think that I should be able to snap my fingers and make hollowgast dance at will. That I was allowing some inner weakness to block my ability. Part of me resented that, and part of me wondered if maybe she was right. The only way to find out for sure was to approach the next hollow with an unshakable belief that I could master it.

"I wish I could see myself the way you do," I whispered.

She hugged me harder, and I resolved to try.

Sharon and Bentham came into the hall. "Ready?" Sharon asked.

We let go of each other. "Ready," I said.

Bentham shook my hand, then Emma's. "I'm so happy you're here," he said. "It's proof, I think, that the stars are beginning to align for us."

"I hope you're right," Emma said.

We were about to go when a question came to me that I'd been meaning to ask the whole time—and it occurred to me that, in a worst-case scenario, this could be my last chance to ask it.

"Mr. Bentham," I said, "we never did talk about my grandfather. How did you know him? Why were you looking for him?"

Bentham's eyebrows shot up and then he smiled quickly, as if to cover his moment of surprise. "I missed him, that's all," he said. "We were old friends, and I hoped I might see him again one day."

I knew that wasn't the whole truth, and I could see in Emma's narrowed eyes that she knew it, too, but there was no time to dig any further. Right now the future was of much greater concern than the past.

Bentham raised his hand goodbye. "Be careful out there," he said. "I'll be here, preparing my Panloopticon for its triumphant return to service." And then he hobbled back into his library, and we could hear him shouting at his bear. "PT, up! We have work to do!"

Sharon led us down a long hall, his wooden staff swinging and his massive bare feet slapping the stone floor. When we came to the door that led outside, he stopped, bent down to match our height, and laid out his ground rules.

"It's dangerous where we're going. There are very few unowned peculiar children left in Devil's Acre, so people will notice you. Don't speak unless spoken to. Don't look anyone in the eye. Follow me at a slight distance, but never lose sight of me. We'll pretend you're my slaves."

"What?" said Emma. "We will *not*."

"It's the safest thing," said Sharon.

"It's demeaning!"

"Yes, but it will raise the fewest questions."

"How do we do it?" I said.

"Just do whatever I say, immediately and without question. And keep a slightly glazed expression."

"Yesss, master," I said robotically.

"Not like that," Emma said. "He means like the kids in that awful place on Louche Lane."

I let my face slacken and said in a flat voice: "Hello, we're all very happy here."

Emma shuddered and turned away.

"Very good," said Sharon, and then he looked at Emma. "Now you try."

"If we must do this," she said, "I'll pretend to be mute."

That was good enough for Sharon. He opened the door and swept us out into the dying day.

CHAPTER FIVE

The air outside was a toxic-looking yellowish soup, such that I couldn't tell the position of the sun in the sky except to say it must've been getting toward evening, the light slowly leaking away. We walked a few paces behind Sharon, struggling to keep up whenever he saw someone he knew on the street and sped up to avoid conversation. People seemed to know him; he had a reputation, and I think he was concerned that we might do something to ruin it.

We made our way down oddly cheerful Oozing Street, with its window-box flowers and brightly painted houses, then turned onto Periwinkle Street, where the pavement gave way to mud and the houses to shabby, sagging flats. Men with hats pulled low over their eyes were congregating around the end of a seedy cul-de-sac. They appeared to be guarding the door to a house with its windows blacked out. Sharon told us to stay put, and we waited while he went to talk with them.

The air smelled faintly of gasoline. In the distance loud, laughing voices swelled and fell away, swelled and fell away. It was the sound of men in a sports bar watching a game—only it couldn't have been; that was strictly a modern sound, and there were no televisions here.

A man in mud-splashed pants came out of the house. As the door swung open, the voices grew louder and then faded when it slammed shut. He walked across the street carrying a bucket. We turned, watching as he walked toward something I hadn't noticed: a pair of bear cubs chained to a sawed-off lamppost at the edge of the street. They were terribly sad looking, with only a few feet of slack on their chains, and they sat on the muddy ground watching the man approach with something like dread, their furry ears flattened back. The man dumped some putrid table scraps before them and left without a word. The whole scene made me unutterably depressed.

"Those there are training grims," Sharon said, and we turned to find him standing behind us. "Blood sport is big business here, and fighting a grimbear is considered the ultimate challenge. Young fighters have to train somehow, so they start out fighting the cubs."

"That's awful," I said.

"The bears have the day off, though, thanks to your beastie." Sharon pointed at the little house. "He's in there, out through the back. But before we go in, I should warn you: this is an ambrosia den, and there'll be peculiars in there who are lit out of their minds. Don't talk to them, and whatever you do, don't look them in the eye. I know people who've been blinded that way."

"What do you mean, blinded?" I said.

"Just what it sounds like. Now follow me and don't ask any more questions. Slaves don't question their masters."

I saw Emma grit her teeth. We fell in behind Sharon as he crossed to the men clustered around the door of the house.

Sharon talked with the men. I struggled to overhear while maintaining a slavelike distance and averting my eyes. One of them told Sharon there was an "admission fee," and he dug a coin from his cloak and paid it. Another asked about us.

"I haven't given them names yet," Sharon said. "Just got 'em yesterday. They're still so green, I don't dare let them out of my sight."

"Is that right?" the man said, approaching us. "Don't have names?"

I shook my head no, playing mute along with Emma. The man looked us up and down. I wanted to squirm out of my skin. "Haven't I seen you somewhere?" he said, leaning closer.

I said nothing.

"Maybe in the window at Lorraine's," Sharon offered.

"Nah," the man said, then waved his hand. "Ah, I'm sure it'll come to me."

I only risked a direct look at him once he'd turned away. If he was a Ditch pirate, he wasn't one of those we'd tangled with. He had a bandage over his chin and another over his forehead. Several of the other men were similarly bandaged, and one sported an eyepatch. I wondered if they'd been injured fighting grims.

The man with the eyepatch opened the door for us. "Enjoy yourselves," he said, "but I wouldn't send them into the cage today, unless you're ready to scrape them off the ground."

"We're just here to watch and learn," said Sharon.

"Smart man."

We were waved in and hurried close at Sharon's heels, anxious to escape the door lurkers' stares. Seven-foot Sharon had to duck to pass through the doorway, and he stayed ducked the entire time we were inside, so low were the ceilings. The room we entered was dark and reeked of smoke, and until my eyes adjusted all I could see were pinpricks of orange light glowing here and there. Slowly the room came into view, lit by oil lamps trimmed so low they gave no more light than matches. It was long and narrow, with bunk beds built into the walls like you might find in the lightless bowels of an ocean-going ship.

I tripped over something and nearly lost my balance.

"Why is it so dark in here?" I muttered, already breaking my promise not to ask questions.

"The eyes get sensitive as the effects of ambro wear off," Sharon explained. "Even weak daylight is nearly unbearable."

That's when I noticed the people in the bunks, some sprawled and sleeping, others sitting up in nests of rumpled sheets. They watched us, smoking listlessly and speaking in murmurs. A few talked to themselves, reeling out incomprehensible monologues. Several had bandaged faces, like the doormen, or wore masks. I wanted to ask about the masks, but I wanted to get that hollow and get out of there even more.

We pushed through a curtain of hanging beads and entered a room that was somewhat brighter and considerably more crowded than the first. A burly man stood on a chair at the opposite wall, directing people to one of two doors. "Fighters to the left, spectators to the right!" he shouted. "Place your bets in the parlor!"

I could hear voices yelling a few rooms away, and a moment later the crowd parted to allow three men to pass, two of whom were dragging the third, who was unconscious and bleeding. Whistles and catcalls followed them.

"That's what losers look like!" the man on the chair bellowed. "And that," he said, pointing into a side room, "is what cowards look like!"

I peeked into the room, where two men under guard stood miserably for all to see. They were covered in tar and feathers.

"Let them be a reminder," said the man. "All fighters must spend two minutes in the cage, minimum!"

"So which are you?" Sharon asked me. "A fighter or a spectator?"

I felt my chest tighten as I tried to imagine what was about to happen: I wasn't just going to tame this hollow, but do it in front of a rowdy and potentially hostile audience—and then try and get out. I found myself hoping that it wasn't too injured, because I had a feeling I'd need its strength to clear us an exit. These peculiars weren't going to give up their new toy without a fight.

"A fighter," I said. "To really control it, I'm going to have to get close."

Emma met my eyes and smiled. *You can do this*, her smile said, and I knew, in that moment, that I could. I strode through the door meant for fighters, buoyed with new confidence, Sharon and Emma following behind me.

That confidence lasted approximately four seconds, which was the length of time it took me to walk into the room and notice the blood that was puddled and smeared all over the floors and walls. A river of it led down a light-filled hall and out an open door, through which I could see another crowd and, just beyond them, the bars of a large cage.

A shrill call came from outside. The next combatant was being summoned.

A man emerged from a darkened room to our right. He was stripped to the waist and wore a plain white mask. He stood at the top of the hall for a moment as if gathering his courage. Then he tipped back his head and raised his hand above it. In his hand he held a small glass vial.

"Don't look," Sharon said, backing us against a wall. But I couldn't help myself.

Slowly the man poured black liquid from the vial into each of his mask's eye holes. Then he dropped the empty vial, lowered his head, and began to groan. For a few seconds he seemed paralyzed, but then his body shuddered and two cones of white light shot from the eye holes of his mask. Even in the bright room they were distinct.

Emma gasped. The man, who had thought he was alone, turned toward us in surprise. His eye-beams arced over our heads and the wall above us sizzled.

"Just passing through!" Sharon said, the tone of which managed to say, *Howdy, friend!* and *Please don't kill us with those things!* at the same time.

"Pass through, then," the man snarled.

By then his eye beams were starting to fade, and just as he turned away they flickered and winked out. He walked down the hall and went out the door, leaving two wisps of smoke curling in his wake. When he'd gone I ventured a look at the wallpaper above our heads. A pair of caramel singe marks traced the path his eyes had made across the wall. Thank God he hadn't looked me in the eye.

"Before we go a step farther," I said to Sharon, "I think you'd better explain."

"Ambrosia," Sharon said. "Fighters take it to give themselves enhanced abilities. Trouble is, it doesn't last long, and when it wears off you're left weaker than before. If you make a habit of it, your ability wears down to almost nothing—until you take more ambro.

Pretty soon you're taking it not just to fight, but to function as a peculiar. You become dependent on whoever's selling it." He nodded to the room on our right, where murmuring voices created an odd counterpoint to the full-throated shouts outside. "It was the greatest trick the wights ever pulled, making that stuff. No one here will ever betray them, so long as they're addicted to ambrosia."

I peeked into the side room to see what a peculiar drug dealer looked like, and I caught a glimpse of someone in a bizarre bearded mask flanked by two men holding guns.

"What happened with that man's eyes?" Emma asked.

"The burst of light is a side effect," Sharon said. "Another is that, over a period of years, the ambro melts your face. That's how you know the hard-core users—they wear masks to hide the damage."

As Emma and I shared a look of disgust, a voice inside the room summoned us. "Hello out there," the dealer called. "Come in here, please!"

"Sorry," I said, "We have to go—"

Sharon poked my shoulder and hissed, "You're a slave, remember?"

"Uh, yes sir," I said, and went as far as the door.

The masked man was sitting in a little chair in a room with frescoed walls. He held himself with unsettling stillness, one arm resting on a side table and his legs crossed delicately at the knee. His gunmen occupied two corners of the room, and in another stood a wooden chest on wheels.

"Don't be afraid," the dealer said, beckoning me in. "Your friends can come, too."

I took another few steps into the room, Sharon and Emma just behind me.

"I haven't seen you around before," the dealer said.

"I just bought him," Sharon said. "He doesn't even have a—"

"Was I speaking to you?" the dealer said sharply.

Sharon went quiet.

"No, I wasn't," the dealer said. He stroked his fake beard and seemed to study me through the hollowed eyes of his mask. I wondered what he looked like underneath, and just how much ambrosia you'd have to pour into your face before you melted it. Then I shuddered and wished I hadn't.

"You're here to fight," he said.

I told him that I was.

"Well, you're in luck. I just got a prime batch of ambro, so your chances of survival have shot up dramatically!"

"I don't need any, thank you."

He looked at his gunmen for a reaction—they remained stone-faced—and then he laughed. "That's a hollowgast out there, you know. You've heard of them?"

They were all I could think about, especially the one outside. I was desperate to be on my way, but this creepy guy clearly ran the place, and making him angry was more trouble than we needed.

"I've heard of them," I said.

"And how do you think you'll do against one?"

"I think I'll do okay."

"Just okay?" The man crossed his arms. "What I want to know is: should I put money on you? Are you going to win?"

I told him what he wanted to hear. "Yes."

"Well, if I'm going to put money on you, you're going to need some help." He stood up, went to the medicine cabinet, and opened its doors. The interior glittered with glass vials—rows of them, all brimming with dark liquid, the tops plugged with tiny corks. He plucked one out and brought it to me. "Take this," he said, holding out the vial. "It takes all your best attributes and magnifies them times ten."

"No thank you," I said. "I don't need it."

"That's what they all say at first. Then, after they get beaten—if they survive—everyone takes it." He turned the vial in his hand and held it to the weak light. The ambrosia inside swam with sparkling, silvery particles. I stared, despite myself.

"What's it made of?" I asked.

He laughed. "Snips and snails and puppy dog's tails." He held it toward me again. "No charge," he said.

"He said he doesn't want any," Sharon said sharply.

I thought the dealer would lash out at him, but instead he cocked his head at Sharon and said, "Don't I know you?"

"I don't think so," Sharon said.

"Sure I do," the dealer said, nodding. "You were one of my best customers. What happened to you?"

"I kicked the habit."

The dealer stepped toward him. "Looks like you waited too long," he said, and pulled teasingly on Sharon's hood.

Sharon snatched the dealer's hand. The guards raised their guns.

"Careful," the dealer said.

Sharon held him a moment longer, then let go.

"Now," the dealer said, turning toward me. "You're not going to refuse a free sample, are you?"

I had no intention of ever uncorking the stuff, but it seemed like the best way to end this was to take it. So I did.

"Good boy," the dealer said, and he shooed us from the room.

"You were an addict?" Emma hissed at Sharon. "Why didn't you tell us?"

"What difference would it have made?" Sharon said. "Yes, I had some bad years. Then Bentham took me in and weaned me off the stuff."

I turned to look at him, trying to imagine. "Bentham did?"

"Like I said, I owe the man my life."

Emma took the vial and held it up. In the stronger light, the silvery bits inside the black liquid shone like tiny flakes of sun. It was mesmerizing, and despite the side effects, I couldn't help but wonder how a few drops might enhance my abilities. "He wouldn't say what was in it," Emma said.

"We are," Sharon said. "Little bits of our stolen souls, crushed up and fed back to us by the wights. A piece of every peculiar they kidnap winds up in a vial like that one."

Emma thrust the vial away in horror, and Sharon took it and

tucked it into his cloak. "Never know when one of these might come in handy," he said.

"Knowing what it's made of," I said, "I can't believe you'd ever take that stuff."

"I never said I was proud of myself," Sharon said.

The whole diabolical scheme was perfect in its evilness. The wights had turned the peculiars of Devil's Acre into cannibals, hungry for their own souls. Addicting them to ambrosia ensured their control and kept the population in check. If we didn't free them soon, our friends' souls would be the next to fill those vials.

I heard the hollow roar—it sounded like a cry of victory—and the man we'd watched take ambro a minute earlier was dragged through door and past us down the hall, bleeding and unconscious.

My turn, I thought, and a thrill of adrenaline shot through me.

* * *

Out back of the ambro den was a walled courtyard, the centerpiece of which was a freestanding cage about forty feet square, its sturdy bars easily capable, it seemed to me, of containing a hollowgast. A line had been painted in the dirt approximately as far from the cage bars as a hollow's tongues could reach, and the crowd, made up of forty or so rough-looking peculiars, had wisely planted themselves behind it. The courtyard's walls were ringed with smaller cages, and inside a tiger, a wolf, and what looked like a full-grown grimbear—animals of lesser interest, at least compared to a hollowgast—were being held to fight another day.

The main attraction could be seen pacing inside the big cage, tethered to a heavy iron post by a chain around its neck. It was in such a sorry state that I was tempted to feel bad for it. The hollowgast had been splashed with white paint and daubed here and there with mud, which made it visible to everyone but also a bit ridiculous looking, like a Dalmatian or a mime. It was limping badly and leaving trails of black blood, and its muscular tongues, which in anticipation of a fight would normally have been whipping around in the air, were dragging limply behind it. Hurt and humiliated, it was far from the nightmare vision I had become accustomed to, but the crowd, having never seen a hollow, seemed impressed nevertheless. Which was just as well: even in this much-reduced state, the hollow had managed to knock out several fighters in a row. It was still plenty dangerous, and very unpredictable. Which is why, I assumed, men armed with rifles were stationed around the courtyard. Better safe than sorry.

I huddled with Sharon and Emma to strategize. The problem, we agreed, wasn't getting me into the cage with the hollow. It wasn't even controlling the hollow—we were working under the assumption that I could do it. The problem would be getting the hollow out, and away from these people.

"Think you could melt through that chain around its neck?" I asked Emma.

"If I had two days to do it," she said. "I don't suppose we could just explain to everyone that we really need the hollow and we'll bring it back when we're finished?"

"You wouldn't even get that whole sentence out," said Sharon, eyeing the rowdy crowd. "This is more fun than these blighters have had in years. No chance."

"Next fighter!" shouted a woman standing watch from a second-story window.

Away from the crowd, a small clutch of men argued about which of them would fight next. There was already plenty of blood soaking the ground inside the cage, and none seemed in a hurry to contribute more. They'd been drawing straws, and a well-built man who was stripped to the waist had just picked the short one.

"No mask," Sharon said, noting the man's bushy mustache and relatively unscarred face. "He must be just starting out."

The man gathered his courage and strutted toward the crowd.

In a loud, Spanish-accented voice, he told them he'd never been beaten in a fight, that he was going to kill the hollow and keep its head for a trophy, and that his peculiar ability—ultraquick healing—would make it impossible for the hollow to inflict a mortal wound.

"See these beauty marks?" he said, turning to show off a collection of nasty, claw-shaped scars on his back. "A grim gave them to me last week. They were an inch deep," he claimed, "and healed the same day!" He pointed at the hollow in the cage. "That wrinkled old thing doesn't stand a chance!"

"Now it's *definitely* going to kill him," Emma said.

The man poured a vial of ambro into his eyes. His body stiffened and light beams shot from his pupils, leaving a cataract of burn marks on the ground. A moment later they winked out. Thus fortified, he strode confidently to the cage door, where a man with a large key ring met him to unlock it.

"Keep an eye on the guy with the keys," I said. "We might need those."

Sharon reached into his pocket and drew out a wriggling rat by its tail. "Did you hear that, Xavier?" he said to the rat. "Go get the keys." He dropped the rodent on the ground and it scurried away.

The boastful fighter entered the cage and began to face off with the hollow. He'd taken a small knife from his belt and assumed a bent-kneed stance, but other than that he showed little appetite for a fight. Instead, he seemed to be running out the clock by running his mouth, giving a speech with all the blowhard bluster of a professional wrestler. "Come at me, you animal! I am not afraid! I'll slice out your tongues and make a belt to hold up my pants! I'll pick my teeth with your toenails and mount your head on my wall!"

The hollow watched him boredly.

The fighter made a show of drawing his knife across his forearm, and as blood began to well he held up the wound. It healed and closed before a single drop could reach the ground. "I am invincible!" he cried. "I am not afraid!"

Suddenly the hollow faked toward the man and roared, which so startled him that he dropped his knife and threw his arms across his face. It seemed the hollow had grown tired of him.

The crowd burst into riotous laughter—and so did we—and the man, red-faced with embarrassment, bent to pick up his knife. Now the hollow was moving toward him, chains clinking as it went, tongues extended and curled like clenched fists.

The man realized he'd have to engage the monster if he was to salvage his dignity, so he took a few tentative steps forward while brandishing the knife. The hollow flicked one of its painted tongues at him. The man swiped at it with his knife—and connected. Cut, the hollow squealed and retracted the tongue, then hissed at the man like an angry cat.

"That'll teach you to attack Don Fernando!" the man shouted.

"This guy never learns," I said. "Taunting hollows is a bad idea."

He seemed to have the hollow on the run. It backed away while the man approached, still hissing and waving his knife. When the hollow could retreat no farther, its back against the bars of the cage, the man raised his knife. "Prepare to die, demon spawn!" he shouted, and charged.

For a moment I wondered if I'd have to step in and save the hollow, but soon it became clear that it had set a trap. Snaking beneath the man was all the slack of the hollow's chain, which the hollow grabbed and swept violently to one side, sending Don Fernando flying head-first into a metal post. *Clonk*—and he was out, limp on the ground. Another KO.

He'd been such a shameless braggart that the crowd couldn't help cheering.

A team of men with torches and electric-tipped taser poles ran into the cage and kept the hollow at bay while the unconscious fighter was dragged out.

"Who's next?" the referee woman shouted.

The remaining fighters traded looks of apprehension, then resumed arguing. Now no one wanted to enter the cage.

Except me.

The man's ridiculous performance and the hollow's trick had given me an idea. It wasn't a sure-fire plan, or even a good one, but it was something, and that was better than nothing. We—meaning the hollow and I—were going to fake its death.

*　　*　　*

I screwed up my courage and, as tends to happen while I'm doing something either slightly brave or very foolish, my brain disengaged from my body. I seemed to watch myself from afar as I waved an arm at the referee and shouted, "I'll go next!"

Before then I'd been invisible; now the crowd and the fighters all turned to stare.

"What's your plan?" Emma whispered to me.

I had one but had been so caught up with working it out that I'd failed to share it with Emma or Sharon, and now I had no time to lay it out for them. Which was probably for the best. If spoken aloud, I feared it might sound ridiculous or, worse yet, impossible, and then I'd lose my nerve.

"I think it's better if I just show you," I said. "But it definitely won't work unless we get those keys."

"Don't worry, Xavier's on the job," said Sharon. We heard a squeak and looked down to see the rat in question with a piece of cheese in its mouth. Sharon picked him up and scolded him. "*Keys*, I said, not cheese!"

"I'll get them," Emma assured me. "Just promise you'll come back in one piece."

I promised. She wished me luck and kissed me on the lips. Then I looked at Sharon, who tilted his head at me as if to say, *I hope you're not expecting a kiss from me, too,* and I just laughed and walked toward the fighters.

They were looking me up and down. I was sure they thought I was crazy, and yet none of them tried to stop me. After all, if this ill-prepared kid, who wasn't even going to take a vial of ambro before his fight, wanted to throw himself at the beast and wear it down a little, that was a gift they were willing to accept. And if I died trying, I was just a slave anyway. Which made me hate them and put me in mind of the poor kidnapped peculiars whose extracted souls were swimming around in the vials they all clutched—which made me even angrier. I did my best to channel all that rage into unwavering determination and focus, but it was mostly just distracting.

And yet. While the man with the keys was working to open the cage, I looked inward and found, to my surprise and delight, that I was not racked with doubt, nor haunted by visions of my impending death, nor battling waves of terror. I had met and exerted control over this hollow twice before; this would be the third time. Despite my anger, I was calm and quiet, and within this quiet I found that the words I needed were waiting for me, ready to be spoken.

The man opened the door and I stepped into the cage. He'd only just closed it when the hollow started toward me, rattling its chain like an angry ghost.

Tongue, don't fail me now.

I raised a hand to hide my mouth and said, in guttural Hollow: *Stop.*

The hollow stopped.

Sit, I said.

It sat.

A wave of relief washed over me. I'd had nothing to worry about; reestablishing the connection was as easy as picking up the reins of an old compliant mare. Controlling the monster was a bit like wrestling someone much smaller than I: it was pinned and wriggling to get free, but so outmatched by my strength that it posed little danger. But then the ease with which I controlled the hollow was its own sort of problem. There was no simple way to get it out of the cage unless everyone believed it was dead and no longer a threat, and there was no way anyone would believe it was dead if my victory came too easily. I was a scrawny, un-ambro-enhanced kid; I couldn't just slap it and have it keel over. For this ruse to be properly convincing, I needed to put on a show.

How was I going to "kill" it? Definitely not with my bare hands. Searching the cage for inspiration, my eyes fell upon the previous fighter's knife, which he'd dropped by the metal post. The hollow was sitting next to the post, which was a problem—so I picked up a handful of gravel, ran toward it suddenly, and threw it.

Corner, I said, again covering my mouth. The hollow turned and darted into the corner, which made it seem as though the handful of rocks had startled it. Then I dashed to the post, snatched the knife from the ground, and retreated, a bit of bravery that earned me a whistle from someone in the crowd.

Angry, I said, and the hollow roared and waved its tongues as if infuriated by my bold move. I glanced behind me to find Emma in the crowd, and I saw her moving furtively toward the man with the keys.

Good.

I needed to make things tough for myself. *Come at me*, I ordered, and once the hollow had lurched a few paces in my direction, I told it to lash out a tongue and grab me by the leg.

It did, the tongue connecting with a sting and wrapping twice around my calf. Then I made the hollow pull me off my feet and drag me toward it through the dirt while I pretended to grasp for a handhold.

As I passed the metal post, I threw my arms around it.

Pull up, I said—*not hard.*

Though my words weren't very descriptive, the hollow seemed to understand exactly what I meant, as if just by picturing an action in my head and speaking a word or two aloud I could convey a paragraph's worth of information. So when the hollow pulled upward as I clung to the post, raising my body into the air, it was precisely as I'd imagined it.

I'm getting good at this, I thought with some satisfaction.

I struggled and groaned for a few seconds in what I hoped sounded like authentic pain, then released the post. The crowd, expecting that I was about to be killed in what was probably the shortest match yet, began to jeer and call me names.

It was time for me to get in a hit.

Leg, I said. The hollow again lashed a tongue around my leg.

Pull.

It began to drag me toward it as I kicked and flailed.

Mouth.

It opened its mouth as if to swallow me whole. I quickly turned my body and slashed at the tongue around my ankle. I hadn't really cut the hollow, but I told it to quickly let go and scream so that it would look like I had. The hollow complied, screeching and then reeling its tongues back into its mouth. It felt like bad pantomime to me—there'd been a second of lag between my command and the hollow's response—but apparently the crowd bought it. The jeers turned to cheers for a match that was getting interesting, with an underdog who maybe had a fighting chance after all.

In what I hoped didn't seem like a fight scene from a low-budget movie, the hollow and I squared off and traded a few blows. I ran at it and it knocked me down. I slashed at it and it backed off. It howled and waved its tongues in the air as we circled each other. I even had it pick me up with a tongue and (gently) shake me, until I (pretended to) stab the tongue and it (probably too gently) dropped me again.

I risked another glance at Emma. She was standing in the middle of the group of fighters near the man with the keys. She made a line-across-the-throat gesture at me.

Quit messing around.

Right. Time to end this. I took a deep breath, gathered my courage, and went for the big finish.

I ran at the hollow with my knife raised. It swung a tongue at my legs, which I jumped over, then another at my head, which I ducked.

All as planned.

What was supposed to happen next was that I would jump over another tongue at my feet, then pretend to stab the hollow in the heart—but instead the tongue hit me directly in the chest. It connected with the force of a heavyweight boxer, flinging me onto my back and knocking the wind out of me. I lay there stunned, unable to breathe as the crowd booed.

Back, I tried to say, but I didn't have the breath.

And then it was on top of me, jaws wide and bellowing with anger. The hollow had thrown off my yoke, if only for a moment, and it was not happy. I had to regain control, and fast, but its tongues had pinned my arms and one leg, and its arsenal of gleaming teeth was closing in on my face. I was only just drawing breath—a gagging lungful of the hollow's stink—and instead of speaking I choked.

That might've been the end of me but for the strange anatomy of hollows: fortunately, it couldn't close its jaws around my head with its tongues extended. It had to release my limbs before it could bite off my head, and the moment I felt its tongue release my arm— the arm with the hand that still held the knife—I did the only thing I could think of to preserve myself. I thrust the knife upward.

The blade plunged deep into the hollow's throat. It screeched and rolled away, tongues flipping and grasping at the knife.

The crowd went crazy with excitement.

I was finally able to draw a full, clean breath, and I sat up to see the hollow writhing on the ground a few yards away, black blood spurting from its wounded neck. I realized, with none of the satisfaction I might've felt under different circumstances, that I had probably just killed the thing. *Really* killed it, which was not even re-motely the plan. From the corner of my eye I saw Sharon shaking his open hands at me, the universal sign for *you just ruined everything.*

I stood up, determined to salvage what I could. Reexerting my control over the hollow, I told it to relax. That it felt no pain. Grad-ually it quit struggling, its tongues sinking toward the ground. Then I walked over to it, pulled my bloody knife from its neck, and held it up to show the crowd. They screamed and cheered, and I did my best to look triumphant when really I felt like a giant failure. I was deathly afraid I'd just botched our friends' rescue.

The man with the keys opened the cage door, and two men ran

over to check the hollow.

Don't move, I murmured as they examined it, one of them aiming a shotgun at its head while the other poked it with a stick and then held a hand below its nostrils.

Don't breathe, either.

It didn't. In fact, the hollow did such a great job pretending to be dead that I, too, would've been convinced if not for the ongoing connection between us.

The men bought it. The examiner tossed away his stick, held up my arm like the victor in a boxing match, and declared me the winner. The crowd cheered again, and I could see money changing hands, the disappointed people who'd bet against me grumbling as they shelled out bills.

Soon spectators were entering the cage to get a better look at the supposedly dead hollow, Emma and Sharon among them.

Emma threw her arms around me. "It's okay," she said. "You had no choice."

"It's not dead," I whispered to her. "But it's hurt. I don't know how long it has. We've got to get it out of here."

"Then it's a good thing I managed to get these," she said, slipping a ring of keys into my pocket.

"Ha," I said, "you're a genius!"

But when I turned to unlock the hollow's chain, I found myself blocked by a swarm of people all clamoring to get close to it. Everyone wanted to get a good look at the thing, to touch it, to take a wisp of its hair or a clod of blood-soaked dirt as a memento. I started to shove my way through, but people kept stopping me to shake my hand and slap me on the back.

"That was unbelievable!"

"You got lucky, kid."

"You *sure* you didn't take ambro?"

All the while I was chanting under my breath for the hollow to stay down and stay dead, because I could feel it beginning to squirm, like a little kid who'd sat still for too long. It was antsy and hurt, and it required every spare ounce of my concentration to keep it from leaping up and filling its jaws with all the tempting peculiar flesh that surrounded it.

I'd finally reached the hollow's chain and was looking for the padlock when the ambro dealer accosted me. I turned to see his creepy bearded mask just inches from my face.

"You think I don't know what you're doing?" he said. He was flanked by his two armed guards. "You think I'm blind?"

"I don't know what you're talking about," I said. For a queasy second I thought he was on to me and knew the hollow wasn't really dead. But his men weren't even looking at it.

He grabbed me by my jacket collar. "No one hustles me!" he said. "This is *my* place!"

People were starting to back away. This guy clearly had a bad reputation.

"No one's hustling anyone," I heard Sharon say behind me. "Just calm down."

"You can't trick a trickster," the dealer said. "You come in here claiming he's fresh meat, never fought so much as a grim cub before, and then this?" He swept his arm toward the fallen hollow. "Not in a million years!"

"He's dead," I said. "Check for yourself if you want to."

The dealer let go of my jacket and put his hands around my throat instead.

"HEY!" I heard Emma say.

The guards pointed their guns at her.

"My only question," said the dealer, "is what are you selling?"

He began to squeeze.

"Selling?" I croaked.

He sighed, irritated at being forced to explain. "You come into *my* place, kill *my* hollow, and convince *my* customers they don't need to buy *my* product?"

He thought I was a rival drug dealer, there to steal his business. Madness.

He squeezed harder.

"Let the boy go," Sharon pleaded.

"If you're not on ambro, then what is it? What are you selling?"

I tried to respond but couldn't. I looked down at his hands. He took my hint and loosened his grip slightly.

"Speak," he said magnanimously.

What I said next probably sounded to him like a choked cough.

The one on the left, I said in hollowspeak. And then the hollow sat up stiff and straight like Frankenstein's monster come to life, and the few peculiars still nearby screamed and ran. The dealer turned to look and I punched him in the mask; the guards didn't know who to shoot first, me or the hollow.

That split second of indecision was their undoing. In the time it took for them to turn their heads, the hollow had flung all three of its tongues at the closest guard. One disarmed him while the remaining two grabbed him by the waist, picked him up, and used him like a battering ram to knock down the other.

Then it was just the dealer and me. It seemed to dawn on him that I was the one controlling the hollow. He dropped to his knees and began to beg.

"This might be your place," I said to him, "but that's *my* hollow."

I made it wrap a tongue around the dealer's neck. I told him we would be leaving with the hollowgast, and the only way he would survive is if we were allowed to go in peace.

"Yes, yes," he agreed, his voice shaking. "Yes, of course . . ."

I unlocked the padlock and unchained the hollow. With the crowd looking on, Emma, Sharon, and I led the limping hollow toward the open cage door, the dealer in front of us saying, "Don't shoot! No one shoot!" as best he could with a hollowgast's tongue collared around his neck.

We locked the cage behind us with most of the spectators still inside, then walked out through the ambro den, back the way we'd come, and onto the street. I was tempted to make a pit stop to destroy the dealer's ambro supply but decided it wasn't worth the risk. Let them choke on it. Besides, maybe it was better not to waste the stuff, if there was even a tiny chance that those stolen souls could one day be reunited with their owners.

We left the dealer on his hands and knees in the gutter, gasping for air, his mask dangling from one ear. We were about to put the whole filthy scene behind us when I heard a tiny growl and remembered the grimcubs.

I looked back at them, torn. They were at the end of their chains, straining to come with us.

"We can't," Sharon said, urging me on.

I might've left them if Emma hadn't caught my eye. *Do it*, she mouthed.

"It'll just take a second," I said.

It took fifteen, in the end, to make the hollow uproot the post the cubs were chained to, and by then a gang of angry addicts had gathered outside the ambro den. It seemed worth it, though, when we left with those cubs trailing after, chains and post dragging behind them—slow and encumbered until my hollow, in a gesture all its own, scooped them into its arms and whisked them along.

* * *

It quickly became obvious that we had a problem. We'd walked only a few blocks, but already people on the street had noticed the hollow. To anyone but me it was just a half-visible collection of paint splotches, but it still attracted attention. And because we didn't want anyone to see where we were going, we had to figure out a subtler way to get it back to Bentham's.

We ducked into a back street. The moment I stopped forcing it to walk, the hollow sank into an exhausted squat. It looked so frail there on the ground, bleeding, its body curled into itself, tongues tucked away in its mouth. Sensing its distress, the cubs it had rescued snuffled against it with their wet wiggling snouts, and the hollow reacted with a quiet snarl that seemed almost tender. I couldn't help feeling a pulse of affection for all three—estranged siblings of a sort.

"I hate to say it, but that's almost cute," Emma said.

Sharon snorted. "Dress it up in a pink tutu if you like. It's still a killing machine."

We brainstormed ways to get it to Bentham's without it dying en route. "I could close that wound in its neck," Emma said, offering a hand that was just starting to glow.

"Too risky," I said. "The pain could snap it out of my control."

"Bentham's healer might be able to help it," Sharon said. "We'll just have to get to her quickly."

My first thought was to run across the rooftops. If only the hollow had the strength, it could've carried us up the side of a building and bounded to Bentham's out of sight. But right now I wasn't even sure walking was an option. Instead I suggested we wash off the hollow's white paint so that no one could see it but me.

"Absolutely not, no way, no sir," said Sharon, shaking his head vigorously. "I don't trust that thing. I want to keep an eye on it."

"I've got it under control," I said, slightly offended.

"So far," Sharon shot back.

"I agree with Sharon," said Emma. "You're doing marvelously, but what happens when you're in another room, or fall asleep?"

"Why would I leave the room?"

"To relieve yourself?" said Sharon. "Are you planning on taking your pet hollowgast into the water closet?"

"Um," I said, "I guess I'll cross that bridge when I come to it?"

"The paint stays on," said Sharon.

"Fine," I said irritably. "So what do we do?"

A door banged open down the alley and a cloud of steam came billowing out. A man emerged pushing a wheeled cart, which he parked in the alley before going back inside.

I ran to take a look. The door belonged to a laundry, and the cart was filled with dirty linens. It was just large enough to fit a small person—or a curled-up hollowgast.

I'll admit it: I stole the cart. I wheeled it back to the others, emptied it, and made the hollow climb in. Then we piled the dirty laundry on top, lifted the bear cubs in, and wheeled the whole thing down the street.

No one gave us a second look.

CHAPTER SIX

*W*hen we reached the house it was nearly dark. Nim rushed us into the entrance hall, where Bentham waited anxiously. He didn't even bother to greet us.

"Why have you brought these grims?" he said, his eyes darting to the laundry cart. "Where's the creature?"

"It's here," I said. Lifting out the cubs, I began to pull back the linens.

Bentham looked but kept his distance. The sheets on top were white but grew bloodier as I dug, becoming a black cocoon as I reached the bottom. I pulled back the last and there it was, a small, withered thing in a fetal curl. It was hard to believe this pathetic creature was the same one that had given me such nightmares.

Bentham stepped closer. "My God," he said, looking at the bloody sheets. "What did they do to him?"

"Actually, I did that," I said. "I didn't really have a choice."

"It was about to swallow Jacob's head," Emma explained.

"You didn't kill it, did you?" Bentham said. "It's no use to us dead."

I said, "I don't think so," and then told the hollow to open its eyes, and very slowly, it did. It was still alive, but weak. "I don't know how much longer it'll last, though."

"In that case, we've not a moment to waste," said Bentham. "We must send for my healer right away and hope to heaven her dust works on hollows."

Nim was sent running to fetch the healer. While we waited, Bentham led us into his kitchen and offered us biscuits and canned fruit. Either because of nerves or all the squeamish things we'd seen, neither Emma nor I had an appetite. We picked at the food out of politeness while Bentham filled us in on what had happened while we were gone. He'd made all necessary preparations to his machine, he said, and everything was ready—all he needed was to plug in the hollowgast.

"Are you sure it'll work?" Emma said.

"Sure as I can be without ever having tried it," he replied.

"Will it hurt him?" I asked, feeling oddly protective of the hollow, if only because I'd gone to such trouble to rescue it.

"Of course not," Bentham said with a dismissive wave.

The healer arrived, and upon seeing her I nearly shouted in surprise. Not because she was so unusual looking—though she was— but because I was absolutely certain I had seen her before, though I couldn't say where or how I'd managed to forget an encounter with someone so strange.

Her only visible body parts were her left eye and left hand. The rest was hidden beneath acres of fabric: shawls, scarves, a dress, and a bell-shaped hoop skirt. She seemed to be missing her right hand, and the left was in the grip of a young man with brown skin and wide, bright eyes. He wore a jaunty silk shirt and a wide-brimmed hat, and he was leading the healer as if she were blind or otherwise disabled.

"I'm Reynaldo," said the young man in a crisp French accent, "and this is Mother Dust. I speak for her."

Mother Dust leaned toward Reynaldo and whispered something in his ear. Reynaldo looked at me and said, "She hopes you are feeling better."

That's when I realized where I'd seen her: in my dreams—or what I thought had been dreams—while recovering from my attack.

"Yes, much better," I said, unnerved.

Bentham skipped the formalities. "Can you heal one of these?" he said, leading Reynaldo and Mother Dust to the laundry cart. "It's a hollowgast, visible to us only where it's been painted."

"She can heal anything with a beating heart," said Reynaldo.

"Then, please," Bentham said. "It's very important that we save this creature's life."

Via Reynaldo, Mother Dust issued orders. Take the beast out of the cart, they said, so Emma and I tipped the hollowgast onto the floor. Put it in the sink, they said, so Emma and Sharon helped me lift it and place it in the basin of the long, deep sink. We cleaned its wounds with water from the tap, careful not to wash away too much of the white paint. Next, Mother Dust examined the hollowgast as Reynaldo asked me to identify all the places it was hurt.

"Now, Marion," Bentham said, addressing Mother Dust informally, "you needn't heal every last cut and bruise. We don't want the creature in top health; we only want to keep it alive. You see?"

"Yes, yes," Reynaldo said dismissively. "We know what we are doing."

Bentham harrumphed and turned his back, making a show of his unhappiness.

"Now she will make the dust," Reynaldo said. "Stand back, and be careful not to breathe it in. It will put you to sleep instantly."

We backed away. Reynaldo strapped a dust mask over his nose and mouth and then untied the shawl that wrapped what was left of Mother Dust's right arm. The stump beneath was only a few inches long, and it came to an end well above what would have been her elbow.

With her left hand Mother Dust began to rub the stump, which released a fine white powder that hung in the air. Holding his breath, Reynaldo combed the air with one hand and collected the dust. We watched, fascinated and slightly repulsed, until he'd gathered about an ounce of the stuff and the size of Mother Dust's stump had been reduced by the same amount.

Reynaldo transferred the dust into his mistress's hand. She leaned over the hollow and blew some of it in its face—as I remembered her doing to me. The hollow inhaled and then jerked suddenly. Everyone but Mother Dust leapt back.

Stay down, stay still, I said, but I needn't have—it was an automatic reaction to the powder, Reynaldo explained: the body downshifting into lower gear. As Mother Dust sprinkled more into the gash on the hollow's neck, Reynaldo told us that the powder could heal wounds and induce sleep, depending on how much was used. As he spoke, a white foam developed around the hollow's wound and began to glow. Mother Dust's dust, Reynaldo said, was *her*, and of inherently limited quantity. She wore herself away a little every time she healed someone.

"I hope this doesn't seem like a rude question," Emma said, "but why do you do it if it hurts you?"

Mother Dust stopped work on the hollow for a moment, turned so that her good eye could see Emma, and spoke as loudly as we'd ever heard her—in the mushy garble of someone who had no tongue.

Reynaldo translated. "I do it," he said, "because this is how I was chosen to serve."

"Then . . . thank you," Emma said humbly.

Mother Dust nodded and turned back to her task.

* * *

The hollow's recovery would not be instantaneous. It was deeply sedated and would wake only after the direst of its wounds had healed, a process that would likely take all night. Because the hollow had to be awake when Bentham "plugged it in" to his machine, phase two of our rescue plan would have to wait several hours. Until then, most of us were stuck in the kitchen: Reynaldo and Mother Dust, who had to reapply her powder to the hollow's wounds every so often, and Emma and me, because I didn't feel comfortable leaving the hollow alone, even though it was deeply asleep. The hollow was my responsibility now, the way an unhousebroken pet was the responsibility of whoever brought it home. Emma stayed close, too, because I had in some sense become *her* responsibility (and she mine), and if I fell asleep she would tickle me awake or tell me stories about the good old days in Miss Peregrine's house. Bentham checked in occasionally but was mostly off doing security sweeps of the house with Sharon and Nim, paranoid that his brother's foot soldiers might attack at any time.

As the night wore on, Emma and I talked about what the coming day might hold. Assuming Bentham could get his machine working again, it was possible that in a matter of hours we would find ourselves inside the wights' fortress. We might see our friends again, and Miss Peregrine.

"If we're very sneaky, and very, very lucky," Emma said. "And if . . . "

She hesitated. We were sitting side by side on a long wooden bench against a wall, and now she shifted so that I couldn't see her face.

"What?" I said.

She looked back at me, her face pained. "If they're still alive."

"They are."

"No, I'm tired of pretending. By now the wights could've harvested their souls for ambrosia. Or realized the ymbrynes are useless and decided to torture them instead, or milk their souls, or made an example of someone for trying to escape . . . "

"Stop it," I said. "It hasn't been *that* long."

"By the time we get there it'll have been forty-eight hours, at least. And a lot of awful things can happen in forty-eight hours."

"We don't have to imagine every single one of them. You sound like Horace with all these worst-case scenarios. There's no use tormenting ourselves until we know for sure what's happened."

"Yes, there is," she insisted. "There's a perfectly good reason to torment ourselves. If we've considered all the worst possibilities and one turns out to be true, we won't be completely unprepared for it."

"I don't think I could ever prepare myself for those kinds of things."

She put her head in her hands and let out a shaky sigh. It was all too much to think about.

I wanted to tell her then that I loved her. I thought that might help, by grounding us in something we were sure about rather than everything we weren't—but we hadn't said the words to each other many times, and I couldn't bring myself to say them now in front of two perfect strangers.

The more I thought about loving Emma, the shakier and sicker it made me feel, precisely because our future was so uncertain. I needed to imagine a future for myself with Emma in it, but it was impossible to picture our lives even a day from now. It was a constant struggle for me, having no idea what tomorrow held. I'm cautious by nature, a planner—someone who likes to know what's around the next corner and the corner after that—and this entire experience, from the moment I ventured into the abandoned shell of Miss Peregrine's house to now, had been one long free-fall into the void. To survive it I'd had to become a new person, someone flexible and sure footed and brave. Someone my grandfather would've been proud of. But my transformation had not been total. This new Jacob was grafted onto the old one, and I still had moments—plenty of them—of abject terror and wishing I'd never heard of any damned Miss Peregrine and needing very badly for the world to stop spinning so I could just hang on to something for a few minutes. I wondered, with a sinking ache, which Jacob loved Emma. Was it the new one, who was ready for anything, or the old one, who just needed something to hang on to?

I decided that I didn't want to think about it right now—a distinctly old-Jacob way of handling things—and focused instead on the distraction nearest at hand: the hollow, and what would happen when it woke. I would have to give him up, it seemed.

"I wish I could take him with us," I said. "He would make it so easy to smash anyone who got in our way. But I guess he has to stay behind to keep the machine running."

"So it's a *him* now." She raised an eyebrow. "Don't get too attached. Remember, if you gave that thing half a chance, it would eat you alive."

"I know, I know," I said, sighing.

"And maybe it wouldn't be so easy to smash everything. I'm sure the wights know how to handle hollows. After all, they used to *be* hollows."

"It's a unique gift you have," said Reynaldo, speaking to us for the first time in over an hour. He had taken a break from monitoring the hollow's wound to rummage through Bentham's cabinets for food, and now he and Mother Dust were seated at a small table, sharing a block of blue-veined cheese.

"It's a strange gift, though," I said. I'd been thinking about how strange it was for a while but hadn't quite been able to articulate it until now. "In an ideal world, there wouldn't be any hollows. And if there weren't any hollows, my special sight would have nothing to see, and no one would understand the weird language I can speak. You wouldn't even know I had a peculiar ability."

"Then it's a good thing you're here now," Emma said.

"Yeah, but . . . doesn't it seem almost too random? I could've been born anytime. My grandfather, too. Hollows have existed for only the last hundred years or so, but it just so happens that we were both born now, right when we were needed. Why?"

"I guess it was meant to be," Emma said. "Or maybe there have always been people who can do what you do, only they never knew it. Maybe lots of people go through life never knowing they're peculiar."

Mother Dust leaned toward Reynaldo and whispered.

"She says it's neither," said Reynaldo. "Your true gift probably isn't manipulating hollowgast—that's just its most obvious application."

"What do you mean?" I said. "What else could it be?"

Mother Dust whispered again.

"It's simpler than that," said Reynaldo. "Just as someone who's a gifted cellist wasn't born with an aptitude for only that instrument but for music in general, you weren't born only to manipulate hollows. Nor you," he said to Emma, "to make fire."

Emma frowned. "I'm over a hundred years old. I think I know my own peculiar ability by now—and I definitely can't manipulate water, or air, or dirt. Believe me, I've tried."

"That doesn't mean you can't," Reynaldo said. "Early in life we recognize certain talents in ourselves, and we focus on those to the exclusion of others. It's not that nothing else is possible, but that nothing else was nurtured."

"It's an interesting theory," I said.

"The point is, it's not so impossibly random that you have a talent for hollowgast manipulation. Your gift developed in that direction because that's what was needed."

"If that's true, then why can't all of us control hollows?" Emma said. "Every peculiar could use some of what Jacob's got."

"Because only *his* basic talent was capable of developing that way. In the times before hollows, the talents of peculiars with souls akin to his probably manifested some other way. It's said that the Library of Souls was staffed by people who could read peculiar souls like they were books. If those librarians were alive today, perhaps they'd be like him."

"Why do you say that?" I said. "Is there something about seeing hollows that's like reading souls?"

Reynaldo conferred with Mother Dust. "You seem to be a reader of hearts," he said. "You saw some good in Bentham's, after all. You chose to forgive him."

"Forgive him?" I said. "What would I have to forgive him for?"

Mother Dust knew she'd said too much, but it was too late to hold back. She whispered to Reynaldo.

"For what he did to your grandfather," he said.

I turned to Emma, but she seemed just as confused as I was.

"And what did he do to my grandfather?"

"I'll tell them," said a voice from the doorway, and then Bentham hobbled in by himself. "It's my shame, and I should be the one to confess it."

He shuffled past the sink, pulled a chair away from the table, and sat down facing us.

"During the war, your grandfather was highly valued for his special facility with hollows. We had a secret project, some technologists and I—we thought we could replicate his ability and give it to other peculiars. Inoculate them against hollows, like a vaccine. If we could all see and sense them, they would cease to be a threat, and the war against their kind would be won. Your grandfather made many noble sacrifices, but none so great as this: he agreed to participate."

Emma's face was tense as she listened. I could see she'd never heard any of this before.

"We took just a little bit," Bentham said. "Just a piece of his second soul. We thought it could be spared, or would be replenished, like when someone gives blood."

"You took his soul," Emma said, her voice wavering.

Bentham held his finger and thumb a centimeter apart. "*This* much. We split it up and administered it to several test subjects. Although it had the desired effect, it didn't last long, and repeated exposure began to rob them of their native abilities. It was a failure."

"And what about Abe?" Emma said. In her tone was the special malice she reserved for those who hurt people she loved. "What did you do to him?"

"He was weakened, and his talent diluted," said Bentham. "Before the procedure, he was much like young Jacob. His ability to control hollows was a deciding factor in our war with the wights.

After the procedure, however, he found he couldn't control them any longer, and his second sight became blurred. I'm told that soon afterward he left peculiardom altogether. He worried he would be a danger to his fellow peculiars, rather than a help. He felt he could no longer protect them."

I looked at Emma. She was staring at the floor, her face unreadable.

"A failed experiment is nothing to be sorry for," Bentham said. "It's how scientific progress is made. But what happened to your grandfather is one of the great regrets of my life."

"That's why he left," Emma said, her face tilting upward. "It's why he went to America." She turned to me. She didn't look angry, but wore an expression of dawning relief. "He was ashamed. He said so in a letter once and I never understood why. That he felt ashamed, and unpeculiar."

"It was taken from him," I said. Now I had an answer to another question: how a hollowgast could've bested my grandfather in his own backyard. He wasn't senile, or even particularly frail. But his defenses against hollows were mostly gone, and had been for a long time.

"That's not what you should be sorry for," said Sharon, standing in the doorway with his arms crossed. "One man wasn't going to win that war. The real shame is what the wights did with your technology. You created the precursor to ambrosia."

"I've tried to repay my debt," Bentham said. "Didn't I help you? And you?" He looked at Sharon and then Mother Dust. Like Sharon, it seemed she, too, had been an ambro addict. "For years I've wanted to apologize," he said, turning to me. "To make it up to your grandfather. That's why I've been looking for him all this time. I hoped he would come back to see me, and I might figure out a way to restore his talent."

Emma laughed bitterly. "After what you did to him, you thought he'd come back for more?"

"I didn't consider it likely, but I hoped. Fortunately, redemption comes in many forms. In this case, in the guise of a grandson."

"I'm not here to redeem you," I said.

"Nevertheless, I am your servant. If I can do anything, it is yours for the asking."

"Just help us get our friends back, and your sister."

"Gladly," he said, seeming relieved I hadn't demanded more or stood up and screamed in his face. I still might've—my head was spinning, and I hadn't quite sorted out how to react. "Now," he said, "as for how to proceed from here . . . "

"Can we have a moment?" Emma said. "Just Jacob and me?"

We exited into the hall to talk in private—out of sight of the hollow, but only just.

"Let's make a list of all the terrible things this man is responsible for," Emma said.

"Okay," I said. "One: he created hollows. Without meaning to, though."

"But he did. And he created ambrosia, and he took away Abe's power, or most of it."

Without meaning to, I nearly said again. But Bentham's intentions were beside the point. I knew what she was getting at: after all these revelations, I wasn't so confident about putting our fates and those of our friends in Bentham's hands—or his plans. He may have been well-meaning, but he had a dismal track record.

"Can we trust him?" Emma said.

"Do we have a choice?"

"That wasn't my question."

I thought for a moment. "I think we can," I said. "I just hope he's used up all his bad luck."

* * *

"COME QUICKLY! IT'S WAKING UP!"

Shouts echoed from the kitchen. Emma and I dashed through the doorway to find everyone cowering in a corner, terrified of a groggy hollowgast that was struggling to sit up but had managed only to droop its upper body over the edge of the sink. Only I could see its open mouth, its tongues lolling limply across the floor.

Close your mouth, I said in Hollow. Making a sound like it was slurping spaghetti, it sucked them back into its jaws.

Sit up.

The hollow couldn't quite do it, so I took it by the shoulders and guided it into a seated position. It was recovering with remarkable speed, though, and after another few minutes it had regained enough motor skill to be coaxed out of the sink and onto its feet. It no longer limped. All that was left of the gash in its neck was a faint white line, not unlike the ones fast disappearing from my own face. As I relayed this, Bentham couldn't hide his irritation that Mother Dust had healed the hollow so thoroughly.

"Can I help it if my dust is potent?" Mother Dust said via Reynaldo.

Exhausted, they went off to find beds. Emma and I were tired, too—it was nearing dawn and we hadn't slept—but the progress we were making was exciting and hope had given us a second wind.

Bentham turned to us, eyes alight. "Moment of truth, friends. Shall we see if we can get the old girl running again?"

By that he meant his machine, and there was no need to ask.

"Let's not waste another second," Emma said.

Bentham summoned his bear and I rallied my hollowgast. PT appeared in the doorway, scooped his master into his arms, and together they led us through the house. What a strange sight we would've made, had anyone been watching: a dapper gentleman cradled in the arms of a bear, Sharon in his billowing black cloak, Emma stifling yawns with a hand that kept smoking, and plain old me muttering at my white-daubed hollowgast, who even in perfect health shuffled as he walked, as if his bones didn't quite fit his body.

Through the halls and down the stairs we went, into the bowels of the house: rooms crowded with clanking machinery, each smaller than the last, until finally we came to a door that the bear couldn't fit through. We stopped. PT set his master down.

"Here it is," Bentham said, beaming like a proud father. "The heart of my Panloopticon."

Bentham opened the door. PT waited outside while the rest of us followed him in.

The small room was dominated by a fearsome machine made of iron and steel. Its guts stretched from wall to wall, a baffling array of flywheels and pistons and valves glistening with oil. It looked like a machine capable of making unholy noise, but for now it sat cold and silent. A greasy man stood between two giant gears, tightening something with a wrench.

"This is my assistant, Kim," said Bentham.

I recognized him: he was the man who'd chased us out of the Siberia Room.

"I'm Jacob," I said. "We surprised you in the snow yesterday."

"What were you doing out there?" Emma asked him.

"Freezing half to death," the man said bitterly, and he went on wrenching.

"Kim's been helping me search for a way into my brother's Panloopticon," said Bentham. "If such a door exists in the Siberia Room, it's likely at the bottom of a deep crevasse. I'm certain Kim will be grateful if your hollowgast succeeds in bringing some of our other rooms online, where there are sure to be doors in more accessible places."

Kim grunted, his face skeptical as he looked us up and down. I wondered how many years he'd spent battling frostbite and combing the crevasses.

Bentham got down to business. He issued clipped orders to his assistant, who twisted a few dials and pulled a long lever. The gears of the machine gave a hiss and sputter, then turned a degree.

"Bring in the creature," Bentham said in a low voice.

The hollow had been waiting outside, and I called him in. He shuffled through the doorway and let out a low gravelly growl, as if he knew something unpleasant was about to happen to him.

The assistant dropped his wrench but quickly retrieved it.

"Here is the battery chamber," Bentham said, drawing our attention to a large box in the corner. "You must guide the creature inside, where he'll be restrained."

The chamber resembled a windowless phone booth made of cast iron. A nest of tubes sprouted from its top and connected to pipes that ran along the ceiling. Bentham grasped the heavy door's handle and pulled it open with a grating rasp. I peered inside. The walls were smooth gray metal perforated with small holes, like the interior of an oven. Along the back hung a collection of thick leather straps.

"Will it hurt him?" I asked.

I surprised myself with the question, and Bentham, too.

"Does that matter?" he replied.

"I'd rather it didn't. If we have a choice."

"We don't," Bentham said, "but it won't feel any pain. The chamber fills with anesthetic sleeping gas before anything else happens."

"And then what?" I said.

He smiled and patted my arm. "It's very technical. Suffice to say, your creature will leave the chamber alive, in more or less the condition he entered it. Now, if you would kindly have it step inside."

I wasn't sure I believed him, nor why it mattered to me. The hollows had put us through hell and seemed so lacking in feeling that inflicting pain on them should have been a pleasure. But it wasn't.

I didn't want to kill the hollow any more than I wanted to kill a strange animal. In the course of leading this creature around by the nose, I had gotten close enough to understand that there was more than just void inside it. There was a tiny spark, a little marble of soul at the bottom of a deep pool. It wasn't hollow—not really.

Come, I said to it, and the hollow, which had been lurking shyly in the corner, stepped around Bentham to stand before the booth.

Inside.

I felt it waver. It was healed now, and strong, and if my hold on it faltered for even a moment, I knew what it might do. But I was stronger, and a battle of wills between us would've been no contest. It wavered, I think, because I had.

I'm sorry, I said to it.

The hollow didn't move; *sorry* was input it didn't know what to do with. I just needed to say it.

Inside, I said again, and this time the hollow complied and stepped into the chamber. Since no one else would touch it, from that point Bentham told me what to do. Per his instructions, I pushed the hollow against the back wall and crossed the leather straps over its legs, arms, and chest, buckling them tight. They were clearly designed to restrain a human being, which raised questions to which I didn't want the answers right now. All that mattered was moving forward with the plan.

I stepped out, feeling stifled and panicky from the few moments I'd spent inside.

"Close the door," Bentham said.

When I hesitated the assistant moved to do it, but I blocked his way. "It's my hollow," I said. "I'll do it."

I planted my feet and grabbed the handle and then—though I tried not to—looked into the hollow's face. Its great black eyes were wide and frightened, all out of proportion with its body, small and shriveled like a cluster of figs. It was still and would always be a disgusting creature, but it looked so pathetic that I felt unaccountably terrible, like I was about to put to sleep a dog who didn't understand why it was being punished.

All hollowgast need to die, I told myself. I knew I was right, but it didn't make me feel any better.

I pulled on the door and it screamed shut. Bentham's assistant hooked a giant padlock through its handles, then went back to the machine's controls and began twiddling dials.

"You did the right thing," Emma whispered in my ear.

Gears began to turn, pistons to pump, the machine itself to thrum with a rhythm that shook the entire room. Bentham clapped his hands and grinned, happy as a schoolkid. Then from inside the chamber came a scream the likes of which I'd never heard.

"You said it wouldn't hurt him!" I shouted at Bentham.

He turned to shout at his assistant. "The gas! You forgot the anesthesia!"

The assistant scrambled to pull another lever. There was a loud hiss of compressed air. A wisp of white smoke curled from a crack in the chamber door. The hollow's screams gradually faded.

"There," said Bentham. "Now it feels nothing."

I wished for a moment that Bentham was in that chamber instead of my hollow.

Other pieces of the machine came alive. There was the sound of liquid sloshing through the pipes above our heads. Several small valves near the ceiling rang like bells. Black fluid began dripping down through the machine's guts. It wasn't oil, but something even darker and more pungent—the fluid that the hollowgast produced almost constantly, that wept from its eyes and dripped from its teeth. Its blood.

I'd seen enough and walked out of the room feeling sick to my stomach. Emma followed me.

"Are you okay?"

I couldn't expect her to understand my reaction. I hardly understood it myself. "I'll be fine," I said. "This is the right thing."

"It's the only thing," she said. "We're so close."

Bentham hobbled out of the room. "PT, upstairs!" he said, and he tipped himself into the bear's waiting arms.

"Is it working now?" Emma said.

"We're going to find out," Bentham replied.

With my hollow restrained, sedated, and locked inside an iron chamber, there was little danger in leaving him behind—and yet I lingered by the door.

Sleep, I said. *Sleep, and don't wake up until this is over.*

I followed the others out through the machine rooms and up several flights of stairs. We came to the long, carpeted hallway that was lined with exotically named rooms. The walls hummed with energy; the house seemed alive.

PT set Bentham on the carpet. "Moment of truth!" he said.

He marched to the nearest door and flung it open.

A humid breeze blew into the hall.

I stepped forward to look inside. What I saw gave me goose-bumps. Like the Siberia Room, it was portal to another time and place. The room's simple furniture—bed, wardrobe, side table—was caked with sand. The rear wall was missing. Beyond it was a curving palm-fringed beach.

"I give you Rarotonga, 1752!" Bentham declared proudly. "Hello, Sammy! Long time!"

Squatting in the near distance was a small man cleaning a fish. He regarded us with mild surprise, then raised the fish and waved to us with it. "Long time," he agreed.

"This is good, then?" Emma said to Bentham. "This is what you wanted?"

"What I wanted, what I've been dreaming of . . . " Bentham laughed as he hurried off to throw open another door. Inside was a yawning, tree-filled canyon, a narrow bridge suspended across it. "British Columbia, 1929!" he crowed.

He pirouetted down the hall to open a third door—by now we

were chasing him—inside which I could see hulking stone pillars, the dusty ruins of an ancient city.

"Palymra!" he shouted, slapping his hand against the wall. "Huzzah! The damned thing works!"

Bentham could hardly contain himself. "My beloved Panloopticon," he cried, throwing his arms wide. "How I missed you!"

"Congratulations," Sharon said. "I'm glad I could be here to witness this."

Bentham's excitement was infectious. It was an astounding thing, his machine: a universe contained in a single hallway. Looking down it, I could see hints of other worlds peeking out—wind moaning behind one door, grains of sand blowing into the hall from beneath another. At any other time, under any other circumstances, I would've run and thrown them open. But right now there was only one door I cared about opening.

"Which of these leads inside the wights' fortress?" I asked.

"Yes, yes, to business," Bentham said, reining himself in. "My apologies if I got a bit carried away. I've put my life into this machine, and it's good to see it up and running again."

He leaned against a wall, suddenly sapped of energy. "Getting you into the fortress should be a simple enough proposition. Behind these doors are at least a half dozen crossover points. The question is, what will you do once you get there?"

"That depends," Emma said. "What are we going to find when we get there?"

"It's been a long time since I was inside," Bentham said, "so my knowledge is dated. My brother's Panloopticon doesn't look like mine—it is arranged vertically, in a high tower. The prisoners are kept elsewhere. They'll be in separate cells under heavy guard."

"The guards will be our biggest problem," I said.

"I may be able help with them," said Sharon.

"You're coming with us?" Emma said.

"Absolutely not!" Sharon said. "But I'd like to do my bit somehow—with minimal risk to myself, of course. I'll create a disturbance outside the fortress walls that will draw the guards' attention.

That should make it easier for you to skulk about unnoticed."

"What kind of disturbance?" I asked.

"The wights' least favorite kind: a civil one. I'll get those layabouts on Smoking Street to catapult nasty, flaming things at the walls until we've got the whole guard force after us."

"And why would they help you?" Emma said.

"Because there's lots more where this came from." He reached into his cloak and pulled out the vial of ambro he'd snatched from Emma. "Promise them enough of it and they'll do just about anything."

"Put it away, sir!" Bentham snapped. "You know I don't allow that in my house."

Sharon apologized and stuffed the vial back into his cloak.

Bentham consulted his pocket watch. "Now, it's just after four-thirty in the morning. Sharon, I imagine your disturbers of the peace are asleep. Could you have them riled and ready by six?"

"Absolutely," Sharon said.

"Then see to it."

"Happy to be of service." And with a swoosh of his cloak, Sharon turned and hurried away down the hall.

"That gives you an hour and a half to prepare," Bentham said—though it wasn't immediately clear what preparations could be made. "Anything I have is at your disposal."

"Think," Emma said. "What would be useful in a raid?"

"Do you have any guns?" I asked.

Bentham shook his head. "PT here is all the protection I need."

"Explosives?" Emma said.

"I'm afraid not."

"I don't suppose you have an Armageddon chicken," I said, only half kidding.

"A stuffed one, among my displays."

I imagined throwing a stuffed chicken at a gun-toting wight and wasn't sure whether to laugh or cry.

"Perhaps I'm confused," Bentham said. "Why would you need guns and explosives when you can control hollows? There are many inside the fortress. Tame them and the battle is won."

"It's not that easy," I said, weary of explaining. "It takes a long time to take control of even one . . . "

My grandfather could've done it, I wanted to say. *Before you broke him.*

"Well, that's your business," Bentham said, sensing he'd stepped on my toes. "However you accomplish it, the ymbrynes must be your priority. Bring them back first—as many as you can, starting with my sister. They're the most wanted, the biggest prize, and they're in the worst danger."

"I agree with that," Emma said. "Ymbrynes first, then our friends."

"And then what?" I said. "Once they notice we're stealing back our peculiars, they're going to come after us. Where do we go from here?" It was like robbing a bank: getting the money was only half the job. Then you had to get *away* with the money.

"Go anywhere you like," Bentham said, gesturing down the length of the hall. "Pick any door, any loop. You have eighty-seven potential escape routes in this hallway alone."

"He's right," Emma said. "How would they ever find us?"

"I'm sure they'd find a way," I said. "This will only slow them down."

Bentham held up a finger to stop me. "Which is why I'll lay a trap for them, and make it look as if we've hidden ourselves in the Siberia Room. PT has a large extended family there, and they'll be waiting just inside the door, good and hungry."

"And if the bears can't finish them off?" Emma said.

"Then I suppose we'll have to," said Bentham.

"And Bob's your uncle," Emma said, a Britishism that would've been incomprehensible if not for her sarcastic tone of voice. Translation: *your nonchalant attitude strikes me as insane.* Bentham spoke as if the whole thing were no more complicated than a trip to the grocery store: storm in, rescue everyone, hide, finish off the bad guys, and Bob's your uncle. Which was, of course, insane.

"You realize we're just two people," I said. "Two kids."

"Yes, exactly," Bentham said, nodding sagely. "That's to your advantage. If the wights are expecting resistance of any kind, it's an army at their gates, not a couple of children in their midst."

His optimism was beginning to wear me down. Maybe, I thought, we did have a chance.

"Hullo, there!"

We turned to see Nim running down the hall toward us, panting for breath. "Bird for Mr. Jacob!" he called. "Messenger bird . . . for Mr. Jacob . . . just winged in . . . waiting downstairs!" Upon reaching us, he doubled over and launched into a coughing fit.

"How could I have a message?" I said. "Who even knows I'm here?"

"We'd better find out," said Bentham. "Nim, lead the way."

Nim fell over in a heap.

"Oh, lord," said Bentham. "We're getting you a calisthenics trainer, Nim. PT, give the poor man a lift!"

*   *   *

The messenger was waiting in a foyer downstairs. It was a large green parrot. It had flown into the house through an open window several minutes before and begun squawking my name, at which point Nim had caught it and put it in a cage.

It was still squawking my name.

"JAYY-cob! JAYY-cob!"

Its voice sounded like a rusty hinge.

"He won't talk to anyone but you," Nim explained, hurrying me toward the cage. "Here he is, you silly bird! Give him the message!"

"Hello, Jacob," the parrot said. "This is Miss Peregrine speaking."

"What!" I said, shocked. "She's a parrot now?"

"No," Emma said, "the message is *from* Miss Peregrine. Go ahead, parrot, what does she say?"

"I'm alive and well in my brother's tower," said the bird, speaking now in an eerily human-sounding voice. "The others are here, too: Millard, Olive, Horace, Bruntley, Enoch, and the rest."

Emma and I glanced at one another. *Bruntley?*

Like a living answering machine, the bird went on: "Miss Wren's dog told me where I might find you—you and Miss Bloom. I want to dissuade you from any rescue attempts. We are in no danger here, and there's no need to risk your life with silly stunts. Instead, my brother has made this offer: give yourselves up to his guards at the Smoking Street bridge and you won't be harmed. I urge you to comply. This is our only option. We will be reunited, and under my brother's care and protection, we'll all be part of the new peculiardom."

The parrot whistled, indicating the message was over.

Emma was shaking her head. "That didn't sound like Miss Peregrine. Unless she's been brainwashed."

"And she never calls the kids by only their first or last names," I said. "That would've been *Miss* Bruntley."

"You don't believe the message is authentic?" Bentham said.

"I don't know *what* that was," Emma replied.

Bentham leaned toward the cage and said, "Authenticate!"

The bird said nothing. Bentham repeated his command, wary, and cocked his ear toward the bird. Then, suddenly, he straightened.

"Oh, hell."

And then I heard it, too: ticking.

"BOMB!" Emma screamed.

PT knocked the cage into a corner, swept us into a protective embrace, and turned his back to the bird. There was a blinding flash and a deafening bang, but I felt no pain; the bear had taken the brunt of the blast. Other than a pressure wave that popped my ears and blew off Bentham's hat, followed by a searing but mercifully brief sensation of heat, we'd been spared.

It was raining paint flakes and parrot feathers as we stumbled out of the room. We were all unscathed but the bear, who sank onto all fours and showed us his back with a trembling whimper. It was seared black and stripped of fur, and when Bentham saw it he cried out in anger and hugged the animal by its neck.

Nim ran off to wake Mother Dust.

"Do you know what this means?" Emma said. She was shaking, eyes wide. I'm sure I looked the same; surviving a bomb attack will do that to a person.

"I'm pretty sure it wasn't Miss Peregrine who sent that parrot," I said.

"Obviously . . . "

"And Caul knows where we are."

"If he didn't before, he does now. Messenger birds are trained to find people even if the sender doesn't have their exact address."

"It definitely means he caught Addison," I said, my heart sinking at the thought.

"Yes—but it means something else, too. Caul's scared of us. He wouldn't have bothered trying to kill us otherwise."

"Maybe," I said.

"Definitely. And if he's scared of us, Jacob . . . " She narrowed her eyes at me. "That means there's something to be scared of."

"He isn't frightened," said Bentham, lifting his head from the folds of PT's neck. "He should be, but he isn't. That parrot wasn't meant to kill you, only to incapacitate. It seems my brother wants young Jacob alive."

"Me?" I said. "What for?"

"I can think of only one reason. Word of your performance with the hollowgast reached him, and it convinced him you're quite special."

"Special how?" I said.

"My hunch is this: he believes you may be the last key to the Library of Souls. One who can see and manipulate the soul jars."

"Like Mother Dust said," whispered Emma.

"That's crazy," I said. "Could it be true?"

"All that matters is that he believes it," said Bentham. "But it changes nothing. You'll execute the rescue as planned, and then we'll get you, your friends, and our ymbrynes as far from my brother and his mad schemes as possible. But we must hurry: Jack's foot soldiers will trace the exploded parrot to this house. They'll be coming for you shortly, and you must be gone before they arrive." He consulted his pocket watch. "Speaking of which, it's nearly six o'clock."

We were about to go when Mother Dust and Reynaldo rushed in.

"Mother Dust would like to give you something," he said, and Mother Dust held out a small object wrapped in cloth.

Bentham told them we had no time for gifts, but Reynaldo insisted. "In case you run into trouble," he said, pressing the item into

Emma's hand. "Open it."

Emma peeled back the rough cloth. The small thing inside looked at first like a stub of chalk, until Emma rolled it in her palm.

It had two knuckles and a small, painted nail.

It was a pinky finger.

"You shouldn't have," I said.

Reynaldo could see we didn't understand. "It's Mother's finger," he said. "Crush it up and use it as you will."

Emma's eyes widened and her hand dropped a little, as if the finger had just tripled in weight. "I can't accept this," she said. "It's too much."

Mother Dust reached out with her good hand—it was smaller than before, a bandage covering the knuckle where her pinky used to be—and closed Emma's hand around the gift. She mumbled and Reynaldo translated: "You and he might be our last hope. I'd give you my whole arm if I could spare it."

"I don't know what to say," I said. "Thank you."

"Use it sparingly," Reynaldo said. "A little goes a long way. Oh, and you'll want these." He pulled two dust masks from his back pocket and dangled them. "Otherwise you'll put yourselves to sleep along with your enemies."

I thanked him again and accepted the masks. Mother Dust gave us a little bow, her enormous skirt dusting the floor.

"And now we really must be going," Bentham said, and we left PT in the company of the healers and the two bear cubs, who had come in to snuggle their ailing elder.

We returned upstairs to the hall of loops. When we came off the landing I felt a brief whirl of vertigo, a sudden cliff's-edge dizziness in recognition of where I was standing, eighty-seven worlds behind eighty-seven doors all stretching out before us, all those infinities connecting back here like nerves to a brain stem. We were about to go into one and maybe never come out again. I could feel old Jacob and new Jacob wrestling over that, terror and exhilaration coming at me in successive waves.

Bentham was talking, walking quickly with his cane. Telling us which door to use and where to find the door inside that door that would cross over to Caul's side of the loop and how to get out again into the Panloopticon machine inside Caul's stronghold. It was all very complicated, but Bentham promised that the route was short and marked with signs. To make doubly sure we didn't get lost, he'd send along his assistant to guide us. The assistant was summoned from tending the machine's gears and stood grim and silent while we said goodbye.

Bentham shook our hands. "Goodbye, good luck, and thank you," he said.

"Don't thank us yet," Emma replied.

The assistant opened one of the doors and waited beside it.

"Bring back my sister," Bentham said. "And when you find the ones who have her . . . " He raised his gloved hand and made a fist with it, the leather creaking as it tightened. "Don't spare their feelings."

"We won't," I said, and walked through the doorway.

CHAPTER SEVEN

*W*e followed Bentham's assistant into the room, past the usual furnishings, through the missing fourth wall, and out into a thick grove of evergreens. It was midday, late fall or early spring, the air chill and tinged with wood smoke. Our feet crunched along a well-worn path, the only other sounds a songbird's whistle and the low but rising roar of falling water. Bentham's assistant said little and that was fine by us; Emma and I were filled with a high, buzzing tension and had no interest in idle conversation.

We passed through the trees and out onto a track that curved around a mountainside. A desaturated landscape of gray rocks and patches of snow. Distant pines like rows of bristling brushes. We jogged at a moderate pace, careful not to exhaust ourselves too soon. After a few minutes we rounded a bend and found ourselves standing before a thundering waterfall.

Here was one of the signs Bentham had promised. THIS WAY, it read, plain as day.

"Where are we?" Emma asked.

"Argentina," the assistant replied.

Obeying the sign, we followed a path that became gradually overgrown with trees and thickets. We pushed aside the brambles and trudged on, the waterfall quieting behind us. The path ended at a small stream. We followed the stream a few hundred yards until it, too, ended, the water flowing into a low opening in a hillside, the entrance to which was hidden by ferns and moss. The assistant knelt on the stream bank and pulled back a curtain of weeds—then froze.

"What is it?" I whispered.

He pulled a pistol from his belt and fired three shots into the opening. A chilling cry came back, and then a creature rolled out into the stream, dead.

"What is it?" I asked again, staring at the creature. It was all fur and claws.

"Dunno," said the assistant. "But it was waiting for you."

It was nothing I could identify—it had a lumpy body, fanged teeth, and giant bulbous eyes, and even they seemed to be covered with fur. I wondered if Caul put it there—if maybe he'd anticipated his brother's plan and booby-trapped all the shortcuts into his Panloopticon.

The stream carried the body away.

"Bentham said he didn't have any guns," Emma said.

"He doesn't," the assistant said. "This one's mine."

Emma looked at him expectantly. "Well, could we *borrow* it?"

"No." He put it away. Pointed to the cave. "Go through there. Retrace your steps backward to the place we came from. Then you'll be with the wights."

"Where will you be?"

He sat down in the snow. "Here."

I looked at Emma and she looked back, both of us trying to hide how vulnerable we felt. Trying to grow a sheath of steel around our hearts. For what we might see. Might do. Might be done to us.

I descended into the stream and helped Emma in. The water was numbingly cold. Bending to peer into the cave, I saw daylight glinting dimly at the other end. Another changeover, darkness into light, pseudo-birth.

There appeared to be no more toothy creatures waiting inside, so I lowered myself into the water. The stream rushed up over my legs and waist in a freezing swirl that took away my breath. I heard Emma gasp behind me as she did the same, and then I grabbed the lip of the cave and slid inside.

Being immersed in cold, rushing water hurts like being stabbed with needles all over your body. All pain is motivating, and this type especially so; I scrabbled and pushed myself through the stone tunnel with a quickness, over slick sharp rocks and low under-hangs, half choking as water flowed over my face. Then I was out, and turned to help Emma.

We jumped out of the freezing stream and looked around. The place was identical to the other side of the cave except there was no assistant, no bullet casings in the snow, no footprints. As if we'd stepped through a mirror and into the world it reflected, minus a few details.

"You're blue," Emma said, and she pulled me up onto the bank and held me. Her warmth coursed through me, bringing feeling back to numbed limbs.

We walked, retracing every step of the route we'd taken. We found our way back through the brambles, up the hill, past the waterfall—all the scenery just the same except for the THIS WAY sign Bentham had set out for us. It was not here. This loop did not belong to him.

We arrived again at the small forest. Darted from tree to tree, using each one as cover until we reached the place where the path ended and became a floor and then a room, framed and hidden by a pair of crossed firs. But this room was different from Bentham's. It was spartan—no furnishings, no poppy-laced wallpaper—and the floor and walls were smooth concrete. We stepped inside and searched the darkness for a door, running our hands along the walls until I happened to hook a small recessed handle.

We pressed our ears to the door, listening for voices or footsteps. I heard only vague echoes.

Slowly, carefully, I slid the door open a crack. Inched my head through the gap to peek out. Here was a wide curving hall of stone, hospital clean and blindingly bright, its smooth walls toothed with tall, black, tomblike doors, dozens of them curving away sharply.

This was it: the wights' tower. We had made it inside the lion's den.

I heard footsteps approaching. Pulled my head back inside the door. There was no time to close it.

Through the crack I glimpsed a flash of white as a man walked by. He was moving quickly, dressed in a lab coat, head down to read a paper in his hand.

He didn't see me.

I waited for his footsteps to recede and then squeezed into the hall. Emma followed, pulling the door shut behind us.

Left or right? The floor ran uphill to the left, downhill to the right. According to Bentham we were in Caul's tower, but his prisoners were not. We needed to get out. Down, then. Down and right.

We turned right, hugging the inner wall as the hallway spiraled downward. The rubber soles of my shoes squeaked. I hadn't noticed the noise until now, and in the amplified quiet of the hard-walled hallway, each step was cringe-inducing.

We went on for a short while, and then Emma tensed and threw her arm across my chest to stop me.

We listened. With our footsteps silenced, we could hear others. They were ahead of us, and close. We rushed to the closest door. It slid open easily. We dove inside, closed it, threw our backs against it.

The room we'd entered was round, walls and ceiling both. We were inside a huge drainage pipe, thirty feet wide and still under construction—and we weren't alone. Where the pipe ended and broke into rainy daylight, a dozen men sat on a pipe-shaped scaffold, staring at us, dumbfounded. We'd interrupted them during their lunch break.

"Hey! How'd you get in there?" one shouted.

"They're kids," said another. "Hey, this ain't a playground!"

They were American, and they didn't seem to know what to make of us. We didn't dare respond for fear that the wights in the hall might hear us, and I worried that the workers' shouting would attract their attention, too.

"Have you got that finger?" I whispered to Emma. "Now seems like a good time to test it out."

So we gave them the finger. By which I mean we put on the dust masks (wet from the stream but still serviceable), Emma crushed a tiny bit of Mother Dust's pinky, and we walked down the pipe toward the men and attempted to launch the powder at them. First Emma tried blowing it out of her cupped hand, but it just swirled into a cloud around our heads, which made my face tingle and go a bit numb. Next I tried throwing it, which didn't work at all. The dust, it seemed, wasn't much good as an offensive weapon. By now the pipe builders were growing impatient, and one had jumped down from the scaffold to remove us by force. Emma tucked the finger away and made a flame with her hand—there was a *poof!* as Emma's flame ignited the dust hanging in the air, turning it instantly to smoke.

"Woah!" the man said. He began coughing and soon slumped to the floor, fast asleep. When a few of his friends ran to help him, they too fell victim to the cloud of anesthetizing smoke and fell to the ground beside him.

Now the remaining workmen were afraid, angry, and shouting at us. We ran back to the door before the situation could devolve further. I checked that the coast was clear and we slipped into the hall.

When I closed the door behind us, the sound of the men's voices was muted completely, as if it hadn't just shut them inside but had somehow turned them off.

We ran a short way, then stopped and listened for footsteps, then ran, then stopped and listened, spiraling down the tower in stuttering bursts of action and silence. Twice more we heard people coming and ran to hide behind doors. Inside one was a steaming jungle echoing with the screams of monkeys, and another opened into an adobe room, beyond which lay hard-packed ground and looming mountains.

The floor leveled and the hallway straightened. Around the last bend was a pair of double doors with daylight gleaming beneath them.

"Shouldn't there be more guards around?" I said nervously.

Emma shrugged and nodded toward the doors, which appeared to be the only way out of the tower. I was about to push them open when I heard voices on the other side. A man telling a joke. I could hear only the burble of his voice, not words, but it was definitely a joke, because when he finished there was an eruption of laughter.

"Your guards," Emma said, like a waiter presenting a fancy meal.

We could either wait and hope they went away, or open the door and deal with them. The latter option was braver and faster, so I summoned New Jacob and told him we were going to throw open the door and fight, and to please not discuss the matter with Old Jacob, who inevitably would whine and resist. But by the time I'd gotten it all settled, Emma was already doing it.

Silently and quickly, she pulled open one of the swinging doors. Arrayed before us were the backs of five wights in mismatched uniforms, all wearing modern police-issue-type pistols at their waists. They were standing casually, facing away from us. None had seen the door open. Beyond them was a courtyard surrounded by low barracks-like buildings, and rising in the farther distance was the fortress wall. I jabbed my finger toward the finger hidden in Emma's pocket—*sleep*, I mouthed, by which I meant that rendering these wights unconscious and then dragging them inside the tower seemed the most expedient course of action. She understood, pulled the door halfway closed, and began to dig out the finger. I reached for the dust masks, which were stuffed into my waistband.

And then a flaming mass of something flew over the fortress wall in the distance, sailed toward us through the air in a graceful arc, and fell *splat* in the middle of the courtyard, spraying dribbly blobs of fire everywhere and sending the guards into a state of excitement. Two ventured to see what had landed, and as they bent over to examine the flaming muck, another hunk came sailing over the wall and hit one of them. He was sent sprawling, his body aflame. (From the smell of it, which was pungent and traveled fast, it was a mixture of gasoline and excrement.)

The remaining guards ran to extinguish him. A loud alarm began to sound. Within seconds, wights were flying out of the buildings around the courtyard and rushing toward the wall. Sharon's assault had begun, bless him, and not a moment too soon. With any luck, it would give us enough cover to search unimpeded—at least for a few minutes. I couldn't imagine it would take longer than that for the wights to repel a few ambro addicts armed with catapults.

We scanned the courtyard. It was surrounded on three sides by low-slung buildings, each more or less identical to the next. There were no flashing arrows or neon signs advertising the presence of ymbrynes. We would have to search, as fast as we could, and hope we got lucky.

Three of the wights had run off to the wall, leaving two behind to extinguish the one covered in flaming excrement. They were rolling him in the dirt, their backs to us.

We chose a building at random—the one on the left—and ran to its door. Inside was a large room suffocatingly packed with what looked and smelled like secondhand clothes. We ran down an aisle lined with racks of clothes of every description, from all different time periods and cultures, all labeled and organized. A wardrobe, perhaps, for every loop the wights had infiltrated. I wondered if the cardigan Dr. Golan always wore to our meetings had hung in this room.

But our friends weren't here and the ymbrynes weren't either, so we tore through the aisles looking for a way into the next building that didn't lead back through the exposed courtyard.

There were none. We'd have to risk another dash outside.

We went to the door and watched through the crack, waiting as a straggler ran through the courtyard, pulling on his guard's uniform as he went. Once the coast was clear, we ran out into the open.

Catapulted objects landed all around us. Having run out of excrement, Sharon's improvised army had begun to launch other things—bricks, garbage, small dead animals. I heard one such projectile utter a string of profanities as it smacked into the ground and recognized the shriveled form of a bridge head spinning across the ground. If my heart hadn't been thrumming so tremendously I might've laughed out loud.

We made it across the courtyard to the building opposite. Its door seemed promising: heavy and metal, it would surely have been guarded had the guard not abandoned his post to go to the wall. Surely there was something important inside.

We opened it and slipped into a small white-tiled laboratory that smelled strongly of chemicals. My eyes were drawn to a cabinet filled with terrifying surgical tools, all steely and shining. There was a deep hum coming through the walls, the dissonant heartbeat of machines, and something else, too—

"Do you hear that?" Emma said, tense, listening.

I did. It was sustained and chattering, but distinctly human. Someone was laughing.

We traded a baffled look. Emma gave Mother Dust's finger to me and lit a flame in her hand, and we each put on our masks. Ready for anything, we thought, though in retrospect we were not at all prepared for the house of horrors that lay waiting for us.

We moved through rooms I struggle to describe now because

I've tried to erase them from my memory. Each was more nightmarish than the last. The first was a small operating theater, the table armed with straps and restraints. Porcelain tubs along the walls stood ready to collect drained fluids. Next was a research area where tiny skulls and other bones were connected to electrical equipment and gauges. The walls were papered in Polaroids documenting experiments conducted on animals. By then we were shuddering, shielding our eyes.

The worst was yet to come.

In the next room was an actual, ongoing experiment. We surprised two nurses and a doctor as they were performing some ghastly procedure on a child. They had a young boy stretched between two tables, newspapers spread below him to catch drips. A nurse held his feet while a doctor gripped his head and peered coldly into his eyes.

They turned and saw us with our dust masks and flaming hands and shouted for help, but no one was there to hear them. The doctor dashed for a table full of cutting tools but Emma beat him to it, and after a brief scramble he gave up and raised his hands. We pinned the adults in the corner and demanded they tell us where the prisoners were kept. They refused to say a word, so I blew dust in their faces until they slumped into a pile on the floor.

The child was dazed but unhurt. He couldn't seem to generate more than a whimper in response to our hurried questions—*Are you okay? Are there more like you? Where?*—so we thought it best to hide him for now. Wrapping him in a sheet for warmth, we stowed him in a small closet, with promises to return that I hoped we could keep.

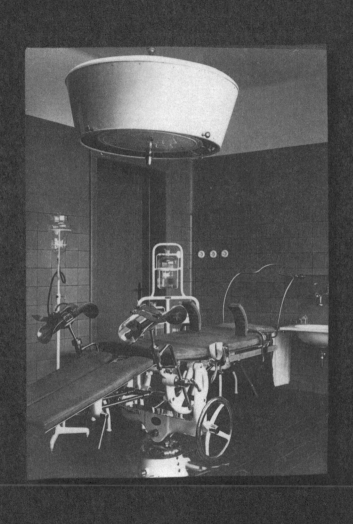

The next room was wide and open like a hospital ward. Twenty or more beds were chained to the walls, and peculiars, adults and children alike, were strapped into the beds. None appeared conscious. Needles and tubes snaked from the soles of their feet to bags that were filling slowly with black liquid.

"They're being drained," Emma said, her voice shaking. "Their souls drawn out."

I didn't want to look at their faces, but we had to. "Who's here, who's here, who are you," I muttered as we raced from bed to bed.

I hoped, shamefully, that none of these poor wretches were our friends. There were several we recognized: the telekinetic girl, Melina. The pale brothers, Joel-and-Peter, separated so there was no chance of another destructive blast. Their faces were twisted, their muscles tense and fists clenched even in sleep, as if both were in the grip of terrible dreams.

"My God," Emma said. "They're trying to fight it."

"Then let's help them," I said, and stepping to the end of Melina's bed I drew the needle carefully from her foot. A tiny drop of black liquid leaked from the wound. After a moment her face relaxed.

"Hello," said a voice from elsewhere in the room.

We spun around. In the corner sat a man in leg shackles. He was curled in a ball and rocking, and he laughed without smiling, his eyes like shards of black ice.

It was his cold laugh we'd heard echoing through the rooms.

"Where are the others being held?" Emma said, dropping to her knees in front of him.

"Why, they're all right here!" the man said.

"No, the others," I said. "There have to be more."

He laughed again, his breath coming out in a little puff of frost—which was strange, because it wasn't cold in the room. "You're standing on top of them," the man said.

"Make sense!" I shouted, losing my temper. "We don't have time for this!"

"Please," Emma begged. "We're peculiars. We're here to help you, but first we have to find our ymbrynes. Which building are they in?"

He repeated himself very slowly. "You're. Standing. On top of them." His words blew a steady stream of icy air in our faces.

Just as I was about to grab him and shake him, the man raised an arm and pointed to something behind us. I turned around and noticed, camouflaged in the tile floor, a handle—and the square outline of a hatch door.

On top of them. Literally.

We ran to the handle, turned it, and pulled up a door in the floor. A set of metal stairs spiraled into darkness.

"How do we know you're telling the truth?" Emma asked.

"You don't," the man said, which was true enough.

"Let's give it a try," I said. There was, after all, nowhere else to go but back the way we'd come.

Emma looked torn, her gaze traveling from the stairs below to the beds around us. I knew what she was thinking, but she didn't even ask—there was no time to go bed to bed, unhooking everyone. We'd have to come back for them. I just hoped that when we did, there would be something to come back to.

* * *

Emma lowered herself onto the metal stairs and descended into the dark hole in the floor. Before I followed, I locked eyes with the madman and raised a finger to my lips. He grinned and copied my gesture. I hoped he meant it. Guards would be there soon, and if he kept his mouth shut, maybe they wouldn't follow us into the hatch. I started down the stairs and pulled the door shut after me.

Emma and I huddled near the top of a narrow cylinder of spiraling stairs and peered down. It took a moment for our eyes to transition from the bright room above to this mostly lightless dungeon walled in rough rock.

She gripped my arm and whispered in my ear.

"Cells."

She pointed. Dimly it came into view: the bars of a prison cell.

We crept down the stairs. The space began to reveal itself: we were at the end of a long, subterranean hallway lined with cells, and though we couldn't see yet who was in them, I had a soaring moment of hope. This was it. This was the place we'd hoped to find.

Then came a sudden slap of boots in the hall. Adrenaline surged through me. A guard was patrolling, rifle over his shoulder, pistol at his hip. He hadn't seen us yet, but he would, any moment now. We were too far from the hatch to escape the way we'd come, and too far from the ground to easily leap down and fight him, so we hunkered and shrank back, hoping the stairs' spindly railing would be enough to hide us.

But it couldn't be. We were nearly at his eye level. He was twenty steps away, then fifteen. We had to do something.

So I did.

I stood up and walked down the stairs. He noticed me right away, of course, but before he could get a good look I started talking. Loud and bossy, I said: "Didn't you hear the alarm? Why aren't you outside defending the walls?"

By the time he realized that I was not someone he took orders from I had reached the floor, and by the time he'd started to grab for his gun I had already closed half the distance between us, barreling toward him like a quarterback. I hit him with my shoulder just as he pulled the trigger. The gun roared, the shot ricocheting behind me. We sprawled to the ground. I made the mistake of trying to stop him from squeezing off another shot while trying to give him the finger—I had it now—which was stuffed deep in my right pocket. I didn't have enough limbs to do both, and he threw me off him and stood up. I'm sure that would've been the end of me if he hadn't seen Emma running toward him, hands aflame, and turned to shoot her instead.

He squeezed off a round but it was wild, too high, and that gave me just the opportunity I needed to scramble to my feet and charge him again. I tackled him and we fell across the hallway, his back slamming into the bars of one of the cells. He hit me—hard, in the face, with his elbow—and I spun and fell. And then he was raising the gun to shoot me, and neither Emma nor I were close enough to stop him.

Suddenly, a pair of meaty hands reached out of the darkness, through the bars, and grabbed the guard by his hair. His head snapped back hard and rung the bars like a bell.

The guard went limp and slid to the ground. And then Bronwyn came forward inside the cell, pressed her face to the bars, and smiled.

"Mr. Jacob! Miss Emma!"

I had never been so glad to see anyone. Her large, kind eyes, her strong chin, her lank brown hair—it was Bronwyn! We stuck our arms through the bars and hugged her as best we could, so excited and relieved that we started babbling—"Bronwyn, Bronwyn," Emma gasped, "is it really you?"

"Is that *you*, miss?" said Bronwyn. "We've been praying and hoping and, oh, I was so worried the wights had got you—"

Bronwyn was squeezing us against the bars so hard I thought I might pop. The bars were thick as bricks and made of something stronger than iron, which I realized was the only reason Bronwyn hadn't broken out of her cell.

"Can't . . . breathe," Emma groaned, and Bronwyn apologized and let us go.

Now that I could get a proper look at her, I noticed a bruise on Bronwyn's cheek and a dark stain that might've been blood spotting one side of her blouse. "What did they do to you?" I said.

"Nothing serious," she replied, "though there's been threats."

"And the others?" Emma said, panicked again. "Where are the others?"

"Here!" came a voice from down the hallway. "Over here!" came another.

And then we turned and saw, pressed against the bars of the cells lining the hall, the faces of our friends. There they were: Horace and Enoch, Hugh and Claire, Olive, gasping through the bars at us from the top of her cell, her back against the ceiling—all there, all of them breathing and alive, except poor Fiona—lost when she fell from the cliff at Miss Wren's menagerie. But mourning her was a luxury we didn't have right then.

"Oh, thank the birds, the miraculous bloody birds!" Emma cried, running to take Olive's hand. "You can't imagine how worried we've been!"

"Not half as worried as we've been!" Hugh said from down the hall.

"I told them you'd come for us!" Olive said, near tears. "I told them and told them, but Enoch kept saying I was a loony for thinking so . . . "

"Never mind, they're here now!" said Enoch. "What took you so bloody long?"

"How in Perplexus's name did you find us?" said Millard. He was the only one the wights had bothered to dress in prisoners' garb—a striped jumpsuit that made him easy to see.

"We'll tell you the whole story," said Emma, "but first we need to find the ymbrynes and get you all out of here!"

"They're down the hall!" said Hugh. "Through the big door!"

At the end of the hall was a huge metal door. It looked heavy enough to secure a bank vault—or hold back a hollowgast.

"You'll need the key," said Bronwyn, and she pointed out a ring on the unconscious guard's belt. "It's the big gold one. I've been watching him!"

I scrambled to the guard and tore the keys from his belt. Then I stood frozen with them in my hand, my eyes darting between the cell doors and Emma.

"Hurry up and let us out!" Enoch said.

"With which key?" I said. The ring held dozens, all identical save the big gold one.

Emma's face fell. "Oh, no."

More guards would be coming soon, and unlocking every cell would cost precious minutes. So we ran to the end of the hall, unlocked the door, and gave the keys to Hugh, whose cell was closest. "Free yourself and then the others!" I said.

"Then stay here until we come back to get you," Emma added.

"No chance!" Hugh said. "We're coming after you!"

There was no time to argue—and I was secretly relieved to hear it. After all this time struggling on our own, I was looking forward to having some backup.

Emma and I heaved open the big bunker-like door, took a last look at our friends, and slipped away.

*   *   *

On the other side of the door was a long rectangular room cluttered with utilitarian furniture and lit from above by greenish fluorescent bulbs. It was doing its best impression of an office, but I wasn't fooled. The wall was spongy with foam soundproofing. The door was thick enough to withstand a nuclear blast. This was no office.

We could hear someone moving around at the far end of the room, but our view was blocked by a bulky filing cabinet. I touched Emma's arm and nodded my head—*let's go*—and we began to advance quietly, hoping to sneak up on whoever was in here with us.

I caught a glimpse of a white coat and a man's balding head. Definitely not an ymbryne. Had they not heard the door opening? No, they hadn't, and then I realized why: they were listening to music. A woman's voice sang a soft, slinky rock song—an old one I'd heard before but couldn't name. So strange, so dislocating, to hear it here, now.

We slid forward, the song just loud enough to mask our footsteps, passing desks crowded with papers and maps. A rack mounted to a wall held hundreds of glass beakers, silver-flecked black liquid spinning inside. Lingering, I saw that each was labeled, the names of the victims whose souls they contained printed in small type.

Peeking around the filing cabinet, we saw a lab-coated man seated at a desk shuffling papers, his back to us. All around him was a horror-show of random anatomy. A skinned arm with musculature exposed. A spine hung like a trophy on the wall. A few bloodless organs scattered like lost puzzle pieces on the desk. The man was writing something, nodding his head, humming along with the song—something about love, something about miracles.

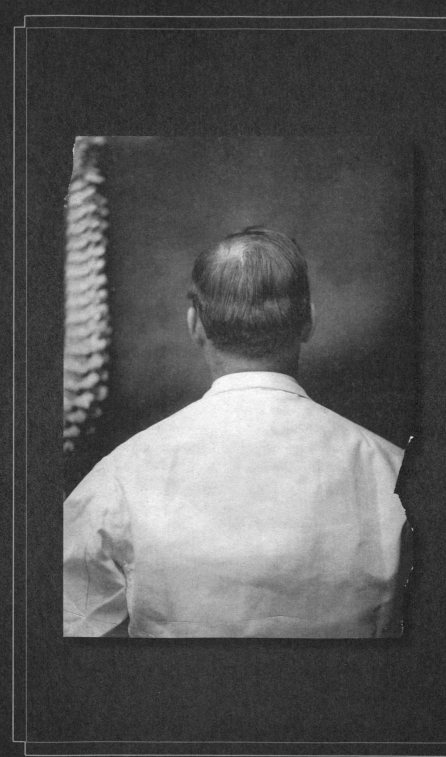

We stepped into the open and moved toward him across the floor. I remembered where I'd last heard the song: at the dentist, while a metal pick stabbed at the soft, pink flesh of my gums.

"*You Make Loving Fun.*"

Now we were only a few yards away. Emma held out a hand, ready to light it. But just before we got within reach of the man, he spoke to us.

"Hello, there. I've been expecting you."

It was a slimy-smooth voice I would never forget. Caul.

Emma summoned flames that shot from her palms with the sound of a whip-crack. "Tell us where the ymbrynes are, and I might spare your life!"

Startled, the man spun around in his chair. What we saw startled us, too: below his wide eyes, his face was a ruin of melted flesh. This man was not Caul—he wasn't even a wight—and it couldn't have been him who'd spoken. The man's lips were fused together. In his two hands he held a mechanical pencil and a small remote control. Pinned to his coat was a name tag.

Warren.

"Gee, you wouldn't hurt old Warren, would you?" Caul's voice again, coming from the same place as the music: a speaker in the wall. "Though it wouldn't matter much if you did. He's only my intern."

Warren sank low into his swivel chair, looking fearfully at the flame in Emma's hand.

"Where are you?" Emma shouted, looking around.

"Never mind that!" Caul said through the speaker. "What matters is that you've come to see me. I'm delighted! It's so much easier than hunting you down."

"We've got a whole army of peculiars on their way!" Emma bluffed. "The crowd at your gates is just the tip of the spear. Tell us where the ymbrynes are and maybe we can settle this peacefully!"

"Army!" Caul said, laughing. "There aren't enough fight-ready peculiars left in London to form a fire brigade, much less an army. As for your pathetic ymbrynes, save your empty threats—I'll gladly show you where they are. Warren, would you do the honors?"

Warren pushed a button on the remote in his hand, and with a loud *whoosh* a panel slid aside in the wall to one side of us. Behind it was a second wall made of thick glass, which looked into an expansive room engulfed in shadow.

We pressed against the glass, cupping our hands around our faces to see. Gradually, there came into view a space like a neglected basement, jumbled with furnishings and heavy drapes and human forms frozen in strange postures, many of which appeared, like the spare parts on Warren's desk, to have been stripped of their skin.

Oh God what's he done to them—

My eyes darted around the dark, my heart racing.

"That's Miss Glassbill!" Emma cried, and then I saw her, too. She sat in a chair off to one side, mannish and flat-faced, perfectly symmetrical braids falling down either side of her head. We pounded on the glass and called to her, but she merely stared, in a daze, unresponsive to our shouts.

"What have you done to her?" I shouted. "Why won't she answer?"

"She's had bit of her soul removed," Caul said. "Tends to
numb the brain."

"You bastard!" Emma shouted, and punched the glass. Warren
backed his rolling chair into the corner. "You black-hearted, despi-
cable, cowardly . . . "

"Oh, calm down," Caul said. "I only took a *little* of her soul,
and the rest of your nursemaids are in top health, if not spirits."

A harsh overhead light flicked on in the jumbled room, and it
became suddenly clear that most of the figures were just dummies—
no, obviously not real—mannequins or anatomical models of some
kind, posed like statues with their tendons and muscles all flexed and
popping. But in among them, gagged, bound to chairs and wooden
posts, flinching and squeezing their eyes shut against the sudden light,
were real, living people. Women. Eight, ten—I hadn't time to count
them all—most of them older, disheveled but distinguished-looking.

Our ymbrynes.

"Jacob, it's them!" Emma cried. "Can you see Miss—"

The light flicked off before we could find Miss Peregrine, and
now my eyes, ruined for the dark, could see nothing through the
glass.

"She's there, too," Caul said with a bored sigh. "Your pious
bird, your wet-nurse . . . "

"Your *sister*," I said, hoping that might inject some humanity
into him.

"I would hate to kill her," he said, "and I suppose I won't—
provided you give me what I want."

"And what's that?" I said, pulling away from the glass.

"Nothing much," he said casually. "Just a little bit of your
soul."

"What!" Emma barked.

I laughed out loud.

"Now, now, hear me out!" Caul said. "I don't even want the entire thing. Merely an eyedropper's worth. Less even than I took from Miss Glassbill. Yes, it'll make you a bit dopey for a while, but in a few days you will have fully recovered your faculties."

"You want my soul because you think it'll help you use the library," I said. "And take all that power."

"I see you've been talking to my brother," Caul replied. "You might as well know: I've nearly accomplished it now. After a lifetime of searching, I've finally found Abaton, and the ymbrynes—this perfect combination of ymbrynes—have unlocked the door for me. Alas, it was only then that I learned I needed still another component. A peculiar with a very specific talent, not often seen in the world these days. I had nearly despaired of ever finding such a person when I realized that a certain peculiar's grandson might fit the bill, and that these ymbrynes, otherwise useless to me now, could act as a lure. And so they have! I do believe it's fate, my boy. You and I, we'll go down in peculiar history together."

"We're not going anywhere together," I said. "If you get that kind of power, you'll make the world a living hell."

"You misunderstand me," he continued. "That's not surprising; most people do. Yes, I've had to make the world a hell for those who've stood in my way, but now that I've nearly achieved my goal, I am prepared to be generous. Magnanimous. Forgiving."

The music, still warbling below Caul's voice, had faded into a calm instrumental number, so at odds with the panic and terror I was feeling that it gave me a chill.

"We'll finally live in peace and harmony," he said, his voice smooth and reassuring, "with me as your king, your god. This is peculiardom's natural hierarchy. We were never meant to live like this, decentralized and powerless. Ruled by women. There will be no more hiding when I'm in charge. No more pathetic cowering beneath the skirts of ymbrynes. Our rightful place as peculiars is at the head of the human table. We'll rule the earth and all its people. We'll finally inherit what's ours!"

"If you think we're going to play any role in that," said Emma, "you're out of your gourd."

"I expected as much from you, girl," said Caul. "You're so typical of ymbryne-raised peculiars: no ambition, and no sense at all but one of entitlement. Quiet yourself, I am speaking to the male."

Emma's face went as red as the flame in her hand.

"Get on with it," I said tersely, thinking of the guards that were probably on their way, and our friends, still fumbling with keys in the hallway.

"Here's my offer," said Caul. "Allow my specialists to perform their procedure on you, and when I've got what I want, I'll let you and your friends go free—and your ymbrynes, too. They'll pose me no threat then, anyhow."

"And if I refuse?"

"If you won't let me remove your soul the easy and painless way, then my hollows would be more than happy to do it. They aren't known for their bedside manner, though, and once they're through with you, I'm afraid I'll be powerless to stop them from moving on to your ymbrynes. So you see, I'll get what I want either way."

"That won't work," Emma said.

"Are you referring to the boy's little trick? I've heard he's been able to control one hollow, but how about two at once? Or three, or five?"

"As many as I want," I said, trying to sound confident, unflappable.

"That I would very much like to see," said Caul. "Shall I take that as your answer, then?"

"Take it however you like," I said. "I'm not helping you."

"Oh, goody," Caul said. "This will be loads more fun!"

We could hear Caul laughing over the PA, and then I startled at the sound of a loud buzzer.

"What've you done now?" Emma said.

I felt a sharp pulse in my gut, and without Caul having to explain anything, I could picture exactly what was happening: in a tunnel below the ymbrynes' room, a hollow had been released from deep within the bowels of the complex. It was coming closer, climbing toward a grate in the floor that was scraping open. It would be among the ymbrynes soon.

"He's sending up a hollow!" I said. "It's coming into that room!"

"We'll start with just one hollowgast," said Caul. "If you can manage him, I'll introduce you to his friends."

I banged on the glass. "Let us in!"

"With pleasure," said Caul. "Warren?"

Warren pushed another button on the remote. A door-sized section of the glass wall slid open.

"I'm going!" I said to Emma. "You stay here and guard him!"

"If Miss Peregrine's in there, I'm coming, too."

It was clear there was no talking her out of it.

"Then we're bringing him with us," I said.

Warren tried to dart away, but Emma caught him by the back of his coat.

I ran through the door, into the dark and jumbled room, and Emma was behind me with the squirming, mouthless intern collared in one hand.

I heard the glass door bang shut behind us.

Emma swore.

I turned to look.

On the other side of the door, on the floor, lay the remote. We were locked in.

*　　*　　*

We'd only been inside the room a few seconds when the intern managed to wriggle from Emma's grasp and tumble off into the darkness. Emma started to chase him, but I held her back—he didn't matter. What mattered was the hollow, which was nearly out of its hole now and into the room.

It was starving. I could feel its gnawing hunger as if it were my own. In moments it would start feasting on ymbrynes, unless we could stop it. Unless *I* could stop it. First, though, I would have to find it, and the room was so crowded with junk and shadows that my ability to see hollows wasn't of great advantage.

I asked Emma for more light. She strengthened the flames in her hands as much as she could, but it seemed to only lengthen the shadows.

To keep her safe, I asked her to stay by the door. She refused. "We stick together," she said.

"Stick together behind me, then. Way behind me."

That, at least, she granted me. As I moved past catatonic Miss Glassbill and deeper into the room, Emma hung back several paces, holding one hand high above her head to light our way. What we could see of the room looked like a bloodless battlefield hospital, deconstructed human forms scattered everywhere.

My foot kicked an arm. It rung dully and spun away—plaster. Here was a torso on a table. There a head in a liquid-filled jar, its eyes and mouth agape, almost certainly real but not of recent vintage. This seemed to be Caul's lab, torture chamber, and storage closet all in one. He was a hoarder, like his brother, of strange and ghastly things—only where Bentham was organized to a tee, Caul badly needed a maid.

"Welcome to the hollows' play space," Caul said, his amplified voice echoing through the room. "We conduct experiments on them here, feed them, watch them disassemble their food. I wonder what part of you they'll eat first? Some hollows start with the eyes . . . a little amuse-bouche . . . "

I tripped over a body, which yelped as my foot dug into it. Looking down, I saw the scared-to-death face of a middle-aged woman peeping back at me, wild-eyed—an ymbryne I didn't know. Without stopping I bent down and whispered, "Don't worry, we'll get you out of here," but no, I thought, we would not; this chaos of forms and mad shadows would be the scene of our death—Old Jacob ascending, doom-saying, un-shut-uppable.

I heard something shift deeper in the room, followed by the wet draw of a hollowgast's mouth opening. It was here among us. I aimed myself toward it and ran—tripping, catching myself, Emma running too, saying, "Jacob, hurry!"

Caul, over the PA, mocking us: "Jacob, hurry!"

He had turned up the music: driving, upbeat, deranged.

We passed three, four more ymbrynes, all tied and struggling, before I finally saw it.

I stopped, breathless, my mind reeling at its sheer size. The hollow was a giant—several heads taller than the one I'd tamed, its skull nearly scraping the ceiling despite its hunched frame. It was twenty feet away, its jaws wide and tongues raking the air. Emma stumbled a few feet ahead of me and stuck out her hand, pointing at something and lighting it at the same time.

"There! Look!"

It wasn't the hollow she'd seen, of course, but what it was moving toward: a woman, upside down and twisting, hung up like a side of beef, her black skirts blooming about her head. Even like that, even in the dark, I knew her—it was Miss Wren.

Addison was hanging right next to her. They were struggling, gagged, and mere feet from a hollowgast whose tongues were now stretching toward them, slipping around Miss Wren's shoulders, drawing her into its jaws.

"STOP!" I screamed, first in English, then in the rasping language the hollow could understand. I shouted again, then again, until it did stop—though not because it was under my control, but because I had suddenly become more interesting prey.

It released the ymbryne and she swung away like a pendulum. The hollow turned its tongues toward me.

"Cut down Miss Wren while I draw the hollow away," I said.

I moved away from Miss Wren while talking to the hollow in a constant stream, hoping to draw it away from her and keep its attention on me.

Close your mouth. Sit down. Lie down.

It turned away from Miss Wren as I moved—*good, good*—and then as I backed away, it came forward.

Yes. Okay. Now what?

My hands went to my pockets. In one I had what remained of Mother Dust's finger. In the other, a secret—a vial of ambro I'd swiped from the previous room while Emma wasn't looking. I'd taken it during a momentary lapse of confidence. What if I couldn't do this on my own? What if I needed a boost?

Sit down, I said. *Stop.*

The hollow whipped one of its tongues at me. I ducked behind a mannequin and the tongue lassoed that instead, lifted it up and flung it against a wall, where it shattered.

I dove away from a second tongue. Banged my shins on a tipped-over chair. The tongue slapped the empty floor where I'd just been. The hollow was toying with me now, but soon it would go in for the kill. I had to do something, and there were two somethings I could do.

The vial or the finger.

There was no way I'd be able to control this hollow without the boost in my abilities a vial of ambro could give. Mother Dust's crushed finger, on the other hand, wasn't something I could launch away from me, and I'd lost my mask. If I tried to use it, I'd only put myself to sleep; it was worse than useless.

As another tongue smashed into the ground beside me, I slid beneath a table and pulled the vial from my pocket. I fumbled to uncork it, my hands shaking. Would it make a hero of me, or a slave? Could one vial really addict me for life? And what would be the worse outcome, being an addict and a slave, or being dead in this hollow's stomach?

The table was ripped away, leaving me exposed. I leapt to my feet. *Stop, stop,* I shouted, taking small hops backward as the hollow's tongues lashed at me, missing by mere inches.

My back hit the wall. There was nowhere left to go.

I took a blow to the stomach, and then the tongue that had hit me uncurled and moved to wrap around my neck. I needed to run but I was stunned, doubled over, breath knocked out of me. Then I heard an angry snarl—one that hadn't come from the hollow—and a stout, echoing bark.

Addison.

Suddenly the tongue that was reaching for my neck stiffened, as if in pain, and retracted across the room. The dog, that brave little boxer, had bitten it. I heard him growling and yelping as he began to do battle with an invisible creature twenty times his size.

I slid to the floor, back against the wall, breath filling my lungs again. I held up the vial, determined now. Convinced I had no chance without it. I pulled the cork, raised the bottle above my eyes, and tilted back my head.

And then I heard my name. "Jacob," softly spoken in the dark, a few feet away.

I turned to look, and there on the floor, lying amidst a pile of parts, was Miss Peregrine. Bruised, tied, struggling to speak through a haze of pain or drugs, but there nonetheless and gazing at me with those piercing green eyes.

"Don't," she said softly. "Don't do that." Her voice barely audible, barely there.

"Miss Peregrine!"

I lowered the vial, corked it, scrambled on my hands to where she lay. This second mother of mine, this peculiar saint. Fallen, hurt.

Dying, perhaps.

"Tell me you're okay," I said.

"Put that down," she said. "You don't need it."

"Yes, I do. I'm not like he was."

We both knew who I meant: my grandfather.

"Yes, you are," she said. "Everything you need is inside you already. Put it down and take that instead." She nodded at something lying between us: a jagged stake of wood from a broken chair.

"I can't. It's not enough."

"It is," she assured me. "Just aim for the eyes."

"I can't," I said, but I did. I put down the vial and took the stake.

"Good lad," she whispered. "Now, go and do something gruesome with it."

"I will," I said, and she smiled, her head sinking back to the floor.

I stood up, determined now, the wooden stake gripped in my hand. Across the room, Addison had his teeth clamped deep into one of the hollow's tongues and was riding it like a rodeo cowboy, clinging valiantly and snarling as the hollow whipped him back and forth. Emma had cut down Miss Wren from the rope where she'd been hanging and was standing guard over her, swinging her flaming hands blindly.

The hollow smacked Addison into a pole, and the dog was flung loose.

I started toward the hollow, running as fast as I could through an obstacle course of scattered limbs. But like a moth to flame, the creature seemed more interested in Emma. It was starting to close in on her, and so I shouted at it, first in English—"Hey! Over here!"—and then in Hollow: *Come and get me, you bastard!*

I picked up the closest thing at hand—which happened to be a hand—and threw it. It bounced off the hollow's back, and the thing turned around to face me.

Come and get me come and get me

For a moment the hollow was confused, which was just enough time for me to get close to it without getting caught up in its tongues. I stabbed it with the stake, once, twice in the chest. It reacted as if it'd been stung by a bee—no worse than that—and then knocked me to the ground with a tongue.

Stop, stop, stop, I shouted in Hollow, desperate for something to get through, but the beast seemed bulletproof, totally inoculated against my suggestions. And then I remembered the finger, the little chalk-stub of dust in my pocket. As I reached for it, a tongue wrapped around me and hoisted me into the air. I could hear Emma shouting at it to put me down—and Caul, too. "Don't you eat him!" he screeched over the PA. "He's mine!"

As I drew Mother Dust's finger from my pocket, the hollow dropped me into its open jaws.

I was trapped in its mouth from knees to chest, its teeth pinning me in place, starting to cut into my flesh, its jaws quickly expanding to swallow me.

This would be my last act. My last moment. I crushed the finger in my hand and shoved it down what I hoped was the hollow's throat. Emma was beating it, burning it—and then, just before it could close its jaws and saw me in half with its teeth, the creature began to choke. It stumbled away from Emma, burned and gagging, retreating toward the grate in the floor from which it had crawled. Bounding back to its nest, where it would have all the time it wanted to devour me.

I tried to stop it, to shout (*Let me go!*) but it was biting down and the pain was so blacking that I couldn't think—and then we were there, at the grate, slipping down into it. Its mouth so full of me that it couldn't catch hold of the rungs on the wall and it was falling, falling and choking, and I was still, somehow, alive.

When we hit bottom, it was with a great, bone-breaking crack that flattened our lungs and sent all the sedative dust I'd shoved down the hollow's gullet blowing into the air around us. As it snowed down I could feel it working, numbing my pain and dulling my brain, and it must've been doing the same to the hollow because it was hardly biting me at all now, its jaws slackening.

As we lay in a stunned and tranquilized pile, racing toward sleep, I could see forming before me, through all those billowing white particles, a dank and lightless tunnel heaped with bones. The last thing I saw before the dust took me was a throng of hollows, hunched and curious, shuffling forward.

CHAPTER EIGHT

I woke up. That in itself is worthy of note, I think, given the circumstances.

I was in the hollows' burrow, and piled around me were the bodies of many hollowgast. They might've been dead, but it was likelier they'd breathed what remained of Mother Dust's pinky finger, and the result was tangled in a spaghetti of stinking, snoring, mostly unconscious hollowflesh.

I gave a silent prayer of thanks for Mother Dust and then wondered, with rising alarm, how long I'd been down here. An hour? A day? What had happened to everyone above?

I had to go. A few of the hollows were beginning to stir from sleep, like me, but they were still woozy. With great effort, I stood. Apparently my wounds were not so grave, my bones not so broken. I swayed, dizzy, then caught my balance and began to move through the enmeshed hollows.

I kicked one in the head by accident. With a grunt it came awake and opened its eyes. I froze, thinking that if I ran it would only chase me down. It seemed to register me—but as neither a threat nor a potential meal—then closed its eyes again.

I continued on, placing each foot with care until I had passed the carpet of hollows and reached a wall. Here the tunnel ended. The way out was above me: a chute leading upward a hundred feet or so to an open grate and that cluttered room. There were holds along the chute, but they were spaced too far apart, built for hollows' acrobatic tongues, not human hands and feet. I stood peering up at a ring of dim light far overhead, hoping a friendly face might appear there, but I dared not shout for help.

In desperation I jumped, scrabbling at the hard wall and grasping for the first hold. Somehow I reached it. Pulled myself up. Suddenly I was more than ten feet off the ground. (*How had I done that?*) I jumped again and reached the next hold—and the next one. I was climbing the chute, my legs launching me higher and my arms reaching farther than I knew was possible—*this is insane*—and then I was at the top, poking my head out, pushing myself up into the room.

I wasn't even breathing hard.

I looked around, saw Emma's firelight, and ran toward it across the cluttered floor. I tried calling out but couldn't seem to make the words. No matter—there she was, on the other side of the open glass door, in the office. Warren was on this side, tied to the chair Miss Glassbill had sat in, and when I came close he groaned fearfully and knocked himself over. Then their faces were at the door, suspicious and peering—Emma and Miss Peregrine and Horace, and behind them other ymbrynes and friends, too. All there, alive, beautiful. They had been freed from their cells only to be imprisoned once more in here, locked behind Caul's bomb-proof bunker door, safe from wights (for now) but trapped.

Their expressions were fearful, and the closer I got to the glass door, the more terrified they became. *It's me*, I tried to say, but the words didn't come out right, and my friends jumped back.

It's me, it's Jacob!

What came out instead of English was a husky snarl and three long, fat tongues, waving in the air before me, spat from my own mouth in my attempt to speak. And then I heard one of my friends—Enoch, it was Enoch—say aloud the terrible thing that had just occurred to me:

"It's a hollow!"

I'm not, I tried to say, *I'm not*—but all evidence was to the contrary. I had somehow *become one of them*, been bitten and turned, like a vampire, or been killed, eaten, recycled, reincarnated—*oh god oh god oh god it can't be . . .*

I tried to reach out with my hands, to make some sign that might be recognized as human now that my mouth had failed me, but it was my tongues that reached out.

I'm sorry, I'm sorry, I don't know how to drive this thing

Emma swiped blindly at me with her hand—and connected. Sudden, searing pain flashed through me.

And then I woke up.

Again.

Or rather, jolted by sudden pain, I woke back into my body— my hurt, human body, still lying in the dark in the slack jaws of a sleeping hollow. And yet I was still the hollow above, too, snatching my hurt tongue back into my mouth and stumbling away from the door. I was somehow dually present in both my mind and the hollow's, and I found now that I could control both—could lift my own arm and the hollow's, turn my own head and the hollow's, and do it all without saying a word aloud, but merely by thinking.

Without realizing it—without consciously trying—I had mastered the hollow to such a degree (seeing through its eyes, feeling through its skin) that it had felt, for a time, like I *was* the hollow. But now a distinction was becoming clear. I was this fallible and broken-bodied boy, deep in a hole surrounded by groggy monsters. They were waking, all but the one who had brought me down here in its jaws (it had so much dust in its system that it might sleep for years), and they were sitting up now, shaking the numbness from their limbs.

But they didn't seem interested in killing me. They were watching me, quiet and attentive. Semicircled around like well-behaved children at storytime. Waiting for input.

I rolled myself out of the hollow's jaws and onto the floor. I could sit up but was too hurt to stand. But *they* could stand.

Stand.

I didn't say it, didn't even think it, really. It felt like *doing*, only it wasn't me who did it. They did it, eleven hollowgast all rising to their feet before me in perfect synchrony. This was astounding, of course, and yet I felt a profound sense of calm spreading through me. I was relaxing into the purest depths of my ability. Something about shutting down all our minds at once, then bringing them back online together—a collective reboot—had brought us into a kind of harmony, allowing me to tap into the unconscious heart of my power, as well as into the hollows' minds at just the moment their defenses were down.

And now they were mine. Marionettes I could control with invisible strings. But how much could I do? What were the limits? How many could I control at once, discretely?

To find out, I began to play.

In the room above, I lay the hollow down.

He lay down.

(They were all *he*s, I had decided.)

I made the ones in front of me jump.

They jumped.

They were two distinct groups now, the loner above and the ones before me. I tried controlling each individually, making one raise a hand without the rest doing it. It was a bit like asking just one toe on your foot to wiggle—difficult, not impossible—but before long I'd gotten the hang of it. The less conscious I was of trying, the easier it became. The control came most naturally when I simply imagined an action being performed.

I sent them away into the bone-piles farther down the tunnel, then had them pick up bones with their tongues and toss them to one another: first one at a time, then two, then three and four, piling action upon action until I'd gotten up to six. It was only when I made the hollow upstairs stand and do jumping jacks that the bone-tossers began to miss catches.

I don't think it would be bragging to say I was very good at this.

A natural, even. I could tell that with more time to practice, I had the capacity to become masterful. I could've played both sides of an all-hollow basketball game. I could've made them dance every role in *Swan Lake*. But there was no more time to practice; this would have to do. And so I gathered them around me, had the strongest one pick me up and saddle me to its back with a wrapped-around tongue; and one by one my monstrous little army bounded up the chute and into the room above.

*　　*　　*

The overhead lights had been turned on in the cluttered room, and in their harsh glow I could see that the only bodies remaining were mannequins and models—the ymbrynes had all been taken out. The glass door to Caul's observation room was closed. I made the hollows hang back while I approached it alone, save the hollow I was riding, then called out to my friends—this time with my own voice, in English.

"It's me! It's Jacob!"

They rushed to the door, Emma's face circled by the others'.

"Jacob!" Her voice was muffled behind the glass. "You're alive!" But as she studied me her face turned strange, as if she couldn't understand what she was seeing. Because I was on the hollow's back, I realized, it looked to Emma like I was floating above the ground.

"It's all right," I said, "I'm riding a hollowgast!" I slapped its shoulder to prove there was something solid and fleshy beneath me. "He's completely under my control—and so are these."

I brought the eleven hollows forward, stamping their feet to announce themselves. My friends' mouths went oval-shaped with wonder.

"Is that really you, Jacob?" Olive asked.

"What do you mean you're controlling them?" Enoch said.

"You've got blood on your shirt!" said Bronwyn.

They opened the glass door just wide enough to talk through. I explained how I fell into the hollows' pit, was nearly bitten in half, was numbed and put to sleep, and woke up with a dozen of them under my control. As further demonstration I had the hollows pick up Warren, the chair he was tied to and all, and toss him back and forth a few times, the chair flipping end over end until the kids were cheering and Warren was groaning as if he was going to be sick. Finally I had them set him down.

"If I hadn't seen it with my own eyes, I'd never have believed it," Enoch said. "Not in a million years!"

"You're fantastic!" I heard a little voice say, and there was Claire.

"Let me get a look at you!" I said, but when I approached the open door she shrank away. Impressed with my skills though they were, overcoming a peculiar's natural fear of hollowgast is no easy thing—and the smell probably didn't help, either.

"It's safe," I said, "I promise."

Olive came right to the door. "*I'm* not scared."

"Me, neither," said Emma, "and me first."

She stepped through the door and came to meet me. I made the hollow kneel, leaned away from it, and managed somewhat awkwardly to put my arms around Emma. "Sorry, I can't quite stand up on my own," I said, my face against her cheek, my closed eyes brushing her soft hair. It wasn't enough, but for now it would have to be.

"You're hurt." She pulled away to look me over. "You've got cuts everywhere—and they're deep."

"I can't feel them. I got dust all over me . . . "

"That could mean you're only numb, not healed."

"I'll worry about it later. How long was I down there?"

"Hours," she whispered. "We thought you were dead."

I nudged her forehead with mine. "I made you a promise, remember?"

"I need you to make me a new promise. Quit scaring the hell out of me."

"I'll do my best."

"No. *Promise.*"

"Once this is over, I'll make any promise you like."

"I'm going to remember that," she said.

Miss Peregrine appeared at the door. "You two had better come in here. And leave that beast outside, please!"

"Miss P," I said, "you're on your feet!"

"Yes, I'm recovering," she replied. "I was spared by my late arrival here, and by some nepotistic favoritism on my brother's part. Not all my fellow ymbrynes were so lucky."

"I wasn't sparing you, sister," said a booming voice from above—Caul again, through the PA system. "I was merely saving the tastiest dish for last!"

"You shut up!" Emma shouted. "When we find you, Jacob's hollows will eat you for breakfast!"

Caul laughed. "I doubt that," he said. "You're more powerful than I imagined, boy, but don't be fooled. You're surrounded with no way out. You've only delayed the inevitable. But if you give up now, I might consider sparing some of you . . . "

With a quick flick of their tongues, I made the hollows rip the speakers from the ceiling and smash them on the ground. As wires and parts sprang everywhere, Caul's voice went dead.

"When we find him," Enoch said, "I'd like to pull out his fingernails before we kill him. Anyone have a problem with that?"

"As long as I can send a squadron of bees up his nose first," said Hugh.

"That's not our way," Miss Peregrine said. "When this is all over, he'll be sentenced by ymbrynic law to rot in a punishment loop for the rest of his unnatural life."

"Where's the fun in that?" said Enoch.

Miss Peregrine gave him a withering look.

I made the hollow let me go, and with Emma's help I limped through the door and into the observation room. My friends were all there—all but Fiona. Ranged along the walls and resting on office chairs, I could see pale, frightened faces watching me. The ymbrynes.

But before I could go to them, my friends blocked my way. They threw their arms around me, holding up my tottering body with their embraces. I gave in to it. I hadn't felt anything so sweet in a long time. Then Addison came trotting up as nobly as he could with two hurt paws, and I broke away to greet him.

"That's twice now you've saved me," I said, putting a hand on his furry head. "I don't know how I'll ever repay you."

"You can start by getting us out of this bloody loop," he growled. "I'm sorry I ever crossed that bridge!"

Those who heard him laughed. Maybe it was his canine nature, but Addison had no filter; he always said just what he meant.

"That stunt you pulled with the truck was one of the bravest things I ever saw," I said.

"I was captured the minute I got inside the compound. I'm afraid I let you all down."

There was a sudden, loud boom from outside the heavy door. The room shook. Small items tumbled off shelves.

"The wights are trying to blow in the door," Miss Peregrine explained. "They've been at it for some time."

"We'll deal with them," I said. "But first I want to know who's unaccounted for. Things will get out of hand when we open that door, so if there are peculiars elsewhere in this compound who need rescuing, I want to keep them in mind as we go into battle."

It was so dark and crowded that we resorted to a roll call. I called our friends' names twice, just to make doubly sure they were all here. Then I asked after the peculiars who'd been snatched from Miss Wren's ice house alongside us: the clown (thrown into the chasm, Olive told us through hitching sobs, for refusing orders from the wights), the folding man (left on the Underground in grave condition), telekinetic Melina (upstairs and unconscious, having had some of her soul drained), and the pale brothers (same). Then there were the kids Miss Wren had rescued: the plain-looking boy in the floppy hat and the frizzy-haired snake-charmer girl. Bronwyn said she'd seen them being led off to another part of the compound, where other peculiars were being held.

Lastly, we counted the ymbrynes. There was Miss Peregrine, of course, whose side the kids had not left since they were reunited. There was so much I wanted to talk with her about. All that had happened to us since we last saw her. All that had happened to her. Though there was no time to say any of it, something did pass between us, in the brief moments our eyes would meet in passing. She regarded Emma and me with a certain pride and wonder. *I trust you*, her eyes said.

But Miss Peregrine, as deeply glad as we were to see her, wasn't the only ymbryne we had to be concerned about. There were twelve in all. She introduced her friends: Miss Wren, whom Emma had cut down from the ceiling, was wounded but coherent. Miss Glassbill was still staring in her vague and mindless way. The eldest, Miss Avocet, who hadn't been seen since she and Miss Peregrine were kidnapped together on Cairnholm, occupied a chair near the door. Miss Bunting, Miss Treecreeper, and several others fussed over her, adjusting blankets around her shoulders.

Nearly all of them looked frightened, which seemed distinctly unymbrynelike. They were supposed to be our elders and our leaders, but they'd been in captivity here for weeks, and they had seen things and had things done to them that had left them shell-shocked. (They also didn't share my friends' confidence in my ability to control a dozen hollowgast and were keeping as far away from my creatures as the dimensions of the room would allow.)

At the end of it, there was still one person among us who hadn't been named: a bearded, small-statured man who stood silently by the ymbrynes, watching us through dark glasses.

"And who's this?" I said. "A wight?"

The man became incensed. "*No!*" He tore off the glasses to show us his eyes, which were severely crossed. "I am *heem*!" he said, his accent thick and Italian. There was a large, leather-bound book on a table next to him, and he pointed to it, as if this somehow explained his identity.

I felt a hand on my arm. It was Millard, invisible now, his suit of stripes removed. "Allow me to introduce history's foremost temporal cartographer," he said grandly. "Jacob, this is Perplexus Anomalous."

"*Buongiorno*," said Perplexus. "How do you do."

"It's an honor to meet you," I said.

"Yes," he said, nose rising in the air. "It is."

"What's he doing here?" I whispered to Millard. "And how is he still alive?"

"Caul found him living in some fourteenth-century loop in Venice that no one knew existed. He's been here two days, though, which means he could age forward very soon."

As I had come to understand such things, Perplexus was in danger of aging forward because the loop he'd been living in was considerably older than the one we were in now, and the difference between those times would eventually catch up with him.

"I'm your biggest fan!" Millard said to Perplexus. "I have all your maps . . . "

"Yes, you tell me already," Perplexus said. "*Grazie.*"

"None of that explains what he's doing here," said Emma.

"Perplexus wrote about finding the Library of Souls in his journals," said Millard, "so Caul tracked him down, kidnapped him, and made him tell where it was."

"I made oath of blood to never say nothing," Perplexus said miserably. "Now I am cursed forever!"

"I want to get Perplexus back to his loop before he ages," said Millard. "I won't be responsible for the loss of peculiardom's greatest living treasure!"

From outside the door came another boom, this one even bigger and louder than before. The room trembled and pebbly bits of rock rained from the ceiling.

"We'll do our best, dear," Miss Peregrine said. "But we've got other things to see about first."

*   *   *

We quickly hatched a plan of action, such as it was: throw open the big door and use my hollows to clear the way. They were expendable, seemed in good working order, and my connection with them was only growing stronger. As for what could go wrong, I dared not even wonder. We would find Caul if we could, but our priority was escaping the compound alive.

I brought my hollows into the little room. Everyone gave them a wide berth, pressing their backs to the walls and their hands over their noses as the creatures shuffled past and gathered round the heavy door. The largest hollow knelt down and I saddled myself to him once more, which made me so tall I had to hunch forward to keep my head from scraping the ceiling.

We could hear the voices of wights outside in the corridor. No doubt they were planting another bomb. We decided to wait until they set it off before going out, so we stood by, waiting, a taut silence filling the room.

Finally, Bronwyn broke the tension. "I think Mr. Jacob should say something to all of us."

"Like what?" I said, making my hollow turn so I was facing everyone.

"Well, you're about to lead us into battle," said Bronwyn. "Something leader-ly."

"Something inspiring," said Hugh.

"Something that'll make us less terrified," said Horace.

"That's a lot of pressure," I said, feeling a bit self-conscious. "I don't know if this will make anyone less terrified, but it's something I've been thinking about. I've only known you for a few weeks, but it feels like so much longer than that. You're the best friends I've ever had. And it's weird to think that just a couple of months ago I was back at home, and I didn't even know you were real. And I still had my grandfather."

There were noises outside in the hall, muffled voices, the thud of something metal being dropped on the ground.

I continued, louder. "I miss my grandfather every day, but a very smart friend once told me that everything happens for a reason. If I hadn't lost him, well, I never would've found you. So I guess I had to lose one part of my family to find another. Anyway, that's how you make me feel. Like family. Like one of you."

"You *are* one of us," Emma said. "You're our family."

"We love you, Jacob," said Olive.

"It's been quite something knowing you, Mr. Portman," Miss Peregrine said. "You would've made your grandfather very proud."

"Thanks," I said, getting emotional and a bit embarrassed.

"Jacob?" said Horace. "May I give you something?"

"Of course," I said.

The others, sensing that something private was unfolding between us, began to murmur amongst themselves.

Horace came as close to the hollow as he could bear and, trembling slightly, held out a folded square of cloth. I took it, reaching down from my high place on the hollow's back.

"It's a scarf," said Horace. "Miss P was able to smuggle me a pair of needles, and I knitted it while I was in my cell. I reckon that making it kept me from going mad in there."

I thanked him and unfolded it. The scarf was simple and gray with knotted tassels on the ends, but it was well made and even had my initials monogrammed in one corner. *JP.*

"Wow, Horace, it's . . . "

"It's no great work of art. If I'd had my book of patterns I could've done better."

"It's amazing," I said. "But how did you know you'd even see me again?"

"I had a dream," he said, smiling coyly. "Will you wear it? I know it isn't cold, but . . . for luck?"

"Of course," I said, and wrapped it clumsily around my neck.

"No, that'll never stay on. Like this." He showed me how to fold it in half lengthwise, then loop it around my neck and back through itself so that it knotted perfectly at my throat and the loose ends hung neatly down my shirt. Not exactly battle-wear, but I didn't see the harm.

Emma sidled up to us. "Did you dream about anything besides men's fashion?" she said to Horace. "Like where Caul might be hiding?"

Horace shook his head and started to answer—"No, but I did have a fascinating dream about postage stamps"—but before he could tell us more, there was a noise from the corridor like a dump truck crashing into a wall, a sonic thud that shook us to the marrow. The big bunker door in the end of the room blew open, flinging hinges and bits of shrapnel into the opposite walls. (Thankfully, everyone had been standing clear of it.) There followed a blank moment while the smoke cleared and everyone slowly uncrouched themselves. Then, through the ringing of my ears, I heard an amplified voice say, "Send the boy out alone and no one gets hurt!"

"Somehow I don't believe them," said Emma.

"Definitely not," said Horace.

"Don't even think about it, Mr. Portman," said Miss Peregrine.

"I wasn't," I replied. "Is everyone ready?"

Murmurs of assent. I moved the hollows to either side of the door, their great jaws hinging open, tongues at the ready. I was about to launch my surprise attack when I heard Caul's voice through a PA in the hallway: "They have control of the hollows! Fall back, men! Defensive positions!"

"Damn him!" Emma cried.

The sound of retreating boots filled the corridor. Our surprise attack had been spoiled.

"It doesn't matter!" I said. "When you've got twelve hollows, you don't need surprise."

It was time to use my secret weapon. Rather than a welling-up of tension before the strike, I felt the opposite, a loosening of my full and present self as my awareness relaxed and split among the hollows. And then, while my friends and I hung back, the creatures began hurling themselves through the jagged, blasted door into the hall, running, snarling, jaws gaping, their invisible bodies carving tunnels in the curling bomb smoke. The wights fired at them, their gun barrels flashing, then fell back. Bullets whizzed through the open doorway and into the room where I and the others were taking cover, cracking into the wall behind us.

"Tell us when!" Emma shouted. "We'll go at your word!"

My mind in a dozen places at once, I could muster hardly a word of English in reply. I was them, those hollows in the hall, my own flesh stinging in sympathy with every shot that tore theirs.

Our tongues reached them first: the wights who had not run fast enough and the brave-but-foolish ones who'd lingered to fight. We pummeled them, smacked their heads into the walls, and a small number of us stopped to—here I tried to disconnect my own senses—to sink our teeth into them, swallowing their guns, silencing their screams, leaving them gashed and gaping.

Bottlenecked at the stairs at the end of the corridor, the guards fired again. A second curtain of bullets passed through us, deep and painful, but we ran on, tongues flailing.

Some of the wights escaped through the hatch. Others weren't so lucky, and when they'd stopped screaming we tossed their bodies clear of the stairs. I felt two of my hollows die, their signals blanking from my mind, the connection lost. And then the corridor was clear.

"Now!" I said to Emma, which at the moment was the most complex speech I could manage.

"Now!" Emma shouted, turning to the rest of our group. "This way!"

I drove my hollow into the corridor, clutching at its neck to keep from being thrown off its back. Emma fell in behind me with the others, using her flaming hands as signals in the smoke. Together we charged down the hall, my battalion of monsters before me, my army of peculiars behind. First among them were the strongest and the bravest: Emma, Bronwyn, and Hugh, then the ymbrynes and grumbling Perplexus, who insisted on bringing his heavy Map of Days. Last came the youngest children, the timid, the injured.

The corridor smelled of gunpowder and blood.

"Don't look!" I heard Bronwyn say as we began to pass the bodies of dead wights.

I counted them as we ran: there were five, six, seven of them to my two fallen hollows. Those were encouraging numbers, but how many wights were there in total? Forty, fifty? I worried that there were too many of them to kill and too many of us to protect, and that aboveground we'd be easily overwhelmed, surrounded, and confused. I had to kill as many wights as I could before they broke into the open and this fight turned into something we couldn't win.

My awareness slid to the hollows again. Bounding up the spiral steps, the first one was up through the hatch—then searing pain, blankness.

It had been ambushed as it came out.

I made the next one out of the hatch pick up the dead one's body to use as a shield. It soaked up a volley of gunfire, pushing forward into the room as other hollows leapt from the hatch behind it. I had to push the wights out fast, to get them away from the peculiars who lay everywhere in hospital beds. With a few lashes of our tongues, the closest ones were struck down, and the rest ran.

I sent my hollows after them as we peculiars emerged from the hatch. There were so many of us now, so many hands, that unhooking our bedridden brethren from their soul-drains would be easy. We spread out and made quick work of it. As for the chained madman and the boy we'd stashed in a closet, they were safer here than with us. We'd be back.

Meanwhile, my remaining hollows chased the wights toward the building's exit. The wights fired wildly behind them as they fled. Snatching at their heels with our tongues, we were able to trip two or three, who met a quick but gruesome end once my hollows caught up with them. One wight had hidden himself behind a counter, where he was arming a bomb. A hollow rooted him out, then bundled both the wight and his bomb into a side room. The bomb went off moments later. Another hollow winked out of my consciousness.

The wights had scattered and more than half had escaped, diving through windows and out side doors. We were losing them; the fight was shifting. We'd finished unhooking the bedridden peculiars and had nearly caught up to my hollows, which now numbered seven, plus the one I was riding. We were near the exit, in the room of horrible tools, and we had a choice. I posed the question to those closest to me—Emma, Miss Peregrine, Enoch, Bronwyn.

"Do we use the hollows as cover and run for the tower?" I said, my language coming back as the hollows I had to keep track of dwindled. "Or do we keep fighting?"

Surprisingly, they all agreed. "We can't stop now," Enoch said, wiping blood from his hands.

"If we do, they'll just keep chasing us forever," Bronwyn said.

"No, we won't!" said an injured wight, who was cowering on the floor nearby. "We'll sign a peace treaty!"

"We tried that in 1945," said Miss Peregrine. "It wasn't worth the lavatory paper it was written on. We must keep fighting, children. We may not have such an opportunity again."

Emma raised a flaming hand. "Let's burn this place to the ground."

*　　*　　*

I sent my hollows racing out of the lab building, into the courtyard, after the remaining wights. The hollows were ambushed again and another was killed, going dark from my mind as it died. Save the one I was riding, by now all my hollows had taken at least a bullet apiece, but despite their wounds most were still going strong. Hollows, as I had learned several times the hard way, are tough little buggers. The wights, on the other hand, seemed to be running scared, but that didn't mean I could count them out. Not knowing precisely where they were only made them more dangerous.

I tried to keep my friends inside the building while I sent the hollows to do reconnaissance, but the peculiars were angry and charged up, itching to get into the fight.

"Out of my way!" said Hugh, trying to push past Emma and me, who were blocking the door.

"It ain't fair for Jacob to do everything!" Olive said. "You've killed near half the wights now, but I hate 'em just as much as you do! If anything I've hated 'em longer—near a hundred years! So come *on!*"

It was true: these kids had a century of wight hatred to work out of their systems, and I was hogging all the glory. This was their fight, too, and it wasn't my place to keep them from it. "If you really want to help," I said to Olive, "here's what you can do . . . "

Thirty seconds later we were out in the open courtyard, and Horace and Hugh were reeling Olive up into the air by a rope around her waist. Right away she became our invaluable eye in the sky, shouting back intel that my ground-bound hollows could never have gathered.

"There's a couple to the right, past the little white shed! And another on the roof! And some running toward the big wall!"

They hadn't scattered to the winds but were mostly out beyond the courtyard. With any luck they could still be caught. I called my six remaining hollows back to us. Spread four of them into a phalanx that would march before us and two behind us as a guard against rear attacks. That left my friends and me to sweep the space between and deal with any wights that might breach our wall of hollows.

We began marching, toward the edge of the courtyard. Astride my personal hollow, I felt like a general commanding his troops from horseback. Emma was at my side, and the other peculiars were just behind: Bronwyn collecting loose bricks to hurl, Horace and Hugh hanging on to Olive's rope, Millard attaching himself to Perplexus, who was unleashing a constant stream of Italian profanities while shielding himself with his Map of Days. At the back, the ymbrynes whistled and made loud bird calls in attempt to recruit winged friends to our cause, but Devil's Acre was such a dead zone that there were few wild birds to be found. Miss Peregrine had taken charge of old Miss Avocet and the few shell-shocked ymbrynes. There was nowhere to leave them; they'd have to accompany us into battle.

We came to the edge of the courtyard, beyond which was a run of open ground about fifty meters long. In all that space was just one small building, all that stood between us and the outer wall. It was a curious structure with a pagoda roof and tall, ornate doors, into which I saw a number of wights flee. According to Olive, nearly all the remaining wights had taken up positions inside the little building. One way or another, we were going to have to flush them out.

A quiet had settled over the compound. There were no wights visible anywhere. We lingered behind a protective wall to discuss our next move.

"What are they doing in there?" I said.

"Trying to lure us out into the open," Emma said.

"No problem. I'll send the hollows."

"Won't that leave us unguarded?"

"I don't know that we have a choice. Olive counted twenty wights going in there at least. I need to send enough hollows to overwhelm them or they'll just get slaughtered."

I took a breath. Scanned the tense, waiting faces around me. I sent the hollows out one by one, sliding across the open yard on tiptoe, hoping light footsteps might allow them to surround the building unnoticed.

It seemed to work: the building had three doors, and I managed to place two hollows at each one without a single wight showing his face. The hollows stood guard outside the doors while I listened through their ears. Inside, I could hear someone with a high voice speaking, though I couldn't make out the words. Then a bird whistled. My blood went cold.

There were ymbrynes inside. More that we hadn't known were here.

Hostages.

But if that was true, why weren't the wights trying to negotiate?

My original plan had been to break down all the doors at once and charge inside. But if there were hostages—especially ymbryne hostages—I couldn't risk such rash action.

I decided to have one of the hollows risk a look inside. All the windows were shuttered, though, which meant I'd have to send it through a door.

I chose the smallest hollow. Reeled out its dominant tongue. It licked the knob, gripped it.

"I'm sending one inside," I said. "Just one, to look around."

Slowly, the hollow turned the knob. On my silent count of three, the hollow pushed open the door.

It leaned forward and pressed its black eye to the crack.

"I'm looking inside."

Through its eye I could see a slice of wall lined with cages. Heavy, black birdcages of various shapes and sizes.

The hollow pressed the door open farther. I saw more cages, and now birds, too, in the cages and out of them, chained to perches.

But no wights.

"What do you see?" Emma said.

There wasn't time to explain, only to act. I made all my hollows throw open the doors at once, and they burst inside.

There were birds everywhere, startled and squawking.

"Birds!" I said. "The room's full of ymbrynes!"

"What?" Emma said. "Where are the wights?"

"I don't know."

The hollows were turning, smelling the air, searching every nook and cranny.

"That can't be!" Miss Peregrine said. "All the kidnapped ymbrynes are right here."

"Then what are these birds?" I said.

Then, in a scratchy parrot voice, I heard one sing, "Run, rabbit, run! Run, rabbit, run!" And I realized: these were not ymbrynes. These were parrots. And they were *ticking.*

"HIT THE DIRT!" I shouted, and we all dove to the ground behind the courtyard wall, the hollow pitching backward and taking me with it.

I flung my hollows at the doors but the parrot-bombs went off before they could get through them, ten at once, obliterating the building and the hollows in a terrible clap of thunder. As dirt and brick and bits of building flew through the courtyard and rained down on us, I felt the hollows' signals go dead together, all but one blacking from my mind.

A cloud of smoke and feathers blew over the wall. The peculiars and ymbrynes were streaked with dirt, coughing, checking one another for holes. I was in shock, or something like it, my eyes locked on a splattered patch of ground where a bit of pulped and quivering hollowgast had been flung. For an hour my mind had been stretching to accommodate twelve of them, and their sudden death had created a disorienting vacuum that left me feeling dizzy and strangely bereft. But crisis has a way of focusing the mind, and what happened next had my last remaining hollow and me sitting bolt upright.

From beyond the wall came the sound of many voices shouting together—a great and rising battle cry—and beneath it a thunder of stampeding boots. Everyone froze and looked at me, dread furrowing their faces.

"What is *that*?" said Emma.

"Let me see," I said, and crawled away from my hollow to peer around the edge of the wall.

A horde of wights was charging toward us across the smoking ground. Twenty of them in a cluster, running with rifles and pistols raised, their white eyes and white teeth shining. They were unscathed by the explosion, having escaped, I assumed, into some underground shelter. We'd been lured into a trap, of which the parrot bombs were only the first component. Now that our best weapon had been stripped from us, the wights were making their final assault.

There was a panicked scramble as others looked around the wall to see the charging horde for themselves.

"What do we do?" cried Horace.

"We fight!" said Bronwyn. "Give 'em everything we've got!"

"No, we must run while we can!" said Miss Avocet, whose bent back and deeply lined face made it hard to imagine her running from anything. "We can't afford to lose another peculiar life!"

"Excuse me, but I was asking Jacob," said Horace. "He got us this far, after all . . . "

Instinctively I looked to Miss Peregrine, whom I considered the final authority on matters of authority. She returned my gaze and nodded. "Yes," she said, "I think Mr. Portman should decide. Quickly, though, or the wights will make the decision for you."

I nearly protested. My hollows were all dead but one—but I suppose this was Miss Peregrine's way of saying she believed in me, hollows or no. Anyway, what we should do seemed obvious. In a hundred years, the peculiars had never been so close to destroying the wight menace, and if we ran away now, I knew that chance may never come again. My friends' faces were scared but determined—ready, I thought, to risk their lives for a chance to finally eradicate the wight scourge.

"We fight," I said. "We've come too far to give up now."

If there was someone among us who would rather have fled, they stayed quiet. Even the ymbrynes, who had sworn oaths to keep us safe, didn't argue. They knew what sort of fate awaited any of us who were recaptured.

"You give the word," said Emma.

I craned my neck around the wall. The wights were closing fast, no more than a hundred feet away now. But I wanted them closer still—close enough that we might easily knock the guns from their hands.

Shots rang out. A piercing scream came from above.

"Olive!" Emma shouted. "They're shooting at Olive!"

We'd left the poor girl hanging up there. The wights were taking potshots at her while she squealed and waved her limbs like a starfish. There was no time to reel her in, but we couldn't just leave her for target practice.

"Let's give them something better to shoot at," I said. "Ready?"

Their answer was resounding and affirmative. I shimmied onto the back of my crouched hollow. "LET'S GO!" I shouted.

The hollow leapt to its feet, nearly bucking me off, then launched forward like a racehorse at the starting gun. We burst from behind the wall, the hollow and I leading the charge, my friends and our ymbrynes close behind. I let out a screaming war cry, not so much to scare the wights as to tear down the fear that was clawing at me, and my friends did the same. The wights balked, and for a moment they couldn't seem to decide whether to keep charging or stop and shoot at us. That bought the hollow and me enough time to clear much of the open ground that separated us.

It didn't take long for the wights to make up their minds. They stopped, leveled their guns at us like a firing squad, and let loose a volley of bullets. They whizzed around me, pocking the ground, lighting up my pain receptors as they slammed into the hollow. Praying it hadn't been hit anywhere vital, I sank low to shield myself behind its body and urged it forward, faster, using its tongues like extra legs to speed us on.

The hollow and I closed the remaining gap in just a few seconds, my friends close behind. Then we were among them, fighting hand-to-hand, and the advantage was ours. While I concentrated on knocking the guns out of the wights' hands, my friends put their peculiar talents to good use. Emma swung her hands like flaming clubs, cutting through a line of wights. Bronwyn hurled the bricks she'd gathered, then punched and pummeled the wights with her bare hands. Hugh's lone bee had recently made some friends, and as he cheered them on ("Go for the eyes, fellows!") they swirled around and dive-bombed our enemy wherever they could. So did the ymbrynes, who'd turned themselves into birds after the first gunshots. Miss Peregrine was most fearsome, her huge beak and talons sending wights running, but even small, colorful Miss Bunting made herself useful, ripping one wight's hair and pecking his head hard enough to make him miss the shot he was taking—which allowed Claire to leap up and bite him on the shoulder with her wide, sharp-toothed backmouth. Enoch did his part, too, revealing from under his shirt three clay men with forks for legs and knives for arms, which he sent hacking after the wights' ankles. All the while, Olive shouted advice to us from her bird's-eye view. "Behind you, Emma! He's going for his gun, Hugh!"

Despite all our peculiar ingenuity, however, we were outnumbered, and the wights were fighting as if their lives depended on it—which likely they did.

Something hard crashed into my head—the butt of a gun—and I hung limp from the hollow's back for a moment, the world spinning around me. Miss Bunting was caught and thrown to the ground. It was chaos, awful bloody chaos, and the wights were beginning to take the momentum, forcing us back.

And then, from behind me, I heard a familiar roar. My senses returning, I looked and saw Bentham, galloping toward the fight astride the back of his grimbear. Both were soaking wet, having come through the Panloopticon the same way Emma and I had.

"Hullo, young man!" he called, riding up next to me. "In need of some assistance?"

Before I could reply, my hollow was shot again, the bullet passing through the side of its neck and grazing my thigh, painting a bloody line through my torn pants.

"Yes, please!" I shouted.

"PT, you heard the boy!" Bentham said. "KILL!"

The bear dove into the fight, swinging his giant paws and knocking wights aside like they were bowling pins. One ran up and shot PT point-blank in the chest with a small handgun. The bear seemed merely annoyed, then picked up the wight and sent him flying. Soon, with my hollow and Bentham's grim working together, we had the wights on the defensive. When we'd picked off enough of them that it became clear they were outnumbered, their ranks whittled to no more than ten, they took off and ran.

"Don't let them escape!" Emma cried.

We tore after the wights on foot, on wing, on bearback and hollowback. We chased them through the smoking ruins of the parrot house, across ground stippled with catapulted rodents from Sharon's insurrection, toward an arched gate built into the looming outer wall.

Miss Peregrine screamed overhead, dive-bombing fleeing wights. She pulled one off his feet by the back of his neck, but this, and more attacks from Hugh's bees, only made the nine that were left run even faster. Their lead was growing and my hollow was beginning to fail, leaking black fluid from a half dozen wounds.

The wights crashed on blindly, the gate's iron portcullis rising as they neared it.

"Stop them!" I shouted, hoping that beyond the gate, Sharon and his unruly crowd might hear.

And then I realized: the bridge! There was still another hollow-gast left—the one inside the bridge. If I could get control of him in time, maybe I could stop the wights from escaping.

But no. They were already through the gate, running up the bridge, and I was hopelessly behind. By the time I passed through the gate, the bridge hollow had already picked up and tossed five of them across to Smoking Street, where only a thin crowd of ambro addicts was lingering—not enough to stop them. The four wights who hadn't yet crossed were stuck at the bridge gap, waiting their turn to be flung.

As my hollow and I started running up the bridge, I felt the bridge hollow come online inside me. It was picking up three of the four wights and lifting them across.

Stop, I said aloud in Hollow.

Or at least that's what I thought I said, though maybe something got lost in translation, and maybe *stop* sounds a lot like *drop* in hollowspeak. Because rather than stopping midair and then bringing the three kicking and terrified wights back to our side of the bridge, the hollow simply let them go. (How strange!)

All the peculiars on our side of the chasm and the addicts on the other side came to the edge to watch them fall, howling and flailing all the way down through layers of sulfurous green mist until—*ploop!*—they plunged into the boiling river and disappeared.

A cheer went up on both sides, and a grating voice I recognized said, "Serves 'em right. They were lousy tippers, anyway!"

It was one of two bridge heads that were still on their pikes. "Didn't your mum ever tell you not to swim on a full stomach?" said the other. "WAIT TWENTY MINUTES!"

The lone wight remaining on our side threw down his gun and

raised his hands in surrender, while the five who'd made it across were quickly vanishing into a cloud of ash the wind had kicked up.

We stood watching them go. There was no way we'd catch them now.

"Curse our luck," Bentham said. "Even that small number of wights could wreak havoc for years to come."

"Agreed, brother, though honestly I didn't realize you gave a titmouse what happened to the rest of us." We turned to see Miss Peregrine walking toward us, returned to human form, a shawl clasped modestly around her shoulders. Her eyes were locked on Bentham, her expression sour and unwelcoming.

"Hello, Alma! Fantastic to see you!" he said with overeager cheerfulness. "And of course I give a . . . " He cleared his throat awkwardly. "Why, I'm the reason you're not still in a prison cell! Go on, children, tell them!"

"Mr. Bentham helped us a lot," I admitted, though I didn't really want to insert myself into a sibling spat.

"In that case, all due thanks," Miss Peregrine said coldly. "I'll ensure the Council of Ymbrynes is made aware of the role you played here. Perhaps they'll see fit to lighten your sentence."

"Sentence?" Emma said, looking sharply at Bentham. "What sentence?"

His lip twisted. "Banishment. You don't think I'd live in this pit if I was welcome anywhere else, do you? I was framed, unjustly accused of—"

"Collusion." Miss Peregrine said. "Collaboration with the enemy. Betrayal after betrayal."

"I was acting as a double agent, Alma, mining our brother for information. I explained this to you!" He was whining, his palms out like a beggar's. "You know I have every reason to hate Jack!"

Miss Peregrine raised her hand to stop him. She'd heard this story before and didn't want to again. "When he betrayed your grandfather," she said to me, "that was the last straw."

"That was an *accident*," Bentham said, drawing back in offense.

"Then what became of the suul you drew from him?" said Miss Peregrine.

"It was injected into the test subjects!"

Miss Peregrine shook her head. "We reverse-engineered your experiment. They were given suul from barnyard animals, which can only mean that you kept Abe's for yourself."

"What an absurd allegation!" he cried. "Is that what you told the council? That's why I'm still rotting in here, isn't it?" I couldn't tell if he was genuinely surprised or just acting. "I knew you felt threatened by my intellect and superior leadership capabilities. But that you'd stoop to such lies to keep me out of your way . . . do you know how many years I've spent fighting to eradicate the scourge of ambrosia use? What on earth would I want with that poor man's suul?"

"The same thing our brother wants with young Mr. Portman," Miss Peregrine said.

"I won't even honor that accusation with a denial. I only wish this haze of bias would clear so that you could see the truth: I'm on your side, Alma, and I've always been."

"You're on whatever side fits your interests at the moment."

Bentham sighed and aimed a hangdog look at Emma and me. "Goodbye, children. It's been a distinct pleasure knowing you. I'll go back home now; saving all your lives has taken quite a toll on this old man's body. But I hope one day, when your headmistress comes to her senses, we'll meet again."

He tipped his hat, and he and his bear began to walk away through the crowd, back through the compound toward the tower.

"What a drama queen," I muttered, though I did feel a little bad for him.

"Ymbrynes!" Miss Peregrine called. "Watch him!"

"Did he really steal Abe's soul?" Emma asked.

"Without proof we can't be certain," replied Miss Peregrine. "But the rest of his crimes taken together would earn him more than a lifetime's banishment." Watching him go, her hard expression gradually melted away. "My brothers taught me a hard lesson. No one can hurt you as badly as the people you love."

*　　*　　*

The wind shifted, sending the ash cloud that had aided the wights' escape in our direction. It came faster than we could react, the air around us howling and stinging, the daylight dimming away. There was a sharp flutter of wings as the ymbrynes changed form and flew up above the storm. My hollow sank to its knees, bowed its head, and shielded its face with its two free tongues. It was accustomed to ash storms, but our friends were not. I could hear them panicking in the dark.

"Stay where you are!" I shouted. "It'll pass!"

"Everyone breathe through your shirts!" said Emma.

When the storm began to subside a little, I heard something from across the bridge that made the hairs on my neck stand up. It was three baritone voices united in a song, the lines of which were punctuated by thuds and groans.

"Hark to the clinking of hammers . . . "

Thwack!

"Hark to the driving of nails!"

"Gahh, my legs!"

"What fun to build a gallows . . . "

"Let me go, let me go!"

" . . . the cure for all that ails!"

"Please, no more! I give up!"

And then, as the ash began to clear, Sharon and his three burly cousins appeared, each of them dragging a subdued wight. "Morning, all!" Sharon called. "Did you lose something?"

Wiping ash from their eyes, our friends saw what they'd done and began to cheer.

"Sharon, you brilliant man!" shouted Emma.

All around us the ymbrynes were landing and resuming human form. As they slipped quickly into the clothes they'd dropped, we respectfully kept our eyes on the wights.

Suddenly, one of them broke away from his captor and ran. Rather than chasing him, the rigger calmly selected a small hammer from his tool belt, planted his feet, and threw it. It tumbled end over end straight toward the wight's head, but what would've been a perfect takedown was spoiled when the wight ducked. He darted toward the chaos of scrap at the road's edge. Just as the wight was about to disappear between two shanty houses, a crack in the road erupted and the wight was engulfed in a belch of yellow flame.

Though it was a grisly sight, everyone whooped and cheered.

"You see!" said Sharon. "The Acre itself wants to be rid of them."

"That's wonderful," I said, "but what about Caul?"

"I agree," said Emma. "None of these victories will matter if we can't catch him. Right, Miss P?"

I glanced around but didn't see her. Emma looked, too, her eyes scanning the crowd.

"Miss Peregrine?" she said, panic creeping into her voice.

I made my hollow stand tall so I could get a better view. "Does anyone see Miss Peregrine?" I shouted. Now everyone was looking, checking the sky in case she was still airborne, the ground in case she'd landed but not yet turned human.

Then from behind us, a high, gleeful shout cut through our chatter.

"Look no further, children!" For a moment I couldn't pinpoint the voice. It came again: "Do as I say and no harm will come to her!"

Then I saw emerge, from beneath the branches of a small, ash-blackened tree just inside the wights' gate, a familiar figure.

Caul. A twig of a man with no weapons in his hand nor guards by his side. His face pale and contorted into an unnatural grin, his eyes capped by bulging sunglasses, insectine. He was dandied up in a cloak, a cape, loops of gold jewelry, and a bouffant silk tie. He looked flamboyantly insane, like some mad doctor from gothic fiction who'd performed too many experiments on himself. And it was his evident madness, I think—and that we all knew him to be capable of true evil—that stopped us from rushing to tear him apart. A man like Caul was never as defenseless as he seemed.

"Where's Miss Peregrine?" I shouted, inspiring a chorus of similar demands from the ymbrynes and peculiars behind me.

"Right where she belongs," Caul said. "With her family."

The last of the ash cloud gusted out of the compound behind him, revealing Bentham and Miss Peregrine, the latter in human form, held captive in the arms of Bentham's bear. Though her eyes flashed with rage, she knew better than to struggle against a sharp-clawed, short-tempered grimbear.

It seemed a recurring nightmare we were doomed to dream again and again: Miss Peregrine kidnapped, this time by Bentham. He stood slightly behind the bear with eyes downcast, as if ashamed to meet our looks.

Cries of shock and anger rippled through the peculiars and ymbrynes.

"Bentham!" I shouted. "Let her go!"

"You traitorous bastard!" cried Emma.

Bentham raised his head to look at us. "As recently as ten minutes ago," he said in a high and imperious tone, "you had my loyalty. I could have betrayed you to my brother days ago, but I didn't." He narrowed his eyes at Miss Peregrine. "I chose *you*, Alma, because I believed—naively, it seems—that if I helped you and your wards, you might see how unfairly you'd judged me, might finally rise above past differences and let bygones be bygones."

"You'll be sent to the Pitiless Waste for this!" Miss Peregrine shouted.

"I'm not frightened of your little council anymore!" Bentham said. "You won't keep me down any longer!" He stamped his cane. "PT, muzzle!"

The bear clamped its paw over Miss Peregrine's face.

Caul strode toward his brother and sister, his arms and smile spreading. "Benny's made a choice to stand up for himself, and I, for one, congratulate him! There's nothing like a family reunion!"

Suddenly, Bentham was pulled backward by an unseen force. A

knife flashed at his throat. "Make the bear release Miss Peregrine or else!" a familiar voice shouted.

"Millard!" someone gasped, one of many that rippled through our crowd.

It was Millard, disrobed and invisible. Bentham looked terrified, but Caul seemed merely annoyed. He drew an antique pepper-box pistol from one of the deep pockets in his cloak and pointed it at Bentham's head. "Let her go and *I'll* kill you, brother."

"We made a pact!" Bentham protested.

"And you caving to the demands of a nude boy with a dull knife would be breaking that pact." Caul cocked the gun, walked it forward until it was pressed against Bentham's temple, and addressed Millard. "If you make me kill my only brother, consider your ymbryne dead, too."

Millard hesitated for a moment, then dropped the knife and ran. Caul made a grab for him but missed, and Millard's footsteps curved away in a trail of divots.

Bentham composed himself and straightened his mussed shirt. Caul, his good humor gone, turned the gun on Miss Peregrine.

"Now listen to me!" he barked. "You there, across the bridge! Let those guards go!"

They had little choice but to do as he asked. Sharon and his cousins released their collared wights and backed away, and the wight who'd been standing on our side of the bridge lowered his hands and picked his gun up off the ground. Within seconds the balance of power had been reversed completely, and there were four guns aimed at the crowd and one at Miss Peregrine. Caul could do what he wanted.

"Boy!" he said, pointing at me. "Pitch that hollow into the chasm!" His shrill voice a needle in my eardrum.

I walked my hollow to the edge of the chasm.

"Now make him leap!"

It seemed I didn't have a choice. It was an awful waste, but perhaps just as well: the hollow was suffering badly now, its wounds leaking black blood that flowed around its feet. It wouldn't have survived.

I unwrapped its tongue from my waist, unsaddled myself, and stepped down. My strength had returned enough for me to stand on my own, but the hollow's was going fast. As soon as I was off its back it bellowed softly, sucked its tongues back into its mouth, and sank to its knees, a willing sacrifice.

"Thank you, whoever you were," I said. "I'm sure that if you'd ever become a wight, you wouldn't have been a completely evil one."

I put my foot on its back and pushed. The hollow tumbled forward and dropped silently into the misty void. After a few seconds, I felt its consciousness disappear from my mind.

The wights across the bridge rode over to our side on the hollow's tongues, Miss Peregrine's life threatened again if I interfered. Olive was yanked out of the sky. The guards set about herding us into a tight and easily controllable cluster. Then Caul shouted for me, and one of the guards reached into the crowd and dragged me out.

"He's the only one we really need alive," Caul said to his guards. "If you must shoot him, shoot him in the knees. As for the rest of them . . . " Caul swung his gun toward the tightly packed crowd and fired. There were screams as the crowd surged. "Shoot them anywhere you please!"

He laughed and twirled with his arms poised like a squat ballerina. I was about to run at him, ready to dig out his eyes with my bare hands and damn the consequences, when a long-barreled revolver appeared front and center in my field of view.

"Don't," grunted my monosyllabic guard, a wight with broad shoulders and a shiny bald head.

Caul fired his own gun into the air and shouted for quiet, and every voice fell away but the whimpers of whomever he'd shot.

"Don't cry, I have a treat for you people!" he said, addressing the crowd. "This is a historic day. My brother and I are about to culminate a lifetime's worth of innovation and struggle by crowning ourselves the twin kings of peculiardom. And what would a coronation be without witnesses? So we're bringing you along. Provided you behave yourselves, you'll see something no one has witnessed for a thousand years: the domination and expropriation of the Library of Souls!"

"You have to promise one thing, or I won't help you," I said to Caul. I didn't have much negotiating power, but he believed he needed me, and that was something. "Once you get what you want, let Miss Peregrine go."

"I'm afraid that won't do," Caul said, "but I'll let her live. Peculiardom will be more fun to rule with my sister in it. Once I clip your wings I'll keep you as my personal slave, Alma, how would you like that?"

She tried to respond, but her words were lost beneath the bear's meaty paw.

Caul cupped a hand behind his ear and laughed. "What's that? I can't hear you!" Then he turned and began walking toward the tower.

"Let's go!" the guards shouted, and soon we were all stumbling after him.

CHAPTER NINE

We were herded toward the pale tower at a brutal pace, the wights encouraging stragglers with shoves and kicks. Without my hollow I was a limping, hobbling mess: I had nasty bite wounds across my torso and the dust that had kept me from feeling them was beginning to wear off. I forced myself forward anyway, my mind spinning out ways we might save ourselves, each more implausible than the last. Without my hollows, all our peculiar powers were outmatched by the wights and their guns.

We stumbled past the wrecked building where my hollows had died, over bricks misted with the blood of parrots and wights. Marched through the walled courtyard, into the tower door and then up and up its winding hallway past a blur of identical black doors. Caul paraded before us like a deranged bandleader, high-stepping and swinging his arms one moment and turning to hurl profane insults at us the next. Behind him, the bear waddled along with Bentham riding in the crook of one arm and Miss Peregrine slung over its shoulder.

She pled with her brothers to reconsider their course of action.

"Remember the old stories of Abaton, and the ignominious end that came to every peculiar who stole the library's souls! Its power is cursed!"

"I'm not a child anymore, Alma, and I'm no longer frightened by old ymbrynes' tales," Caul scoffed. "Now hold your tongue. That is, if you want to keep it!"

She soon gave up trying to convince them and stared silently at us over the bear's shoulder, her face projecting strength. *Don't be afraid*, she seemed to telegraph. *We'll survive this, too.*

I worried not all of us would survive even the trip to the top of the tower. Turning around, I tried to see who it was that had been shot. Amidst the tight-packed group behind me, Bronwyn was carrying someone limp in her arms—Miss Avocet, I think—and then a meaty hand smacked me in the head.

"Face forward or lose a kneecap," growled my guard.

Finally we came to the top of the tower and its very last door. In the hallway beyond, pale daylight shone on the curving wall. There was an open deck above us, a fact I filed away for future reference.

Caul stood beaming before the door. "Perplexus!" he called. "*Signor* Anomalous—yes, there in the back! Since I owe this discovery in part to your expeditions and hard work—credit where credit is due!—I think you should do the honors and open the door."

"Come now, we've no time for ceremony," said Bentham. "We've left your compound unguarded . . . "

"Don't be such a ninny-willow," Caul said. "This won't take but a moment."

One of the guards dragged Perplexus out of the crowd and up to the door. Since I'd last seen him, his hair and beard had turned alabaster white, his spine had curved, and deep wrinkles grooved his face. He'd spent too long away from his loop, and now his true age was beginning to catch up to him. Perplexus seemed about to open the door when he was struck by a fit of coughing. Once he'd regained his breath, he faced Caul, drew in a snorting lungful of air, and spat a glistening wad of phlegm onto his cloak.

"You are an ignorant pig!" Perplexus cried.

Caul raised his pistol to Perplexus's head and pulled the trigger. There were screams—"Jack, don't!" Bentham shouted—and Perplexus threw up his hands and spun away, but the only sound the gun made was a dry click.

Caul opened the gun and peered into its chamber, then shrugged. "It's an antique, like yourself," he said to Perplexus, then used its barrel to flick the spittle from his jacket. "I suppose fate has intervened on your behalf. Just as well—I'd rather watch you turn to dust than bleed to death."

He motioned for the guards to take him away. Perplexus, muttering oaths at Caul in Italian, was dragged back to the group.

Caul turned to the door. "Oh, to hell with it," he muttered, and opened it. "Get in there, all of you!"

Inside was the same familiar gray-walled room, only this time its missing fourth wall extended into a long, dark corridor. With a few shoves from the guards, we were hurrying along it. The smooth walls became rough and uneven, then widened into a primitive, day-lit room. The room was made from rock and clay, and I might've called it a cave but for its approximately rectangular door and two windows. Someone had carved them, and this room, using tools to dig it out of soft rock.

We were herded outside into a hot, dry day. The view opened dizzyingly. We were high in a landscape that could've been an alien world: everywhere around us, towering on one side and rolling away into valleys on the other, were humps and spires of strange, reddish rock, all honeycombed with crude doors and windows. A constant wind blew through them, producing a human-sounding moan that seemed to emanate from the earth itself. Though the sun was nowhere near setting, the sky glowed orange, as if the end of the world were brewing just beyond the horizon. And despite evidence here of a civilization, other than ourselves there was no one in sight. I had a heavy, watched feeling, like we were trespassing someplace we were not meant to be.

Bentham climbed down from his bear and removed his hat in awe. "So this is the place," he said, gazing across the hills.

Caul threw a big-brotherly arm across his shoulders. "I told you this day would come. We certainly put each other through hell getting here, didn't we?"

"We did," Bentham agreed.

"But I say all's well that ends well, because now I get to do this." Caul turned to face us. "Friends! Ymbrynes! Peculiar children!" He let his voice echo away into the strange, moaning canyons. "Today will go down in history. Welcome to Abaton!"

He paused, waiting for applause that didn't come.

"You're standing now in the ancient city that once protected the Library of Souls. Until recently, it hadn't been seen in over four hundred years, nor conquered in a thousand—until I rediscovered it! Now, with you as my witnesses . . . "

He stopped, looked down for a moment, then laughed. "Why am I wasting my breath? You philistines will never appreciate the gravity of my achievement. Look at you—like donkeys contemplating the Sistine Chapel!" He patted Bentham on the arm. "Come on, brother. Let's go and take what's ours."

"And ours as well!" said a voice behind me. One of the guards. "You won't forget us, will you, sir?"

"Of course I won't," Caul said, attempting a smile and failing. He couldn't disguise his irritation at having been challenged in front of everyone. "Your loyalty will be repaid tenfold."

He turned with Bentham and started down a footpath, the guards pushing us after them.

*   *   *

The sunbaked path split and split again, sending branches and feeders into the spiked hills. Following a route he'd no doubt forced Perplexus to reveal and had trod many times in recent days, Caul led us down obscure and bramble-choked lanes with certainty, his every step oozing the arrogance of a colonizer. The watched feeling I had only grew. As if the rough openings bored into the rock were a colony of half-closed eyes, some ancient intelligence encased in stone, waking slowly from a thousand-year sleep.

I was fevered with anxiety, my thoughts tripping over one another. What happened next would be up to me. The wights needed me, after all. What if I refused to handle the souls for them? What if I found a way to trick them?

I knew what would happen. Caul would kill Miss Peregrine. Then he'd start killing the other ymbrynes, one after another until I gave him what he wanted. And if I didn't, he'd kill Emma.

I wasn't strong enough. I knew I'd do anything to stop them from hurting her—even hand Caul the keys to untold power.

Then I had a thought that scared the bejesus out of me: what if I *couldn't* do it? What if Caul was wrong and I couldn't see the soul jars, or I could see them but not handle them? He wouldn't believe me. He'd think I was lying. He'd start murdering my friends. And even if I somehow convinced him it was true—that I couldn't—he might get so livid that he'd kill everyone anyway.

I said a silent prayer to my grandfather—can you pray to dead people? Well, I did—and I asked, if he was watching me, to see me through this, and to make me as strong and as powerful as he once was. *Grandpa Portman*, I prayed, *I know this sounds crazy, but Emma and my friends mean the world to me, the whole damned world, and I would gladly give every bit of it to Caul in exchange for their lives. Does that make me evil? I don't know, but I thought you might understand. So please.*

Looking up, I was surprised to see Miss Peregrine watching me from over the bear's shoulder. As soon as she met my eyes she looked away, and I could see tears tracking through the grime on her pale cheeks. As if somehow she'd heard me.

Our route wound through an ancient maze of twisting paths

and stairways cut into the hills, their steps worn into crescent moons. In some places the path all but disappeared, swallowed by weeds. I heard Perplexus complain that it had taken him years to puzzle out the way to the Library of Souls, and to have this ungrateful thief tromping along it now with no regard—a terrible insult!

And then I heard Olive say, "Why did no one ever tell us the library was real?"

"Because, my dear," replied an ymbryne, "it wasn't allowed. It was safer to say . . . "

The ymbryne paused to catch her breath.

" . . . that it was just a story."

Just a story. It had become one of the defining truths of my life that, no matter how I tried to keep them flattened, two-dimensional, jailed in paper and ink, there would always be stories that refused to stay bound inside books. It was never just a story. I would know: a story had swallowed my whole life.

We'd been walking for several minutes along a plain-looking wall, the wind's eerie moan rising and falling, when Caul raised a hand and shouted for everyone to stop.

"Have we gone too far?" he said. "I could've sworn the grotto was along here somewhere. Where's the cartographer?"

Perplexus was hauled forth from the crowd.

"Aren't you glad you didn't shoot him?" Bentham muttered.

Caul ignored him. "Where's the grotto?" he demanded, getting in Perplexus's face.

"Ahh, perhaps it's hidden itself from you," Perplexus teased.

"Don't test me," Caul replied. "I'll burn every copy of your Map of Days. Your name will be forgotten by next year."

Perplexus knotted his fingers together and sighed. "There," he said, pointing behind us.

We had passed it.

Caul stomped down to a vine-choked patch of wall—an opening so humble and well-hidden that anyone might've missed it; not so much a door as a hole. He pushed aside the vines and poked his head through. "Yes!" I heard him say, and then he pulled out his head again and began giving orders.

"Essential persons only are allowed past this point. Brother, sister." He pointed at Bentham and Miss Peregrine. "Boy." He pointed at me. "Two guards. And . . ." He searched the crowd. "It's dark in there, we'll need a flashlight. You, girl." He pointed at Emma.

As my stomach turned knots, Emma was pulled out of the group.

"If the others give you trouble," Caul said to the guards, "you know what to do." Caul raised his pistol at the crowd. They all screamed and ducked their heads. Caul howled with laughter.

Emma's guard pushed her through the hole. Bentham's bear would never fit through, so Miss Peregrine was set down and my wight given double duty guarding both her and me.

The youngest children began to weep. Who knew if they would ever see her again? "Be brave, children!" Miss Peregrine called to them. "I'll be back!"

"That's right, children!" Caul sang mockingly. "Listen to your headmistress! Ymbryne knows best!"

Miss Peregrine and I were pushed through the opening together, and there was a moment, tangled in the vines, when I was able to whisper to her unnoticed.

"What should I do when we get inside?"

"Anything he asks," she whispered back. "If we don't anger him, we may yet survive."

Survive, yes—but at what cost?

And then we were parting the vines and stumbling into a strange new space: a stone room open to the sky. For an instant my breath abandoned me, so shocked was I by the giant, misshapen face staring back at us from opposite wall. A wall—that's all it was—but one with a gaping mouth for a door, two warped eyes for windows, a pair of holes for nostrils, and grown over with long grass that resembled hair and an unruly beard. The moaning wind was louder than ever here, as if the mouth-shaped door were trying to warn us away in some ancient language made of vowels a week long.

Caul indicated the door. "The library awaits."

Bentham removed his hat. "Extraordinary," he said, hushed and reverent. "It almost seems to be singing to us. Like all the resting souls here are coming awake to welcome us."

"Welcoming," said Emma. "I doubt that."

The guards pushed us toward the door. We ducked through the low opening and into another cavelike room. Like the others we'd seen in Abaton, it had been dug by hand from soft rock, untold ages ago. It was low-ceilinged and bare, empty but for some scattered straw and broken shards of pottery. Its most unique feature was the walls, into which had been dug many dozens of small coves. They were oval-topped and flat on the bottom, large enough to hold a bottle or a candle. At the back of the room, several doors forked away into darkness.

"Well, boy?" said Caul. "Can you see any?"

I looked around. "Any what?"

"Don't trifle with me. Soul jars." He stepped to a wall and swept his hand inside one of the coves. "Go and pick one up."

I turned slowly, scanning the walls. Every cove appeared to be empty. "I don't see anything," I said. "Maybe there aren't any."

"You're lying."

Caul nodded to my guard. The guard punched me in the stomach.

Emma and Miss Peregrine shouted as I fell to my knees, groaning. Looking down at myself, I saw blood trickling through my shirt—not from the punch, but from my hollow bite.

"Please, Jack!" cried Miss Peregrine. "He's just a boy!"

"Just a boy, just a boy!" Caul said mockingly. "That's the very heart of the problem! You've got to punish them like men, water them with a bit of blood, and then the shoot begins to spring up, the plant to grow." He strode toward me while spinning the barrel of his odd, antique pistol. "Straighten his leg. I want a clean shot at the knee."

The guard shoved me to the ground and grabbed ahold of my calf. My cheek ground into the dirt, my face aimed at the wall.

I heard the gun's hammer pull back. And then, as the women begged Caul for mercy, I saw something in one the coves in the wall. A shape I hadn't noticed before—

"Wait!" I shouted. "I see something!"

The guard flipped me over.

"Come to your senses, have you?" Caul was standing over me, looking down. "What do you see?"

I looked again, blinking. Forced myself to be calm, my vision to focus.

There in the wall, coming gradually into view like a Polaroid photo, was the faint image of a stone jar. It was a simple, unadorned thing, cylindrical in shape with a tapered neck and a cork plugging its top, its stone the same reddish color as the strange hills of Abaton.

"It's a jar," I said. "Just one. It was tipped over, that's why I didn't notice it at first."

"Stand," Caul said. "I want to see you pick it up."

I drew my knees to my chest, rocked forward onto my feet, and stood, pain rioting through my midsection. I shuffled across the room and reached slowly into the cove. I slid my fingers around the jar, then got a shock and pulled my hand away.

"What is it?" Caul said.

"It's *freezing*," I replied. "I wasn't expecting it."

"Fascinating," murmured Bentham. He'd been lingering near the door, as if reconsidering this whole endeavor, but now he took a step closer.

I reached into the cove again, ready for the cold this time, and removed the jar.

"This is wrong," Miss Peregrine said. "There's a peculiar soul in there, and it should be treated with respect."

"To be eaten by me would be the greatest respect a soul could be paid," Caul said. He came and stood next to me. "Describe the jar."

"It's very simple. Made of stone." It was starting to freeze my right hand, so I passed it to my left, and then I saw, written across the back in tall, spidery letters, a word.

Aswindan.

I wasn't going to mention it, but Caul was watching me like a hawk and had seen me notice something. "What is it?" he demanded. "I warn you, hold nothing back!"

"It's a word," I said. "Aswindan."

"Spell it."

"A-s-w-i-n-d-a-n."

"Aswindan," Caul said, his brow furrowing. "That's Old Peculiar, isn't it?"

"Obviously," Bentham said. "Don't you remember your lessons?"

"Of course I do! I was a quicker study than you, remember? Aswindan. The root is *wind*. Which doesn't refer to the weather but denotes quickness, as in quickening—as in strengthening, invigoration!"

"I'm not so sure about that, brother."

"Oh you're *not*," Caul said sarcastically. "I think you want it for yourself!"

Caul reached out and tried to snatch the jar from me. He managed to get his fingers around it, but as soon as the jar left my hand his fingers closed on themselves, as if there were suddenly nothing between them, and the jar dropped to the floor and smashed.

Caul swore and looked down, dumbfounded, as blue and brightly glowing liquid puddled at our feet.

"I can see it now!" he said excitedly, pointing at the blue puddle. "That, I can see!"

"Yes—yes, me too," said Bentham, and the guards concurred. They could all see the liquid, but not the jars that contained and protected it.

One of the guards bent down to graze the blue liquid with his finger. The moment he touched it he cried out and jumped back, flapping his hand to shake the stuff off. If the jar was freezing, I could only imagine how cold the blue stuff was.

"What a waste," Caul said. "I would have liked to combine that with a few other choice souls."

"Aswindan," Bentham recited. "Root word *swind*. Meaning *shrink*. Be glad you didn't take that one, brother."

Caul frowned. "No. No, I'm certain I was right."

"You're not," said Miss Peregrine.

His gaze darted between them, paranoid, as if he were weighing the possibility they might somehow be in league against him. Then he seemed to let it go. "This is just the first room," he said. "The better souls are deeper in, I'm sure."

"I agree," said Bentham. "The farther we go, the older the

souls will be, and the older the soul, the more powerful."

"Then we shall plumb the very heart of this mountain," said Caul, "and eat it."

* * *

We were prodded through one of the black doors, pistols at our ribs. The next room was much like the first, with coves combing its walls and doors leading into the dark. There were no windows, though, and just a single blade of afternoon sun slicing down the dusty floor. We were leaving daylight behind us.

Caul ordered Emma to make a flame. He ordered me to inventory the contents of the walls. I duly reported three jars, but my word wasn't enough; he made me tap each one with my fingernail to prove it was there, and pass my hand through dozens of empty coves to prove they were vacant.

Next he made me read them. *Heolstor. Unge-sewen. Meaganwundor.* The words were meaningless to me, unsatisfactory to him. "The souls of piddling slaves," he complained to Bentham. "If we're to be kings, we need the souls of kings."

"Onward, then," said Bentham.

We plunged into a baffling and seemingly endless maze of caverns, daylight a memory, the floor sloping ever downward. The air grew colder. Passageways branched off into the dark like veins. Caul seemed to navigate by some sixth sense, confidently bounding left or right. He was insane, manifestly insane, and I was sure he was getting us so lost that even if we managed to escape him, we could expect to spend eternity trapped in these caves.

I tried to imagine the battles that had been waged over these souls—ancient, titanic peculiars clashing among the spires and valleys of Abaton—but it was too mind-boggling. All I could think of was how terrifying it would be to be trapped down here without a light.

The farther we went, the more jars were in the walls, as if plunderers had long ago raided the outermost rooms but something had stopped them from getting too far—a healthy sense of self-preservation, maybe. Caul barked at me for updates, but he'd stopped demanding proof of which coves were occupied and which were vacant, and only occasionally made me read a jar's label aloud. He was hunting bigger game and seemed to have decided there was little worth bothering with in this part of the library.

We went on in silence. The rooms grew larger and grander, in their crude way, the ceilings rising and walls widening. The jars were everywhere now: filling every cove, stacked in totemic pillars in the corners, wedged into cracks and crevices, the cold that seeped from them refrigerating the air. Shivering, I pulled my arms close to my body, my breath pluming before me, the watched feeling that had haunted me earlier creeping back. This library, so-called, was a vast underworld, a catacomb and hiding place for the second soul of every peculiar who had ever lived, prior to the last millennium—hundreds of thousands of them. That great accretion of souls had begun to exert a strange pressure on me, compressing the air spaces in my head and lungs as if I were sinking gradually into deep water.

I wasn't the only one feeling out of sorts. Even the guards were skittish, startling at small noises and checking constantly over their shoulders.

"Did you hear that?" mine said.

"The voices?" said the other one.

"No, more like water, rushing water . . . "

While they talked I stole a quick glance at Miss Peregrine. Was she frightened? No—she seemed to be biding her time, waiting and watching. I took some comfort in that, and in the fact that she could have taken bird form and escaped her captors long ago, but hadn't. So long as Emma and I were prisoners, she would be. Maybe that was more than just her protective instinct at work. Maybe she had a plan.

The air grew colder still, a thin sweat on my neck turning steadily to ice water. We trudged through a chamber so littered with jars I had to hopscotch around them to keep from kicking them over—though everyone else's feet passed right through them. I felt suffocated by the dead. It was standing-room only here, the platform of a rush hour train station, Times Square on New Year's Eve, all the revelers slack-faced and staring, unhappy to see us. (I could *feel* this, if not quite see it.) Finally, even Bentham lost his nerve.

"Brother, wait," he said, breathless, holding Caul back. "Don't you suppose we've gone far enough?"

Caul turned slowly to look at him, his face split evenly by shadow and fire-glow. "No, I do not," he said.

"But I'm sure the souls here are sufficiently—"

"We haven't found it yet." His voice sharp, brittle.

"Found what, sir?" my guard ventured.

"I'll know it when I see it!" Caul snapped.

Then he tensed, excited, and ran away into the dark.

"Sir! Wait!" the guards shouted, shoving us after him.

Caul vanished briefly before reappearing at the end of the chamber, illuminated by a shaft of faint blue light. He stood half-rimmed in it, transfixed by something. When we caught up to him and rounded a corner, we saw what it was: a long tunnel shining with azure light. A square opening at the other end was ablaze with it. I could hear something, too, a vague white noise like rushing water.

Caul clapped his hands and whooped. "We're close, by God!"

He skipped down the corridor, manic, and we were forced after him at a stumbling run. When we came to the end, the light that enveloped us was so dazzling that we all staggered to a stop, too blinded to see where we were going.

Emma let her flames die. They weren't needed here. Squinting through my fingers, the space came slowly into view. Bathed in undulating curtains of gauzy blue light, it was the largest cavern we'd seen—a huge, circular space like a beehive, a hundred feet across at the bottom but tapering to a single point at its top, several stories above. Ice crystals gleamed on every surface, in every cove and on every jar—of which there were thousands. They climbed to impossible heights, festooning the walls.

Despite the freeze, there was free-flowing water here: it sprung from a tap shaped like a falcon's head, tumbled into a small channel that circled the room at the base of the walls, and flowed into a shallow pool at the edge of the room, ringed by smooth black stone at the far edge of the room. This water was the source of the cavern's heavenly light. Like the stuff inside soul-jars, it glowed a ghostly blue, and it pulsed dimmer and brighter in regular cycles, as if breathing. It might've been oddly soothing, all this, like some Nordic spa experience, if it weren't for the distinct and human sound moaning at us beneath the water's pleasant burble. It was exactly like the moan we'd heard outside—the one I'd dismissed as wind whistling through doors—but there was no wind here, nor any possibility of hearing wind. This was something else.

Bentham hobbled into the cavern behind us, winded and shielding his eyes, while Caul strode to the middle of the room. "VICTORY!" he cried, seeming to enjoy the way his voice ricocheted between the towering walls. "This is it! Our treasure house! Our throne room!"

"It's magnificent," Bentham said weakly, shuffling to join his brother. "I see now why so many were willing to give their lives fighting for it . . . "

"You're making a terrible mistake," Miss Peregrine said. "You mustn't desecrate this sacred place."

Caul sighed dramatically. "Must you spoil every moment with your schoolmarmish moralizing? Or are you simply jealous and mourning the end of your reign as the more-gifted sister? *Look at me, I can fly, I can make time loops!* A generation from now, no one will remember there was ever such a silly creature as an ymbryne!"

"You're wrong!" Emma shouted, no longer able to hold her

tongue. "It's you two who will be forgotten!"

Emma's guard moved to strike her, but Caul told him to leave her be. "Let her speak," he said. "It may be her last opportunity."

"Actually, you won't be forgotten," said Emma. "We'll write a new chapter in the *Tales* about you. The Greedy Brothers, we'll call it. Or the Horrible Awful Traitors Who Got What They Deserved."

"Hmm, a bit flat," Caul said. "I think we'll call it How the Magnificent Brothers Overcame Prejudice to Become the Rightful God-Kings of Peculiardom, or something to that effect. And you're fortunate that I'm in such excellent humor right now, girl."

His attention turned to me. "Boy! Tell me about the jars here, and skip no detail, however small." He demanded an exhaustive description, which I gave, reading aloud many dozens of their spidery, hand-scripted labels. If only I spoke Old Peculiar, I thought, I could've lied about what was written on them, maybe tricked Caul into taking a soul that was weak and silly. But I was the perfect automaton: blessed with ability but cursed with ignorance. The only thing I could do was try to divert his attention from the most obviously promising jars.

Though most of them were small and plain, a few were large, ornate, and heavy, with hourglass shapes and double handles and gem-toned wings painted on their surfaces; it seemed clear they contained the souls of powerful and important (or self-important) peculiars. The larger size of their coves was a giveaway, though, and when Caul made me rap on them with my knuckle, they rang deep and loud.

I had no tricks left. Caul would get what he wanted, and there was nothing I could do about it. But then he did something that surprised everyone. Something that seemed, at first, bizarrely generous. He turned to his guards and said, "Now! Who would like first crack at this?"

The guards looked at each other, confused.

"What do you mean?" said Bentham, hobbling toward him in

alarm. "Shouldn't it be you and I? We've worked so long . . . "

"Don't be greedy, brother. Didn't I tell them their loyalty would be repaid?" He looked again to the guards, grinning like a game show host. "So which of you will it be?"

Both of their hands shot up.

"Me, sir, me!"

"I'd like to!"

Caul pointed to the wight who'd been guarding me. "You!" he said. "I like your spirit. Get over here!"

"Thank you, sir, thank you!"

Caul pointed his gun at me, thus relieving my guard of his duty. "Now, which of those souls sounds like your cup of tea?" He remembered where I'd identified certain jars and began to point them out. "*Yeth-Faru*. Something to do with water, flooding. Good one if you've ever fancied a life under the sea. *Wolsenwyrsend*. I believe that's a sort of centaurish half-horse, half-man creature who controls clouds? Ben, sound familiar?"

Bentham mumbled something in reply, but Caul was hardly listening.

"*Styl-hyde*, that was a good one. Metal skin. Could be useful in a fight, though I wonder if you'd have to oil yourself . . . "

"Sir, I hope you don't mind my asking," the guard said meekly, "but what about one of the larger urns?"

Caul wagged his finger. "I like a man with ambition, but those are for my brother and me."

"Of course, sir, of course," the guard said. "Then . . . um . . . were there any others?"

"I gave you the best options," said Caul, his tone edging toward warning. "Now choose."

"Yes, yes, sorry, sir . . . " The guard looked anguished. "I choose *Yeth-faru*."

"Excellent!" Caul boomed. "Boy, retrieve the jar."

I reached into the cove Caul indicated and removed the jar. It was so cold, I pulled the cuff of my jacket over my hand like a glove, but even through the fabric it felt like the jar was stealing all the warmth left in my body.

The guard stared at my hand. "What do I do with it?" he said. "Take it like ambrosia?"

"I'm not certain," Caul said. "What do you think, brother?"

"I'm not sure, either," said Bentham. "It's not mentioned in any of the old texts."

Caul scratched his chin. "I think . . . yes, I think you should take it like ambrosia." He nodded, suddenly sure of himself. "Yes, that's the ticket. Just like ambro."

"Are you sure?" asked the guard.

"Absolutely one hundred percent sure," said Caul. "Don't be nervous. You'll go down in history for this. A pioneer!"

The guard locked eyes on me. "No tricks," he said.

"No tricks," I said.

I uncorked the jar. Blue light shone out of it. The guard put his hand around mine, guided it and the jar above his head, and tilted back his face.

He took a long, shuddering breath. "Here goes nothing," he muttered, and tipped my hand.

The liquid poured from the jar in a viscous stream. The instant it reached his eyes, his hand clenched so tight around mine that I thought my fingers would break. I wrenched free and leapt backward, and the jar fell to the ground and smashed.

The guard's face was smoking and turning blue. He screamed and fell to his knees, his body shuddering, and then he pitched forward. When his head smacked the ground, it shattered like glass. Bits of frozen skull shot out around my feet. And then he was silent—and very, very dead.

"Oh, my God!" cried Bentham.

Caul clucked his tongue as if someone had spilled a glass of expensive wine. "Well, drat," he said. "I guess it's not like taking ambrosia after all." His gaze roved around the room. "Well, now someone else has got to try it . . . "

"I'm quite busy, milord!" cried the other guard, who had his gun trained on both Emma and Miss Peregrine.

"Yes, I can see you've got your hands full there, Jones. Perhaps one of our guests, then?" He looked at Emma. "Girl, do this for me and I'll make you my court jester!"

"Go to hell," Emma snarled.

"That can be arranged," he snarled back.

Then there was a loud hiss and a brightening of light at one edge of the room, and everyone turned to look. The liquid from the broken jar was dripping into the channel by the wall, and where the water and blue liquid had mixed, a reaction was taking place. The water bubbled and churned, glowing brighter than ever.

Caul was gleeful. "Look at this!" he exclaimed, bobbing on the balls of his feet.

The quickly flowing channel pushed the bright, bubbling water around the edges of the room. We turned, watching it go, until it reached the shallow, stone-rimmed pool at the far end of the room— and then the pool itself began to churn and glow, a column of strong blue light rising from it all the way to the ceiling.

"I know what this is!" Bentham said, his voice trembling. "It's called a spirit pool. An ancient means of summoning and communicating with the dead."

Hovering above the pool's surface in the column of light was a ghostly white vapor, and it was coalescing, slowly, into the form of a man.

"But if a living person enters the pool during the summoning . . . "

"He absorbs the spirit being summoned," Caul said. "I do believe we've found our answer!"

The spirit hovered, motionless. It was dressed in a simple tunic that revealed scaly skin and a dorsal fin that jutted from his back.

This was the soul of the *Yeth-faru*, the merman chosen by the guard. The column of light seemed a sort of prison from which it could not escape.

"Well?" Bentham said, gesturing at the pool. "Are you going?"

"I'm not interested in another man's leftovers," Caul said. "I want *that* one." He pointed to the jar I'd rung for him earlier, the largest of them all. "Tip it into the water, boy." He pointed his gun at my head. "*Now.*"

I did as I was told. Reaching into the oversized cove, I took the urn by both handles and tipped it toward me—carefully, lest it splatter and ruin my face.

Bright blue liquid ran down the wall into the channel. The water went crazy, hissing and bubbling, the light it produced so bright that I had to squint. As the urn's liquid flowed around the room toward the spirit pool, my eyes darted to Miss Peregrine and Emma. This was our last chance to stop Caul, and there was only one guard left—but he wasn't taking his eyes or his gun off the women, and Caul still had his pistol aimed squarely at my head. It seemed we were still at their mercy.

The great urn's liquid reached the spirit pool. The pool frothed and heaved as if a sea creature was about to break the surface. The column of light rising from it grew brighter still, and *Yeth-faru* evaporated into nothing.

A new vapor began to coalesce, much larger than the one it replaced. If this was taking the shape of a man, it was a giant one, twice as tall as any of us, its chest twice as broad. Its hands were claws, and they were raised, palms upturned, in a way that implied great and terrible power.

Caul looked at the thing and smiled. "And that, as they say, is my cue." He reached into his cloak with his free hand, pulled out a folded piece of paper, and shook it open. "I just have a word or two I'd like to say first, before I officially change stations in life."

Bentham hobbled toward him. "Brother, I think we'd better

not dally any longer . . . "

"I don't believe it!" Caul shouted. "Will no one allow me a moment to glory in all this?"

"*Listen!*" Bentham hissed.

We listened. For a moment I heard nothing, but then, distantly, there came a high, sharp sound. I saw Emma tense and her eyes widen.

Caul scowled. "Is that . . . a *dog*?"

Yes! A dog! It was the bark of a dog, far away and lost in echoes.

"The peculiars had a dog with them," Bentham said. "If it's following our scent, I doubt it's alone."

Which could mean only one thing: our friends had overpowered their guards, and led by Addison, they were coming after us. Yes—the damned *cavalry* was coming! But Caul was moments from taking power, and who knew how far echoes traveled in these caverns. They could still be minutes away, and by then it would be too late.

"Well, then," Caul said, "I suppose my remarks will have to wait." He tucked the paper back into his pocket. He seemed in no particular hurry, and it was driving Bentham mad.

"Go, Jack! Take your spirit and then I'll take mine!"

Caul sighed. "About that. You know, I've been thinking: I'm not sure you could handle all this power. You're weak-minded, see. By which I don't mean unintelligent. On the contrary, you're more intelligent than I am! But you *think* like a weak person. Your *will* is weak. It isn't enough to be smart, you know. You've got to be vicious!"

"No, brother! Don't do this!" Bentham begged. "I'll be your number two, your loyal confidant . . . anything you need me to be . . . "

Serves you right, I thought. *Keep talking . . .*

"This groveling is precisely what I mean," said Caul, shaking his head. "It's the sort of thing that could only change the mind of a weak-willed person, like yourself. But I am not susceptible to emotional entreaties."

"No, this is about revenge," Bentham said bitterly. "As if breaking my legs and enslaving me for years wasn't enough."

"Oh, it was, though," Caul said. "True, I was cross with you for turning us all into hollowgast, but having an army of monsters at my disposal turned out to be quite useful. But if I'm being honest, it's not even about your weak character. It's just . . . it's my own failing as a brother, I suppose. Alma can speak to this. I don't like to share."

"Then do it!" Bentham spat. "Get it over with and shoot me!"

"I could do that," Caul said. "But I think it would be more effective if I shot . . . him."

And he aimed the gun at my chest and pulled the trigger.

* * *

I felt the impact of the bullet almost before I heard the gun roar. It was like being walloped by giant, invisible fists. I was knocked off my feet and thrown backward, and then everything became abstract. I was looking up at the ceiling, my vision tunneled to a pinhole. Someone was screaming my name. Another gun fired, then fired again.

More screams.

I was dimly aware that my body was experiencing a great deal of pain. That I was dying.

Then Emma and Miss Peregrine were kneeling over me, anguished, shouting, the guard out of the picture. I couldn't understand their words, as if my ears were underwater. They were trying to move me, to drag me by the shoulders toward the door, but my body was limp and heavy. Then came a howl like hurricane winds from the direction of the spirit pool, and despite unbearable pain, I managed to turn my head and look.

Caul was standing calf-deep in the pool, his arms outstretched and head tilted back, in a state of paralysis as the vapor gripped him, merged with him. It poured into every opening in his face—tendrils of it sliding down his throat, ropes of it reeling up his nose, clouds of it settling into his eyes and ears. Then, in a matter of seconds, it was gone, the blue light that had shone throughout the cavern dimming to half strength, as if Caul had soaked up its power.

I could hear Miss Peregrine shouting. Emma picked up one of the guards' guns and emptied it at Caul. He wasn't far and she was a good shot. She must have hit him, but Caul didn't so much as flinch. Rather than falling, he seemed to be doing the opposite—he was *growing*. He was growing very quickly, doubling in height and breadth in just a few seconds. He let out an animal scream as his skin split open and healed, split open and healed. Soon he was a tower of raw pink flesh and tattered clothes, his giant eyes electric blue, a stolen soul having finally filled the old blankness he'd nurtured so long. Worst of all were his hands. They had become huge, gnarled things, thick and twisted like tree roots, ten fingers each.

Emma and Miss Peregrine tried again to drag me toward the door, but now Caul was coming after us. He stomped out of the spirit pool and bellowed in a bone-rattling voice: *"ALMA, COME BACK HERE!"*

Caul raised his awful hands. Some unseen force ripped Miss Peregrine and Emma away from me. They were pulled into the air and hovered there, flailing, ten feet off the ground, until Caul flipped his palms down again. Quick as a bounced ball, they slammed back to earth.

"I'LL GRIND YOU BETWEEN MY TEETH!" Caul howled, starting across the cavern toward them, his every footfall an earthquake.

Adrenaline, it seemed, had begun to focus my vision and hearing. I could imagine no crueler death sentence than this: to spend my last moments watching the women I loved be torn apart. And then

I heard a dog bark, and something worse occurred to me: watching my friends die, too.

Emma and Miss Peregrine ran. They had no choice. To come back for me now was impossible.

The others began pouring out of the corridor. Kids and ymbrynes, all mixed up. Sharon and the gallows riggers, too. Addison must have led them here, as he led all of them now, a lantern dangling from his mouth.

They had no idea what they were up against. I wished I could warn them—*don't bother fighting it, just run*—but they wouldn't have listened to me. They saw the towering beast and threw all they had at it. The gallows men pitched their hammers. Bronwyn hurled a chunk of wall she'd carried in, winding back and letting it go like a shot-put. Some of the kids had guns they'd taken from the wights, which they fired at Caul. The ymbrynes transformed into birds and swarmed his head, pecking him wherever they could.

None of it had the slightest effect on him. The bullets bounced off. He batted away the chunk of wall. He caught the hammers between his giant teeth and spat them out. Like a swarm of gnats, the ymbrynes seemed merely to irritate him. And then he spread his arms and his knotty fingers, the little feeder roots that dangled from them dancing like live wires, and slowly brought his palms together. As he did, all the ymbrynes circling his head were pushed away, and all the peculiars were smashed together in a clump.

He brought his palms together and folded them over and over as if crumpling a piece of paper. The ymbrynes and the peculiars rose from the ground in a spherical crush of limbs and wings. I was the only one left alone (except Bentham—where was Bentham?) and I tried get up, to stand and do something, but I could only lift my head. My God, they were being pulverized, their terrified screams echoing off the walls—and I thought that was it, that in a moment blood would pour from them like juice from a squeezed fruit, but then one of Caul's hands flew up and began to flap in front of his face, waving something away.

It was bees. A stream of Hugh's bees had flown out of the crush and now they were in Caul's eyes, stinging him as he let out a shattering howl. The ymbrynes and peculiars fell to the ground, the ball they'd formed collapsing, bodies spilling out everywhere. They hadn't been crushed, thank God.

Miss Peregrine, screeching and flapping in bird form, pulled people to their feet and propelled them toward the corridor. *Run. Run. Go!*

Then she winged off for Caul. He had dealt with the bees and was again spreading his arms, ready to scoop everyone up and splatter them against a wall. Before he could, Miss Peregrine dive-bombed him with her talons and raked deep cuts across his face. He spun to take a lumbering swipe at her, smacking her so hard she flew across the room, bounced off the wall, and fell to the ground, where she lay motionless.

By the time he turned back to deal with the others, they had nearly disappeared into the corridor. Caul extended his palm toward them, closed his hand and scooped it back—but they were farther away, apparently, than his powers of telekinesis would reach. Bellowing in frustration, he ran after them, then flopped onto his belly and tried to wriggle into the corridor after them. He could just fit inside, though it was a tight squeeze.

That's when, finally, I saw Bentham. He had rolled into the channel of water to hide, and now he was climbing out again, soaking wet but otherwise unaffected. He was bent over, his back to me, working at something—I couldn't see what.

I felt like I was coming back to life. The pain in my chest was receding. I tried to move my arms—an experiment—and found that I could. I slid them up my body and over my chest, expecting to find a couple of holes and a lot of blood. But I was dry. Instead of holes, my hands found a piece of metal flattened like a coin. I closed my hands around it, picked it up to look.

It was a bullet. It had not pierced my body. I was not dying. The bullet had embedded itself in my scarf.

The scarf Horace had knit for me.

He had known, somehow, that this would happen and had made me this scarf from the wool of peculiar sheep. Thank God for Horace . . .

I saw something flash across the room and lifted my head—I could just do it—to see Bentham standing with his eyes ablaze, cones of hot white light beaming from his sockets. He dropped something and I heard a tinkle of glass.

He'd taken a vial of ambro.

I used all my strength to turn onto my side, then curled and began to sit up. Bentham hurried along the walls, looking up at the jars. He was studying each one carefully.

As if he could see them.

And then I realized what he'd done, what he'd taken. He'd been saving my grandfather's stolen soul all these years, and now he'd consumed it.

He *could* see the jars. He could do what I did.

I was on my knees. Palms to the ground. Pulled one foot under me, then pushed myself up to standing. I was back, risen from the dead.

By then Caul had wriggled into the corridor and was halfway down it. I could hear my friends' voices echoing from the other end. They hadn't escaped yet. Perhaps they refused to leave Miss Peregrine behind (or me, possibly). They were still fighting.

Bentham was running now, as best he could. He'd spied the other large urn and was heading right for it. I took a few limping steps toward him. He reached the urn and tipped it over. Its blue liquid hissed into the channel and began circulating toward the spirit pool.

He turned and saw me.

He limped for the pool and I limped for him. The urn's liquid reached the pool. Its water began to rage and a column of blinding light shot up toward the ceiling.

"WHO IS TAKING MY SOULS!" Caul bellowed from the corridor. He began to worm his way back into the chamber.

I tackled Bentham—or fell on him, whichever you prefer. I was weak and dizzy, and he was old and brittle, and we were just about a match for each other. We struggled briefly, and when it was clear I had him pinned, he gave up.

"Listen to me," he said. "I've got to do this. I'm the only hope you have."

"Shut up!" I said, grabbing at his hands, which were still flailing. "I won't listen to your lies."

"He'll kill us all if you don't let me go!"

"Are you insane? If I let you go, you'll just help him!" I grabbed his wrists, finally. He'd been trying to get something from his pocket.

"No, I won't!" he cried. "I've made so many mistakes . . . but I can put them right if you let me help you."

"*Help* me?"

"Look in my pocket!"

Caul was backing slowly out of corridor, roaring about his souls.

"My vest pocket!" Bentham shouted. "There's a paper in it. One I carry with me always, just in case."

I let go of one of his hands and reached into his pocket. I found a small piece of folded paper, which I tore open.

"What is this?" I said. It was written in Old Peculiar; I couldn't read it.

"It's a recipe. Show it to the ymrbynes. They'll know what to do."

A hand reached over my shoulder and snatched the paper from me. I spun around to see Miss Peregrine, battered but human.

She read the paper. Her eyes flashed at Bentham. "You're certain this will work?"

"It worked once," he said. "I don't see why it shouldn't again. And with even more ymbrynes . . . "

"Let him go," she said to me.

I was shocked. "What? But he's going to—"

She put a hand on my shoulder. "I know."

"He stole my grandfather's soul! He's taken it . . . it's in him, right now!"

"I know, Jacob." She looked down at me, her face kind but firm. "That's all true and worse. And it was a good thing you caught him. But now you must let him go."

So I released his hand. Stood up, with help from Miss Peregrine. And then Bentham stood, too, a sad, bent-backed old man with the starry black drippings of my grandfather's soul running down his cheeks. For a moment I thought I could see a flash of Abe in his eyes—a little of his spirit there, sparking back at me.

Bentham turned and ran for the column of light and the spirit pool. The vapor was gathering into the shape of a giant almost as large as Caul, but with wings. If Bentham reached the pool in time, Caul would have a worthy challenger.

Caul was nearly out of the corridor now, and he was raging mad. "*WHAT HAVE YOU DONE!*" he cried. "*I'LL KILL YOU!*"

Miss Peregrine pushed me flat to the ground and lay beside me. "There's no time to hide," she said. "Play dead."

Bentham stumbled into the pool, and immediately the vapor began funneling into him. Caul had finally wriggled out of the corridor and lurched heavily to his feet, then ran toward Bentham. We were nearly crushed as one of his enormous feet crashed down not far from our heads, but Caul arrived at the pool too late to stop Bentham from merging with whatever old, great soul had been in that urn. Miss Peregrine's younger, weaker brother was already rocketing up to twice his original height.

Miss Peregrine and I helped each other up. Behind us, Caul and Bentham began to clash, the sound erupting like bombs. No one had to tell me to run.

We were halfway to the corridor when Emma and Bronwyn sped out of it to meet us. They caught us by the arms and whisked us toward safety faster than our weak and battered bodies could've managed alone. We didn't speak—there was no time to do anything but run, no way to shout loud enough to be heard—but Emma's face, electrified with wonder and relief at the simple fact that I was alive, said it all.

The black tunnel enveloped us. We'd made it. I looked back just once, to catch a glimpse of the riot exploding behind us. Through clouds of dust and vapor I saw two creatures, taller than houses, trying to murder each other: Caul choking Bentham with one spiky hand, gouging his eyes with the other. Bentham, insect-headed, thousands of eyes to spare, feeding on Caul's neck with long, flexible mandibles and battering him with great leathery wings. They danced, a tangle of limbs, slamming together into walls, the room coming down around them, the contents of countless shattered soul jars flying, a luminous rain.

With that preview of my nightmares thus cemented in my brain, I let Emma pull me into the dark.

*   *   *

We found our friends in the next chamber, swallowed by the dark, their only light a fading gleam from the lantern in Addison's mouth. When Emma fired a flame and they saw us loping toward them, worse for wear but alive, they let out a great whooping cheer. I saw them in her light and winced. They were in rough shape themselves, bloodied and bruised from being slammed around by Caul, a few limping on sprained or broken legs.

There was a momentary lull in the blasting noises coming from the cavern, and Emma was finally able to hug me. "I saw him shoot you! By what miracle are you alive?"

"By the miracle of peculiar sheep's wool and Horace's dreams!" I said, and then I kissed Emma and broke away to find Horace in the crowd. When I did, I hugged him so hard his patent leather shoes lifted off the ground. "I hope one day I'll be able to repay you for this," I said, tugging on my scarf.

"I'm so glad it helped!" he said, beaming at me.

The destruction resumed, the sound immense, unbelievable. Rocky debris rolled out of the corridor at us. Even if Caul and Bentham couldn't reach us from where they were, they could still bring the whole place crashing down on our heads. We had to get out of the library—and then out of this *loop*.

We ran, scraping and hobbling back the way we'd come, half of us a limping mess, the others acting as human crutches. Addison guided us with his nose, back through the maze and out the way we'd come. The sound of Caul and Bentham's battle seemed to pursue us, growing louder even as we got farther away, as if they were growing. How big could they get, and how strong? Perhaps the souls from all the jars they'd broken were raining into the pool, feeding them, making them even more monstrous.

Would the Library of Souls bury them? Would it be their grave, their prison? Or would it crack open like an eggshell and birth these horrors into the world?

We reached the grotto exit and dashed once again into the orange daylight. The rumble behind us had become constant, a quake that reverberated through the hills.

"We must keep going!" Miss Peregrine shouted. "To the loop exit!"

We were halfway there, stumbling through a clearing, when the ground beneath us shook so violently that we were all thrown off our feet. I'd never heard a volcano erupt in person, but it couldn't have sounded much scarier than the thunderous boom that echoed from the low hills behind us. We turned in shock to see acres of pulverized rock flying into the air—and then we heard, clear as day, the screams of Bentham and Caul.

They were free of the library now. They had torn through the cavern ceiling, and untold depths of stone, to daylight.

"We can't wait any longer!" Miss Peregrine cried. She picked herself up and held aloft Bentham's crumple of paper. "Sisters, it's time to close this loop!"

That's when I realized what it was he'd given us, and why Miss Peregrine had let him go. *A recipe*, he'd called it. *It worked once . . .*

It was the procedure he'd tricked Caul and his followers into enacting, all those years ago in 1908. The one that had collapsed the loop they were in, rather than resetting their internal clocks as they'd hoped. This time the collapse would be intentional. There was only one problem . . .

"Won't that turn them into hollows?" asked Miss Wren.

"A hollow's no problem," I said, "but last time someone collapsed a loop this way, didn't it make an explosion big enough to flatten half of Siberia?"

"The ymbrynes my brother coerced into helping him were young and inexperienced," Miss Peregrine said. "We'll do a better job."

"We'd better," said Miss Wren.

Over the hill, a giant face rose like a second sun peeking over the horizon. It was Caul, large as ten houses now. In a terrible voice that trumpeted across the hills, he bellowed, "*ALMAAAAAAAAA!*"

"He's coming for you, miss!" Olive cried. "We must get to safety!"

"In a moment, dear."

Miss Peregrine shooed all of us peculiar children (and Sharon and his cousins) a good distance away, then gathered the ymbrynes around her. They looked like some mystical secret society about to enact an ancient ritual. Which, I suppose, they were. Reading from the paper, Miss Peregrine said, "According to this, once we start the reaction, we'll have only a minute to escape the loop."

"Will that be that enough time?" said Miss Avocet.

"It'll have to be," said Miss Wren grimly.

"Perhaps we should get closer to the exit before we try," suggested Miss Glassbill, who had just recently come to her senses.

"There isn't time," said Miss Peregrine. "We have to—"

The rest of her sentence was drowned out by a distant-but-thunderous shout from Caul, his words gibberish now, his mind likely melting from the extraordinary stress of rapid growth. His breath reached us a few seconds after his voice, a foul yellow wind that curdled the air.

Bentham hadn't been heard from in a few minutes. I wondered if he'd been killed.

"Wish your elders luck!" Miss Peregrine shouted to us.

"Good luck!" we all cried.

"Don't blow us up!" Enoch added.

Miss Peregrine turned to her sisters. The twelve ymbrynes formed a tight circle and joined hands. Miss Peregrine spoke in Old Peculiar. The others replied in unison, all their voices rising in an eerie, lilting song. This went on for thirty seconds or more, during which time Caul started to climb out of the cavern, rubble tumbling down the hills where his massive hands grasped for purchase.

"Well, this is fascinating," Sharon said, "and you're all free to stay and watch, but I think my cousins and I will be going." He began to walk away, then saw that the path ahead split five ways, and the hard ground had captured none of our footprints. "Um," he said, turning back, "does anyone happen to remember the way?"

"You'll have to wait," Addison growled. "No one leaves until the ymbrynes do."

Finally they unclasped their hands and broke their circle.

"That's it?" Emma said.

"That's it!" Miss Peregrine replied, hurrying toward us. "Let's be on our way. We don't want to be here fifty-four seconds from now!"

Where the ymbrynes had been standing a crack was splitting open in the ground, the clay falling away into a quickly widening sinkhole from which a loud, almost mechanical buzz issued forth. The collapse had begun.

In spite of exhaustion and broken bodies and faltering steps, we ran, pushed faster by terror and awful, apocalyptic noises—and by the giant, lumbering shadow that fell across our path. We ran over ground that was splitting open, down ancient stairways that crumbled beneath our feet, back into the first house we'd exited from, choked with red dust from pulverizing walls, and finally into the passageway that led back to Caul's tower.

Miss Peregrine herded us through, the passageway disintegrating around us, and then out the other side, into the tower. I looked back to see the passage cave in behind us, a giant fist smashing down through its roof.

Miss Peregrine, frantic: "Where's the door gone? We must close it, or the collapse may spread beyond this loop!"

"Bronwyn kicked it in!" Enoch tattled. "It's broken!"

She'd been the first to reach it and, for Brownyn, kicking down the door had been faster than turning its knob. "I'm sorry!" she cried. "Have I doomed us all?"

The loop's shaking had begun to spread to the tower. It swayed, spilling us from one side of the hall to the other.

"Not if we can escape the tower," Miss Peregrine said.

"We're too high!" cried Miss Wren. "We'll never make it to the bottom in time!"

"There's an open deck just above us," I said. Though I wasn't sure why I said it, because leaping to our deaths seemed no better than being crushed in a collapsing tower.

"Yes!" cried Olive. "We'll jump!"

"Absolutely not!" Miss Wren said. "We ymbrynes would be just fine, but you children . . . "

"I can float us!" Olive said. "I'm strong enough!"

"No way!" Enoch said. "You're tiny, and there are too many of us!"

The tower rocked sickeningly. Ceiling tiles crashed down around us and cracks spidered through the floor.

"Fine, then!" Olive said. "Stay behind!"

She started upstairs. It took the rest of us only a moment, and one more wobble of the tower, to decide that Olive was our only hope.

Our lives were now in the dainty hands of our smallest member. Bird help us.

We ran up the sloping hallway, then out into open air and what remained of the day. Below us spread a commanding view of Devil's Acre: the compound and its pale walls, the misty chasm and its hollow-gapped bridge, the black tinders of Smoking Street and the packed tenements beyond—and then the Ditch, snaking along the loop's edge like a ring of scum. Whatever happened next, whether we lived or died, I'd be happy at least to see the last of this place.

We bellied up to the circular railing. Emma gripped my hand. "Don't look down, eh?"

One by one the ymbrynes turned to birds and perched on the rail, ready to help however they could. Olive took hold of the railing with both hands and slipped out of her shoes. Her feet bobbed upward until she was doing a weightless headstand on the rail, her heels aimed at the sky.

"Bronwyn, take my feet!" she said. "We'll make a chain. Emma grabs Bronwyn's legs, and Jacob Emma's legs, and Horace Emma's, and Horace Hugh's . . . "

"My left leg's hurt!" Hugh said.

"Then Horace will grab your right one!" Olive said.

"This is madness!" said Sharon. "We'll be much too heavy!"

Olive started to argue, but a sudden tremor shook the tower so hard that we had to cling to the rail or be shaken off.

It was Olive's way or nothing.

"You get the idea!" Miss Peregrine shouted. "Do as Olive says and, most importantly, don't let go until we reach the ground!"

Little Olive bent her knees, kicked one foot down toward Bronwyn, and offered it to her. Bronwyn took Olive's foot, then reached up and grabbed the other one. Olive let go of the rail and stood up in Bronwyn's hands, pushing toward the sky like a swimmer kicking off the wall of a pool.

Bronwyn was lifted off her feet. Emma quickly grabbed hold of Bronwyn's legs, and then she was lifted, too, as Olive strained upward, gritting her teeth, willing herself higher. Then it was my turn—but Olive, it seemed, was running out of lift power. She struggled and groaned, dog-paddling toward the sky, but she was out of juice. That's when Miss Peregrine turned into a bird, flapped into the air, hooked her talons through the back of Olive's dress, and lifted.

My feet came off the ground. Hugh grabbed onto my legs and Horace onto his legs and Enoch onto his and so on, until even Perplexus and Addison and Sharon and his cousins had caught a ride. We strung out into the air like a strange, wiggling kite, Millard its invisible tail. The other, smaller ymbrynes hooked into our clothes here and there and flapped furiously, adding what lift they could.

The last of us had only just left the tower when the whole thing began to crumble. I looked down in time to see it fall. It happened quickly, tumbling in on itself, the top section seeming to implode as if it had been sucked into the collapsing loop. After that the rest just went, tipping over in one section before breaking in the middle and slumping into a huge cloud of dust and debris, the sound like a million bricks being poured into a quarry. By then Miss Peregrine's strength was flagging and we were falling slowly toward the ground, the ymbrynes pulling us hard to one side for a soft landing away from the wreckage.

We touched down in the courtyard, Millard first and then finally Olive, who was so spent that she landed on her back and stayed there, breathing like she'd just run a marathon. We gathered around, cheering and applauding her.

Her eyes got big and she pointed up. "Look!"

In the air behind us, where the top of the tower had been just moments before, there spun a small vortex of shimmering silver, like a miniature hurricane. It was the last of the collapsing loop. We watched hypnotized as it shrank, spinning faster and faster. When it became too small to see, there issued from it a sound like the crack of a sonic boom:

"*ALMAAAAAAAAAA . . . *"

And then the whirlwind winked out, sucking Caul's voice away with it.

CHAPTER TEN

*A*fter the loop collapsed and the tower fell, we weren't allowed to stand shell-shocked and gaping—at least not for long. Though it seemed the worst dangers were behind us and most of our enemies had been felled or captured, there was chaos all around and work to be done. Despite our exhaustion and bruises and sprains, the ymbrynes set about doing what ymbrynes do best, which was to create order. They changed into human form and took charge. The compound was searched for hidden wights. Two surrendered outright, and Addison discovered another—a miserable-looking woman hiding in a hole in the ground.

She came out with her arms raised, begging for mercy. Sharon's cousins were employed constructing a makeshift jail to hold our small but growing number of prisoners, and they set happily to work, singing while they hammered. Sharon was interrogated by Miss Peregrine and Miss Avocet, but after just a few minutes of questioning, they were satisfied that he was merely a mercenary, not a secret operative or a traitor. Sharon had seemed as shocked by Bentham's betrayal as the rest of us.

In short order the wights' prisons and laboratories were emptied and their machines of terror smashed. The subjects of their horrible experiments were brought out into the open and attended to. Dozens more were freed from another block of cells. They emerged from the underground building where they'd been held looking thin and ragged. Some wandered in a daze and had to be corralled and watched, lest they walk away and get lost. Others were so over-

whelmed by gratitude that they couldn't stop thanking us. One small girl spent half an hour going from one peculiar to another, surprising us with hugs. "You don't know what you did for us," she kept saying. "You don't know what you did."

It was impossible not to be affected by it, and as we gave them what comfort we could, we were beset by sniffles and sighs. I could not begin to imagine what my friends had been through, much less those who'd spent weeks or months in Caul's keeping. Compared to that, my bruises and traumas were inconsequential.

The rescued peculiars I'll remember most were three brothers. They seemed in fair health but were so shocked by what they'd experienced that they would not speak. At the first opportunity they retreated from the crowd, found a bit of rubble to hunker on, and stared hollowly around them, the oldest with his arms stretched around the younger two. As if they could not quite square the scene before them with the hell they had accepted as reality.

Emma and I crossed to where they were sitting. "You're safe now," she said gently.

They looked at her as if they didn't know the meaning of the word.

Enoch saw us talking to them and came over with Bronwyn. She was dragging a barely conscious wight behind her, a white-coated lab worker with his hands tied. The boys recoiled.

"He can't hurt you anymore," Bronwyn said. "None of them can."

"Maybe we should leave him here with you awhile," said Enoch with a devilish grin. "I'll bet you'd have a lot to talk about."

The wight lifted his head. When he saw the boys, his blackened eyes widened.

"Stop it," I said. "Don't torment them."

The youngest boy's hands curled into fists and he started to get up, but the oldest boy held him back and whispered something in his ear. The younger boy closed his eyes and nodded, as if putting something away, then tucked his fists tightly under his arms.

"No thank'y," he said in a polite Southern drawl.

"Come on," I said, and we let them be, Bronwyn dragging the wight along behind her.

We milled about the compound, awaiting instructions from the ymbrynes. It was a relief, for once, not to be the ones who decided everything. We felt spent but energized, exhausted beyond belief but charged with the crazy knowledge that we had survived.

There were spontaneous bursts of cheering, laughter, songs. Millard and Bronwyn danced across the scarred ground. Olive and Claire clung to Miss Peregrine, who carried them in her arms as she buzzed around, checking on things. Horace kept pinching himself, suspicious that this was just one of his dreams, some beautiful future that hadn't yet come to be. Hugh wandered off by himself, no doubt missing Fiona, whose absence had left a hole in us all. Millard was busy fretting over his hero, Perplexus, whose rapid aging had stopped when we entered Abaton and, strangely, not yet resumed. But it would, Millard assured us, and now that Caul's tower was destroyed, it was unclear how Perplexus would reach his old loop. (There was Bentham's Panloopticon, of course, but which of its hundred doors was the right one?)

Then there was the matter of Emma and me. We were attached at the hip and yet hardly exchanged a word. We were afraid to talk to each other, I think, because of what we had to talk about.

What would happen next? What would become of us? I knew Emma couldn't leave peculiardom. She would have to live inside a loop for the rest of her life, be it Devil's Acre or some other, better place. But I was free to go. I had family and a home waiting for me. A life, or the pale approximation of one. But I had a family here, too. And I had Emma. And there was this new Jacob I had become, was still becoming. Would he survive back in Florida?

I needed all of it. Both families, both Jacobs—all of Emma. I knew I would have to choose, and I was afraid it would split me in half.

It was all too much, more than I could face so soon after the trials we'd just endured. I needed a few more hours, a day, to pretend. So Emma and I stood shoulder to shoulder and looked outward, throwing ourselves into whatever the ymbrynes needed of us.

The ymbrynes, overly protective by nature, decided we'd been through enough. We needed rest, and besides, there were tasks, they said, that peculiar children had no business taking part in. When the tower fell it had crushed a smaller building beneath it, but they didn't want us combing the wreckage for survivors. Elsewhere in the compound there were ambro vials to be recovered, which they didn't want us going near. I wondered what they'd do with them, or if those stolen souls could ever be reunited with their rightful owners.

I thought about the vial made from my grandfather's soul. I'd felt so violated when Bentham used it—and yet, if he hadn't, we never would have escaped the Library of Souls. So in the end, really, it was my grandfather's soul that had saved us. It was gratifying to know that at least it had not gone to waste.

There was work to be done outside the wights' compound, as well. Along Louche Lane and elsewhere in Devil's Acre, enslaved peculiar children needed to be freed, but the ymbrynes insisted they should be the ones to do it, along with some peculiar adults. As it happened, they would face no resistance: the slavers and other turncoats had fled the Acre the moment the wights fell. The children would be collected and brought to a safe house. The traitors hunted down and brought before tribunals. None of this was our concern, we were told. Right now we needed a place to recuperate, as well as a base of operations from which the reconstruction of peculiardom could begin—and none of us wanted to stay in the wights' fear-haunted fortress any longer than we had to.

I suggested Bentham's house. It had tons of space, beds, facilities, a live-in doctor, and a Panloopticon (which, you never know, might come in handy for something). We moved as dark was falling, loading one of the wights' transport trucks with those of us who couldn't walk, the rest marching behind it. We crossed out of the fortress with a little help from the bridge hollow, which lifted the truck across the gap first and the rest of us in groups of three. Some of the kids were frightened of the hollow and needed coaxing. Others couldn't wait and clamored for another ride once they'd crossed. I indulged them. My control over hollows had become second nature, which was satisfying if slightly bittersweet. Now that hollows were nearly extinct, my peculiar ability seemed obsolete—this manifestation of it, anyway. But I was okay with that. I didn't care about having a showy power; it was just a party trick now. I'd have been much happier if hollows had never existed.

We traveled through Devil's Acre in a slow procession, those of us on foot surrounding the vehicle like a float in a parade, others riding its bumpers and roof. It felt like a victory lap, and the Acre's peculiars flooded out of their homes and hovels to watch us pass by. They had seen the tower fall. They knew things had changed. Many applauded. Some gave salutes. Others lurked in the shadows, ashamed of the role they'd played.

When we arrived at Bentham's house, Mother Dust and Reynaldo met us at the door. We were welcomed warmly and told the house was ours to use as we needed. Mother Dust immediately began treating the injured, showing them to beds, making them comfortable, anointing them with dust. She offered to heal my bruises and the bite wounds across my stomach first, but I told her I could wait. Others were worse off.

I told her how I'd used her finger. How it had saved my life, and the lives of others. She shrugged it off and turned back to her work.

I insisted. "You deserve a medal," I said. "I don't know if peculiars give medals, but if they do I'll make sure you get one."

She seemed taken aback by this somehow, and let out a choking sob before hurrying away.

"Did I say something wrong?" I asked Reynaldo.

"I don't know," he said, concerned, and went after her.

Nim meandered about the house in a daze, unable to believe

what Bentham had done. "There must be some mistake," he kept repeating. "Mr. Bentham would *never* betray us like that."

"Snap out of it!" Emma said to him. "Your boss was a slime-ball."

The truth was a bit more nuanced, I thought, but making an argument for the complexity of Bentham's moral character wasn't going to make me terribly popular. Bentham didn't have to give up that recipe or take on his monstrous brother. He made a choice. In the end he'd damned himself in order to save the rest of us.

"He just needs time," Sharon said of Nim. "It's a lot to process. Bentham had a lot of us fooled."

"Even you?" I said.

"Me especially." He shrugged and shook his head. He seemed conflicted and sad. "He weaned me off ambrosia, pulled me out of addiction, saved my life. There was good in him. I suppose I let that blind me to the bad."

"He must've had *one* confidant," Emma said. "You know, a henchman. An Igor."

"His assistant!" I said. "Has anyone seen him?"

No one had. We searched the house for him, but Bentham's stone-faced right-hand man had disappeared. Miss Peregrine gathered everyone together and asked Emma and me describe him in detail, in case he returned. "He should be considered dangerous," she said. "If you see him, do not engage. Run and tell an ymbryne."

"Tell an ymbryne," Enoch muttered. "Doesn't she realize that *we* saved *them*?"

Miss Peregrine overheard him. "Yes, Enoch. You were brilliant, all of you. And you've grown up remarkably. But even grown-ups have elders who know better."

"Yes, miss," he said, chastened.

Afterward I asked Miss Peregrine if she thought Bentham had planned to betray us from the beginning.

"My brother was an opportunist above all else," she said. "I think part of him did want to do the right thing, and when he helped you and Miss Bloom, he did so genuinely. But all along he'd been making preparations to betray us, in case that turned out to be advantageous for him. And when I told him where to stuff it, he decided that it was."

"It wasn't your fault, Miss P," said Emma. "After what he did to Abe, I wouldn't have forgiven him, either."

"Still, I could have been kinder." She frowned, her eyes wandering. "Sibling relationships can be complex. I wonder, sometimes, if my own actions had some bearing upon the paths my brothers chose. Could I have been a better sister to them? Perhaps, as a young ymbryne, I was too focused on myself."

I said, "Miss Peregrine, that's"—and then stopped myself from using the word *ridiculous*, because I'd never had a brother or sister, and maybe it wasn't.

*   *   *

Later we took Miss Peregrine and some of the ymbrynes down to the basement to show them the heart of Bentham's Panloopticon machine. I could feel my hollow inside the battery chamber, weak but alive. I felt awful for it and asked if I could take it out, but Miss Peregrine said that for now they needed the machine working. Having so many loops accessible under one roof would allow them to spread news of our victory quickly throughout peculiardom, to assess the damage done by the wights and to begin rebuilding.

"I hope you understand, Mr. Portman," said Miss Peregrine.

"I do . . . "

"Jacob has a soft spot for that hollow," Emma said.

"Well," I said, a little embarrassed. "He was my first."

Miss Peregrine looked at me strangely but promised she'd do what she could.

The bite wound across my stomach was becoming too unbearable to ignore, so Emma and I joined the line to see Mother Dust, which snaked out of her makeshift clinic in the kitchen and down the hall. It was amazing to watch person after person hobble in, battered and bruised, nursing a broken toe or a mild concussion—or in Miss Avocet's case, a bullet from Caul's antique pistol lodged in her shoulder—only to stride out a few minutes later looking better than new. In fact, they were looking so good that Miss Peregrine pulled Reynaldo aside and asked him to remind Mother Dust that she was not a renewable resource, and not to waste herself on minor wounds that would heal just fine on their own.

"I tried to tell her myself," he replied, "but she's a perfectionist. She won't listen to me."

So Miss Peregrine went into the kitchen to have a word with Mother Dust in person. She came out again five minutes later looking sheepish, several cuts on her face having disappeared and her arm, which hadn't hung straight since Caul had slammed her into that cavern wall, swinging freely at her side. "What a stubborn woman!" she exclaimed.

When it was my turn to go in and see her, I almost refused treatment—she only had a thumb and forefinger left on her good hand. But she took one look at the zagging, blood-encrusted cuts across my belly and practically shoved me onto the cot they'd set up by the sink. The bite was becoming infected, she told me through Reynaldo. Hollow teeth were crawling with nasty bacteria, and left untreated I would get very sick. So I relented. Mother Dust sprinkled her powder across my torso, and in a few minutes I was feeling much improved.

Before I left, I tried to tell her again how much her sacrifice had meant, and how the piece of herself she'd given to me had saved us. "Really, without that finger, I never would've been able to—"

But she turned away as soon as I started talking, as if the words *thank you* burned her ears.

Reynaldo hurried me out. "I'm sorry, Mother Dust has many

other patients to see."

Emma met me in the hall. "You look marvelous!" she said. "Thank the birds, I was really starting to worry about that bite . . . "

"Be sure and tell her about your ears," I said.

"What?"

"Your *ears*," I said louder, pointing to them. Emma's ears hadn't stopped ringing since the library. Because she'd had to keep her hands aflame to light our way as we escaped, she hadn't been able to block out the terrific noise—which, I worried, had literally been deafening. "Just don't mention the finger!"

"The what?"

"The finger!" I said, holding up my finger. "She's very touchy about it. No pun intended . . . "

"Why?"

I shrugged. "No idea."

Emma went in. Three minutes later she came out snapping her fingers by her ears. "Amazing!" she said. "Clear as a bell."

"Thank goodness," I said. "Shouting is no fun."

"Ha. I mentioned the finger, by the way."

"What! Why?"

"I was curious."

"And?"

"Her hands started shaking. Then she mumbled something Reynaldo wouldn't translate, and he practically chased me out."

We might've pursued it further, I think, if we hadn't been so tired and hungry, and if at that moment the smell of food had not wafted its way past our noses.

"Come and get it!" Miss Wren shouted from down the hall, and the conversation was tabled.

*   *   *

As night fell we gathered to eat in Bentham's library, the only room big enough to hold all of us comfortably. The fire was stoked and a feast donated by grateful locals brought in, roast chicken and potatoes and wild game and fish (which I avoided, on the off chance they might have been caught in the Ditch). We ate and talked and rehashed the adventures of the past few days. Miss Peregrine had heard only a little about our journey from Cairnholm to London, and then across bombed-out London to reach Miss Wren, and wanted to know every last detail. She was a great listener, always laughing at the funny parts and reacting with satisfying gasps to our dramatic flourishes.

"And then the bomb fell right on the hollow and blew it to *smithereens*!" Olive cried, leaping out of her chair as she reenacted the moment. "But we had Miss Wren's peculiar sweaters on, so the shrapnel didn't kill us!"

"Oh my heavens!" Miss Peregrine said. "That was very lucky!"

When our stories had finished, Miss Peregrine sat quietly for a time, studying us with a mixture of sadness and awe. "I'm so very, very proud of you," she said, "and so sorry for all that happened. I can't tell you how much I wish it had been me by your side, and not my deceitful brother."

We observed a moment of silence for Fiona. She wasn't dead, Hugh insisted, but merely lost. The trees had cushioned her fall, he said, and she was probably wandering in the forest somewhere near Miss Wren's menagerie. Or had knocked her head on the way down and forgotten where she came from. Or was hiding . . .

He looked around hopefully at us, but we avoided his eyes.

"I'm sure she'll turn up," Bronwyn assured him.

"Don't give him false hope," Enoch said. "It's cruel."

"You would know about cruel," Bronwyn replied scornfully.

"Let's change the subject," Horace said. "I want to know how the dog rescued Jacob and Emma in the Underground."

Addison hopped gamely onto the table and began to narrate

the story, but he embellished it with so many asides about his own heroism that Emma was forced to take over. Together, she and I told them how we'd found our way to Devil's Acre, and how with Bentham's help we'd mounted our mini-invasion of the wights' compound. Then everyone had questions for me—they wanted to know about the hollows.

"How did you teach yourself their language?" Millard asked.

"What's it like to control one?" asked Hugh. "Do you imagine you're one of them, like I do my bees?"

"Does it tickle?" asked Bronwyn.

"Do you ever wish you could keep one as a pet?" asked Olive.

I answered as best I could but was feeling tongue-tied because it was a hard thing to describe, my connection with the hollows, like piecing together a dream the morning after. I was distracted, too, by the talk Emma and I had been putting off. When I'd finished, I caught Emma's eye and nodded to the door, and we excused ourselves. As we walked away from the table, I could feel the eyes of the room on our backs.

We ducked into a lantern-lit cloakroom cramped with coats, hats, and umbrellas. It was not a spacious or comfortable place, but it was at least private; somewhere we wouldn't be walked in on or overheard. I felt suddenly and irrationally terrified. I had a difficult choice to make, one I had not fully grappled with until now.

We were silent for a moment, facing each other, the room so deadened by fabric that I thought I could hear the beating of our hearts.

"So," Emma said, because of course she would start first. Emma, always direct, never afraid of an awkward moment. "Will you stay?"

I did not know what I would say until the words left my mouth. I was running on autopilot, no filter. "I have to see my parents."

That was unquestionably true. They were hurting and frightened and didn't deserve to be, and I had left them dangling too long.

"Of course," Emma said. "I understand. Of course you do."

A question hung in the air, unasked. *See my parents* had been a half-measure, a non-answer. *See* them, sure. And then what? What would I say to them?

I tried to imagine telling my parents the truth. In that regard, the phone conversation I'd had with my father in the Underground had been a preview of coming attractions. *He's lost it. Our son is insane. Or on drugs. Or maybe not on enough drugs.*

No, the truth wouldn't work. So, what? I would see them, assure them I was alive and well, make up a story about sightseeing in London, then tell them to go home without me? Ha. They would chase me. They'd have cops hiding in the bushes at our meeting place. Men in white coats with Jacob-sized nets. I'd have to run. Telling them the truth would only make things worse. Seeing them only to run away again would torture them more. But the idea of not seeing my parents at all, of never going home again—I couldn't get my mind around it. Because, if I was really being honest with myself, as much as it hurt to think about leaving Emma and my friends and this world, part of me wanted to go home. My parents and their world represented a return to sanity and predictability, something I was longing for after all this madness. I needed to be normal for a while. To catch my breath. Just for a while.

I had repaid my debt to the peculiars and Miss Peregrine. I had become one of them. But I wasn't *only* one of them. I was also my parents' son, and as imperfect as they were, I missed them. I missed home. I even sort of missed my dumb, ordinary life. Of course, I would probably miss Emma more than any of those things. The problem was, I wanted too much. I wanted both lives. Dual citizenship. To be peculiar, and learn everything there was to learn about the peculiar world, and to be with Emma, and explore all the loops Bentham had catalogued in his Panloopticon. But also to do the stupid, ordinary things normal teenagers do, while I could still pass for one. Get my driver's license. Make a friend my own age. Finish high school. Then I'd be eighteen, and I could go anywhere I wanted—or any*when*. I could come back.

Here was the truth, the root and bone of it: I couldn't live the rest of my life in a time loop. I didn't want to be a peculiar child forever. But one day, maybe, I could be a peculiar adult.

Maybe, if I was very careful, there was a way to have it all.

"I don't want to go," I said, "but I think I might need to, for a while."

Emma's expression flattened. "Then go," she said.

I was stung. She hadn't even asked what "a while" meant.

"I'll come visit," I said quickly. "I can come back anytime."

Theoretically, this was true: now that the wight menace had been crushed, there would—bird willing—always be something to come back to. But it was hard to imagine my parents signing off on more trips to the U.K. anytime soon. I was lying to myself—to both of us—and Emma knew it.

"No," she said. "I don't want that."

My heart dropped. "What?" I said quietly. "Why not?"

"Because that's what Abe did. Every few years he'd come back. And every time he was older and I was the same. And then he met someone and got married . . . "

"I wouldn't do that," I said. "I love you."

"I know," she said, turning away. "So did he."

"But we're not . . . it won't be like that with us . . . " I grasped blindly for the right words, but my thoughts were a muddle.

"It would, though. You know I'd go with you if I could, but I can't—I would age forward. So I'd just be waiting for you. Frozen in amber. I can't do that again."

"It wouldn't be long! Just a couple of years. And then I could do what I wanted. I could go to college somewhere. Maybe here in London!"

"Maybe," she said. "Maybe. But now you're making promises you might not be able to keep, and that's how people in love get very badly hurt."

My heart was racing. I felt desperate and pathetic. Screw it, I'd never see my parents again. Fine. But I couldn't lose Emma.

"I wasn't thinking straight," I said. "I didn't mean it. I'll stay."

"No, I think you were being honest," she said. "I think if you stay you won't be happy. And eventually you'll come to resent me for it. And that would be worse."

"No. No, I would never . . . "

But I'd shown my hand, and now it was too late to take it back.

"You should go," she said. "You have a life and a family. This was never supposed to be forever."

I sat down on the floor, then leaned back into the wall of coats and let them swallow me up. For a few long seconds I pretended none of this was happening, that I wasn't here, that my entire world was woolen and black and smelled of mothballs. When I surfaced again to breathe, Emma was sitting cross-legged on the floor beside me.

"I don't want this either," she said. "But I think I understand why it has to be. You have your world to rebuild, and I have mine."

"But it's mine too, now," I said.

"That's true." She thought for a moment, kneading her chin. "That's true, and I very much hope you do come back, because you've become a part of us, and our family won't feel whole without you. But when you do, I think you and I should just be friends."

I thought about that for a moment. Friends. It sounded so pale and lifeless.

"I guess it's better than never talking again."

"I agree," she said. "I don't think I could bear that."

I scooted next to her and put my arm around her waist. I thought she might pull away, but she didn't. After a while, her head tipped onto my shoulder.

We sat like that for a long time.

*　　*　　*

When Emma and I finally emerged from the cloakroom, most everyone was asleep. The hearth in the library was burned down to embers, the platters overflowing with food reduced to scraps, the room's high ceilings echoing with contented snores and murmurs. Kids and ymbrynes lay draped across couches and curled upon the rug, even though there were plenty of comfortable bedrooms upstairs. Having nearly lost one another, they weren't about to let go again so soon, even if just for the night.

I would leave in the morning. Now that I knew what had to happen between Emma and me, a longer delay would only torment us. Right now, though, we needed sleep. How long had it been since we'd closed our eyes for more than a minute or two? I couldn't remember feeling more exhausted.

We piled some cushions in a corner and fell asleep holding each other. It was our last night together, and I clung tight, my arms locked around her, as if by squeezing hard enough I could lock her into my sense memory. How she felt, how she smelled. The sound of her breathing as it slowed and evened. But sleep pulled me down hard, and it seemed I'd only just closed my eyes when suddenly I was squinting against glaring yellow daylight pouring in from a bank of high windows.

Everyone was awake and milling around the room, talking in whispers so as not to disturb us. We untangled ourselves in a hurry, self-conscious without the privacy of the dark. Before we'd had a chance to compose ourselves, in breezed Miss Peregrine with a pot of coffee and Nim with a tray of mugs. "Good morning, all! I trust you're well-rested, because we've got lots of—"

Miss Peregrine saw us and stopped midsentence, her eyebrows rising.

Emma hid her face. "Oh, *no*."

In the exhaustion and emotion of last night, it hadn't occurred

— ⟫⟩◆⟨⟪ **423** ⟫⟩◆⟨⟪ —

to me that sleeping in the same bed as Emma (even if sleeping is all we did) might offend Miss Peregrine's Victorian sensibilities.

"Mr. Portman, a word." Miss Peregrine set down the coffeepot and crooked a finger at me.

Guess I was taking the rap for this one. I stood up and smoothed my rumpled clothes, color rising in my cheeks. I wasn't ashamed in the least, but it was hard not to feel a little embarrassed.

"Wish me luck," I whispered to Emma.

"Admit nothing!" she whispered back.

I heard giggles as I crossed the room, and someone chanting, "Jacob and Emma, sittin' in a tree . . . y-m-b-r-y-n-e!"

"Oh, grow up, Enoch," said Bronwyn. "You're just jealous."

I followed Miss Peregrine into the hall.

"Nothing happened," I said, "just so you know."

"I'm sure I'm not interested," she said. "You're leaving us today, correct?"

"How did you know?"

"I may, strictly speaking, be an elderly woman, but I've still got my wits about me. I know you feel torn between your parents and us, your old home and your new one . . . or what's left of it. You want to strike a balance without choosing sides, and without hurting any of the people you love. But it isn't easy. Or even, necessarily, possible. Is that about the size of it?"

"It's . . . yeah. That's pretty much it."

"And where have you left things with Miss Bloom?"

"We're friends," I said, testing the word uneasily.

"And you're unhappy about it."

"Well, yeah. But I understand . . . I think."

She cocked her head. "Do you?"

"She's protecting herself."

"And you," Miss Peregrine added.

"That I don't get."

"You're very young, Jacob. There are many things you're not

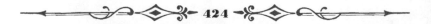

likely to 'get.'"

"I don't see what my age has to do with it."

"Everything!" She laughed, quick and sharp. And then she saw that I really didn't understand, and she softened a bit. "Miss Bloom was born near the turn of the last century," she said. "Her heart is old and steady. Perhaps you worry she'll soon replace you—that some peculiar Romeo will turn her head. I wouldn't count it likely. She's fixed on you. I've never seen her as happy with anyone. Even Abe."

"Really?" I said, a surge of warmth building in my chest.

"Really. But as we've established, you're young. Only sixteen—sixteen for the first time. Your heart is just waking up, and Miss Bloom is your first love. Is she not?"

I nodded sheepishly. But yes, undoubtedly. Anyone could see it.

"You may have other loves," Miss Peregrine said. "Young hearts, like young brains, can have short attention spans."

"I don't," I said. "I'm not like that."

I knew it sounded like something an impulsive teenager would say, but at that moment, I was as sure about Emma as I'd ever been about anything.

Miss Peregrine nodded slowly. "I'm glad to hear that," she said. "Miss Bloom may have given you permission to break her heart, but I have not. She's very important to me, and not half as tough as she lets on. I can't have her mooning about and setting things on fire should you find yourself distracted by the feeble charms of some normal girl. I've been through that already, and we simply haven't the furniture to spare. Do you understand?"

"Um," I said, caught off guard, "I think so . . . "

She stepped closer and said it again, her voice dropping low and stony. "Do you understand?"

"Yes, Miss Peregrine."

She nodded sharply, then smiled and patted my shoulder. "Okay, then. Good talk." And before I could respond she was marching back into the library and calling out, "Breakfast!"

*　　*　　*

I left an hour later, accompanied to the dock by Emma and Miss Peregrine and a full complement of our friends and ymbrynes. Sharon was waiting with a new boat left behind by fleeing Ditch pirates. There was a long exchange of hugs and tearful goodbyes, which ended with me promising I would come and see everyone again—even though I didn't know how I'd manage that anytime soon, what with international flights to pay for and parents to convince.

"We'll never forget you, Jacob!" Olive said, sniffling.

"I shall record your story for posterity," Millard promised. "That will be my new project. And I'll see that it's included in a new edition of the *Tales of the Peculiar*. You'll be famous!"

Addison approached with the two grimbear cubs trailing him. I couldn't tell if he had adopted them or they him. "You're the fourth-bravest human I've ever known," he said. "I hope we'll meet again."

"I hope so, too," I said, and meant it.

"Oh, Jacob, may we come and visit you?" begged Claire. "I've always wanted to see America."

I didn't have the heart to explain why it wasn't possible. "Of course you can," I said. "I'd love that."

Sharon rapped his staff on the side of the boat. "All aboard!"

Reluctantly I climbed in, and then Emma and Miss Peregrine boarded, too. They had insisted on staying with me until I met my parents, and I hadn't put up a fight. It would be easier to say goodbye in stages.

Sharon unmoored the boat and we pushed off. Our friends waved and called to us as we floated away. I waved back, but it hurt too much to watch them recede, so I half closed my eyes until the current had taken us around a bend in the Ditch, and they were gone.

None of us felt like talking. In silence we watched the sagging buildings and rickety bridges pass. After a while we came to the crossover, were sucked rudely through the same underpass by which we'd entered, and spat out the other side into a muggy, modern afternoon. The crumbling tenements of Devil's Acre were gone, glass-fronted condos and shining office towers risen up in their place. A motorboat buzzed past.

The sounds of a busy, preoccupied present-day filtered in. A car alarm. A cell phone ringing. Jangly pop music. We passed a fancy canal-side restaurant, but thanks to Sharon's enchantment, the diners on the patio didn't see us as we floated by. If they had, I wondered what they would've thought of us: two teenagers in black, a woman in Victorian formalwear, and Sharon in his Grim Reaper cloak, poling us out of the underworld. Who knows—maybe the modern world was so jaded that no one would have batted an eye.

My parents were another story, though—and now that we were back in the present, just what that story would be was starting to concern me. They already thought I'd lost my mind, or gotten into hard drugs. I'd be lucky if they didn't ship me off to a mental hospital. Even if they didn't, I'd be doing damage control for years. They would never trust me again.

But it was my struggle, and I would find a way to deal with it. The easiest thing for *me* would be to tell them the truth—but again, I couldn't. My parents would never understand this part of my life, and to try and force them to could land *them* in a mental hospital.

My dad already knew more about the peculiar children than was good for him. He'd met them all on Cairnholm, though he'd thought he was dreaming. Then Emma had left him that letter and a photo of herself with my grandfather. As if that weren't bad enough, over the phone I'd actually *told* my dad I was peculiar. That had been a mistake, I realized, and selfish. And now here I was heading to meet them with Emma and Miss Peregrine at my side.

"On second thought," I said, turning to them in the boat, "Maybe you shouldn't come with me."

"Why not?" Emma said. "We won't age forward *that* quickly . . ."

"I don't think my parents should see me with you. This is all going to be hard enough to explain as it is."

"I've given some thought to this," said Miss Peregrine.

"To what? My parents?"

"Yes. I can help you with them, if you like."

"How?"

"One of an ymbryne's myriad duties is dealing with normals who become problematically curious about us, or otherwise trouble-some. We have ways of making them uncurious, of making them forget they've seen certain things."

"Did you know about this?" I asked Emma.

"Sure. If it wasn't for the wipe, peculiars would be in the news every other day."

"So it . . . wipes people's memories?"

"It's more a selective cherry-picking of certain inconvenient recollections," said Miss Peregrine. "It's quite painless and has no side effects. Still, it may strike you as extreme. I leave it to your discretion."

"Okay," I said.

"Okay what?" said Emma.

"Okay, please do the memory wipe thing to my parents. That sounds amazing. And while you're at it, there was this time when I was twelve that I crashed my mom's car into the garage door . . . "

"Let's not get carried away, Mr. Portman."

"Just kidding," I said, though I'd only sort of been. Either way, I was hugely relieved. Now I wouldn't have to spend the rest of my adolescence apologizing for the time I ran away, made my parents think I was dead, and nearly ruined their lives forever. Which was nice.

CHAPTER ELEVEN

*S*haron dropped us off at the same dark, rat-infested under-jetty where we'd first met him. Stepping off his boat there gave me a twinge of bittersweet nostalgia. I may have been terrified and filthy and in various exotic forms of pain every second of the last several days, but I would probably never have an adventure like this again. I would miss it—not so much the trials I'd endured as the person I'd been while I endured them. There was an iron will inside me, I knew that now, and I hoped I could hang on to it even as my life grew softer.

"So long," Sharon said. "I'm glad I met you, despite all the endless trouble you caused me."

"Yeah, me too." We shook hands. "It's been interesting."

"Wait here for us," Miss Peregrine said to him. "Miss Bloom and I will be back within an hour or two."

Finding my parents turned out to be easy. It would've been even easier if I'd still had my phone, but as it was, all we had to do was report to a police station. I was a known missing person, and within half an hour of giving an officer my name and sitting down on a bench to wait, my mother and father arrived. They were wearing rumpled clothes that had clearly been slept in, my mother's normally perfect makeup was a mess, my dad had a three-day beard, and they were both holding stacks of MISSING posters with my face on them. I felt instantly and comprehensively awful for what I'd put them through. But as I tried to apologize, they dropped the posters and wrapped me in a two-way hug, and my words were lost in the folds of my dad's sweater.

"Jake, Jake, ohmygod, my little Jake," my mother cried.

"It's him, it's really him," my father said. "We were so worried, we were *so* worried . . ."

How long had I been gone? A week? Something like that, though it seemed like an eternity.

"Where *were* you?" my mother said. "What were you *doing*?"

The hug broke but still I couldn't get a word in.

"Why did you run away like that?" my father demanded. "What were you thinking, Jacob?"

"You gave me gray hairs!" my mother said, then threw her arms around me a second time.

My dad looked me over. "Where are your clothes? What's this you're wearing?"

I was still in my black adventure clothes. Oops. They'd be easier to explain than nineteenth-century clothes, though, and thankfully Mother Dust had healed all the cuts on my face . . .

"Jacob, say something!" my father demanded.

"I'm really, really sorry," I said. "I would never have put you through this if I could've helped it, but everything's okay now. Things are going to be fine. You won't understand, and that's okay, too. I love you guys."

"You're right about one thing," my dad said. "We don't understand. At all."

"But it's not okay," said my mom. "You *will* give us an explanation."

"We'll need one, too," said a police officer who'd been standing by. "And a drug test."

Things were slipping beyond my control. It was time to pull the rip cord.

"I'll tell you everything," I said, "but first I'd like you to meet a friend of mine. Mom, Dad, this is Miss Peregrine."

I saw my dad's eyes go to Miss P, then to Emma. He must've recognized her, because he looked like he'd seen a ghost. But it was okay—he would forget soon enough.

"Pleased to make your acquaintance," said Miss Peregrine, shaking both my parents' hands. "You have a terrific son, just a top-notch boy. Not only is Jacob a perfect gentleman, he's even more talented than his grandfather."

"His grandfather?" said my dad. "How do you . . . "

"Who is this bizarre woman?" my mother said. "How do you know our son?"

Miss Peregrine gripped their hands and stared deeply into their eyes. "Alma Peregrine, Alma LeFay Peregrine. Now, I understand you've had a dreadful time here in the British Isles. Just an awful trip. I think it would be best for everyone involved if you just forgot it ever happened. Don't you agree?"

"Yes," my mother said, a faraway look in her eyes.

"I agree," said my father, sounding slightly hypnotized.

Miss Peregrine had paused their brains.

"Fantastic, wonderful," she said. "Now cast your eyes upon this, please." She let go of their hands and drew a long, blue-spotted falcon feather from her pocket. And then a hot wave of guilt flashed through me, and I stopped her.

"Wait," I said. "I don't think I want you to do it, after all."

"Are you sure?" She looked a bit disappointed. "It could get very complicated for you."

"It feels like cheating," I said.

"Then what will you tell them?" Emma asked.

"I don't know yet. But it doesn't seem right to just . . . wipe their brains."

If telling them the truth was selfish, it seemed doubly so to sim-ply erase the need for an explanation. And what about the police? My extended family? My parents' friends? Surely they all knew I'd been missing, and for my parents to forget what had happened . . . it would've been a mess.

"That's up to you," said Miss Peregrine. "But I think it would be wise to at least let me wipe the past two or three minutes, so they'll forget Miss Bloom and me."

"Well . . . okay," I said. "So long as they don't lose the English language along with it."

"I'm very precise," said Miss Peregrine.

"What's all this about wiping brains?" said the police officer. "Who are you?"

"Alma Peregrine," said Miss Peregrine, rushing over to shake his hand. "Alma Peregrine, Alma LeFay Peregrine."

The officer's head dropped, and he was suddenly fascinated by a spot on the floor.

"I can think of a few wights you might've done that to," said Emma.

"Unfortunately, it only works on the pliable minds of normals," Miss Peregrine said. "Speaking of which." She held up the feather.

"Wait," I said. "Before you do." I put out my hand for her to shake. "Thank you for everything. I'm really going to miss you, Miss Peregrine."

Miss Peregrine ignored my hand and hugged me. "The feeling is mutual, Mr. Portman. And I'm the one who should be thanking you. If it hadn't been for your and Miss Bloom's heroism . . . "

"Well," I said, "if it hadn't been for you saving my grandfather all those years ago . . . "

She smiled. "Let's call it even."

There was one goodbye left. The hardest one. I put my arms around Emma, and she squeezed back ferociously.

"Can we write to each other?" she said.

"Are you sure you want to?"

"Of course. Friends keep in touch."

"Okay," I said, relieved. At least we could—

And then she kissed me. A big, full-on-the-lips kiss that left my head spinning.

"I thought we were just friends!" I said, pulling back in surprise.

"Um, yes," she said sheepishly. "*Now* we are. I just needed one to remember us by."

We were both laughing, our hearts soaring and breaking at once.

"Children, stop that!" Miss Peregrine hissed.

"Frank," my mother said faintly, "who is that girl Jake's kissing?"

"I haven't the slightest idea," my father mumbled. "Jacob, who is that girl, and why are you kissing her?"

My cheeks flushed. "Um, this is my . . . friend. Emma. We're just saying goodbye."

Emma waved bashfully. "You won't remember me, but . . . hello!"

"Well, stop kissing strange girls and come along," said my mother.

"Okay," I said to Miss Peregrine. "I'd guess we'd better get on with it."

"Don't think this is goodbye," Miss Peregrine said. "You're one of us now. You won't get rid of us that easily."

"I sure hope not," I said, grinning despite a heavy heart.

"I'll write you," Emma said, trying to smile, her voice cracking. "Good luck with . . . whatever it is normal people do."

"Goodbye, Emma. I'll miss you." It seemed so inadequate a thing to say, but at times like this, words themselves were inadequate.

Miss Peregrine turned to finish her work. She raised the falcon feather and tickled my parents under their noses.

"Excuse me!" my mother said, "what do you think you're doooo-AAAAAA-*CHOO*!"

And then both she and my father had a sneezing fit, and while they were sneezing, Miss Peregrine tickled the police officer, and he had a sneezing fit, too. By the time they were all finished, noses running and red in the face, Miss Peregrine and Emma had whisked out the door and were gone.

"As I was saying," my dad said, picking up as if the last few minutes hadn't happened. "Wait . . . what *was* I saying?"

"That we could just go home and talk about all this later?" I said hopefully.

"Not before you answer some questions," the officer said.

We spent a few minutes talking to the police. I kept my answers vague, laced every sentence with an apology, and swore up and down that I hadn't been abducted, abused, or drugged. (Thanks to Miss Peregrine's memory wipe, the officer had forgotten about making me take that drug test.) When my parents explained about my grandfather's death and the "troubles" I'd suffered following it, the police seemed satisfied that I was just a garden-variety runaway who'd forgotten to take his meds. They made us sign a few forms and sent us on our way.

"Yes, yes, let's please go home," my mother said. "But we *will* talk about this, young man. In *depth*."

Home. The word had become foreign to me. Some distant land I could hardly imagine.

"If we hurry," said my dad, "we might be able to catch an evening flight . . . "

He had cemented his arm around my shoulder, as if afraid I'd run away the moment he let go. My mom couldn't stop staring at me, her eyes wide and grateful, blinking back tears.

"I'm okay," said, "I promise."

I knew they didn't believe me, and wouldn't for a long while.

We went outside to hail a black cab. As one was pulling up, I saw two familiar faces watching me from a park across the street. Occupying the dappled shade of an oak were Emma and Miss Peregrine. I raised a hand goodbye, my chest aching.

"Jake?" My dad was holding the cab door open for me.

"What's the matter?"

I turned my wave into a head scratch. "Nothing, Dad."

I got into the cab. My dad turned to stare into the park. When I looked out the window, all I saw under the oak were a bird and some blowing leaves.

*　　*　　*

My return home was neither triumphant nor easy. I had shattered my parents' trust, and piecing it back together would be slow, painstaking work. Considered a flight risk, I was watched all the time. I went nowhere unsupervised, not even for walks around the block. A complicated security system was installed in the house, less to stop thieves from getting in than me sneaking out. I was rushed back into therapy, subjected to countless psychological evaluations, and prescribed new, stronger drugs (which I hid under my tongue and later spat out). But I'd endured far worse deprivations that summer, and if a temporary loss of freedom was the price I had to pay for the friends I'd made, the experiences I'd had, and the extraordinary life I now knew to be mine, it seemed a bargain. It was worth every awkward conversation with my parents, every lonely night spent dreaming about Emma and my peculiar friends, every visit to my new psychiatrist.

She was an unflappable older lady named Dr. Spanger, and I spent four mornings a week in the glow of her face-lifted permasmile. She questioned me incessantly about why I'd run away from the island and how I'd spent the days after, that smile never wavering. (Her eyes, for the record, were dishwater brown, pupils normal, no contacts.) The story I concocted was a temporary insanity plea sprinkled with a dash of memory loss, every bit of which was totally unverifiable. It went like this: frightened by what appeared to be a sheep-murdering maniac loose on Cairnholm, I cracked, stowed away on a boat to Wales, briefly forgot who I was, and hitchhiked to

London. I slept in parks, spoke to no one, made no acquaintances, consumed no mood- or mind-altering substances, and wandered the city for several days in a disoriented fugue state. As for the phone call with my father in which I'd admitted to being "peculiar"—um, what phone call? I couldn't remember any phone call . . .

Eventually Dr. Spanger chalked the whole thing up to a manic episode, characterized by delusions, triggered by stress, grief, and unresolved grandpa issues. In other words: I'd gone a little nuts, but it was probably a one-time thing and I was feeling much better now, thank you. Still, my parents were on pins and needles. They were waiting for me to crack, do something crazy, run away again—but I was on my best behavior. I played the role of good kid and penitent son like I was out to win an Oscar. I volunteered my help around the house. I rose long before noon and hung out in plain view of my watchful parents. I watched TV with them and ran errands and lingered at the table after meals to participate in the inane discussions they liked to have—about bathroom remodeling, homeowners' association politics, fad diets, birds. (There was never more than a glancing allusion to my grandfather, the island, or my "episode.") I was pleasant, kind, patient, and in a hundred ways not quite the son they remembered. They must've thought I'd been abducted by aliens and replaced with a clone or something—but they weren't complaining. And after a few weeks, it was deemed safe to bring the family around, and this uncle or that aunt would drop by for a little coffee and stilted conversation, and so I could demonstrate in person how sane I was.

Weirdly, my dad never mentioned the letter Emma had left for him back on the island, nor the photo of her and Abe tucked inside it. Maybe it was more than he could deal with, or maybe he worried that talking about it with me might trigger a relapse. Whatever the reason, it was like it never happened. As for having actually met Emma and Millard and Olive, I'm sure he'd long ago dismissed that as a bizarre dream.

After a few weeks my parents began to relax. They'd bought my story and Dr. Spanger's explanations for my behavior. They could've probed deeper, probably—asked more questions, gotten a second or third opinion from other psychiatrists—but they really wanted to believe I was doing better. That whatever drugs Dr. Spanger had put me on were working their magic. More than anything, they wanted our lives to return to normal, and the longer I was home, the more that seemed to be happening.

Privately, though, I was struggling to adjust. I was bored and lonely. The days dragged. I had thought, after the hardships of the past few weeks, that the comforts of home would be sweeter, but pretty soon even laundered sheets and Chinese takeout lost their luster. My bed was too soft. My food too rich. There was too *much* of everything, and it made me feel guilty and decadent. Sometimes, wandering mall aisles on an errand with my parents, I would think about the people I'd seen living on the margins of Devil's Acre and get angry. Why did we have more than we knew what to do with, while they had less than they needed to stay alive?

I had trouble sleeping. I woke at odd hours, my mind looping scenes from my time with the peculiars. Though I'd given Emma my address and checked the mailbox several times a day, no letters had arrived from her or the others. The longer I went without hearing from them—two weeks, then three—the more abstract and unreal the whole experience began to seem. Had it really happened? Had it all been a delusion? In dark moments, I wondered. What if I *was* crazy?

So it was much to my relief when, a month after returning home, a letter finally arrived from Emma. It was short and breezy, just filling me in on the rebuilding process and asking me how things were going. The return address was a post office box in London, which Emma explained was close enough to the Devil's Acre loop entrance that she could sneak into the present fairly often and check it. I wrote back the same day, and pretty soon we were exchanging two or three letters a week. As home grew more suffocating, those letters became a lifeline.

I couldn't risk my parents finding one, so every day I stalked the mailman and dashed out to meet him as soon as he appeared at the end of our driveway. I suggested to Emma that we trade e-mails instead, which would have been safer and faster, and I filled several pages attempting to explain what the Internet was and how she might find a public Internet café and create an e-mail address—but it was hopeless; she'd never even used a keyboard. The letters were worth the risk, though, and I came to enjoy communicating by hand. There was something sweet about holding a tangible thing that had been touched and marked upon by someone I loved.

In one letter she included a few snapshots. She wrote:

Dear Jacob, things are finally getting interesting around here again. Remember the people on display in the basement, the ones Bentham said were wax models? Well, he was lying. He kidnapped them from different loops and was using Mother Dust's powder to keep them in suspended animation. We think he'd been trying to power his machine using different types of peculiars as batteries—but nothing worked until your hollowgast. Anyway, Mother Dust confessed to having known about it, which explains why she was acting so strangely. I think Bentham was blackmailing her somehow, or threatening to hurt Reynaldo if she didn't help him. Anyway, she's been helping us wake everyone up and return them to their rightful loops. Isn't that just pure madness?

We've also been using the Panloopticon to explore all sorts of places and meet new people. Miss Peregrine says it's good for us to see how other peculiars live around the world. I found a camera in the house and brought it along on our last excursion, and I've included a few of the photos I took. Bronwyn says I'm already getting good!

*I miss you like mad. I know I shouldn't talk like that . . .
it only makes this harder. But sometimes I can't help it. Maybe
you could come visit soon? I'd like that so much. Or maybe*

She'd scratched out *or maybe* and written: *Uh-oh, I hear Sharon calling my name. He's leaving now and I want to make sure this
letter gets into the post today. Write soon! Love, Emma.*

What was that "or maybe," I wondered?

I looked over the photos she'd included. A few lines of description had been penned on the back of each. The first was a snapshot
of two Victorian ladies standing in front of a striped tent beneath a
sign that read CURIOS. On the back Emma had written: *Miss Bob-
olink and Miss Loon started a traveling exhibit using some of Bentham's old artefacts. Now that peculiars are freer to travel, they've
been doing quite a business. Many of us don't know much about our
history . . .*

The next was a photo of several adults descending a set of narrow steps to a beach and a rowboat. *There's a very nice loop on the
shore of the Caspian Sea*, Emma had written, *and last week Nim
and some of the ymbrynes went on a boating trip there. Hugh and
Horace and I tagged along but stayed on the shore. We've all had
enough of rowboats, thank you.*

The last picture was of conjoined twin girls wearing giant white
bows in their raven-black hair. They were seated next to each other,
their hands pulling aside a bit of their shirts to reveal a section of
shared torso. *Carlotta and Carlita are conjoined*, the back read, *but
that isn't what's most peculiar about them. Their bodies produce an
adhesive glue that's stronger than concrete when it dries. Enoch sat
in some and attached his bottom to a chair for two whole days! He
was so mad I thought his head would pop off. I wish you could've
been there . . .*

I replied right away. *What did you mean by "or maybe"?*

Ten days passed and I didn't hear from her. I worried that she felt she'd gone too far in her letter; had violated our just-friends agreement and was stepping back. I wondered if she'd even sign her next letter *Love, Emma,* two little words I had come to depend on. After two weeks, I began to wonder if there would even *be* another letter.

Then the mail stopped coming altogether. I watched obsessively for the mailman, and when he didn't show for four days, I knew something was up. My parents always got tons of catalogs and bills. I mentioned, casually as I could, that it seemed strange we hadn't gotten any mail recently. My father mumbled something about a national holiday and changed the subject. Then I really started to worry.

The mystery was solved during the next morning's session with Dr. Spanger, which, unusually, my parents had been invited to attend. They were tense and ashen-faced, struggling even to make small talk as we sat down. Spanger began with the usual softball questions. How had I been feeling? Any interesting dreams? I knew she was leading up to something big, and finally I couldn't take the suspense.

"Why are my parents here?" I asked. "And why do they look like they just got back from a funeral?"

For the first time ever, Dr. Spanger's permasmile faded. She reached into a folder on her desk and pulled out three envelopes.

They were letters from Emma. All had been opened. "We need to talk about these," she said.

"We agreed there wouldn't be any secrets," my dad said. "This is bad, Jake. Very bad."

My hands started to shake. "Those are private," I said, struggling to control my voice. "They're addressed to me. You shouldn't have read them."

What was in those letters? What had my parents seen? It was a disaster, an utter disaster.

"Who is Emma?" said Dr. Spanger. "Who is Miss Peregrine?"

"This isn't fair!" I shouted. "You stole my private letters, and now you're using them to ambush me!"

"Lower your voice!" my dad said. "It's out in the open now, so just be honest, and this will be easier for all of us."

Dr. Spanger held up a photograph, one Emma must have included in the letters. "Who are these people?"

I leaned forward to look at it. It was a picture of two older ladies in a rocking chair, one cradling the other in her lap like a baby.

"I have no idea," I said curtly.

"There's writing on the back," she said. It says: 'We're finding new ways to help those who've had parts of their soul removed. Close contact seems to work miracles. After just a few hours, Miss Hornbill was like a new ymbryne.'"

Eyem-brine, she pronounced it.

"It's *imm-brinn*," I corrected her, unable to help myself. "The 'i' sounds are flat."

"I see." Dr. Spanger set the photo down and steepled her fingers beneath her chin. "And what *is* an . . . *imm-brinn?*"

In retrospect maybe it was foolish, but at the time I felt cornered, like I had no choice but to tell the truth. They had letters, they had photos, and all my flimsy stories had blown away in the wind.

"They protect us," I said.

Dr. Spanger glanced at my parents. "All of us?"

"No. Just peculiar children."

"Peculiar children," Dr. Spanger repeated slowly. "And you believe you're one of them."

I stuck out my hand. "I'd like to have my letters now."

"You'll get them. But first we need to talk, okay?"

I retracted my hand and folded my arms. She was talking to me like I had an IQ of seventy.

"Now, what makes you think you're peculiar?"

"I can see things other people can't."

From the corner of my eye, I saw my parents going increasingly pale. They were not taking this well.

"In the letters you mention something called a . . . Pan . . . loopticon? What can you tell me about that?"

"*I* didn't write the letters," I said. "Emma did."

"Sure. Let's switch gears, then. Tell me about Emma."

"Doctor," my mother interrupted, "I don't think it's a good idea to encourage—"

"Please, Mrs. Portman." Dr. Spanger held up a hand. "Jake, tell me about Emma. Is she your girlfriend?"

I saw my dad's eyebrows rise. I'd never had a girlfriend before. Never so much as been on a date.

"She was, I guess. But now we're sort of . . . taking a break."

Dr. Spanger wrote something down, then tapped her pen against her chin. "And when you imagine her, what does she look like?"

I shrank back in my chair. "What do you mean, imagine her?"

"Oh." Dr. Spanger pursed her lips. She knew she'd messed up. "What I mean is . . . "

"Okay, this has gone on long enough," my father said. "We know you wrote those letters, Jake."

I nearly jumped out of the chair. "You think I *what*? That's not even my handwriting!"

My dad took a letter out of his pocket—the one Emma had left for him. "You wrote *this*, didn't you? It's the same writing."

"That was Emma, too! Look, her name's right there!" I grabbed for the letter. My dad whipped it out of reach.

"Sometimes we want things so badly, we imagine they're real," Dr. Spanger said.

"You think I'm crazy!" I shouted.

"We don't use that word in this office," Dr. Spanger said. "Please calm down, Jake."

"What about the postmark on the envelopes?" I said, pointing at the letters on Spanger's desk. "They came all the way from London!"

My father sighed. "You took Photoshop last semester at school, Jakey. I might be old, but I know how easy that sort of thing is to fake."

"And the photos? Did I fake those, too?"

"They're your grandpa's. I'm sure I've seen them before."

By now my head was spinning. I felt exposed and betrayed and horribly embarrassed. And then I stopped talking, because everything I said seemed only to further convince them I had lost my mind.

I sat fuming while they talked about me like I wasn't in the room. Dr. Spanger's new diagnosis was that I'd suffered a "radical break with reality," and that these "peculiars" were part of an elaborate universe of delusions I'd constructed for myself, complete with fantasy girlfriend. Because I was very intelligent, for weeks I'd managed to fool everyone into thinking I was sane, but the letters proved I was far from cured, and could even be a danger to myself. She recommended I be sent to an "in-patient clinic" for "rehabilitation and monitoring" with all due haste—which I understood to be psychiatrist talk for "looney-bin."

They'd had it all planned out. "It'll just be for a week or two," my father said. "It's a really nice place, super expensive. Think of it as a little vacation."

"I want my letters."

Dr. Spanger tucked them back into her folder. "Sorry, Jake," she said. "We think it's best if I hold on to them."

"You lied to me!" I said. Leaping at her desk, I swiped at them, but Spanger was quick and jumped back with the folder in her hand. My dad shouted and grabbed me, and a second later two of my uncles burst through the door. They'd been waiting in the hall the whole time. Bodyguards, in case I made a break for it.

They escorted me out to the parking lot and into the car. My uncles would be living with us for a few days, my mom explained nervously, until a room opened up for me at the clinic.

They were scared to be alone with me. My own parents. Then they'd send me off to a place where I'd be someone else's problem. The *clinic*. Like I was going in to have a hurt elbow bandaged. Call a spade a spade: it was an asylum, expensive though it may be. Not a place I could fake swallowing my meds and spit them out later. Not somewhere I could dupe doctors into believing my stories about fugue states and memory loss. They would dope me with antipsychotics and truth serums until I told them every last thing about peculiardom, and with that as proof that I was irredeemably insane, they'd have no choice but to lock me in a padded cell and flush the key down a toilet.

I was well and truly screwed.

*   *   *

For the next several days I was watched like a criminal, a parent or uncle never more than a room-length away. Everyone was waiting for a call from the clinic. It was a popular place, I guess, but the minute there was an open room—any day now—I would be bundled off.

"We'll visit every day," my mom assured me. "It's just for a few weeks, Jakey, promise."

Just a few weeks. Yeah, right.

I tried reasoning with them. Begging. I implored them to hire a handwriting expert, so I could prove the letters weren't mine. When that failed, I reversed myself completely. I admitted to writing the letters (when of course I hadn't), saying I realized now that I'd invented it all—there were no peculiar children, no ymbrynes, no Emma. This pleased them, but it didn't change their minds. Later I overheard them whispering to each other and learned that in order to secure me a spot on the waiting list, they'd had to pay for the first week of the clinic—the very expensive clinic—in advance. So there was no backing out.

I considered running away. Snatching the car keys and making a break for it. But inevitably I'd be caught, and then things would be even worse for me.

I fantasized about Emma coming to my rescue. I even wrote a letter telling her what had happened, but I had no way to send it. Even if I could've snuck out to the mailbox without being seen, the mailman didn't come to our house anymore. And if I'd reached her, what would it have mattered? I was stuck in the present, far from a loop. She couldn't have come anyway.

On the third night, in desperation, I swiped my dad's phone (I wasn't allowed one anymore) and used it to send Emma an email. Before I'd realized how hopeless she was with computers, I'd set up an address for her—*firegirl1901@gmail.com*—but she was so firmly disinterested that I'd never written her there, nor even, I realized, bothered to tell her the password. A message in a bottle thrown into the sea would've had a better chance of reaching her, but it was the only chance I had.

The call came the following evening: a room had opened up for me. My bags had been packed and waiting for days. It didn't matter that it was nine o'clock at night, or that it was a two-hour drive to the clinic—we would go right away.

We piled into the station wagon. My parents sat in front, and I was squashed between my uncles in the back, as if they thought I might try leaping from a moving car. In truth, I might've. But as the garage door rumbled open and my dad started the car, what little hope I'd been nurturing began to shrivel. There really was no escaping this. I couldn't argue my way out of it, nor run from it—unless I managed to run all the way to London, which would've required passports and money and all sorts of impossible things. No, I would have to endure this. But peculiars had endured far worse.

We backed out of the garage. My father flipped on the headlights, then the radio. The smooth chatter of a DJ filled the car. The moon was rising behind the palm trees that edged the yard. I lowered my head and shut my eyes, trying to swallow back the dread that was filling me. Maybe I could wish myself elsewhere. Maybe I could disappear.

We began to move, the broken shells that paved our driveway crunching beneath the wheels. My uncles talked across me, something about sports, in an attempt to lighten the mood. I shut out their voices.

I'm not here.

We hadn't yet left the driveway when the car jerked to a stop.

"What the heck is this?" I heard my father say.

He honked the horn and my eyes flew open, but what I saw convinced me that I'd succeeded in willing myself into a dream. Standing there before of our car, lined up across the driveway and shining in the glare our headlights, were all my peculiar friends. Emma, Horace, Enoch, Olive, Claire, Hugh, even Millard—and out in front of them, a traveling coat across her shoulders and a carpet-bag in her hand, Miss Peregrine.

"What the hell's going on?" said one of my uncles.

"Yeah, Frank, what the hell is this?" said the other.

"I don't know," said my father, and he rolled down his window. "Get out of my driveway!" he shouted.

Miss Peregrine marched to his door. "We will not. Exit the vehicle, please."

"Who the hell are you?" my dad said.

"Alma LeFay Peregrine, Ymbryne Council leader pro tem and headmistress to these peculiar children. We've met before, though I don't expect you'd remember. Children, say hello."

As my father's jaw dropped and my mother began hyperventilating, the children waved, Olive levitated, Claire opened her back-mouth, Millard twirled, a suit of clothes without a body, and Emma lit a flame in her hand while walking toward my dad's open window. "Hello, Frank!" she said. "My name's Emma. I'm a good friend of your son's."

"See?" I said. "I *told* you they were real!"

"Frank, get us out of here!" my mother screeched, and slapped him on the shoulder.

He'd seemed frozen until then, but now he laid on the horn and jammed his foot on the accelerator, and as shells spit from the back tires, the car lurched forward.

"STOP!" I screamed as we sped toward my friends. They jumped out of the way—all but Bronwyn, who simply planted her feet, stuck out her arms, and caught the front of our car in her hands.

We slammed to a stop, the wheels spinning uselessly while my mother and uncles howled in terror.

The car stalled. The headlights died and the engine went quiet. As my friends surrounded the car, I tried to reassure my family. "It's okay, they're my friends, they're not going to hurt you."

My uncles passed out, their heads slumping onto my shoulders, and my mother's screams gradually faded to whimpers. My dad was jumpy and wide-eyed. "This is nuts this is nuts this is totally *nuts*," he kept muttering.

"Stay in the car," I said, and reaching over an unconscious uncle I opened the door, crawled over him, and slid out.

Emma and I slammed together in a dizzy, twirling embrace. I could hardly speak. "What are you—how did you—"

I was tingling all over, certain I was still dreaming.

"I got your electrical letter!" she said.

"My . . . e-mail?"

"Yes, whatever you call it! When I didn't hear from you I got worried, and then I remembered the machinated postbox you said you'd made for me. Horace was able to guess your password, and—"

"We came as soon as we heard," said Miss Peregrine, shaking her head at my parents. "Very disappointing, but not entirely surprising."

"We're here to save you!" Olive crowed. "Like you saved us!"

"And I'm so glad to see you!" I said. "But don't you have to go? You'll start aging forward!"

"Didn't you read my last few letters?" Emma said. "I explained everything . . . "

"My parents took them. That's why they freaked out."

"What? How awful!" She glared at my parents. "That's stealing, you know! In any case, there's nothing to worry about. We made an exciting discovery!"

"You mean *I* made an exciting discovery," I heard Millard say. "All thanks to Perplexus. It took me days to figure out how to get him back to his loop using Bentham's convoluted machine—during which time Perplexus should have aged forward. But he didn't. What's more, his gray hair even turned black again! That's when I realized something had happened to him while he was in Abaton with us: his true age had been reset. When the ymbrynes collapsed the loop, it wound back his clock, so to speak, so that his body was exactly as old as it looked, rather than his actual age of five hundred and seventy-one."

"And it wasn't just Perplexus's clock that got wound back," Emma said excitedly, "but all of ours! Everyone who was in Abaton that day!"

"Apparently it's a side effect of loop collapse," Miss Peregrine said. "An extremely dangerous Fountain of Youth."

"So this means . . . you won't age forward? Ever?"

"Well, no faster than you!" Emma said, and laughed. "One day at a time!"

"That's . . . amazing!" I said, overjoyed but struggling to take it all in. "Are you sure I'm not dreaming?"

"Quite sure," said Miss Peregrine.

"Can we stay a while, Jacob?" said Claire, bouncing up to me. "You said we could come anytime!"

"I figured we'd make a holiday of it," Miss Peregrine said before I could reply. "The children know almost nothing of the twenty-first century, and besides, this house looks *much* more comfortable than Bentham's drafty old rat-trap. How many bedrooms?"

"Um . . . we have five, I think?"

"Yes, that'll do. That'll do just fine."

"But what about my parents? And my uncles?"

She glanced at the car and waved a hand. "Your uncles can be memory-wiped with ease. As for your parents, I believe the cat's out of the bag, as they say. They'll have to be watched closely for a time, kept on a short leash. But if any two normals can be brought 'round to our way of seeing things, it's the parents of the great Jacob

Portman."

"And the son and daughter-in-law of the great Abraham Port-man!" said Emma.

"You . . . you knew my father?" my dad said timidly, peeping at us from the car window.

"I loved him like a son," said Miss Peregrine. "As I do Jacob."

Dad blinked, then slowly nodded, but I don't think he understood.

"They're going to stay with us for a while," I said. "Okay?"

His eyes widened and he shrank away. "It's . . . uh . . . I think you'd better ask your mother . . . "

She was curled in the passenger seat with her hands blocking her eyes.

I said, "Mom?"

"Go away," she said. "Just go away, all of you!"

Miss Peregrine leaned down. "Mrs. Portman, look at me, please."

Mom peeked through her fingers. "You aren't really there. I had too much wine at dinner, that's all."

"We're quite real, I assure you. And this may be hard to believe now, but we're all going to be friends."

My mom turned away. "Frank, change the channel. I don't like this show."

"Okay, honey," my dad said. "Son, I think I'd better, um . . . um . . . " and then he shut his eyes, shook his head, and rolled up the window.

"Are you sure this isn't going to melt their brains?" I asked Miss Peregrine.

"They'll come around," she replied. "Some take longer than others."

* * *

We walked back toward my house in a group, the moon bright and rising, the hot night alive with wind and cicadas. Bronwyn pushed the dead car along behind us, my family still in it. I walked hand in hand with Emma, my mind reeling from all that had happened.

"One thing I don't understand," I said. "How did you get here? And so quickly?"

I tried to picture a girl with a mouth in the back of her head and a boy with bees buzzing around him getting through airport security. And Millard: had they snuck him onto an airplane? How did they even get passports?

"We got lucky," Emma said. "One of Bentham's rooms led to a loop just a hundred miles from here."

"Some appalling swamp," Miss Peregrine said. "Crocodiles and knee-deep muck. No idea what my brother wanted with the place. Anyhow, from there I managed to effect our exit into the present, and then it was just a matter of catching two buses and walking three and one-half miles. The whole trip took less than a day. Needless to say, we're tired and parched from our journey."

We had arrived on my front porch. Miss Peregrine looked at me expectantly.

"Right! There are sodas in the fridge, I think . . . "

I fumbled the key into door and opened it.

"Hospitality, Mr. Portman, hospitality!" Miss Peregrine said, breezing past me into the house. "Leave your shoes outside, children, we're not in Devil's Acre anymore!"

I stood holding the door as they tramped inside, muddy shoes and all.

"Yes, this will do nicely!" I heard Miss Peregrine say. "Where's the kitchen?"

"What should I do with the car?" Bronwyn said, still standing at its rear bumper. "And, uh . . . the normals?"

"Could you put them in the garage?" I said. "And maybe keep an eye on them for a minute or two?"

She looked at Emma and me, then smiled. "Sure thing."

I found the garage door opener and hit the button. Bronwyn rolled the car and my dazed parents inside, and then Emma and I were left alone on the front porch.

"You're sure it's okay that we stay?" Emma said.

"It'll be tricky with my family," I said. "But Miss P seems to think we can make it work."

"I meant, is it okay with *you*. The way we left things was . . . "

"Are you kidding? I'm so happy you're here, I can hardly speak."

"Okay. You're smiling, so I suppose I believe you."

Smiling? I was grinning like a fool.

Emma took a step toward me. I slipped my arms around her. We held each other, my cheek pressed to her forehead.

"I never wanted to lose you," she whispered. "But I didn't see a way around it. A clean break seemed easier than losing you in slow motion."

"You don't have to explain. I understand."

"Anyway, maybe we don't have to, now. Be just friends. If you don't want to."

"Maybe it's a good idea, though," I said. "Just for a while."

"Oh," she said quickly, disappointed. "Sure . . . "

"No, what I mean is . . . " I pulled away gently, looking at her. "Now that we have time, we can go slow. I could ask you out to the movies . . . we could go for walks . . . you know, like normal people do."

She shrugged. "I don't know too much about what normal people do."

"It's not complicated," I said. "You taught me how to be peculiar. Maybe now I can teach you how to be normal. Well, as normal as I know how to be."

She was quiet for a moment. Then she laughed. "Sure, Jacob. I think that sounds nice." She took my hand, leaned toward me, and kissed me on the cheek. "Now that we have time."

And it occurred to me, standing there, just breathing with her, quiet settling around us, that those might be the three most beautiful words in the English language.

We have time.

About the Photography

The images that appear in this book are authentic, vintage found photographs, and with the exception of a handful that have undergone digital processing, they are unaltered. They were painstakingly collected over the course of several years: discovered at flea markets, vintage paper shows, and in the archives of photo collectors more accomplished than I, who were kind enough to part with some of their most peculiar treasures to help create this book.

The following photos were graciously lent for use by their owners:

PAGE	TITLE	FROM THE COLLECTION OF
32	Wights testing gas	Erin Waters
57	Man with pirates	John Van Noate
113	Floating girl	Jack Mord/The Thanatos Archive
179	Taxidermied girl	Adriana Müller
181	Myron Bentham	John Van Noate
185	Ymbrynes and their grim	Jack Mord/The Thanatos Archive
202	Boy with wings	John Van Noate
225	Bloody hallway	Jack Mord/The Thanatos Archive
264	Bowels of the machine	John Van Noate
278	Parrot in cage	John Van Noate
290	Inside the tower	Peter J. Cohen
293	Drainage pipe	John Van Noate
301	Doctor and nurses	John Van Noate
310	Man with thinning hair	John Van Noate
336	Man in dark glasses	John Van Noate
461	Boy and girl	John Van Noate